IDENTICAL STRANGER

ALICE SHARPE

SPECIAL FORCES: THE SPY

CINDY DEES

This book is produced from independently certified FSC™
paper to ensure responsible forest management.

For more information visit: www.harpercollins.co.uk/green

Printed and bound in Spain
by CPI, Barcelona

MILLS & BOON

First Published in Great Britain 2019
by Mills & Boon, an imprint of HarperCollins*Publishers*
1 London Bridge Street, London, SE1 9GF

Identical Stranger © 2019 Alice Sharpe
Special Forces: The Spy © 2019 Cynthia Dees

ISBN: 978-0-263-27423-3

0619

MIX
Paper from
responsible sources
FSC™ C007454

IDENTICAL STRANGER

ALICE SHARPE

This book is dedicated to Joey, Sam, Koa, Kiwi, Mele, Annie and Bonnie, even though most are no longer with us and none of them could read a word. They each filled our lives and hearts with joy. I mean, really, who doesn't love a dog?

Chapter One

Sophie Sparrow sat very still, the sound of rain hitting the window the only noise in the room. As a young girl, she'd imagined what this moment would feel like. Boy, had she been wrong.

"What do you say?" Danny Privet asked as he knelt on bended knee by her side. A glittering diamond ring sparkled in his hand.

She gulped. When he'd asked to come by this Saturday morning, she'd assumed they would go out to brunch. She had not even imagined this. "Danny, I—"

"Go on, say yes," Sophie's mother prompted from her self-imposed semipermanent residence in a recliner located four feet to Sophie's left.

Danny's head swiveled to her mother and then back to Sophie. "If you're worried about having to move to Seattle, don't. I've secured a position here in Portland. My new job starts in two weeks."

"You quit your job! But what's the rush?" Sophie whispered as she tried to make an intimate moment out of a public one. Her long straight hair fell forward if she leaned her head just so, creating an impromptu curtain between her mother and herself where she could study Danny in privacy. Why had he chosen to propose now? What was going on?

For a second, his soft gray eyes held an unfamiliar edge. She'd always wondered how anyone as agreeable as he was could make it as an attorney, how he could defend a client in a court of law, but this new glimpse into his character suggested he possessed the passion a courtroom would require. "Why should we wait?" he responded. "I've known you were the right woman for me since the minute I saw you in that grocery store. Why not get married now?"

"Now?"

"Well, I know how important a wedding is to you ladies. Plan whatever you want, I'll pay for it, just make sure we tie the knot by Wednesday because Thursday morning, we leave for Hawaii! I remember you mentioned wanting to go there. I've already bought the tickets and made all the arrangements. It'll be a honeymoon you'll never forget!"

Sophie would have gulped again if her throat wasn't so dry. She felt like a contestant on a game show, different curtains lifting to reveal unexpected—and in this case, unwanted—surprises. "Oh, Danny, you shouldn't have—"

"For once in your life," her mother interrupted, "use your head. This boy wants to marry you."

"I certainly do," Danny said. "And, frankly, Sophie, I thought you'd jump at the chance."

Sophie, just about speechless, finally mumbled, "We've only known each other a few weeks. I need more time."

"To wait for a better offer?" her mother scoffed. "Show some spunk! This boy is a wonderful catch, especially for someone of your—well, think about how kind he's been to me. What else do you need?"

I need to love him, Sophie whispered internally, *and I don't. I've been waiting twenty-six years to find someone to complete me, a second half that I've always known existed out there somewhere. Silly? Romantic? Probably, but there you go.*

As usual, when faced with her mother's iron will, Sophie voiced these arguments solely to herself, where they went to work burning a hole in her gut.

"Thank you for your compliments, Margaret," Danny said softly, "but I can't agree with your assessment of Sophie. To me she's a star, the brightest in the heavens, an angel surrounded by a halo of gossamer fawn silk."

Gossamer fawn silk… Did he mean her hair? The flattery sounded like lines lifted from a greeting card, but on the other hand, it was kind of nice to hear positive—if overly flowery—things about herself instead of negative. She smiled appreciation.

Danny apparently mistook her smile for acquiescence. Taking her hand, he slipped the ring on her finger. He got up off his knees and sat down on the sofa beside her, placing himself between Sophie and her mother. He squeezed her hand. The ring was too big and had slipped to the side; the pressure of his grip pinched the stone between her fingers.

"I knew you'd say yes," he said with a smile bordering on a smirk. "I was so confident you'd see how perfect this is that I already bought you a wedding present. You know that house a block over that's for sale? I bought it yesterday. You'll be close enough to keep an eye on your mom."

He'd purchased a ring, a honeymoon and a house before even popping the question and without asking for any input from her. She'd known him about a month. How had he been so sure she'd say yes?

"I've also taken the liberty of looking into hiring full-time live-in help," he added, addressing Margaret. "I hope you don't think it presumptuous of me but I see how you struggle. Would you mind having someone else living here with you?"

Sophie's mother fanned her face with her hand. "I'm

just a disabled old widow, Danny. I know you have your own mother to consider. You shouldn't worry about me. But yes, it would be so nice to have someone to talk to who doesn't prattle on about teaching babies how to read. I'll tell you, a little of that goes a long way."

"I think her enthusiasm is cute." Danny chuckled as he squeezed Sophie's hand again.

His condescending words struck her like poison darts. She pulled her hand free as retorts ransacked her stomach looking for real estate in which to sink new geysers.

And how could her mother not understand that the money Sophie made teaching her adorable first-graders was all that stood between this admittedly small house and a tent on the sidewalk?

"What would you like to talk about instead, Mom? Your sciatica? What a big disappointment I am?"

Was that her voice she just heard? Had her thoughts actually forced their way up her throat and out of her mouth? Her gaze darted from Danny's face to her mother's. Their stunned expressions made it crystal clear she had indeed given voice. Dumbfounded, she stared down at the gaudy ring on her finger.

Margaret didn't miss a beat. "Danny, dear, if you haven't changed your mind about marrying bridezilla over there, perhaps you and I should discuss the details."

He leaned forward. "Don't take her words personally, Margaret. She's just excited. A wedding is the most important day of a woman's life, right?"

Their voices faded to white noise. Sophie couldn't feel her feet. In fact, numbness seemed to be spreading up her legs toward her heart.

She stood abruptly, catching both of their attention. Looking from one pair of startled eyes to the next, she mumbled, "I have to go."

"Where?" her mother demanded.

"The school," she said. Where else would she go?

"Since when is the school open on a Saturday? What's gotten into you?"

"It's a… PTA bake sale," she muttered.

"I'll drive you," Danny said, starting to stand.

"No, thanks," she called over her shoulder as she forced her legs to carry her into the kitchen, where she grabbed her coat and purse from the hook by the door and moved quickly outside. Oscar the cat scooted past her into the warmth of the house before she closed the door and ran through the pouring rain to the curb where she'd parked. For once the aging compact started without trouble and she drove down the street with no plan except escape.

After a couple of miles and ever-increasing traffic, she pulled to the curb, turned off the car but kept an iron-fisted grip on the wheel to still her shaking hands.

Her cell rang and Danny's name flashed onto the screen. Damn if she wasn't tempted to answer the call. As soon as it stopped ringing, she picked up the phone and turned off the power.

The panic that had fueled her this far now began escaping into the atmosphere like steam rising from hot bread. She attempted to review the pieces of what had just happened, who said what, all of that, but the words were muted now, details washed out, a blur. What remained was the one moment when she'd glimpsed her life through a different lens and hated what she saw.

Had she run from her mother's negativity, Danny's condescension or her own sudden fear?

A woman exiting a shop caught her attention. Tall and svelte, what really made Sophie look twice was her crown of platinum curls that seemed to announce to the world that this woman took no prisoners. The shop she had left was a hair salon.

"I want to trade places with her," Sophie said aloud. She got out of the car and walked into the salon.

The hairdresser turned as Sophie entered.

"I need help," Sophie said.

"Honey, all I can do is fix your hair," the woman said with a half smile.

"That's a start," Sophie said. And in her heart she knew she could never go back to the way things had been.

JACKSON TRAVERS SAT across the table from the very pretty wife of his best friend, though right now she looked exhausted. It had taken him hours to drive here from his house in Northern California, and as of yet, he still had no idea why Sabrina had summoned him. What he did know was that there wasn't much he wouldn't do for Buzz and, by extension, Buzz's wife.

"It was really nice of you to come," she said after the waitress delivered coffee. "I'm sorry the hotel is so crazy. As far as I know, this is the first February they've hosted a conference here. I had a reservation but I'm worried you're going to have trouble—"

"Don't worry about it. The front desk connected me with a little place a couple of miles down the road, so it's okay. I have to admit I'm curious why you called," he added. "You sounded spooked on the phone."

As she pushed aside her dark hair, a series of fresh red scratches on her forehead caught his attention. Since he'd already noticed the abrasions on her palms when they shook hands and the stiff way she moved as she preceded him into the coffee shop next to the hotel, his curiosity ran rampant. "I've never called a private investigator before," she said.

He flashed what he hoped was an encouraging smile. "Think of it more as calling a friend. I know we've only met a few times, but you're Buzz's wife and that makes you family."

She smiled. "Thanks."

"So…"

"First of all, I don't want Buzz alarmed," she said quickly. "He has enough going on right now."

"You're referring to him being in Antarctica."

"Yes. The whole scientific team is currently aboard a Russian ship visiting outer islands. I can reach him by radio but holding an in-depth conversation is really hard. He doesn't need to worry about me."

Jack studied her for a second. He'd had a feeling of destiny when she called, something not common to him, something he didn't even believe in. He'd just had the sensation that her call was the catalyst of a crucial moment in his life and he'd rearranged his plans to travel here without a second's hesitation. "I can't promise you I won't notify Buzz until I know what we're talking about," he told her at last. "Why don't you just tell me what's going on."

She swallowed a sigh and fidgeted a bit before finally speaking. "It started a couple months ago when I was in the kitchen cooking lasagna. The neighbors across the backyard were having their porch painted. I was at the window draining pasta when I saw the painter taking photos of me with a big camera. By the time I set aside the strainer, his back was to me and then he left… I just had the strangest feeling he'd been doing more than taking pictures, the feeling of, well, invasion."

"You were cooking?"

"Yes."

A painful lump appeared in his throat as her words awakened painful memories. They had no place in the present and he did his best to ignore them. "Why do you use the word *invasion*?"

She shrugged one shoulder. "It felt...personal. Stupid, huh?"

"I don't know," he told her, the lump refusing to budge. "Did he paint the porch?"

"What do you mean?"

"Did he finish the job?"

She thought for a second. "I don't know."

For a second he just stared at her, forcing himself to let go of out-of-context parallels between Sabrina's issues and his own past. She was sitting here, alive, proof that his imagination was getting the worst of him. "What happened next?" he finally said.

"A day or so later I came home from work to the feeling that someone had just left our house. No one was there, of course, but I swear, there was just some lingering essence, something that sent chills up my spine. It happened the next day, too. I searched the house but nothing was missing, nothing was even out of place. There was just... nothing."

"Did you call the cops?"

"Of course not. What could they do?"

"Well, something made you uneasy," Jack said, not only to reassure her but because he was a firm believer that reasonable people picked up on offbeat vibes they sometimes couldn't even identify.

"I run into burning buildings for a living," she said softly. "I'm not anxious to be tagged as the woman who gets rattled over nothing."

"Buzz calls you unflappable," he said.

She smiled fondly.

"Anything else?"

"Just that same watched feeling. It started to get under

my skin. Last weekend when I walked out of the fire station it was stronger than ever. I looked around, but the only person I saw was sitting in a parked car. He immediately drove off but that afternoon I came home from work and found an origami fox folded out of a dollar bill sitting on the front porch."

Again he stared at her because now the vibe had changed from creepy to sophomoric. *No*, he cautioned himself, *her story is just diverging from the one written in your head. This is her story, not a trashy remake of yours.* "Not inside the house?" he said aloud. "No note or anything?"

"Nothing."

He folded his hands around his cup. "Tell me why we're meeting here in Seaport and not back in Astoria where all of this happened."

"I'm not sure you know this or not, but every February for years I've driven up and down the coast. There aren't many tourists in the winter and the hiking trails are all but empty. Anyway, after Buzz and I got married, we took the trip together. I was dragging my feet about it this year because Buzz is gone, but after I found one of those origami foxes perched on my steering wheel I decided it was time to get away for a while, and since I'd already made all the reservations—well, I just went, a day early, too, which I thought would give me a chance to chill out.

"I drove down to the California border pretty much in a straight line, stayed a couple of nights in Brookings and then started my way back up the coast just like I always do. Everything was going okay until I was hiking a narrow trail down to the beach about fifty miles south of here. A falling boulder appeared out of nowhere. It hit my left side and knocked me to the ground. I had to scramble to keep from going over the edge. It was a long way down to the rocks and I could hear waves breaking." She took a deep breath and continued. "Once I was back on the trail I heard something on the bluff above me."

"Like what?" he asked as he realized the scratches on her face and hands were undoubtedly caused when she fought to keep from tumbling over the edge of the mountain.

"Like footsteps."

"You're thinking some purposely dislodged the rock?"

"I don't know…maybe."

"Did you report the incident to authorities?"

She shook her head. "I climbed up to take a look myself. The spot was within easy walking distance of the parking lot. No one was around. The ground was muddy after this run of wet weather but it was also covered with pebbles— I couldn't see any footprints. What could the police do?"

"Investigate," he said gently. "Also, they'd be in the position to tell you if similar incidents had happened to other hikers due to weather or even vandals. They might have been able to help you understand if the falling rock was personal or accidental."

"Okay, you make a point. But I keep thinking police will question friends and acquaintances and word will get back to Buzz. What's he supposed to do from half a world away and what if the paper foxes are just some stupid prank? Anyway, I woke up ridiculously early this morning and ordered room service to be left in the hall while I took a shower." She retrieved her purse from the floor beside her, grabbed something from its depths and showed it to Jack. "This was on the tray when I uncovered it."

Resting on her deeply scratched palm he found an origami fox folded out of a dollar bill. "I called Housekeeping at once to see if they'd put it there," she continued. "They hadn't, of course. I put the tray back in the hall and called you. Then I left. Once it was light, I stopped for a long walk on the beach. Nothing happened and I almost called you back to cancel but I figured you were already on your way.

"So anyway, I drove to Seaport. I always stay at this hotel and I thought if you and I met here, you could help me figure things out. After I checked in I went up to my room to collapse but the maid wasn't finished cleaning so I came back to the dining room for breakfast. While I was waiting for my order, a man walked into the restaurant, made eye contact with me and immediately took a seat at the bar. I swear he was staying at the same hotel I was at when the rock fell. His being here could be sheer coincidence, of course, except that I have a feeling I've also seen him in Astoria."

"Did you talk to him?"

She shook her head.

"Could he be the painter from your neighbor's porch?"

She thought for a moment. "No. This guy had light brown hair and a trimmed beard… The painter was taller, darker, bigger. And maybe older."

"How about the guy you glimpsed in the parked car?"

She thought again. "Really hard to tell. By the time my backbone rebuilt itself this morning, the man had left the restaurant." She rubbed her eyes and took a deep breath. "If this guy is following me and leaving little gifts, I want to know it before I get home and he invades my house again or drops another rock on my head." She took another breath before adding, "Jack, I know it's a lot to ask but do you think you could help me confront him?"

"Of course. And if it turns out he's just a hapless traveler, I'll drive back to Astoria with you and see what we can do there. First we have to find this guy."

"And you won't tell Buzz."

"We'll leave him out of it as long as we can. That's all

I can promise." He didn't add the same deal would exist concerning police involvement.

"Okay."

"And I have to ask. Could anyone you know be behind all this?"

"What? No!"

"Someone you don't know well, then, someone with whom you're in a legal battle."

"Legal battle?"

"Well, the origami is folded out of money, right? Why? Could it be because someone thinks you or Buzz owe them something?"

She shook her head. "Neither one of us is in any kind of argument with anyone, legal or not. Buzz's friends are all scientists more concerned with sea ice extent than money and none of them live locally. My friends are firefighters. They're family to me. I'm an only child. My parents are deceased. I'm alone in the world, really, except for Buzz."

"And Buzz wasn't having trouble with anyone before he left?"

"No. None of this makes any sense and that makes me think it's all in my head."

"The origami fox isn't in your head," he reminded her.

She rubbed her eyes. "No, it's not."

"Nor was the falling rock."

She looked unsure about that but he wasn't a big fan of coincidences. The boulder could easily have killed her— probably would have if she wasn't in tip-top shape.

And that meant someone wanted her dead.

"I have an idea," he told her. "Why don't I take photos of the men in this hotel while you get some rest. You can look at the pictures later and we'll go from there."

She started to argue with him, but he stood firm. Her eyes were bloodshot and she kept rolling her shoulders as though yesterday's fall had hurt her neck or back. "Please, Sabrina. Get some sleep. In the long run, it will make everything go faster. Trust me."

She finally agreed and he insisted on escorting her to her hotel next door and upstairs. They exited the elevator and turned toward the long, beige hall as a man in coveralls carrying a toolbox entered the freight elevator a few steps away. Jack heard the whirring of the motor as it descended.

"Where's your luggage?" he asked after Sabrina had opened her door and he'd preceded her into her room.

"Still in my car."

He checked the locked door to the balcony, the bathroom and the closet. "What are you driving?"

"Buzz's old SUV. Why?"

"If you'll give me your keys I'll run down and get your things for you," he told her.

"All I want to do is climb under those blankets and sleep. I'll get everything later."

"Okay, but don't forget to slide the dead bolt after me," he added and fervently hoped that when this was all said and done, Buzz would understand why Jack didn't immediately get ahold of him no matter where he was.

Before he settled into a good chair in the lobby, he bought a cup of coffee at a kiosk he suspected had been created to service the dozens of human resource conference attendees milling around the hotel. As far as dropping everything to drive here, that hadn't been all that hard. He was in the middle of two cases but he got a buddy to cover one and the other could simmer a couple of days. The only other thing he'd had to do was cancel a date he hadn't been real interested in going on anyway.

Phone on camera mode, he clandestinely began taking pictures of every adult male he saw, customer or employee, bearded or clean shaven, tagged with a conference badge or not. Some of them seemed highly unlikely when compared with the brief description Sabrina had given—no facial hair, too heavy or tall or short—but all those things could be altered by a clever con man.

He'd just returned from his second run to the coffee kiosk when his roving gaze took in Sabrina moving away from the check-in desk. He set the coffee aside and walked over in time to catch her halfway to the door. "There you are. Ready to look at the pictures I took while you snoozed away the afternoon?" She had changed clothes, put on a coat and acquired a smattering of raindrops in her hair and on her shoulders. She'd been outside? She must have gone out to her car to retrieve her luggage. How had he missed her leaving the hotel, coming back inside to change and then apparently leaving again?

"I beg your pardon?" she said.

He finally looked past the raindrops. "I stand corrected," he said. "You skipped the nap and went to a salon instead. I hear that can be just as fortifying."

Her hand flew up to touch the lilac strands running through her glossy dark hair. "What I did with my afternoon is none of your business," she said with a defiant tilt of her chin and then ruined the effect by shrinking back. "I'm sorry. That was rude." She raised her hand as if to pat her hair and dropped it. "Does it look as bad as I think?"

He rushed to assure her. "It looks just like it did before, right, except for the purple streak?"

His words were met by another alarmed expression. "It's two shades darker and ten inches shorter." Her brow furled. "I'm sorry," she said again. "I've been in such a fog today. I'm having the hardest time placing how we know each other. Who are you?"

"Who am I? Are you sleepwalking?" She didn't smile

at his attempt at humor. "Okay," he said in a more serious tone. "How about letting me in on the joke."

"Danny has something to do with this, doesn't he?" she said as she glanced around the lobby. "He's not here, is he? Please, tell me he's not here."

"How could he be here?" He shook his head to clear it. Was it even remotely possible that Buzz's wife had a split personality? Had recent stress caused some kind of abnormal blip in her psyche? He touched her shoulder. "Are you sure you're okay? Did you change your mind and call Buzz, I mean Danny, after all?"

She held up one hand. "Wait a second. Why would I call him when all I want is a little space to think? And for that matter, why did you call Danny Buzz?"

"He earned the nickname two decades ago when he knocked a beehive out of a tree and got stung thirteen times, which is why he always carries epinephrine with him—just a second, he never told you about the bees?"

"No. This happened when he was growing up outside Seattle?"

He felt like scratching his head. "Buzz grew up across the street from my house in Napa, California."

"He told me he grew up in Seattle," she said.

"Why would he do that?"

"How should I know? He said his stepfather piloted a ferry on Puget Sound and his mom was—is—a housekeeper. He and his younger half brother—wait a second, why did Danny send you here instead of coming himself?"

Something weird was going on. He lowered his voice as they'd begun to draw attention. "You called me, remember? You asked me to meet you here. You've been feeling threatened and you asked for help figuring things out. You went up to take a nap—"

"I can't even get a room here."

He studied her face for some sign she was messing with him, dissecting her delicate features, aware as he did so that she flinched under the scrutiny, obviously uncomfortable and ready to run. She tried to rake her hair over her face but it was too short.

What was happening? This was the same woman he'd watched walk down the aisle two years earlier to marry his best friend, the same woman who sat across from him two hours before desperate for his help. And yet, somehow, it wasn't her either. She "felt" different, like a lost and impotent version of herself. Two hours ago she'd been Buzz's wife and now she was a complete stranger.

"Did Danny cook this up?" she said in a whisper, and he could feel her anxiety leap to a new level. "Mother must have guessed I'd come here—but why send a stranger?" She looked toward the door before turning back to meet his gaze. "I'd really appreciate it if you'd stop pretending you know me and just be honest."

"Wait a second," he said, ignoring the fact that she'd mentioned her mother in the present tense when the woman had died years before, ignoring everything except her unmarred forehead. "Where are the scratches?"

"What scratches?"

"The ones you got when that boulder fell. Let me see your hands." He caught her left hand before she could move away. "Nothing," he murmured as he studied her palm. Her hand trembled in his grip and he released it. "Where's your wedding band?"

"Do you mean that stupid engagement ring? Because that's in my purse."

"I'm talking about the wedding band Buzz gave you. It belonged to his grandmother." He shook his head. "Sabrina, something is very wrong."

"My name's not Sabrina."

He peered into her deep brown eyes and finally accepted she was as clueless as he was. With the realization came a giant wave of relief. Sabrina hadn't morphed into a delusional head case and he hadn't fantasized that her very essence had changed.

The relief was short-lived as the woman standing inches away narrowed her eyes. But when she spoke, her voice was soft. "Don't you think it's time you explained what's going on?"

"I wish I could," he said.

Chapter Two

Oblivious to the hustle and bustle of the lobby around her, Sophie perched on the edge of an off-white chair and studied the man who had accosted her.

There was no denying he was better-looking than about 98 percent of the men currently walking on planet Earth, but if there was one thing she'd learned the hard way it was this: looks mattered exactly zero. What good were broad shoulders, a lean, fit body and very blue eyes if the person sporting these attributes turned out to be a lunatic or a manipulator…or both?

"I can't believe you're not Sabrina," he said. "The likeness is incredible."

"First things first," she said. "Just who are you?"

"My name is Jack Travers. I'm a private investigator from California."

"For real?"

"Yeah," he said. "Why does that surprise you?"

"I don't know. I guess you don't look like one."

"What does one look like?" he asked.

"Humphrey Bogart," she answered without hesitation.

"Isn't he a little dated for you?"

"My mother watches a ton of cable TV. I grew up watching *The Maltese Falcon*."

"That's a hard act to follow. Now, who are you?"

"Sophia Sparrow. Sophie. When you say this woman and I look alike, you're talking in general terms?"

"Like eye color and height?" he asked and shook his head. "No. I mean identical, like clones, like twins. In fact, that's the only explanation for your startling similarities and why I was so sure you were her."

"Except that I don't even have a sister let alone a twin," she said. "In fact, I'm an only child."

"So is Sabrina."

"You said she's your friend's wife?"

"Yes."

"You also said she felt threatened. What's wrong? Is she in trouble?"

"I think so, yes," he said, "but she talked to me in confidence so I won't go into details."

"You also mentioned a falling boulder."

"Did I?"

Sophie wished he would stop staring at her. She tilted her head but no hair fell forward. Why had she chosen today of all days to cut it? She studied her hands to escape his gaze but looked back up because she wanted to know what he was thinking and so far she wasn't sure. She only knew it was important to figure it out. Something strange was going on in many ways at the same time, leaving her confused and worried.

She'd driven to the coast for one reason—to think. And yet in the back of her mind she admitted that thinking about this mix-up was easier than thinking about herself.

With what sounded like an aha, Jack took his phone out of his pocket and fooled around with it for a second, then turned it so she could see the screen. "This is a photo I took at Sabrina's wedding. The groom is my friend Daniel Cromwell. He's currently in Antarctica. Take a look at the bride's face."

Sophie glanced from Jack's intense gaze to the picture, and in that instant, her world flipped on its axis—again. From the bride's small cowlick near her hairline to her heavily lashed dark eyes, from the shape of her face to her eyebrows to the bump on her nose, everything Sophie could see looked familiar.

Was this a trick? Had an old picture of Sophie somehow been Photoshopped into this format? So many things were different—hairstyle, hair color, makeup, jewelry, dress and, oh yeah, what little she could see of a dark-haired guy whose face was smashed up against hers. This was not a photo of Sophie and yet it looked as though it was.

"She's prettier than me," Sophie said.

"She's a duplicate of you," Jack murmured, his glance darting from the telephone to Sophie. "And you're a duplicate of her."

"She doesn't have a mole on her cheek like I do," Sophie continued, unable to stop staring at the woman on the screen. "Does she color her hair?"

"I don't know. Except that she doesn't have a purple streak."

"Neither did I until this morning. You said her name is Sabrina?"

"Yeah. Sabrina Cromwell. Her maiden name was Long. Sabrina Long. She grew up in Astoria, Oregon, about sixty minutes north of here. How about you?"

Sophie had been digging in her shoulder bag as he spoke and now produced her wallet. She handed him her driver's license. "Born and raised in Portland, Oregon. How old is Sabrina?"

"Eight years younger than Buzz, so around twenty-six or so. Wait, I remember Buzz saying she's a July baby." He scanned her driver's license. "Looks like you were born in July, too."

"Lots of people are born in July," she said as she continued staring at Sabrina's face.

He dug in his pocket and produced his own wallet. "You don't have to take me on face value either," he said, handing her his driver's and private investigator's licenses. She looked them over before returning them. "Are you adopted?" he asked.

"No. Is she?"

"Not that I know of."

"I want to meet her."

"I think she'll want to meet you, too, but I'm pretty sure she turned her phone off when she decided to take a nap. I'll try calling her room."

Sophie popped to her feet. "She's here, in this hotel, right now?"

"Yes."

She blinked several times. Was she up to more shocks and surprises? Did she have a choice? She followed Jack to the desk, where he placed the call but ended up leaving a message. "I'm going upstairs to check on her," Jack said. "I'll be right back."

"May I come with you?" Sophie squeaked, then stiffened her resolve. "I need to see her with my own eyes. This is all so…weird."

"I think she'll need a few minutes to adjust to…things. She's pretty stressed."

"Yeah, well, so am I."

He smiled and the transformation was stunning. Half-surreal before, he now turned into a genuine human being. "I can see how you'd feel that way," he said, and together they rode up to the third floor and walked down the hall.

He finally stopped and knocked on the door of room 302. It was the same room Sophie had stayed in the summer before, the one she'd hoped to get today because it had a great view of the beach. They waited a few seconds and then he knocked again, harder this time. He twisted the knob to no effect. "I'm going to try a credit card," he said as he opened his wallet.

"Shouldn't we just go downstairs and ask for help?"

"Probably, but it's chancy they'll open the door without provocation. I saw this in a movie. It might work, what the heck."

As he ran a variety of cards through the magnetic lock, Sophie heard footsteps and glanced up to find a maid carrying an armload of towels walking toward them. She elbowed Jack, who glanced over his shoulder and quickly stuck the cards in his pockets. Sophie looked back at the maid in time to see a man turn the corner on his way to the elevator. He and Sophie made eye contact. He stopped dead in his tracks. His gaze shifted as he patted his pockets, then he turned on his heels and disappeared back around the corner.

It looked as though he'd forgotten something.

The housekeeper paused midstep. "I saw you earlier today," she said, smiling at Sophie. "Did you leave your key in your room?"

"Yes," Sophie said. The woman had mistaken her for Sabrina Cromwell. The last possibility that Jack might be in cahoots with Danny in some elaborate scheme to accomplish heaven knew what toppled off the edge of probability.

"I can open it for you," the woman said. For a second, Sophie wondered how they would explain the sleeping woman already in the room, but the bed was empty and the maid went on her way.

They closed the door behind them.

Jack glanced at the open door of the bathroom as he strode to the balcony and tried the glass door. It was locked. Planting his hands on his waist, he stated the obvious. "She's not here."

"Where are her things?" Sophie asked because aside from a rumpled bed and a damp hand towel in the bathroom, the room looked untouched.

"In her car. I guess I should go make sure it's still parked outside. Give me your cell number and I'll call you when I get this cleared up."

The impulse to wait in the lobby drew her like a magnet. She could find a corner where she could commence thinking about her life. Waiting felt comfortable. It felt natural.

She looked up into Jack's blue eyes. The anxiety she found there made waiting seem an inconceivable option. "You think something happened to her," she stated flatly.

"I don't see how it could have, but yeah, I'm concerned."

"Then I'm coming with you."

"You don't need to do that. I'll let you know."

"Listen," Sophie said, reaching over to grasp his arm, then removing her hand at once. There must be something on his jacket sleeve, some invisible substance that made her palms tingle. "There aren't any rooms available at the hotel, I'm not going home and I'm not going to risk losing track of you and Sabrina. It's like fate is screaming my name, trying to tell me something. Normally I would ignore such unwanted callouts from things like destiny and all that, but today—I don't know, I think I should listen. I can't explain it, I just have to find out where Sabrina is, who she is. I have to *see* her." She shrugged and slid him a glance to see if he was ready to bolt. He actually nodded and she took a deep breath. "I don't understand how anyone can look so much like me and not actually be—" She stopped short.

"Related," he finished for her and briefly touched her

arm as though he understood. "Nor do I. All right, come with me. Let's see if we can find her car."

"SHE'S DRIVING BUZZ'S old Chevy," he said as they walked out into the rainy afternoon. "Think rusty hulk."

He pulled the hood up on his jacket. She hesitated while still under the protection of the portico, and he realized her coat didn't have a hood and the rain had done nothing but go from bad to worse. "Why don't you wait here while I check the outside lot, then if need be, we can look in the parking garage together."

"Okay," she agreed.

Ten minutes later he jogged back to the front of the hotel to find Sophie gone. Man, he was losing women left and right today, but in this case, he thought it likely Sophie Sparrow had rethought her involvement with this situation and cut her loses. He was disappointed and not only because he was curious about the connection between her and Sabrina. Maybe it was for the better. What good could possibly come from being attracted to a woman who lived hours away, looked just like his best friend's wife and, more to the point, was in the middle of a relationship with a guy named Danny?

Was he attracted? Yeah, for whatever reason, he was. He wanted to know why she'd stuck purple in her hair. He wanted to know why she was timid one minute and brave the next.

Bypassing the valet's offer of help, he entered the parking garage located under the hotel.

Sophie was waiting for him inside the entrance. He was able to stifle the smile that threatened to curve his lips, but there wasn't a thing he could do about the spark of pleasure that flared in his chest.

"It was cold standing out there," she said as she joined

him. "It's not much warmer in here, though. I take it her car isn't in the lot?"

"No. Let's work our way down."

But search as they might, they could not find a rusty white Chevy SUV with a red stripe down its side in among all the sleeker, newer models. By the time they reached the bottom tier, Jack was sure Buzz's car wasn't parked in either the lot or the garage. That meant Sabrina had driven it away from the hotel. Why? What caused her to leave without telling him? It seemed so out of character.

He took out his cell to try Sabrina again but the reception was nonexistent down here.

"Let's go back up to the lobby and see if I can get some coverage. Obviously Sabrina left the hotel for some reason. I guess she couldn't find me to explain why. I'll call her again."

Sophie had to know as well as he that his words didn't explain why she didn't call or text or why she wasn't responding to his repeated attempts to contact her. She nodded but made no comment.

He started up the ramp, unaware until he was nearing the ground floor that Sophie wasn't directly behind him. He turned to look for her right as revving engine noises bellowed up from below. A human scream came right before four thousand pounds of screeching metal shot past Jack and accelerated up the last ramp, leaving behind the acrid smell of burned rubber.

Jack ran back down the ramp half-sick at what he might find. "Sophie?"

She was plastered to one of the brick support pillars, eyes closed, shaking like a leaf. She was missing her right shoe, and her handbag had disappeared from her shoulder. He clutched her arms. Her eyes flew open, and for a second she stared at him as if she'd never seen him before. Then she burst into tears and fell against his chest.

A few seconds later, pounding footsteps heralded the arrival of the parking valet, who stopped short in his tracks and stared at them as he gasped for breath.

"Is everyone here okay?" he finally managed to sputter.

Jack titled Sophie's chin up. Her brown eyes were huge but a resolute expression had begun to chase away the initial fright. "How about it? Are you all right? Are you hurt?"

She shook her head. "No."

"Are you sure?"

"Shaken but recovering," she muttered.

"What happened?"

With a glance at the valet, who seemed to be hanging on their every word, she shook her head again. "Later."

The valet was not as reticent. "I heard a racket down here and then a car came flying out going ninety miles an hour!" he said, his eyes as round as hubcaps. "I thought for sure someone had been run over flatter than a pancake."

"Did you get a license plate number?" Jack asked.

"Are you kidding?"

"How about a glimpse of the driver?"

"As I was ducking out of the way for my life? Nope."

"Was it a car you'd parked?"

"Doubt it. We have valet spaces reserved on the first floor so we can deliver as fast as possible. If it came from down here, chances are good someone parked it themselves."

"How long have you been on duty?" Jack asked.

"Since morning. I'm going home soon."

"Then do you remember a woman who looked a lot like Ms. Sparrow here parking an older white SUV Chevy?"

"Or taking it out," Sophie added, her voice shaky.

"No. I haven't seen a car like that, not that I remember

anyway. There's a parking lot outside. Some people prefer to use that no matter what the weather. Some people really don't like underground garages."

"I may now be one of them," Sophie mumbled, then took a deep breath and straightened up, pushing herself away from Jack's grasp. "I've lost my shoulder bag and my phone," she announced, nose and eyes dripping.

"I'll find them," the valet said, and went to work searching for the bag. With a triumphant whoop, the kid found her purse on top of a car parked a few spaces away and retrieved it. He handed it to Jack, who pressed it into Sophie's hands.

Sophie opened the purse and withdrew a tissue to wipe at her face.

"I'll look for your shoe," the valet offered as he scanned the pavement and kept talking. "You know, we get some awful drivers here, we really do, but this guy took the cake." He leaned way over to shine a penlight under a row of vehicles. He stood again and turned to search the other direction. "That dude peeled out of here like the cops were after him." He knelt again to shine his light. "Found it!" he called as he all but crawled under a van. He stood up grasping the shoe and focused the narrow beam of light on the skid marks scorching the pavement. "I guess you're just lucky he was a good enough driver to miss hitting you," he said as he handed the shoe to Sophie.

Sophie's lips parted. Jack thought she was going to say something but instead she slipped the black loafer on her foot as he steadied her arm.

"Do you have your phone on you?" he asked the valet.

"Sure."

"Sophie, give him your number. Let's see if your phone will ring."

"Good thing I turned it back on," she said as she rattled off her number.

A second later they heard a ring that Jack tracked down to the far side of the garage, where he found it had landed against the tire of a truck. As he picked it up and glanced at the lit screen, he saw numerous alerts that "Danny" had called. He handed it back to Sophie. She scanned the screen momentarily before turning the device off and shoving it in her pocket.

"Let's get out of here," she said as she settled her hand-bag on her shoulder.

"Sure."

She waited until the valet was far ahead of them before tugging on Jack's sleeve. "The car didn't veer to avoid me," she said. "It swerved to hit me."

"WHY DID YOU wait to tell me that?" Jack asked as they took their first deep breath of fresh ocean air. The rain Sophie had previously avoided now created a welcome cleansing, and she closed her eyes to turn her face upward.

"Sophie?"

She let Jack lead her under the portico, relieved when the valet left to help an arriving customer. "I don't know," she said. "I guess I didn't want to make a fuss."

He looked down at her as if to speak, but his expression suddenly softened. With one finger he touched her cheek. A raindrop glistened on his fingertip and he met her gaze. It was a strange moment full of currents Sophie didn't understand, but that was okay. This whole day had been a time out of time, one bewildering moment following another.

"Jack?" she finally said.

He blinked away whatever place he'd been lost in. "You

sound just like Sabrina," he said. "She didn't want to make a fuss either. And now she's gone."

"Well, I'm right here. Weren't you going to try calling her again?"

He pulled out his phone and a moment later shook his head. "It goes right to voice mail."

They walked back into the lobby. Feeling shaky, Sophie took a chair by the door as Jack continued on to the front desk.

After leaving the hairdresser, she'd headed to Seaport almost on autopilot. This town and this hotel were familiar—she'd been vacationing here for years, first with her parents and then alone after she graduated from college. She'd felt sure this was the place she could figure things out before returning to Portland and explaining herself to Danny and her mother.

In light of what had happened within the last hour, that plan now seemed ancient.

She thought again to the parking garage—could she be mistaken about the driver's intentions?

Jack sat down next to her. "Sabrina is still not answering her room phone, her own phone, anything. I've called the town's other hotels and the hospital. The front desk has no record of her checking out. She's just vanished."

"People don't just vanish," Sophie said.

She saw him flinch and wondered what nerve she'd inadvertently touched. "Actually, people do," he said softly. "At least for a while, sometimes forever." He seemed to shake off whatever had distressed him and leaned toward her. "Tell me why you stayed down on the bottom level of the garage and what happened between the time I left and returned."

"You said something about your phone reception and I stopped to dig my phone out of my purse, turn it on and offer it to you," she began. "Then I became aware that an engine had started and I turned around. A whitish car inched out of its spot, then turned and started my way. I was still standing in the middle of the lane so I moved aside. The driver gunned the engine and the car sped up. I dodged farther right—that's when I think I lost my shoe, but the car veered, too, so I tried to get behind the support. As I ran, I think my bag slipped down my arm and then the car tore it out of my hand. It made the corner with screeching brakes and shot upward toward you. I thought it might hit you... I just stood there like an idiot, too rattled to move. And then there you were—well, you know the rest."

"You felt the attack was purposeful?"

She nodded. "Yes."

"Did you see the driver?"

"Kind of."

"Kind of?"

"I think he was about my age. I don't know—it was a blur."

"Sophie, think carefully, does anyone know you're here?"

"In Seaport? No."

"Think for a little longer. You must have told someone you were coming to the coast."

"*I* didn't even know I was coming until I was practically here."

"Okay, you said something about your mother guessing where you were and you've mentioned a guy named Danny a few times."

"My mother could have guessed. I don't know that she did, but she might have."

"Would she have told Danny?"

"If he asked. But he would never try to run me down."

"You positive?"

She thought for a second. "Yes. He's my boyfriend. Sort of. Probably not anymore. He asked me to marry him this morning and I kind of…left. That's no reason to kill someone."

"You'd be surprised," Jack said.

"Come on," she joked as she resisted the urge to elbow him. "Look at me. I'm not the kind of woman to excite men to grand passion."

"You underestimate yourself," he said. "Okay, we're going to the police."

"Why would we—"

"Because you look exactly like Sabrina. If someone wasn't going after you specifically, then it figures they mistook you for her. The next step could be a great big rock falling on your head. Don't argue with me."

She broke into laughter. "You know, that whacko might have been after you, not me *or* Sabrina."

"He didn't aim at me," Jack said softly.

"Oh. Well, since Sabrina is missing, I think going to the police is a reasonable thing to do."

"So glad you agree," he said with sarcasm and she laughed again. She never laughed like this. Obviously the day's events were catching up with her.

They took Jack's car and within minutes were speaking to an anxious-looking police sergeant who kept glancing at the clock. Jack and Sophie both produced their identification and the sergeant looked it over without much interest until he got to Jack's PI license. "Just out of curiosity, were you formerly military or civil police?" he asked.

"I was a cop in Los Angeles for seven years before going out on my own," Jack said.

"I know a guy who did that, too," the sergeant said as he handed back their papers with a quick peek at the wall clock. "What can I do for you folks?"

Sophie was content to let Jack explain her garage encounter. He didn't mention that they'd been searching for Sabrina's vehicle but she figured he'd get around to it eventually.

"Ah, this stuff happens all the time," Sergeant Jones said with another glance at the time and a general shuffling of papers. When he saw their interest in his obsession with the clock, he smiled. "It's my tenth anniversary," he confided. "I completely forgot about it last year, and let me tell you, my friends, that is not a mistake I am ever going to make again. I made a reservation at her favorite restaurant but I keep thinking I should do something else. She's always complaining about how old her mixer is—"

"Don't get her an appliance," Sophie interrupted.

"Really?"

Sophie nodded.

"Buy her flowers," Jack said, and Sophie looked at him in surprise. He smiled. "Red roses for passion," he added as he met her gaze.

The sergeant grinned. "Yeah, and I can pick those up at the grocery store on my way home. Now, what was I saying?"

Sophie spoke up. "Jack just told you about the driver who almost—"

"Oh, yeah. I remember. Thing is, some stupid kid gets all excited because he sees a pretty girl and wants to impress her but he's not nearly as cool as he thinks he is and goes too far." He glanced at Jack and added, "And you feel protective, of course, because she's your girl."

Sophie opened her mouth, but Jack jumped in. "I hope that's all it is," he said. "The guy could have killed her, you know."

Now the policeman glanced at Sophie again. "I wouldn't worry about this, Ms. Sparrow. You aren't hurt, right? And without an ID on the car, there's really not much I can do. I mean, do you have any idea how many newish white sedans are running around in this city?"

Sophie thanked him—for what, exactly? she wondered—and started to stand. That's when Jack brought up Sabrina and revealed what she thought must be the minimal amount to drive home the fact that the woman felt threatened enough to elicit Jack's help. "We were searching for her car when the incident with the wild driver occurred. It's important to remember that Sabrina Cromwell and Sophie Sparrow look very much alike and that Sabrina seems to be missing."

The sergeant once again checked the clock before stifling a sigh. "Did you find her car?"

"No."

Sergeant Jones made a few notes. "Do you have her plate number?"

"It's her husband's SUV so run Daniel Thorne Cromwell, Astoria, Oregon."

"Okay," Jones said as he jotted notes. "We'll keep our eyes open, but honestly, people like this are usually off looking at the beach or shopping or something. You know this, Mr. Travers, from your own experience both as a policeman and as a detective. Chances are good she'll show up. She's an adult, right? No law says she can't get a wild hair. There was no sign of a struggle?"

"No," Jack said.

"Nobody at the hotel is alarmed?"

"No."

"Did you check the hospital?"

"Earlier today."

He made a note. "I'll check again just to be on the safe side. If I learn anything, I'll let you know." The sergeant looked over at the wall clock and they finally took the hint.

Once again they found themselves outside as overhead lights glittered on falling drops of silver rain.

"Why didn't you tell him about Sabrina and the rock?" she asked as he opened the passenger door.

"Because I promised her I'd keep everything she told me quiet as long as I can. I'm doing my best. She's concerned about her husband finding out. He's a long ways away right now."

"In Antarctica," Sophie remembered his saying. "Doing what?"

"He's part of an international team of biologists and other scientists investigating climatic changes. He's been gone a couple of months. Sabrina doesn't want him to worry."

"How do you feel about that?"

"I feel that the stakes have changed. I feel Sabrina needs help and it's clear to me that it's not going to come from Sergeant Jones. He's right that most people who leave suddenly and without explanation usually have a good reason. But most people haven't been followed for days or felt invaded enough to ask for professional help."

"She must have been terrified," Sophie said softly.

He ran a hand through his gorgeous hair and looked her in the eye. "The bottom line is that right now it's clear we represent her best chance of being found."

She noticed he used the word *we*, and as good as it made her feel inside, it frightened her, too. Was she up to the task? Well, she would just have to be. "You're really worried about her," she whispered.

"Yeah," he said, "I am."

Chapter Three

"I forgot about the photos," Jack said as he took his phone out of his jacket pocket. They had just entered the hotel again; maybe that's why he'd finally thought about all the pictures he'd taken earlier today. He and Sophie sat in the lobby once again, only it was now wine and cheese happy hour. While he called up photos, she jumped up to peruse the selection. He also called the hotel Sabrina had mentioned staying at the previous night after her encounter with the rock. What if she'd returned to it for some reason? But the hotel hadn't seen or heard from her since she left earlier that day. Another dead end.

"Things are really picked over," Sophie said as she returned with a tiny cluster of grapes and a couple of crackers. "Tell me about these photos."

"While Sabrina supposedly napped," he explained, "I took pictures of every male I saw. Maybe you'll recognize the driver who almost ran you down. If I photographed him earlier today. He may be a guest here and we may be able to get a name."

She perched on the arm of his overstuffed chair as he scrolled through the more than four dozen cameos he'd taken. "Wow, you didn't miss a beat," she said when a picture of a ten-year-old kid with his mother showed up.

"I thought it might amuse Sabrina. She was so upset I was hoping to get her to smile."

"How well do you know her?" Sophie asked.

"I met her when Buzz and she first got serious and then again at their engagement party. I was Buzz's best man at their wedding and then I stayed with them one night while I was on my way up to Canada on a case. That was last November, before Buzz left for Antarctica. So, to answer your question, not real well. Today was the longest time she and I have ever talked without someone else around."

He'd been scrolling while they spoke and now she said, "Stop. Go back one. One more. There."

"The guy in the hoodie?"

"Yeah."

He looked up at her, alarmed by how often he had to fight the urge to touch her hand or bump her shoulder. It had been a long time since he'd been flooded with impulses so old-fashioned and innocent yet fueled by such desire. Years in fact, ever since Lisa.

Did Sophie remind him of Lisa? Is that what drew him to her? He didn't know for sure.

Now was not the time to give in to retrograde musings. He put aside random thoughts as he casually said, "This is the man who attempted to run you down?"

"No. This is the guy I saw upstairs outside Sabrina's room right before the maid opened the door for us. He came around the corner behind her. He looked at me for a second and then acted as though he'd forgotten something. He turned around and went back the way he'd come. He wasn't wearing a hoodie then. I think he had light brown hair."

"Sounds pretty innocuous," Jack said.

"Yeah. But there was something kind of strange about the whole thing, too," Sophie said. "The more I think about it, the more I get the feeling he recognized me." She shook her head. "Maybe he'd just seen Sabrina enter her room earlier in the day and thought I was her."

"Sabrina talked about seeing a man in the restaurant this morning," Jack mused. "She was sure she recognized him but she also mentioned he had a beard."

"This guy was clean shaven."

"Beards can be shaved off or fake ones can be applied with adhesive," Jack said.

"That's true. So we're at…nowhere?"

"I'm not sure. The first thing to do is ID this guy."

"How?"

"The valet, the people at the desk. If the guy was upstairs in the hall, then he probably has a room here. We'll knock on every door if we have to."

"Or try the maid," Sophie said.

"That's good. I don't recall her name."

"Bonnie," Sophie said immediately. "Fiftyish, fading red hair, green eyes."

Jack whistled softly. "I have to admit I barely remembered what she looked like."

"That's because you were busy trying to hide your attempt to break into Sabrina's room. Let's split up and question people. It'll be faster that way."

He smiled as he got to his feet. "Let's just do it together. Maybe one of us will pick up things the other misses."

They started with the valet, who was a different guy from the one who had helped them earlier. As many of the conference attendees were calling for their cars in order to leave the hotel for dinner elsewhere in town, he didn't have time to ponder the photo. Because he hadn't been on duty since the day before, it seemed a moot point. The housekeeper had gone home for the day, and though Jack protested, they split up with Sophie taking the front desk and Jack going down to the basement to try to find the handyman he'd glimpsed when he and Sabrina first went to her room. Maybe he saw or heard something.

"Ask if Sabrina called or has any messages," he told Sophie before he left her side.

"Will do," Sophie said.

Jack was pretty sure the reason he didn't want Sophie out of his sight was because she was his sole link to Sabrina. At least it felt as though she was. No two women could look that much alike and not have very close connections.

The truth was, however, he suspected it also had to do with the fact that he was worried she was in the line of fire that he felt partially responsible for creating.

The basement was a brightly lit network of rooms portioned off for conference seminars and was all but empty now. He made his way to the housekeeping, kitchen and maintenance facilities and found a small room labeled Maintenance.

"Hank Tyson never showed up today," Jack was informed by a harried-looking man wearing a badge proclaiming he was Jerry Able, head of housekeeping. "I'm filling in for him. I don't know how he handles this job all by himself. With the hotel this crowded, the list of complaints is longer than Santa's naughty list."

"I saw someone in coveralls carrying a toolbox up on three a few hours ago," Jack said.

"Wasn't me. I called in a local guy to help out. Had to. With this many guests, we've got dozens of heater failures, clogged sinks, stuck windows, issues with dead bolts—you name it. Brad Withers and the new guy he hired, Adam something, tried to stay on top of everything. You must have seen one of them." He frowned as he added, "Wait, do you have an emergency? What kind?"

"No emergency," Jack said. He called up the picture of the man in the hoodie. "Is this Brad Withers or Adam?"

"I don't know," Jerry said. "I mean it's not Brad for sure but I've never actually seen Adam."

Jack retraced his steps to the lobby, where he found Sophie. He told her the little bit he'd learned. "How about you? Did the desk have any information? Does Sabrina have any messages?"

She shook her head. "Most of the staff has turned over. No one recognized the photo of the man in the hoodie that you sent to my phone. Only one woman remembers Sabrina and that was just because she checked her in this morning. She thought I was her and issued me a new room key. I let it ride."

"We need people to be looking for her," he said.

"Well, it was the only way I could learn anything about messages. I'll go clear it up."

He caught her arm. "Let me think for a minute."

"I thought I could stay in her room tonight," Sophie explained. "If she comes back, I can let you know. Are you on the same floor?"

"I don't have a room here either," he said. "The hotel found me a place a mile or two down the road. It's called Pine Lodge or Pine Lane or something."

"Pine Ledge," she said and shuddered dramatically. "You don't want to stay there."

"I've probably stayed in worse," he said. "As for you in Sabrina's room…are you forgetting she more or less disappeared from there?"

"I haven't forgotten. She must have answered the door to someone who enticed her away—"

"Or snatched her," he said and even he heard the despair in his voice. This could not be happening, not to Buzz and not on Jack's watch. He was the one who insisted she take a nap and then left her alone. Where was she? Was he wasting time staying in this hotel?

"Wait a second," he said aloud. "How did the guy terrorizing Sabrina get a room here if he was just following her? The hotel has been booked for well over a week. He would have had to already have a reservation, which meant he was privy to her plans and that probably means he's someone Sabrina knows."

She looked uneasy, as though a thought had occurred to her that she was reluctant to voice. "Go on, say whatever it is you're thinking," he prompted her.

"Don't they say it's usually the one closest to a person who—"

"No," he interrupted. "Buzz would never hurt Sabrina or engage someone else to do it for him."

"But—"

"No. The man is as good as a brother to me. I know him. I know how he feels about his wife. Whoever is terrorizing Sabrina is breaking into her house, dropping rocks on top of her, following her and, maybe now, stealing her out of her room. No way does Buzz have anything to do with any of this."

"Okay."

He made a sudden decision. "There's a chair in the hall," he announced. "I'm going to park myself in it. I know I won't sleep if I'm three miles away no matter how good or bad the hotel is so I might as well fidget the night away where I can keep an eye on the door to your—her—room."

Sophie stared at him a second. "I've known you for about three hours. You confronted me in the lobby, called me a nutcase, more or less, and then showed me a picture of a woman who looks a lot like me."

"Identical to you. You keep shying away from that."

She waved an impatient hand. "That's not the point. I'm

not sure why, but I trust you. If you knew me you'd realize how crazy that is because I'm one of those cautious people who drive the rest of the world to drink. Anyway, stay in Sabrina's room with me. If she does come back in the middle of the night, at least she'll recognize one of us."

"Actually, she'll recognize both of us."

"Are you taking the offer or not?"

"You sure?"

"Positive. I plan on calling room service for dinner. I don't know about you, but I'm hungry and tired and I have a lot of deep thinking to accomplish. You in?"

"Absolutely," he said. "Just let me get my suitcase out of the car. Can I get yours for you?"

"I don't have one," she said. "I believe I may have mentioned I left kind of spontaneously."

"Wait right here," he told her. "I'll be right back."

THEY ATE CHICKEN sandwiches while they watched the local news. It wasn't until it was over that Sophie realized Jack had been waiting for some kind of a horrible report that a female body had been discovered on a lonely beach or at the bottom of a cliff. She was glad she hadn't thought of that.

The room came with two queen-size beds so where to sleep didn't pose an issue. A bigger problem was the fact that Sophie didn't have anything to change into. Jack solved that by handing her his pajama top, which brushed her knees, and then putting on his bottoms.

"I saw this very scenario in one of my mother's old movies," Sophie told him as they stood a few feet apart looking each other over. "I believe it's time for you to string a clothesline between our beds so we can drape a blanket to preserve my modesty."

He laughed, then he sat down on the bed and fooled

with the alarm on his phone. She glanced at him again, rather taken aback by all the muscles in his chest and the hypnotizing shape of his well-formed arms. Was he trying to prove something by parading all that male virility so close she could touch—

Wait a second, just stop. Since when had things like rippling muscles and toned abs intimidated her? She wasn't even interested in that kind of thing. A person's mind was the true seat of sensuality.

Really? her subconscious chided. *What about Danny's mind did you find so terribly stimulating?*

That was a tricky one. In fact, she'd be hard-pressed to truly define him. In ways, he'd seemed one faceted, but then again, she'd known him only a few weeks. What he might have lacked in original thought, she decided, he made up for in other endearing qualities. Like the way they always laughed at the same things. Really, they never even disagreed let alone argued.

Until this morning.

In her head, she heard him tell her mother that he found Sophie's enthusiasm about her students and her job "cute."

"Cute" sat heavy in her heart.

"Looks like you're working away on those deep thoughts," Jack said as he checked his phone messages.

"Any word?" she asked, ignoring his remark.

"Just work-related stuff, nothing from Sabrina. So, what were you thinking about?"

"Danny."

He put the phone aside. "Go on. This sounds interesting."

She wished she knew Jack well enough to ask him to put on a T-shirt. His chest with its fine sprinkling of dark hair was distracting. And where did those square shoulders come from? Did he spend half his life in a gym?

Just as though he read her mind—or perhaps her stare—he got up and snatched a forest green T-shirt out of his suitcase, pulled it over his head and returned to his bed. It kind of helped. "You were going to tell me about your Danny," he said with an encouraging smile.

"Not my Danny, not anymore," she said and sat down on the edge of her mattress facing him, making sure their knees didn't touch. They were very close nonetheless, something that might have bothered her more if his comment hadn't driven home the fact that she'd blown it with Danny. He was gone by now, taking her opportunity for marriage and family with him. This hadn't bothered her hours before, but now, as the dark outside the hotel window pressed against the window glass, she suddenly felt adrift.

Instead of telling Jack little or nothing as she had planned, she found herself spilling her guts and, by voicing the events of the morning, reliving them. He didn't say a word as she spoke, and when she was finished she met his gaze. "Do you think I was unfair to him?"

He responded at once. "*You* unfair to *him*? Hardly. I think Danny has to take the heat for this mess. The guy sounds…odd."

She felt a sudden wave of defensiveness for Danny. After all, Jack had heard only her side of the story and as she'd retold it, her own complicity in what happened is what struck her. "I don't know if that's a fair observation," she said.

"Tell me how you met."

She smiled. "It was like a movie in a way, you know, guy trying to figure out what kind of apple to choose, girl—who happened to be a big fan of apples—offering advice. He was very sweet. He explained his company had sent him to Portland for a few weeks and admitted he was lonely. He asked me out to dinner and when I said yes he seemed so pleased. I was craving Italian food. Turns out it was his favorite, too. It was just so—"

"Suspicious?" he said.

She frowned. "Cynic. I thought it was exciting. He asked my opinion about things and listened to my answers—that's a very engaging thing for a guy to do. And he's super kind to my mother. She isn't exactly easy to get along with. She and I—well, we're like oil and water. It would be a war zone if I hadn't learned not to react to every little thing. Anyway, back to Danny. His marriage proposal came with a ready-made honeymoon, a big house one block over for us to live in and financial aid for my mother in the form of live-in help so she can stay in her own house. And he even quit his job with a prestigious law firm up in Seattle to relocate to Portland. That's pretty amazing, right? I don't know why it hit me so hard this morning."

"Then I stand corrected," Jack said. "The guy sounds like a prize. Why *did* you turn him down?"

"It was just so unexpected. And it was hard thinking straight with my mother butting in all the time."

"Why was she there again?"

"She lives with me, or I live with her. It was her and Dad's house and then she lost it after he died. I bought it back when I finished college and started teaching. She has a few health issues that aren't as bad as she thinks they are, but, well, the truth is, she can't afford to live on her own and I can't afford separate housing for her."

"Sounds like you and she have an…uneasy…relationship," he said.

She started to protest but nodded instead. "Yeah, it is. I'm a disappointment."

He looked incredulous. "What?"

She shrugged one shoulder. "I'm not big enough, you know?"

"Physically, you're perfect so what does that mean?"

She fought the moment of pleasure his compliment created. "I'm not smart enough or funny enough or ambitious enough or... You know what I mean. I understand most of her bitterness comes from Dad dying so young and all the burdens of raising a kid falling on her shoulders. He left Mom with few resources."

"Sounds as if you've been trying to make things up to her since then. How old were you when he died?"

"Eleven. He was the one who wanted children. Mom really didn't, she was happy with just the two of them, but he talked her into it. My birth caused all sorts of physical issues for her."

"How do you know all this?"

"She told me."

He stared at her for a long minute, the blue of his eyes filling her whole head. "Sophie, what kind of parent tells their child they didn't want them?"

Sophie blinked. She couldn't think of a word to say. Out of loyalty at the very least, she should defend her mom, but words just escaped her.

"Does Danny know about this?" Jack asked.

She swallowed and, for the second time that day, that stone-like feeling started to creep up her legs toward her heart. She stood abruptly and glanced longingly at the door. She was running out of safe havens. Taking a deep breath, she slowly sat back down. "I think it's kind of hard to miss," she admitted.

"Then why did he propose in front of her?"

"I wondered that, too. I don't know."

"Why didn't he ask you to step outside?"

She gestured toward the window, through which nothing could be seen. "It was cold and pouring down rain."

"Trust me," he said softly. "If I loved a woman enough to ask her to share the rest of my life and I knew someone intimidated her, I would stand in a blizzard to talk to her in private. The only reason I would do it right there in front of that person—" He stopped short. "Well, what do I know?"

"Finish what you were going to say."

"I've said enough," he mumbled. "Only, if this guy is such a dandy listener, then how did he so totally misread your level of commitment?"

"I must have misled him."

"You seem pretty straightforward to me," he said.

"I'm not myself today," she mumbled.

"Maybe you are yourself today."

"What does that mean?"

"Maybe today you got pushed over your own personal edge of tolerance. Maybe today you finally got tired of never being heard."

Once again his blue gaze filled her vision. She rubbed her forehead until it faded away.

"I'm sorry," Jack said into the continuing silence. His voice turned introspective as he added, "I have no right to counsel anyone on romance and love."

Anxious for a chance to focus the spotlight elsewhere, she perked up. "That's a provocative sentence. Care to explain it?"

"No, I do not." He opened the bed and got under the covers. "I'm ready to put an end to this day. How about you?"

"Please."

She lay there in the dark, very aware of Jack just a few feet away, listening to him breathe. It was a nice, steady, reassuring noise, and as her mind drifted she admitted that

although his comments and questions had been probing and painful, she'd enjoyed talking to him. Was there any truth in what he said?

Eventually her thoughts circled back to Danny and she recalled the times she'd basked in his compliments. Now, in retrospect, she'd been like a thirsty flower aching for water. She sometimes found children like this in her classroom and her heart always went out to them. Was that partially because she recognized their need in herself?

Man, that was embarrassing but she could feel the truth lurking in there somewhere. If Danny had seen her only as an easy way to fill a few idle hours, then why quit his job and move, why buy a house, why ask her to marry him?

What if he truly did love her? What if he'd just gotten heavy-handed with the marriage stuff and just wanted to share the moment with her mother, who, face it, was an awfully big part of Sophie's life. She knew he'd tried to call several times today, she'd seen his name on her screen every time she looked… What if she'd just told him she needed a few days to think instead of running away? What if she'd had a backbone and insisted she and Danny go talk in the kitchen? Why was it his problem to figure out her needs?

What had she done?

If she'd been alone in the room, she would have switched on the light, gotten dressed and driven home. She suddenly had no idea what she was doing here.

And then she remembered Sabrina. Sabrina, missing. Sabrina absent from this room without explanation, drawn by someone or something she couldn't ignore. Sophie knew in a moment of insight only two things could do that. Love…or fear. Jack was adamant that his friend would not be behind anything that would harm Sabrina, and she would have to accept he knew what he was talking about. But what if Sabrina had called her husband for comfort? Maybe Buzz knew where she'd gone.

Fear was different. Fear could be generated by something hidden, something Sabrina might not have confessed to her husband or his best friend, a secret, something that caught up with her.

Regardless of anything else, where was Sabrina right now? Sophie fell asleep saying a silent prayer that wherever she was it was because she wanted to be there and she was safe.

It was impossible to tell how much time had elapsed when a voice woke her from her sleep. She sat up immediately, her heart in her throat, and scanned the room. "Sabrina?" she said and was met by nothing but silence. A line of light shone under the door but the rest of the room was dark and still. And then she heard the voice again, and realized it came from Jack.

"Lisa," he moaned, and then, "No!" uttered with a gut-wrenching sob that sent chills washing through Sophie's body.

"No, no," he whispered again, pain dripping from his voice like blood from a wounded animal.

Sophie lay frozen, not sure what to do. As the sound of tossing and turning continued, she slipped out of bed and approached his dark shape. He was mumbling now, his head turning from side to side. She sat down beside him and he immediately clutched her wrist.

"It's okay," she said in a calm voice. "Everything's fine. You're safe."

His grip didn't loosen and his body stayed rigid. She had the feeling he was like a soldier in a trench, lying in wait, uncertain what was coming but geared up to annihilate it in order to stay alive.

She tried to reach the light switch on the lamp but it was

just out of reach. The shifting of her body weight made his grip tighten.

"Jack," she said. "It's me, Sophie, remember? We met earlier today, here in Seaport. I'm the girl with the purple streak in my hair."

For the first time, his fingers relaxed, but he still didn't let go. She took a deep breath and continued prattling on about nothing as she adjusted herself on the bed next to him, propped up on his spare pillow, half sitting with her legs stretched out in front of her. She stroked his hair without considering whether or not it was too personal. He was in pain, that much was clear.

When his restlessness stopped and his breathing returned to normal, she slowly withdrew her hand, but when she shifted her weight to stand, his arm slipped over her legs and his head fell against her hip. Trapped!

But not uncomfortable.

She tugged on a corner of the blanket to get a little coverage, then settled down, her intention to wait until he started snoring and then disengage herself. It seemed like second nature to continue stroking his fine hair as she leaned back and closed her eyes.

Who was Lisa and what in the world had happened to her?

Chapter Four

Jack awoke without the help of his phone alarm. He always did and wasn't even sure why he still bothered to set it except for some superstitious feeling that if he didn't, that would be the one time his internal alarm took a hike.

As he became aware that sunlight actually peeked through the gap in the drapes, he also figured out his pillow was the lap of the woman slumped in bed beside him.

He recalled Sophie's coming to him last night. He'd had a nightmare about Lisa, one so real the dream had crossed into reality. He could remember holding Sophie's hand very tight to keep from slipping back into the void. Her voice had been like a lantern in a lighthouse illuminating a path back to safety. He'd wanted her to keep talking forever.

He hoisted himself up on one elbow and looked at her. A lock of purple hair fell over her right eye. In repose, she looked impossibly young, and when he thought back to the things she'd revealed about her boyfriend and her mother, the very people who seemed to form the core of her support system, he felt anger pump in his veins.

As he watched, she scrunched up her nose and yawned and then her eyes flew open.

"Good morning," he said.

"Hmm—"

"Looks like we have a break in the rain."

"Oh, Lord," she groaned. "Save me from morning people."

Her voice brought him firmly back to the here and now. He scooted off the bed and grabbed his phone, hoping against hope that there would be a message from Sabrina. Sophie's sudden stillness announced her awareness of this possibility, as well. He shook his head. "Not a word. That's it. I'm driving to Astoria."

"That's where she lives."

"It is. I can't sit around here anymore. Probably should have left last night."

She popped to her feet. "I'll take the first shower," she said. "I take short ones. Saves water, you know. That'll give me a chance to dry my hair while you take yours."

"I think—"

"You're not going to argue about this, are you?" she interrupted. "Look, I'll follow your car in mine unless you want to try to go without me, in which case I'll find my own way."

"I'll order breakfast," he said. He hadn't intended to talk her out of it. Instead, he'd been about to agree that until they identified this bozo intent on harming Sabrina, Sophie should stay where he could protect her, but there really wasn't any point in saying that now. Nor would he mention his gut feeling that his, Sophie's and Sabrina's destinies were all tied together in some cosmic knot.

He made the rest of his usual calls—Sabrina's house to leave yet another message on the land phone they still kept for emergencies; the police who had nothing to report; the local hospital; the front desk; valet parking. Nothing. The woman was just flat out not here.

Sophie came back in the room five minutes later, still wearing his pajama top, her hair wrapped up in a towel. He tore his gaze away from her shapely bare legs and her very pretty heart-shaped face. How that very face on Sabrina could seem remote and collected and yet look so vivid and irresistible on Sophie was a mystery to him.

"Breakfast is on the way," he said, and strode past her into the bathroom, a change of clothes in his hands. He turned at the door. "Everything in my suitcase will swim on you but you're welcome to borrow what you need."

SOPHIE SPENT SEVERAL minutes blow-drying her new hair. She loved the darker brown; finally the shade enhanced her skin. She loved the chic bounce of the shorter cut and the new longish bangs. It was the purple streak that jumped out at her but she could recall telling the hairdresser to do what she wanted, just as long as it was different. She couldn't deny the woman's panache and Sophie had to admit that life had certainly gotten more interesting since making the change.

Last night, she'd felt trapped in a web of her own making, a web created by the endless second-guessing that inevitably occurred as a postscript to any act of defiance no matter how small or even justified. Equilibrium had returned with the light of day, and this morning when she thought of going back to Danny it was to apologize for bolting, to return his ring and offer support as he figured out what to do about a honeymoon they wouldn't take, a house they wouldn't live in and a job he'd quit on what had to be a whim.

But right now, Sabrina came first. Where was she?

A knock on the door sounded at the same time the water went off in the bathroom. Sophie stood between the two doors, half-dressed. She ran to the door but without opening hollered, "Yes?"

"Room service."

"Please leave the tray," she said, and ran back to the pile of clothes on a chair to pull on yesterday's leggings and T-shirt before Jack caught her seminude. His open suitcase beckoned her. She looked through his neatly folded belongings until her fingers grazed the cloud-soft fibers of cashmere. She pulled out a sweater the color of a summer sky and tugged it over her head, where it slid down her body to midthigh. Cozy but oversize on her, she bet it molded Jack's arms and torso and highlighted his eyes. This was the kind of sweater a woman might buy for her lover, and with that thought, last night's anguished call for Lisa rang in her ears.

Could she ask him about her? No, she decided. A cry in the night was not an open invitation to pry.

The bathroom door opened and a freshly showered Jack stood framed in the doorway for an instant.

"That sweater looks great on you," he said as he walked back into the room. His own clothes consisted of black boots, gray pants and a charcoal sweater. Damp, black hair curled around his ears. He looked urbane and pulled together and yet now that she knew him a little better, totally approachable.

"Thanks," she said. "I have an idea."

"What's that?"

"I got to thinking that maybe Sabrina called Buzz after you left her to rest. Maybe she realized she needed to be with him. Maybe she left on the run to drive back to Portland to catch a flight—"

"Wait a second," he said. "Slow down. Getting to Antarctica isn't a piece of cake. There are no direct flights. It takes some planning."

"But it could be done."

"Maybe. The airport is three hours from here, though.

In all that time she couldn't stop and contact me or answer one of my calls?"

"There may be a reason. Cell phones run out of battery or break." She studied her feet for a second before adding, "I just realized that I've done the same thing."

"In what way?"

"I left without explanation, although people did see me drive away. I came to the coast without telling anyone where I was going, I'm not registered at any hotel and I haven't answered my phone even once. The people in my life are just as clueless about me as we are about Sabrina."

"You need to call your mother or Danny."

"I know. I will. I've been so wrapped up in myself that it didn't even cross my mind until now. Does that give us hope about Sabrina just wandering off for some reason and not thinking to call?"

"The situation, as far as I know, isn't quite the same. She elicited my help. I don't think she'd leave me hanging. I'm not saying it couldn't happen, it just seems unlikely. And I'm not discounting how much she must have wanted to run to Buzz, but he's currently aboard a Russian ship with a bunch of other scientists from all over the world visiting islands no one else ever goes to. Right now getting to him is a pretty daunting task."

Sophie took a deep breath. "Don't take this the wrong way but is it possible you said something to her yesterday that would cause her to cut you out of the loop?"

If someone had asked her that question, she knew she would have immediately replayed every word she'd uttered the day before, but Jack just shook his head.

Such confidence!

"But you make a good point. Yesterday she was adamant about protecting Buzz but she may have changed her mind. It's possible she contacted him. I'll think of some way to find out if he's heard from her. But we also need to talk to her coworkers. She said they were like family. Maybe she ran to one of them for help." He looked down at Sophie and smiled. "I'm sorry I jumped on your idea when you first broached it. I shouldn't have interrupted you."

Her hand landed on his arm and once again she got that tingly feeling, but this time she knew it had nothing to do with his clothes. It was just him, plain and simple. He probably affected everyone this way. "It's no big deal," she said. "We're both on edge."

He glanced at her hand before meeting her gaze. Something passed between them; Sophie had no idea what. She removed her hand while struggling to think of something to say. He took care of it. "I was hoping the coffee got here. I hate the stuff you make in the room."

She tore her attention away from him, not an easy feat. "It did come," she said. "It's in the hall."

"I'll get it," he told her and broke the connection that had fused them together for a few seconds by striding to the door. She cleared the table.

"Have a seat if you're hungry," he said as he kicked the door closed behind him and carried the lidded tray into the room. "I also ordered bacon and eggs for two."

"Sounds wonderful," she said, claiming one of the chairs. As he set the lid aside, she reached to pour the coffee, then paused as she glanced at the plates of goodies.

"What's wrong?" he asked.

She smiled up at him as she set aside the coffee thermos. "What's that perched beside the salt and pepper? It's so cute." She lowered her fingers.

Jack grabbed her hand. "Don't touch it," he cautioned.

"Why not? Maybe the hotel—"

"The hotel had nothing to do with this," he interrupted, leaning down to look at the little folded figurine.

"Then who did?" she asked.

"I believe we can thank the guy you recognized in the photo."

"The one you think has Sabrina?"

"Not anymore I don't," he said, peering closely at the tray. "Sabrina received a couple of foxes folded out of dollar bills just like this one when she was up in Astoria. Another one showed up on her breakfast tray yesterday morning, sixty miles south of here and following the falling rock incident."

"Odd."

"If the man who is planting them took her or enticed her away, he'd know she wasn't in this room. For that matter, if it's the same guy he'd also know she wasn't in the garage last night. That means he thinks you're Sabrina, which means he doesn't know she's missing, which probably means she isn't missing at all, she's just gone off somewhere and, like you said, something happened to her phone."

"That's good news, right?" Sophie asked.

"I think so." He opened his pocketknife to a pair of tweezers. "Will you please get me one of those plastic sleeves they wrap around the water glasses?" he said as he removed the fox from the tray.

"Fingerprints?" she asked as he slid it into the plastic she fetched. He nodded. "Why would this cute little thing frighten Sabrina?" she asked.

Jack took the plastic from her and tucked it in his suitcase. When he turned back to her, his expression was thoughtful. "She received two or three of these before she left Astoria, all anonymously. And now they're following her on her vacation. It's not the fox that's frightening, it's the intent behind it. Someone thumbing their nose at her, saying, 'I can get to you whenever I want. I'm watching you.'"

"But why fold it out of a dollar bill?"

"I don't know. How long ago did the tray arrive?"

"It came to the door right as you turned off the shower."

"Ten, fifteen minutes," he said. "That means that whoever is stalking Sabrina Long Cromwell stood outside that door waiting for an opportunity to interact with her. The tray being left must have made his day."

She looked from his gaze to the bounty of untouched food. "I don't think I can eat any of that," she said.

"Me neither, but you've started me thinking like a detective again. See if you can find more of the plastic bags. I'll take a sample of everything on that tray and have it analyzed to see if whoever is taunting her with folded money is also trying to poison her. While I do that, why don't you call down for another tray. This time we'll leave the door open."

THE EMPLOYEE WHO delivered the second tray now took away the first. Before he left, Jack showed him the photo of the hooded guy on his phone, but the kid denied ever seeing the man and knew nothing about what happened after he left the tray in the hall.

After picking at their new breakfast, Sophie turned on her phone. "Better get this over with," she said with a glance at Jack, and he could feel her stress level rise. "Mom, hi, it's me," she finally said.

Jack glanced at her face as she obviously listened to her mother. She frowned at last and seemed to measure her words. "I know I'm lucky," she said. "I know he's a great catch."

She listened some more and he found himself feeling fidgety on her behalf.

"Wait, what?" After a few seconds, she took a deep breath. "I don't know. Maybe, I have to think about it… Yeah, I'm crazy, I get it. Listen, I'll be home tonight sometime… No, please don't call Danny. I just didn't want you to worry."

She listened again, her expression now impatient. "Well, I guess it's good I'm so predictable, isn't it?" she finally said and ended the call.

She looked at him immediately and he smiled.

"Feel better?" he asked her.

"No. Let's get out of here."

"Do you want to talk?"

"No," she said. "Last night the desk clerk said Sabrina is booked through Tuesday."

Sophie obviously wanted to get back to business. "Then we won't check her out of the hotel," Jack said after a moment's thought. It was kind of hard to picture her coming back here but if she didn't, what did that say, that she wasn't able to return, that she wasn't able to answer his calls or respond to his messages? There were only three reasons that could be true. She was off on some secret mission, so to speak; she was injured and her situation precluded contacting someone; or she'd been abducted and denied the opportunity.

Face it. Option three was what terrified him. Three was his Lisa.

He stowed his suitcase in his car, then he and Sophie went downstairs to show the photo of the guy in the hoodie to anyone who would stop long enough to look. At the front desk, they asked about the woman who opened their room for them, Bonnie, and was told today was her day off.

Jack wondered if he should get a last name and look her up for questioning and decided to give the information he had to Sergeant Jones at the police station. Let him do the follow-up; Jack was anxious to get to Astoria. A man who usually operated on logic, he found himself being ruled by his gut and his gut said, hit the road.

"How 'bout your maintenance guy, Hank? Is he around today?"

"He didn't show up again. Jerry's still covering for him."

"What about the local guys Jerry called in? Is one of them around?"

"Brad Withers is in the basement. You can catch him there if you hurry," the clerk told them before turning her attention to a tagged conference official who was having trouble with an overhead projector.

They found Withers in an anteroom in the basement digging through a pile of stuff in the corner. He glanced over his shoulder when he heard them in the doorway. His round bald head reflected what little light the overhead bulb produced. Jack had never seen anyone so hairless. Even his eyelashes looked translucent, like the fins of some tiny fish. He sure as heck wasn't the guy Jack had seen upstairs the day before; that must have been the other one.

"You folks need something?" he asked. "Call the desk and tell them. I'll get to you when I can."

Jack flicked on his phone and showed Brad the photo of the guy in the hooded sweatshirt. "Do you recognize him?" he asked.

"Sure, I seen him," Brad said. "Up on three, I think. Yesterday morning, late. Me and Adam were working on a heater unit up there. Adam left to drive into town to hunt down a part. I got bored and wandered out in the hall to sneak a smoke. This guy was standing by the elevator." He turned back to the dark corner. "Turn your phone this way. The light is helping. Lower." He made a triumphant sound. "There's the pipe wrench, right in front of my nose."

"Do you know the guy's name?" Sophie asked.

Brad stuffed the wrench in a bucket with some other tools. "Nope. Ask Bonnie."

"She's off today," Jack said.

"Nah, she's up on three again covering for someone with a sick kid."

"But the front desk—"

"Trust me," Brad interrupted.

Jack and Sophie exchanged quick glances and took off. They found Bonnie just coming out of a room. "You lock yourself out again?" she asked as she caught sight of Sophie.

"Not this time. Would you look at a photo for us?"

Jack pulled out his phone. Bonnie peered at the screen and huffed. "That's Gerald Duff in 308."

"You've met him?" Sophie asked, her voice tinged with excitement.

"Not really but I came up here yesterday to exchange a coffeepot he claimed was broken. He wasn't in the room so I left the new one on the desk right next to a stack of crisp dollar bills. Lot of good it did me."

"What do you mean?" Jack asked.

"He checked out a while ago. It's a holiday tomorrow and that means more people will check in when this group leaves, so I've already cleaned the room and what with the mess he left, I expected a decent tip. This is what I got instead." She dug in her apron pocket and extracted a folded dollar bill. "What do I need a paper dog for?"

"It's a fox," Sophie murmured.

"I don't care what it is," Bonnie declared and shoved it back in her pocket. "Bottom line it's a buck tip for a two-hundred-dollar room. Tightwad."

As she turned to roll her cart down the hall, Jack posed another question. "One more thing. The hotel seems to have been booked solid for the weekend. That means Duff had to have made a reservation, doesn't it?"

She shook her head. "He walked in right after we got a cancellation. I remember because I had to go up to 308 to remove a fruit basket someone had sent for the people who canceled. I bet they would have left a decent tip."

They thanked her for her help and went back to the desk, where the clerk refused to confirm or deny their former guest's name. Jack called the police and gave them the information, which also gave him a chance to remind Sergeant Jones to keep looking for Sabrina.

"Turns out my wife hates red roses," the sergeant said before hanging up. Jack relayed this information to Sophie, who laughed.

Jack felt a huge wave of relief when they finally drove out of Seaport. He decided at once that the trip would be easier if the rain hadn't started again and more interesting if Sophie was in the car with him. As it was, he'd given her the address and now followed her red compact while keeping an eye out for white sedans with murderous drivers. What he discovered was that there were a lot of white cars.

He couldn't get over Duff leaving the origami fox for the maid. Talk about calling attention to himself! He had to be an idiot or incredibly smug…maybe both. With any luck the police would haul him in for questioning. If they didn't and he was following Sophie right now, her driving up to Sabrina's residence would reinforce his belief that Sophie truly was Sabrina.

Jack's thoughts drifted to Sophie's phone conversation with her mother, especially the comments that seemed to concern Danny. She'd said he'd quit his job in Seattle and accepted a new one in Portland. That meant he would have to take and pass a new bar exam. Would he really quit a good job in Washington before making sure he could practice law in Oregon? Something sounded kind of fishy about it.

Jack could understand how a guy in a new city would latch onto a pretty companion, especially someone as warm as Sophie. He could understand how a man would be drawn to her quirky insecurities and ask her to marry him. Unfortunately, the same quirky insecurities that made her lovable also made her vulnerable. If the guy wasn't head over heels in love with her, then what was his angle?

Jack searched his memory for a second and then realized Sophie hadn't said whether or not she loved Danny, and even if she didn't, he knew people drifted into marriage for lots of reasons and only one of them was love.

And what about that phone call? She'd told her mom she had to think about something. Think about what? Danny? Was the guy still hanging around?

Regardless, on a strictly professional level, he was curious. He wanted to meet Danny, size him up. He hoped this desire stemmed solely from wholesome concern and not some irrational spark of jealousy but had to admit he wouldn't bet his life on it.

It was almost noon when they drove into Astoria, Oregon's northernmost coastal town, built where the Pacific Ocean meets the Columbia River. It was a city with a long maritime history, and Jack always enjoyed coming here despite the rain and fog. Sophie seemed to know her way around and it wasn't long before she pulled into a small subdivision in the making.

Up and down the street, still-unbought lots featured small signs with build-to-suit information while a half a dozen complete houses stood on their parcels of land surrounded by relatively new lawns and vegetation. Those residences all included rocked-in cement pillars housing mailboxes at the end of their driveways. When the subdivision was complete, it would look attractive and uniform, making up in civility what it lacked in originality. It looked like the kind of place young families started.

A smattering of vehicles parked in driveways signified people enjoying the long weekend by staying inside out of the rain. The distinct exception was the Cromwell house, whose driveway was empty. Buzz's rusty SUV was not parked outside, which meant Sabrina was not inside armed with a plausible explanation of what she'd been up to.

He pulled in beside Sophie's car and stared at the dark windows of the neat, well-cared-for craftsman-style house that Buzz and Sabrina had bought nine months before. Only the brightly burning front porch light challenged the gloom.

They both got out of their cars and hurried to the protection of the porch.

"I don't think she's here," Sophie said, her voice reflecting his own disappointment. A tabby cat suddenly jumped onto the back of a chair and stared at them through the window. Sophie put her hand against the glass and the cat carried on as though it had been abandoned for months.

"You've got a friend," Jack said.

"He looks a lot like my cat, Oscar."

"*Her* name is Gabby," Jack said. "She's Sabrina's cat. Buzz complains that she won't give anyone else the time of day."

They both watched as the cat rubbed the glass where Sophie's fingers still lingered. "Kitty doesn't seem the standoffish type," Sophie said.

"Not to you." He opened the screen door and tried the knob. This sent the cat flying. A moment later, they heard her scratching the other side of the wood door as if trying to let them in.

"Too bad Gabby doesn't have opposable thumbs," Sophie said. "Now what?"

He scanned the street, checking for loitering white sedans. "I have a lock-pick set in my glove compartment. It's time to break in."

Chapter Five

It took Jack less than thirty seconds to open the lock on the back door. "Well, that's an eye-opener," Sophie said. "Is it always that easy?"

"Not always. They need to install better locks." He held the door open. Sophie stepped inside as a blur of gray and black stripes escaped to the outside.

"I hope she's not strictly an indoor cat," Sophie said. The tabby had already jumped to the top of the fence and disappeared.

"I'm not sure if she is or not," Jack said.

The kitchen they entered was small but tidy and it looked like it would be filled with sunlight if it ever stopped raining. Jack walked to the window over the sink and peered outside.

"What are you looking at?" she asked as she stood by his side.

"The neighbor's porch. Sabrina said they hired someone to paint it. Does it look painted to you?"

"It's hard to tell through all the rain."

"Still, it's an odd time of year to paint, don't you think?"

He walked out of the kitchen without waiting for an answer. He'd gotten cryptic since entering the house and Sophie didn't blame him. Sabrina missing from a hotel room had been one thing, but Sabrina missing from this house was a whole other matter. The cat anxious for her return, a lacy red sweater on the back of a chair, rubber rain boots lined up neatly by the door, a clean coffee mug in the strainer—it was as though Sabrina might have left this room five minutes before. Missing from this house seemed like missing from her life and while Sophie had been concerned for the woman's safety before, she now found anxiety tying her stomach in tight knots.

She followed Jack into what turned out to be the living area, which was one big room full of wood walls and shelves, earth-colored furniture, family photographs and large paintings all depicting local scenic scenes. While Jack searched the house—for uninvited guests, she assumed—Sophie's attention was drawn to a grouping of wood-framed photographs displayed on the wall above a low bookcase.

All together there were ten photos that appeared to capture a life in progression. The first one was taken of a very pretty smiling woman standing on a beach, a swaddled baby in her arms. From there, the pictures included various people but the focus was always on the same child who grew older from shot to shot. Preschool, birthdays, graduations…it was all there. The last photo was of three people who sat side by side on a log. The woman was the same as the one in the first picture only two decades older. A college-age girl sat in the middle with a middle-aged man on her left side.

The girl was Sophie only it wasn't.

"Is it like looking at your own family photos?" Jack asked from beside her.

"More like seeing yourself in an alternate universe," Sophie said softly. "Are these Sabrina's parents?"

"Yeah."

"This last picture can't be more than six or seven years old. Her parents are pretty young. Do they live locally?"

"They're both dead," Jack said. "Sabrina said they were trapped in a house fire about six months after that photo was taken."

"Is that why she became—"

"A firefighter? Probably. I know something like that led to my becoming a cop."

"Lisa," Sophie said, and wished immediately she hadn't allowed the word to slip through her lips.

He took a step back as though she'd punched him in the gut.

"I'm sorry, Jack. I shouldn't have mentioned her name. I don't know why I made the leap to you becoming a cop…"

"It's okay," he said. "It's been ten years and she's acutely responsible for what I've become. Not by design on her part, I can assure you. Don't worry, I'm not going to lose it. Nightmares about her have tapered off dramatically over the years. I don't know why they've returned. Anyway, did you look like Sabrina when you were a kid?"

"According to my dad's photographs, almost exactly. My hair was longer. That's about it. I wish I understood how that's possible." As she spoke, she looked around the room. It was easy to appreciate the woodsy casualness of the interior. When the fireplace was lit, she bet the small love seat pulled up in front of it would provide a cozy spot to cuddle with a special someone. Almost as though she felt the other woman's emotions, she was suddenly washed with a feeling of loneliness.

"Sabrina really misses her husband. I hope he comes home soon."

Jack didn't question how she could say such a thing. "I know she misses him. But right now the main priority is finding her."

"And how do we do that?"

"First we call our old friend Sergeant Jones of the Seaport police and see if he's tracked down Gerald Duff." He took out his phone and walked back into the kitchen. Sophie heard his voice ask for the sergeant. He was frowning when he reentered the room a few minutes later.

"Well?"

"The bad news is that Gerald Duff is a stolen identity. They tried dusting his room for prints, but as we know, it had already been cleaned. The plate number he left is also false. The good news is that they're taking Sabrina's disappearance more seriously. They're sending an officer over here to collect the food samples we took from the breakfast tray."

"It sounds as if they're narrowing their search to the guy I saw in the hall. I don't think he even knows Sabrina is missing."

"Because he thinks you're her. I agree."

"Did you explain?"

"Yeah, but they're going to go about this their own way. And in the end, who knows how much this guy saw? He may not be responsible for Sabrina's disappearance, but if he was stalking her, he might have seen something that would indicate who is. Plus if they get him off the street, it'll be safer for you."

"What do we do in the meantime?"

"Conduct our own investigation. I'm going to tackle Buzz's desk computer. It's time to contact him. Sabrina's been gone for almost twenty-four hours. There isn't a doubt in my mind that something has happened to her."

"Mine either," Sophie said.

"How about you look through the drawers and see if you find anything that sheds light on this situation."

"Okay."

They stared at each other for a long second, then Jack closed the distance between them and gently put his arms around her. For a moment, Sophie froze, but then she slowly melted against his chest. He held her very tight. If she'd been cold, his embrace would have suffused her with warmth. What she gathered from him now was more than warmth—it was courage that flushed through her body, and hope.

As comforting as this was, his arms also sparked awareness she'd so far refused to examine. When he drew back to look down at her, she met his gaze, struggling to understand what was happening. He was a strong, gorgeous, kind man and she liked him, trusted him, cared what he thought.

But honesty bit at her heart. She more than liked and trusted him. It wasn't just that she enjoyed his company— she yearned for it.

"You okay?" he asked as he released his grip on her arms.

"I think this house is getting to me."

"I know. It's so…empty. I'm going out to the car to get those samples for the police. Let's find out what we need to and get out of here."

Sophie nodded and escaped into the bedroom.

EVENTUALLY THE POLICE came and collected the food samples and the origami fox they'd found on their breakfast tray. They related to Sophie and Jack that a search had been launched to find Sabrina's car and, hence, establish her whereabouts. Sophie wasn't sure what Jack thought of their assurances; she only knew they didn't help her a lot. If she stepped back and looked at the situation honestly, however, she wasn't sure what else they could do. The man she thought of as Gerald Duff was still their only lead.

Meanwhile, Sophie found a cat box, food and water dispensers for the cat. That might mean Gabby was a house cat or it might just mean Sabrina kept her in when she traveled. At any rate, Sophie went to the kitchen door and called for the cat, but she didn't appear.

By the time deep shadows fell over the house, Sophie had found bits and pieces of paper scattered around Sabrina's desk computer. Lists, notes on hotel reservations, doodles, scribbled telephone numbers with a single name to identify them…nothing of import until she opened a drawer to reveal a duo of origami foxes tucked in the corner. Looking at the tiny folded dollar bills gave Sophie the willies and she could not imagine why she had ever thought them cute.

As she put everything back in a small closet that had yielded zero information, Jack appeared in the doorway. "She has a computer, too?" he said, and immediately sat down at the desk. "If I can get into her bank account I can find out if she's using her credit cards. Look around for phone information so we can conduct a search on her calls. If she's using her phone, it probably means she's okay."

As they worked, she asked him if he reached Buzz.

"I tried to call him, but that didn't work," he said, and her heart went out to him. In her gut she knew that his distress over Sabrina tied into whatever had happened to Lisa all those years before. She could see it in his eyes and hear it in his voice. And in this scenario, Buzz was Jack.

"To tell you the truth, I'm not positive what time it is there. I think it's twenty hours ahead of us. Since it's four o'clock here that makes it about noon tomorrow there. Anyway, I sent him an email."

"What did you tell him?" she asked as she found a folder labeled Northwoods Credit Union and handed it to Jack.

"Everything," he said. "If she were my wife, I'd want to know. He deserves the truth."

"I can't find anything about her phone," she said as Jack typed in the credit union information. "I did find her planner, though. She has several notes about favorite coworkers. You know, meeting Sue for lunch or going hiking with someone named Kyle."

"Kyle?" he said, brows furled.

Kyle Woods. She smiled. "Don't get all excited. Just because a woman mentions a man doesn't mean she's romantically involved with him."

"I know that but if Sabrina was involved with this Kyle guy it could explain why she disappeared without a word and why she didn't want Buzz to know. Maybe Kyle's girlfriend or wife is behind the foxes. Or maybe Sabrina tried to break it off and—"

"Slow down," Sophie said, mimicking the advice he'd given her that morning, and yet she remembered thinking herself that harboring a secret could compel a person to vanish. She felt strongly that this wasn't the case with Sabrina, at least as far as a boyfriend was concerned, but that was just her gut speaking and her gut didn't have that great a track record. "The guy behind the origami is a man, not a woman," she said.

"Well, you see, we don't really know that, do we?"

"I still think you're stretching."

"I know I'm stretching but people will be people and we all make bad choices occasionally. Okay, I'll get off that tangent for now but trust me, if I thought of it so will the police and they won't be shy about asking questions." He clicked off the computer and stood. "It doesn't look like she's used her credit card since paying for breakfast yesterday morning. There's no way of knowing if that's good or bad. I think we need to go to the fire station and talk to Sue and Kyle."

"Agreed," she said, anxious to leave the house.

As they passed through the kitchen, Jack glanced out the window. "The neighbor's lights are on. I'm going to go take a peek at the porch and ask a question or two."

"I'll go with you," she said.

But once outside, Sophie glimpsed the tabby walking along the top of the fence. A man in the yard next door was apparently taking the break in the rain to bring in firewood. He carried a load in his arms, but managed to free a hand to wave at her. With a start, Sophie realized he probably thought she was Sabrina and she waved back. "I'll catch up," she told Jack and walked toward the cat, calling, "Kitty, kitty."

The neighbor yelled, "Have you heard from Buzz lately?"

"No," she said as the cat jumped into the yard and started toward Sophie.

The man dumped the wood into a wheelbarrow. The resulting clatter spooked the cat, who turned on a dime and darted around the house toward the street.

Sophie followed at a run. She could not be responsible for losing Sabrina's cat, she just couldn't. She reached the front yard as the cat reached the far sidewalk and trotted onto the muddy driveway of the house under construction. Sophie finally caught up with the tabby when the little rascal stopped to wash her tummy. "Gotcha," she said, and swept her up. The cat immediately went into limp mode and started purring.

"Now you're all friendly?" Sophie said as she hugged the tabby in her arms and started back to the house. As she stepped off the curb, a white car suddenly appeared from a side street. A moment of déjà vu assaulted Sophie's nerves and she stopped dead in her tracks to steel herself for another incident like the one in the garage. This car, however, slowed down as it drew closer, and the passenger window lowered.

Another neighbor mistaking her for Sabrina, she thought, until she found herself facing the barrel of a gun.

JACK WALKED ACROSS the wet grass toward the house on the east side of Buzz and Sabrina's place. The only part of the house visible from their window had been the porch, but as Jack approached he could see the house itself was older and smaller than the new ones springing up in the subdivision surrounding it. No doubt it had once sat on this small plateau more or less by itself.

He was looking for a path around the porch when a sliding glass door opened and a pleasant-looking woman in her forties stepped outside. "I saw you coming from Sabrina's house. Is everything okay over there?"

"Why do you ask?" Jack asked, suddenly alert.

"I just haven't seen her around for a few days. I got worried, you know, what with her husband off on that job and everything."

"She decided to take a little trip," he said.

"Down the coast like she does every year?" the woman asked, but it was more a statement. "That girl is amazing. Who else goes hiking in February?"

"No one," he said with a laugh. "My name is Jack. Buzz and I go way back. Sabrina mentioned that you had your porch painted recently and I was hoping you could give me the name of the guy you hired."

Her expression turned quizzical. "My porch?" She gestured at the faded paint. "This porch? When? Did she say?"

"About a month ago. She just happened to see a painter over here. Maybe your husband hired someone."

"Tom? Not likely."

They both peered at the protected walls of the inset

porch. The only new paint consisted of a couple of whitish brush strokes that stood out against the beige paint. Jack turned to look at Sabrina and Buzz's house and found his gaze centered on the kitchen window.

A couple of Sabrina's statements lingered in his mind. *I was at the kitchen window draining pasta when I thought I saw the painter taking photos of me... I just had the strangest feeling he'd been doing more than taking pictures...*

A decade-old image of Lisa cooking pasta for a photographer flashed in his head. She'd survived the photo shoot but soon after—

Where was Sabrina? For that matter, where was Sophie?

"We didn't hire a painter," the woman was saying. "I have no idea—"

"I must have misunderstood Sabrina," Jack interrupted as he turned on his heels and began retracing his steps. The back of Buzz's house looked deserted. He broke into a jog and headed to the front yard, stopping short when he spied Sophie standing in the street, facing his direction, holding the wiggling cat. A car had stopped between him and her and for a second he thought she was arguing with the driver because even from a distance, he detected waves of tension.

He continued moving, wondering if he dared take time to open the trunk and retrieve his gun. It appeared the driver's attention was on Sophie and not him. However, the late-afternoon light made seeing anything inside the car iffy at best.

And then suddenly it looked like Sophie tossed the cat right at the driver. An explosion sounded and the car spurted forward as though the driver's foot reflexively hit the accelerator pedal.

Sophie took off at a run as the cat came flying back out the window. The car crashed into the construction's

trash bin that fell over with a bang, spilling its contents
into the street. The driver overcorrected and his car came
damn close to hitting Jack, who jumped out of the way as
the vehicle continued careening until it smashed into one
of the cement pillars holding a mailbox. Jack ran toward
the stalled car, but the driver got it going again before he
could get there and this time backed up and accelerated
like a race-car driver, speeding off down the street until
lurching around the corner and roaring out of sight.

Jack looked around for Sophie and found her kneeling
by the supine cat. He sprinted over to join her.

"I killed Sabrina's cat!" she said as she lifted the little
animal from the pavement and clutched it to her chest.

He looked down at the cat, who was already beginning
to squirm in her grasp. "No, she's not dead. See, she's
breathing." The cat continued to struggle against Sophie's
hands as Jack helped her stand.

"Did he shoot her?" Sophie demanded.

"There's no blood, at least not hers," Jack said as he
lifted the angry tabby out of Sophie's grasp to save her
from further scratches.

"We have to take her to Dr. London."

"Who?"

"Sabrina's veterinarian. He's on Hyde Street. I saw an
invoice for him in Sabrina's papers."

"The cat seems fine," Jack protested. "How about you?"

"I'm okay."

"Did you get a look at him?" Jack asked but he knew
the answer, for he had also seen the guy through the windshield and knew he'd hidden his face.

"He had one of the ski mask things on," she said.
This conversation was held as they hurried back toward
Jack's car. Sophie got into the passenger seat and held out
her hands to accept the increasingly irate cat, who now

growled and hissed her displeasure. Jack wished he had a box in which to contain the eight pounds of striped fury, but he didn't and it was obvious Sophie was determined to see this through.

"I have to lock their door," he shouted as he ran back around the house and did just that. They arrived at the vet's a little bloodied but in one piece.

THE RECEPTIONIST ASSUMED Sophie was Sabrina. "Love your hair," she said. "Man, Gabby is going nuts. Let me get you a cat carrier."

Sophie explained about the fall and asked that the small animal be examined and boarded but added that she couldn't stay.

"Late for work, huh? No problem. We'll examine her and call for your consent if we need to treat—"

"No, I'll be out, you know, fighting fires, and I may not hear my phone. Just do whatever it takes to make her okay and keep her here until I come for her." As the cat had started howling, this whole conversation had a surreal quality that remained as the receptionist agreed to Sophie's requests and disappeared down the hall with the yowling tabby.

"You're going to have to stop allowing everyone to believe you're Sabrina," Jack cautioned her as they drove to the police station. "When the cops start questioning people they'll all report they saw her today. We need everyone to understand that she's missing."

"I didn't think of it that way," Sophie said. "Okay, I'm now Sophie Sparrow again, unlikely look-alike."

He smiled at her.

At the police station, they spoke to a Detective Reece, a very tall man with a thick thatch of gray hair and a sweet smile that seemed as if it would be better suited for work in the clergy than on the streets. Sophie reported what had transpired outside Sabrina and Buzz's house. "The guy wore a ski mask and gloves. He pointed a gun at me and I threw the poor cat at him. He fired and I ran. He crashed into a dumpster thing and made a huge mess."

"After that, he proceeded to hit a very solid post," Jack said. "I saw the glitter of glass or plastic in the street. He also fired a shot, as Sophie said. The bullet's undoubtedly there somewhere."

"He probably broke a headlight," Detective Reece said. "I'll get someone out there right away to fetch the pieces and find the bullet. License plate?"

"Obscured," Jack said, "both front and back."

"Anything else?"

Sophie took a deep breath. "I think the cat is going to be okay."

Jack smiled to himself as the detective's eyebrows rose on his forehead.

In the end, there was no way to know if it was the same man who had tried to run Sophie over in the hotel garage or if he was responsible for the origami, let alone Sabrina's absence. They were told the lab work on the food samples hadn't come back yet, that there were no prints on the origami fox found on the breakfast tray and that Sabrina's car was still missing. But Detective Reece, as opposed to Sergeant Jones down in Seaport, seemed to take the situation more seriously and Sophie felt as though he would actually see things through.

They left after answering a host of related questions and drove immediately to the fire station, where they were told they could find Sue Landers in the kitchen but that Kyle Woods was off for a few days.

The kitchen was large and well equipped, and at the center of it, a woman stood peering into an open refrigerator. A pile of ingredients sat on the counter next to her. At the sound of her name, she straightened up and turned. They were treated to a blazing-white smile and curious hazel eyes surrounded by an unruly mass of red hair and a galaxy of freckles. She stared openmouthed at Sophie before saying, "Sabrina never told me she had a twin."

"That's kind of up in the air," Sophie said evasively.

"You could have fooled me. Just your hair and the mole on your cheek are different. You aren't Sabrina playing a trick on me, are you?"

"No, definitely not."

"The resemblance is amazing."

Jack got her back on track by showing her the picture of the guy in the hooded sweatshirt and she shook her head as she closed the fridge. "He doesn't look familiar," she said.

"So you never saw him hanging around the station waiting for Sabrina?"

"Are you saying this is *another* friend of hers?"

"Another?" Jack asked.

She shook her head as she opened a cupboard and rifled through the contents. "Never mind. This dude's a friend, though?"

"No," Jack said. "Listen, I'll level with you. The police will be around asking questions sooner or later because Sabrina seems to have disappeared." He explained about being Buzz's friend and that Sabrina had called him to help her but vanished before he could do more than take a few random photos.

"It's hard to tell with Sabrina," Sue said carefully as she closed the cupboard. "She can run hot and cold. I don't mean that in a bad way. She's just, well, independent. If she was having a problem of some sort she'd probably tell Kyle about it before she'd tell me."

"Kyle Woods?" Jack said.

"Yeah. But he's up in Canada visiting his grandfather for a few days."

"So, Sabrina, you and Kyle are close friends?"

"Sort of," she said. "Kyle is married but his wife walked out on him right before the holidays. Since then, he and Sabrina have been hanging out. Well, you know, he's suddenly alone and so is she thanks to Buzz's job." She peered at Sophie again. "You say Sabrina is missing?"

"Yes. She asked Jack for help and then she left the hotel in her car and no one has seen or heard from her since."

"I wouldn't worry," Sue said casually.

"Why not?" Jack asked.

"She may have gotten a wild hair and just taken off. Or she may have met someone she knew. You said the police are looking for her?"

"They will be. I'm sure they'll ask you questions."

Sue shook her head as she glanced back at the fridge. "She has this whole week off. I'm not going to start worrying about her until she doesn't show up for her next shift. Listen, it's my turn to cook and that means enchiladas. I can't find the tortillas. If Rowdy forgot to buy them, I'm going to have to kill him. You guys need anything else?"

"Is there anyone else here who she might have confided in?"

Sue seemed to consider the question before responding. "I don't think so. Kyle will be back by the end of the week. Chances are if she had plans, she told him." She patted her pocket and took out a card. "Feel free to call me if you think I can help. But like I said, Sabrina is a take-no-prisoners type of gal. Try not to worry too much."

They talked to the supervisor and anyone else they could corner, but no one recognized the guy in the photo and no one had heard from Sabrina or expected to.

"Did you get the feeling Sue thinks something is going

on between Kyle Woods and Sabrina?" Sophie asked after they got back in his car.

"Yeah, I did. Well, he's off for a few days, she's off—I don't know. I don't want to think it, but you have to keep an open mind. What she does is her business—and Buzz's. I just want her safe."

"Would you be this easygoing if you suspected your spouse was fooling around?" she asked him as she put on her seat belt.

He turned his head to smile at her as he started the engine. "Hell no."

Sophie stared back at the station house with a million random thoughts flying through her head. Jack let the car idle as he touched her arm. "What is it?" he asked. "What's on your mind?"

"I was just thinking about Sabrina. About her house and her job and her habits… She's a brave woman, isn't she?"

"Well, yes, I suppose she is."

"But she's also a good friend to people. Sue made her sound a little cold and calculating but that's not the woman I saw in her emails. People obviously relied on her in different ways. She drove for Meals on Wheels, she visited a friend's grandmother in a dementia care facility, she helped a friend called Bunny when her marriage broke up… She's a kind person."

He smiled. "It sounds as if you're comparing yourself to her."

"We're nothing alike," Sophie said.

"Other than your appearances, there's the fact that you both love or loved a man named Daniel."

"Love? Maybe she does, but my Danny was never a lover."

"Then what was he, Sophie? What *is* he?"

She met his gaze. "I'm not sure."

He took a deep breath but went back to his original point. "You both have tabby cats, you both vacation at the same seaside town and even stay at the same hotel, albeit at different times of the year."

"Coincidences," Sophie said.

"Perhaps. But you're also both kind and civic minded, and don't shake your head at me. I bet you do a lot more for the kids you teach than show up in the classroom, don't you?"

"Yeah. You know. But I get back so much more than I give."

"That sounds like the essence of compassion to me," he said. "Besides, you're both very beautiful on the outside, too."

She laughed to cover a sudden onslaught of shyness. "I never felt beautiful before meeting you," she said and looked away at once, wishing she could take back her words. They were true, but they also revealed the very vulnerable core at the center of her being.

"I'm not a fool," she added at once so he wouldn't have to figure out how to respond to the neediness of her last comment. "Sabrina and I look too much alike for it to be a fluke. All my life I've been searching for someone—I thought it was a forever guy, you know, true love and all that. But now I think I was searching for Sabrina. And since I can't compare notes with her, I have to talk to my mother, I have to know exactly what she's been keeping from me and why."

"When are you going to talk to her?"

"Tonight. It's time for me to go home and face my family."

"Including Danny?"

"Yes. I have a huge diamond to return."

"I'm going with you," Jack said, and for some reason she wasn't surprised.

"Okay."

"No argument?"

"Until they catch the idiot in the white car, you are more than welcome to watch my back. I guess I have to ask if going to Portland isn't a waste of your time. Your priority is Sabrina."

"My priority is getting her back in her house in time to welcome Buzz home with a giant kiss. You're like a magnet for this white-car guy and at this point he's my sole lead."

"Okay, but I need to go back and get my car. I have a job to return to on Tuesday."

"It'll be harder to throw the guy in the car off the trail if we're driving two cars," he warned her. "He's got to be somewhere close. He always is."

She shuddered as a dozen spidery chills radiated outward from her spinal column. "I have to admit all this is getting to me. I'm normally a fly-under-the-radar type of gal, not the kind anyone tries to kill."

"I don't think anyone wants to actually kill *you*, as in the Sophia Sparrow you," Jack said.

"That's the only me I am. And how do we know what this lunatic is thinking? Maybe he's declared war on all dark-haired girls who own tabby cats."

He laughed softly in his throat.

"I'll just say it," she added, her voice deadly serious. "Sabrina may be courageous, but I'm not Sabrina. I'm a card-carrying chicken."

"Once again you sell yourself short," Jack said. "Okay, we'll go get your car. I'm going to twist and turn all over this city to try to throw him off, so try to keep up."

"Just watch me," she said and took a deep breath.

"That's exactly what I intend to do," he responded.

Chapter Six

By the time they reached the outskirts of Portland, Jack was hungry enough to eat just about anything, including fast food. He passed Sophie's car and signaled as he pulled into a restaurant parking lot, relieved when she followed suit.

They went inside and ordered, then sat at a window table and unwrapped burgers and fries. It was useless trying to maintain a conversation with Sophie; the closer she got to home, the more preoccupied she became. At one point she dug in her purse and brought out an enormous diamond ring that she turned this way and that as she studied it. He had no idea what she was thinking. He began to wonder if it was such a good idea to go with her into what promised to be a powder keg, but when he suggested she drop him off at a hotel and continue on without him, she shook her head.

"Oh, no you don't," she said, stuffing the ring in her pants pocket. "I'm not going in there alone. Besides, what about the phony Gerald Duff?"

"Good point. Okay, I'll stay outside. That way you'll have your privacy and I can keep an eye on the street."

"Cluck, cluck, cluck. Jack, don't wimp out on me," she scolded.

"I just don't want to make things harder for you."

She stuffed her uneaten food in the bag. "I'm finished. Let's go."

He looked longingly at the half of burger he was about to abandon and grabbed a handful of fries as they left.

Sophie's childhood home turned out to be a modest dwelling on a quiet street. Even in the dark with light rain falling, he could see the place reflected its owner's warmth. The shutters were painted bright yellow, the house itself a dove gray, and tubs that probably spent the spring and summer spilling over with flowers sat on either side of the front door.

She parked right in front and immediately got out. He did the same, habitually scanning the road for any sign of a white sedan—now with a broken headlight and dented bumper—before following her up a cement path.

The front door of the house opened while they were still a few feet away. A tall woman stood glowering at them. "I expected you hours ago," she said. "Hurry, there's just time for you to freshen up."

As they walked into the light from the porch fixture, the woman—she had to be Sophie's formidable mother—clutched her throat. "What happened to your hair?" she gasped.

"I dyed it," Sophie said.

"Go wash it."

"Why?" Sophie asked as they both paused on the small porch. The mother still barricaded the door and so far she hadn't paid Jack the least bit of attention.

"Because it looks stupid. Danny will—"

"Danny? You called him? He's coming here? Now?"

"He'll be here any minute. Now go wash that stuff out of your hair." She finally met Jack's gaze and added, "Who are you?"

"This is my friend Jack Travers," Sophie said. "Jack,

my mother, Margaret Sparrow. Mom, it's wet and cold out here. How about you let us in?"

"'Us'?" she repeated, but stepped aside for them to enter. The room Jack found himself in was small, overly warm and dominated by a reclining chair and a television set.

Margaret Sparrow slid Jack a sidelong look. "What is he doing here?" she asked Sophie.

"Like I said, he's a friend. Mom, I need to talk to you about something serious."

"First fetch me a glass of water," Margaret said. "All this stress has taken its toll. Honestly, Sophie, you've been very inconsiderate to everyone."

"I'll get the water," Jack volunteered. Sophie gestured toward an arch to his left.

Margaret's voice followed Jack into the small kitchen.

"The only thing you need to worry about right now," she said, "is making sure you don't blow it again with Danny. Get rid of this other man."

"Mother…"

"Help me sit down. My sciatica is worse than ever."

Jack returned with the water right as Sophie assisted her mother into the recliner. He handed the glass to Sophie, as Margaret was busy sorting through a dozen prescription bottles until she found the one she wanted.

Once the medicine was taken, Sophie tried again. "I need to ask you about a woman named Sabrina Long Cromwell."

"Never heard of her," Margaret said. She glanced at the wall clock and added, "There's no time to fix your hair, although, Lordy, what were you thinking? And where'd you get that sweater? It hides your figure. Go change."

"Mom," Sophie said again. "Forget Danny. Did you

know there's a woman who lives two hours away from here who looks exactly like me? How is that possible?"

"How should I know? Stop going on about nothing and show this guy the door. Your fiancé will be here any moment. Isn't that a lot more important than some girl you don't know?"

Jack thought he detected a little tic in Margaret's left eye that suggested she wasn't as nonplussed about the mention of a Sophie look-alike as she tried to appear.

There was no way he was wading into this fray, however. He strove to make his six-foot-plus frame a little less obtrusive by standing far to the side, but it was a small room in a house with low ceilings.

Sophie stood her ground. "No, Danny is not more important than getting to the bottom of this. Jack, will you please show my mother Sabrina's wedding picture?"

He pulled out his phone and found the photo. Walking to Margaret's side, he turned the phone so she could see. He was standing close enough that he felt her body stiffen as Sabrina's face filled the small screen.

"Remarkable, isn't it?" Sophie asked as she took Jack's phone from his hand and looked at the picture again as if to reacquaint herself.

"There is a surface resemblance," her mother allowed.

"Will you please tell me how this could happen?"

Margaret shook her head. "I don't have the slightest idea." To Jack, her voice sounded sincere, as though she truly was flummoxed.

Sophie perched on the edge of the small sofa next to her mother's recliner. "Mom, just tell me. Am I adopted?"

"Are you adopted? Stop being silly."

"Then how—"

"I don't know!" Margaret snapped.

Sophie laid her free hand atop her mom's arm. "I have a theory," she said softly.

This was news to Jack, who tried once again to disappear into the woodwork.

"Honestly, this isn't the time—" Margaret began, but Sophie cut through her protest.

"If I am truly not adopted, then I think Dad talked you into having a baby. When you found out you were going to have twins, I think the idea of raising two kids when you didn't even really want one was too much for you to handle. I think you gave my sister up for adoption. I don't know how you talked Dad into that. Maybe he didn't even know, maybe you kept it a secret—"

"Listen to yourself," her mother interrupted. "Do you realize how delusional you sound?"

"Then you tell me what happened," Sophie said. "Please, Mom. I need to know. I can't pretend to understand how you might have felt—I've never been in a similar position—but surely you can see that I must know the truth."

Sophie might not think she was as brave as Sabrina, Jack thought, but broaching this subject in the middle of the Danny debacle wasn't exactly an easy thing to do, not when deep inside her world pivoted on this key piece of missing information.

"You want the truth?" Margaret said. "Well, here it is. I had one baby. You. Not two." She stared hard at Sophie as if daring defiance.

"You can't sweep this under the rug," Sophie said. "It's important, damn it."

"How dare you swear at me!"

"And how dare you lie to me," Sophie said. "I'm not leaving here until you tell the truth."

"You want the truth? Come with me."

With that, the older woman waved away Sophie's help

and struggled to her feet. "I'll show you the truth," she muttered, and grabbed a cane. The two women exited the room through another doorway while Jack stood there wondering what he should do.

A soft knock on the door answered that question. He opened it to find a clean-shaven man about his own age. "What can I do for you?" Jack asked the sandy-haired thirtysomething guy, who wore a very expensive Burberry coat. It had to be Danny, and face it, Jack was curious what Sophie had seen in him.

"I'm looking for my fiancée, Sophia Sparrow," he said. "My name is Daniel Privet."

"Come on in." Jack scanned the street for white cars before he closed the door.

The newcomer looked around the empty room. "Where is she?"

Jack waved toward the back of the house. "She and her mother are…visiting." He stared at the guy in the better light. Something about him seemed familiar.

"What are you staring at?" Danny asked, his brows furled.

"Sorry. I was just wondering if we've met."

"I don't recall it if we did."

"You just look kind of familiar."

"I work up in Seattle at a law firm called Finder and Finch," Danny said. "Well, I should say I used to work there. I've recently taken a position here in Portland with another firm. Sophie and I are getting married soon."

"That's not what I heard," Jack said, curious how Danny would react to direct confrontation.

"What's that supposed to mean?"

"Sophie never agreed to marry you."

"She most certainly did. Right here in this room, as a matter of fact. Who in the hell are you?"

"Jack Travers. I'm a friend of Sophie's. I'm curious about something. Why in the world did you propose in front of her mom?"

"I don't see how that's any of your business," Danny said as a red flush began to creep up his neck.

"Was it because you needed her on your side? That's all I can figure. You were unsure what Sophie would say so you used her mother to, well, gang up on her. That's it, right?"

His cheeks were bright pink by now. "I'm quite intimate with this family," he said sternly. "Sophie's never mentioned your name."

"We just met a day or so ago," Jack said as he heard Sophie and her mother returning to the living room.

"Now are you satisfied?" Margaret asked as she headed for her chair.

"No," Sophie said from right behind her.

Danny rushed forward and threw his arms around Sophie. "Darling," he gushed. "You're back!" He caressed her hair, apparently oblivious to the way she tried to push herself free. "If you only knew how worried I've been about you."

Sophie firmly detached herself from his grip. "Danny—"

"Shush, sweetie, I have the most wonderful news! I changed our flight to Hawaii. We leave tomorrow! We can get married out there and have two whole weeks to get used to being Mr. and Mrs. Daniel Privet. I'm sure your mother will understand."

"Of course I do," Margaret chirped from the recliner.

Jack watched all of this as one might view a reality television show. It was downright surreal how the two attempted to cut Sophie out of her own life.

"We're not getting married in Hawaii or anywhere else," she said softly.

Margaret's deep sigh sucked half the air out of the room. "I don't know what's gotten into you," she lamented. Then she looked straight at Jack. "It has to be you. You put some kind of spell on her."

"Do you really think she's that gullible?" Jack asked.

Sophie reached into her jeans pocket and emerged with the diamond ring she'd stuffed there when they ate dinner. She held her hand toward Danny. "I'm sorry, I really am," she said. "You must take this back. I have no intention of marrying anyone. I think it's best if we stop seeing each other."

"You don't mean that," Danny said, refusing to take back the ring.

"Yes, I do mean it."

He shook his head. "I know you love me. We're going to get married just like I…we…planned. I'll make you happy, I swear I will."

For the first time, he seemed to notice the phone Sophie still clutched in her left hand.

"What's that!" he demanded, turning his head to better see Sabrina's picture. He grabbed the phone away and stared openmouthed at her image. "You got married!" he screeched, and then turned to Jack. "Is this you in the picture? Did you two… How could you?" he demanded of Sophie. "After all the time I've invested."

"'Time you've invested'?"

He shook his head.

She narrowed her eyes as she forced the ring into his hand. "This isn't a photo of me."

"How is that possible?"

"I don't know how it's possible. We could be twins we look so much alike."

Danny took a step back.

"Do you know her?" Sophie asked. "Her name is Sabrina Cromwell."

He shook his head but the gesture looked as phony as just about every word that had come out of his mouth except for the line about investing time. To Jack that had been the one real thing the man had uttered.

And Jack was positive Danny knew something about Sabrina. On a hunch, he reclaimed his phone and scrolled through the photos, pausing on the one of the guy in the sweatshirt jacket. He showed it to Danny, who retreated another step. "How about this guy. Do you recognize him?"

"No. I've… No."

"I don't know why I didn't see it before," Sophie said wonderingly, looking between the photo and Danny. "This guy bears a surface resemblance to you."

"No way," Danny said, but a light went off in Jack's head. That was the reason he'd thought he'd recognized Danny when he came through the door.

"I used to be a cop," Jack said slowly. "I'm a PI now. In today's world that means I know my way around a computer. Give me an hour and I can trace your whole family tree back to the gleam in your great-great-grandpa's eyes. You can save me the hour and make it easy on yourself by telling us what you know. Oh, and maybe it will jar your memory if I tell you he tried to kill Sophie."

"Twice," Sophie added.

Danny stared at her. "He tried to hurt you?"

"He tried to *kill* me."

"Why would he do that?"

"Apparently because he thinks I'm Sabrina. By the way, she's missing. The police are looking for this guy in connection to her disappearance and the attacks on me. If you know something you'd better speak up."

Danny reminded Jack of a groundhog who peeks out of his hole and doesn't like what he sees.

"Mr. Privet, face it," Jack said. "You're stuck between a rock and a hard place. Keep in mind we're going to tell the investigating police our suspicion that you have information. To stay silent now makes you an accessory after the fact…"

"He's my half brother," Danny blurted out, "but you're wrong, he couldn't have had anything to do with hurting someone or trying to kill Sophie. That's insane."

"What's his name?"

"I don't know."

"You don't know your brother's name?"

"We were never close, never. He ended up in prison a few years ago. I heard he's out now and I heard he changed his name, you know, for a fresh start. I don't know what he chose because I don't have anything to do with him."

"I thought you just said he'd never hurt anyone," Sophie said. "How do you know that if you're alienated from him?"

Danny bit at his lip and shook his head.

"What about your mother?" she asked. "You said she works for a guy up in Seattle. I can't remember who the guy is, but she'll know your half brother's new name."

"She quit that job. She's…traveling."

"But you can get in touch with her."

It took him a moment to respond. "I doubt it," he finally said.

"How about your half brother's old name?" Jack asked.

"The guy's a loose cannon," Danny grumbled without making eye contact with anyone.

"If your half brother has been in prison I can find his name in about five seconds."

"Then find it," Danny said.

Anger chilled Jack's voice as he looked Danny in the eye. "Whether you like it or not, you're in this up to your eyeballs. Do you know where Sabrina is? So help me if anything happens to her or to Sophie, I'll wring your neck with my bare hands."

Danny collapsed on the small sofa as though his feet would no longer support his weight. "Oh, God," he groaned, covering his head with his hands.

"Stop badgering the poor boy," Margaret Sparrow ordered. Was she really so blinded by Danny's show of wealth that she couldn't see what a complete waste of skin and bones he was? Jack fought an urgent desire to whisk Sophie away. How she had managed to mature into womanhood with even an ounce of self-esteem was a miracle to him.

But the bigger fish that needed frying sat crumpled on the sofa. He obviously knew more than he'd told them so far and even their warnings about the police didn't seem to get to him.

"Tell us his name, new, old, whatever," Jack insisted. "Is it Privet like yours?"

"We're so worried about Sabrina," Sophie added. "If your half brother can help find her—"

Danny slammed his fist against his thigh and shot to his feet. "I don't have to talk to you two," he said, glancing from Sophie to Jack. He stabbed a finger at Sophie. "You blew it, babe." He strode to the door with an attempt at a swagger.

"Danny, wait, where are you going?" Margaret pleaded.

He opened the door and looked back at them all. "If I have to talk to the police, I'll talk to the police, but I'd rather live out my life on a deserted island than spend one more second in this terrible house. You can all go to hell." And at that, he left without closing the door.

Jack glanced over at Sophie, who looked introspective as she watched Danny's retreat. He bet she was wondering what she'd ever seen in the slimeball.

"I'm going to go make a call," Jack announced as he swung the door shut and walked into the kitchen for a little privacy.

By the time he gave the Astoria police Danny's name so they could start tracing his relatives and got caught up on what was happening at their end, he was ready to leave. He returned to the living room to find both women more or less as he had left them. He was desperate to drive to Seattle. He wasn't sure if Sophie would come with him or elect to stay here and try to fix her small family.

"I want you out of my house," Margaret said as she glared at Jack.

"If he goes, I go," Sophie said.

"Did I raise an idiot? We need to put our heads together and figure out a way to fix what's happened with Danny. He'll give you everything you want if you play your cards right."

Sophie looked at her mother as though she'd never seen her before. "You mean he'll give me everything *you* want."

"It's the same thing," Margaret said.

"No, Mom, it isn't. And besides, that ship has sailed— for both of us." She glanced down at the floor as she took a deep breath, then she leaned over and retrieved the diamond ring that must have rolled under the sofa when Danny stood so abruptly. She set it on her mother's tray. "Maybe you can hock this," she said. She picked up her purse from the chair where she'd flung it and without another word, opened the front door and exited the house.

"She can't just leave," Margaret said.

Jack stared at her a moment. "You're lucky she stayed as long as she did," he said, and left to join Sophie before a white car could appear out of nowhere and run her down.

Chapter Seven

The rain had stopped and the skies cleared to the point where a few stars actually glimmered in the sky. But the temperature had dropped and Sophie's coat wasn't really warm enough. Still, she ignored her own car and leaned against Jack's. In retrospect, she wished she'd packed a bag before her big exit, as she was still wearing the clothes she'd dressed in Saturday morning and it was now ten o'clock Sunday night. No way was she going back inside.

"You're going with me?" Jack asked as he approached.

She smiled as she watched his easy gait. The past hour or so had been an exercise in humiliating chaos that was going to take a while to process. But there had been a constant: Jack. He alone stood out as a person without a selfish agenda. He'd defended her without acting like she couldn't take care of herself, treated her like the intelligent, thoughtful human being she was beginning to hope she would become.

That was not to say she'd banished all her insecurities, self-doubts or the persistent desire to hide under a rock, just that she also saw glimmers of confidence and self-worth. Somehow they made her feel stronger, more substantial, and she had Jack, in part, to thank. And, perversely, she also owed Danny. He'd held a mirror up to her face; seeing herself through his eyes was sobering.

But that led to a giant question: What had been the purpose of his "investment" in her? It didn't make any sense.

"Sophie?" Jack asked and she shook her head.

"Sorry, my thoughts wandered."

"I don't doubt it." He looked back at the house and raised his hand. "That whole, uh—"

"Freak show?"

He smiled. "Yeah. It was something else. Frankly, your mother and Danny are made for each other."

"I know. So, how about it, are you driving to Seattle to try to find Danny's mother?"

"It would make more sense to use the internet but if she's as slippery as her son, a phone call would accomplish squat."

"Plus Danny said she was traveling, whatever that means."

"Do you believe him?"

"I don't know what to believe. I need to talk to her, too. It would save gas if we rode together."

"I guess it would," he said as though he might not want the company. She knew he did. He looked up and down the street, no doubt for a white car, before unlocking the doors. The two of them sat in silence for a moment until Jack said, "I guess the only trouble is where do we start?"

"Aha," she said. She'd been waiting for him to ask. "Thanks to Danny's big mouth, I was able to connect the dots. Remember how he said his half brother was a loose cannon? And then he said that whole thing about how he'd rather be stuck on a deserted island than in my house."

"Okay," Jack said. "I'm listening."

"A week or two ago I saw a letter in his car. The return address label said it was from someone named R. H. Cannon, Weather Island, Washington. Someone had crossed out the R. H. Cannon part and handwritten the initials

N.R. above the label. I asked Danny about it and he blew me off. At the time, I thought N.R. might be the name of an old girlfriend but then I remembered his mom's name is Nora. I'm not sure her last name begins with an R, but I'll bet you a dollar that letter was from his mother and that R. H. Cannon is the name of the man she works for. Danny told me the guy lived in Seattle. Well, Weather Island is just a forty-minute ferry ride away."

"I've never heard of Weather Island," Jack said.

Sophie smothered a yawn. "I went there with my dad when I was a kid."

He started the car. "Let's give it a try. But listen, Seattle is only about three or four hours away. Let's get a room for the night on the outskirts of town and drive the distance tomorrow morning."

"We'd have to get an early start if we want to catch the first ferry."

"Then we'll get an early start. It's been a very long day."

"Okay," she said. "Only I'll have to borrow your pajama top again."

"No problem. You look a hell of a lot sexier in it than I do."

She doubted that. "As long as we get up there before Danny has a chance to blow the whistle. I want to be back here by tomorrow night. Maybe by then Sabrina will be home and this whole thing will be over."

"I hope so," he said, but she detected no real confidence in his voice.

"Now you've got me hoping she's having an affair with fireman Kyle. At least that would mean she's safe."

"I got an email from Buzz saying he's coming home. It'll take him a couple of days…but he's on his way."

"Did he sound worried?"

"He didn't say it outright—everyone who knows Sabrina respects that independent streak in her—but if he's cutting the study short, that's a pretty good indicator he's concerned."

To Sophie, the reality of Sabrina's absence seemed to come and go. For hours now she'd clung to Sue's assurances that Sabrina would show up when she wanted to, but now, sitting here in the dark and thinking back over a day that had started with an origami fox on their breakfast tray and still wasn't over, it didn't seem quite so likely. "I should have asked Danny if his half brother knows how to make origami."

"That would have been smart," Jack said as he turned the key. "However, there was quite a bit going on."

"No kidding. Did the Astoria police have information about anything?"

"They told me to call back tomorrow, which is understandable. Detective Reece went home hours ago, so I left a message with all the information. When I call him in the morning, I'll give him Danny's name and his half brother's information again. He'll be able to get a last name for us in case his mother has flown the coop. I'll also give him Kyle Woods's name and ask him to make sure Kyle wasn't using the old guy as a ruse to get away for a private meeting with Sabrina. I just want to know she's safe and bring her home."

"Home," Sophie said, reeling at the mention of the word. Up until an hour ago, she'd had one, but now—no, now she didn't. "I don't have a home anymore," she said aloud to come to terms with it.

"Technically, that house is still yours, not your mother's."

"Do you really believe that?" she asked him as she leaned back against the headrest.

"Not if you don't," he said. He reached over to grip her

arm in support. She caught his fingers and he glanced at her.

"Thank you," she said. "For going in there with me. For…everything."

She liked that he didn't pretend not to understand what she meant. He squeezed her hand in his and then released it. "You're welcome."

They found a hotel easily and without even asking, Jack rented a single room with two beds. Sophie washed out her underwear, put on Jack's pajama top and crawled into bed. She watched his face as he worked on his laptop. He sure was easy to look at but it went deeper than the surface with him. She enjoyed the mobility of his expressions, the untold stories in his eyes.

Up until now, she'd acknowledged to herself that she really liked him. Liked spending time with him, liked talking to him. She felt his protective vibe without being overwhelmed by it, and for the first time since losing her dad, it seemed someone thought her idiosyncrasies endearing rather than stupid.

But there was a wall between them, too, and it wasn't just Sabrina's disappearance or the incident in the street outside Sabrina's house. It was also Danny's belligerence and her own mother's selfish greed. She'd been on a roller coaster the last two days—so much had happened that was making her rethink her entire life.

"The good news is Daniel Privet really was an attorney with Finder and Finch," Jack said. "He's not listed anymore, though, so I guess they took him off their list real fast. I also checked the ferry schedules. It's a private company that services some of the smaller islands, including Weather Island, and it leaves Seattle at seven forty-five." He closed his laptop and got to his feet. "And you're right, a guy named Randall Harrison Cannon lives there.

I couldn't get a name on a housekeeper. Not knowing her last name is problematic. I could run further searches on Danny to get to his mom but since we're going there anyway, I'll save that for later. I'm bushed," he added as he set the alarm on his phone.

A few minutes later he came out of the bathroom wearing his pajama bottoms. No T-shirt tonight. A light coating of fine dark hair highlighted his pectoral muscles and his taut torso. Last night she'd found his nudeness an annoying distraction. Tonight she found it absolutely captivating.

He sat down on the edge of his bed, put his phone on the nightstand and looked at her. She waited for him to say something but he didn't. The fact that his gaze didn't make her squirm kind of stunned her.

"What are you thinking?" she asked at last.

"I'm thinking you're an amazing woman," he said.

She smiled. "Do you think so?"

"You've conquered a lot of negativity and you've done it with your sanity intact. I admire that."

"Thank you," she whispered.

"How did you do it?" he asked.

"I had a wonderful father. To this day I don't know how he and Mother ever got together. He was nurturing and kind and sweet tempered, but just like me, he was never enough for her. He sold shoes for a living, the same job for twenty years. He was so proud when someone specifically sought his help…but he didn't make a lot of money and Mom was always pressuring him to make something out of himself."

"She couldn't see that he already had," Jack said.

She nodded. "He was happy."

"And he adored you."

She nodded as tears flooded her eyes.

Jack got down on his knees beside her. He swept hair

from her forehead and kissed the exposed skin. "I think he lives inside of you," Jack said. "Is there any better gift to give a beloved child?"

"What if I'm not his child?"

"You mean, what if you're adopted?"

"Yes."

"So what?" Jack said. "He was your dad, and like it or not, Margaret is your mother. They raised you, they loved you, well, each in their own way."

"I know," she said. "I'm sorry about the tears."

He plucked a tissue from the box on the nightstand and handed it to her as she sat up. The warmth of his blue eyes was a hypnotic embrace that drew her to him. "Danny was using me," she said as she dabbed the moistness from her eyes.

"I know."

"Why?"

"You're beautiful and sexy. No man could resist you."

"Jack, you know that's not true. He didn't find me alluring at all. I was an investment to him. But in what way? It doesn't make sense."

"We're going to find out," he said. "It's too big a coincidence that his half brother has apparently been stalking Sabrina and now is going after you. Hopefully the police will wring the truth out of Danny and we can get this thing wrapped up."

His focus had dropped to her mouth as he spoke. She could read his mounting desire as clearly as if it was written on his face. Was that because she shared it?

His face drifted toward hers and their lips touched. They separated immediately. Sophie smiled. He kissed her again as they fell back together on her bed.

She had never been kissed with such abandon, with such intensity or purpose. His fingers stroked the soft flesh of her throat, down to the hollow at the base, under the pajama top to brush along her clavicles... His lips followed their path and for a moment she was lost in the sheer ecstasy of unexpected and glorious sensations.

"Jack," she heard herself say. Her voice sounded as though it came from a distant knoll.

Time seemed to stop for a moment or two, then they both started speaking at the same time. "You first," he said.

With a mental kick to her stupid psyche, she whispered the truth. "No matter how good this feels on the outside, on the inside I'm just not ready. I can't go from Danny to you in one day. It's not who I am."

"I hate that guy," he whispered.

"This isn't about him."

"I know that." He propped himself up on his elbow, gazed into her eyes and gently brushed her face with his fingers as though unable to keep from touching her. As her own hand currently ran along his biceps, she understood the compulsion completely.

"The first time we met I thought you were someone else," he said in a soft sexy voice that reverberated inside Sophie. "What was really confusing was that to me, at that time, you were my best friend's wife who I'd always thought pretty but distant. And then suddenly you'd grown warm and desirable. It really shook me. I can't tell you what a relief it was when you turned out to be...well, you."

Her smile deepened. "You felt something that soon?"

"Yeah. Now don't laugh, but I'd had the premonition, if you want to call it that, that answering Sabrina's call was kind of like responding to the call of destiny. When I met you—well, I knew I'd been right. It felt as though everything in my life had been leading to that moment. We were meant to meet each other. There's a bigger plan for us. Does that sound whacky?"

"Yeah, it does," she said. "But I kind of get it. The flip side of that is I never dreamed you'd look twice at a woman like me."

"And I can't take my eyes off you," he said, smiling. He leaned forward and kissed her lips, then gently grasped her chin and looked into her eyes. "When the time is right, I want you. All of you. Tell me when the moment arrives that you feel the same way about me and I don't care where we are or what we're doing, I'm going to take your body to places it's never been."

"That's quite a promise," she said.

He smiled and kissed her nose. "I'm good for my word."

"I'll make sure to buy some sexy lingerie," she added as he slipped out of her arms and stood up.

He stared down at her. "You won't need any lingerie."

She watched him get in the other bed, and once again their gazes met. She was already second-guessing her judgment.

"Good night, Sophia Sparrow," he said softly as he turned off the light.

"Good night," she whispered and closed her eyes.

Instead of sleep, she found herself reentering what would always be Margaret Sparrow's house no matter who held the mortgage papers. Her mother's refusal to acknowledge Sophie's very real concerns about discovering a look-alike still rankled her. As proof that Sophie was being ridiculous, she'd produced a picture of herself sitting atop a bed holding a newborn in a pink blanket. "See?" she'd said. "One baby. Not two."

"This proves nothing," Sophie had responded.

"It proves everything. If you still don't believe me, look at this."

She'd turned the page to reveal a picture of her father holding her in his arms. He was standing in the kitchen, warming a baby bottle in a pan on the stove. He held a six-month-old Sophie against his chest and his smile jumped from the page.

There was a single high chair to his left. Not two. One. *Your father would never have given away a baby.* That was the unspoken message between Sophie and her mother. *You don't trust me, I get it, but you do trust him, don't you?*

And the answer was yes, she did trust her father, his big heart, his homespun wisdom, his love. He'd been her rock and she'd missed him every day since an untimely heart attack stole him away.

But that trust didn't obliterate the fact that as far as Sophie could tell, Sabrina and she were identical except for a mole on Sophie's cheek. If her parents didn't have two babies of their own, then they adopted her. Why keep that a secret?

Maybe it was Sabrina's mother who had been unable to care for two. Maybe she'd shared her windfall of babies and exacted a promise of silence. "Back in the day, did you know a woman with the last name of Long?" Sophie had whispered.

Her mother hadn't flinched. "Long? No. Why?"

"I need Sabrina," Sophie mumbled.

Jack's voice responded although she couldn't understand what he was saying. Her eyes flicked open and she realized she'd been dreaming and that she hadn't spoken aloud.

"Lisa," he moaned in the same forsaken voice as the night before.

His cry was what had awoken her.

And right that second, Sophie realized why she'd really turned Jack away. She wasn't the only one with bridges to burn and demons to excise.

She got out of bed. This time when her weight hit the mattress he reached for her. No tight grasp, just open arms.

She slid beneath the covers to lie beside him, her goal to comfort, but his goal was different. His hot mouth claimed hers, his hands moved down her body, grasping her rear, pulling her so close even the layers of cloth between them seemed to burn away. She felt his hand reach under the pajama top, travel up her thigh, across her belly, cup her breast. He pulled her closer and she was enveloped by a man bigger, hotter and sexier than any she could have ever created in her imagination.

In a moment, he would make love to her.

"Sophie," he whispered into her hair. "Sophie, Sophie." She kissed him hard and long, his voice floating her name like a blanket to warm her heart. He knew exactly who she was, exactly whose body he touched, whose arms encircled him.

His hand sliding between her legs drove all thought from her mind. She pulled at his pajama bottoms as he pushed aside the pajama top.

One hand tangled in her hair, the other touched her breasts tenderly. In a moment he would be inside her. She felt conflicted, half ready and half worried that for him, lovemaking had started with a memory of one woman before distilling into the realization of another. Of her. It was even possible he might still think she was Lisa even though he'd called out Sophie's name.

He'd told her what he wanted from her—absolute commitment to the moment—not doubt and indecision.

The whites of his eyes as he gazed down at her glistened and he grew still as if sensing her sudden detachment. He kissed her lips briefly as he lowered his head next to hers. His weight seemed to double before he rolled onto his back beside her. His fingers entwined with hers.

After a minute, he kissed her forehead and gripped her shoulders. "Lisa, right?"

"You woke with another nightmare."

"Damn."

"Jack?"

"You want to know about her."

"Yes."

He sighed. "I don't even know where to start."

"What was she like?"

"Pretty. Dark hair, blue eyes, smart, funny. She was studying prelaw because her father wanted her to. What she wanted was to be a famous chef with her own television show. She worked at this little bistro to try to get experience. Someone from a magazine saw her in the kitchen and offered her a spread in a series they were doing called 'Coeds Cook!' She was very excited—this was her big chance. They said they'd send a photographer to take a few informal pictures of her whipping up a marinara sauce to make sure she came across sexy enough."

"Sexy enough? For a cooking magazine?"

"Yeah. That's what I thought. But the magazine turned out to be one of those titillating college girl things. I told her the article would include two sentences about cooking and two pages of photos of her wearing damn near nothing but an apron. She went ballistic, told me I didn't respect her decisions, etcetera. I don't know, maybe she was right, maybe I didn't understand then how important it all was to her. Anyway, I saw her a couple of days later and she said the photo shoot had gone great and she was on her way to see the pictures. She'd completely forgotten we had a longstanding date to go to a concert. I stormed off. That was the last time I ever saw her."

Sophie knew there was more. She could feel his despair in her own bones, pumping through her own veins. She waited.

"She disappeared that night. No one knew where she was. She was just…gone."

"Like Sabrina," Sophie said softly.

"Like Sabrina. I was the major suspect, of course, until the cops discovered the magazine's photographer had given them an alias and a false address. No one could find out anything about the guy and he was as gone as Lisa was. They made a composite sketch—the guy was tall, dark, walked with a limp. The people who hired him said he didn't talk a lot. One of the typists there said he creeped her out. Long story short, Lisa was found out in the desert a week later. Her body had been set on fire. They had to identify her with dental records. An autopsy determined she'd suffered broken bones before her death… When I think of what she endured before she finally died it breaks my heart."

"And the photographer?"

"They never found him. A composite sketch linked him to another young woman's disappearance although no trace of her body was ever found. After Lisa, apparently, he changed his MO or got run over by a truck, or just flat quit… He just disappeared. No one has ever identified him."

"No wonder Lisa's death haunts you," Sophie said softly, squeezing his fingers with hers.

He turned on his side again, his presence little more than the gleam of his eyes and the musky warm fragrance of his skin. "If I hadn't belittled her big chance, I might have been around during the supposed photo shoot. I might have sensed something about the guy. She might still be alive."

There was no way to respond. He might be right. He might also be wrong but he knew that. She inched closer and he raised his arm so she could nestle against his side.

"I don't have nightmares all the time," he told her softly as he stroked her hair with his free hand. She had thrown one arm across his chest and felt the beat of his heart in her wrist. "It's just that Sabrina said a big man with dark hair had been taking pictures of her while she drained pasta water and then she vanished into thin air. It brought everything back."

"You talked about destiny," Sophie said. "Maybe somehow your past and Sabrina's present are merging."

"That would mean that against all odds she's with a human monster right now. I don't know how to save her from that."

"If it's at all possible, you will," Sophie said, and she glanced at the clock. "We have two hours before we have to leave for Seattle."

"Stay here with me," he whispered.

"Of course," she said simply.

But there was nothing simple about anything.

THEY DROVE TO Seattle under leaden skies, the steely pavement slick with ice as the windshield wipers tried to keep up with the sleet. Sophie was not looking forward to riding a ferry in her thin coat.

Today was a holiday and the schools were closed, but just to be safe, Sophie used the time they spent waiting for the ferry to load to call her principal and arrange for a last-minute substitute-teacher replacement for her class, saying she was indisposed for a week, hoping that was silly, that by tonight they'd have found Sabrina and put this whole thing to rest.

Jack called Detective Reece and found out the detective wasn't in the office.

It was finally their turn to drive aboard and park. The lower deck of the ferry was packed tight with vehicles except for the empty middle lane, as this was a ferry that made four different stops at four different islands. They got out of the car and Sophie studied the other vehicles.

"He couldn't have known we were coming here," Jack said, pulling his coat closer. Sophie knew how he felt. The bottom deck was open on both ends to allow vehicles to move off and on the boat. An icy wind that felt like it carried ice in its gusts blew straight down the middle, whipping loose hair and clothing and torturing warm-blooded creatures. If she wasn't still wearing Jack's blue cashmere sweater, she was certain she would turn into a Popsicle.

"We're the second-to-last stop," Jack added as they climbed the inboard stairs to the second floor.

The heaters were working but the cold still seeped inside. They found an empty bench and sat down. Jack immediately went to work on his phone and Sophie looked through the windows at the sleet-driven skies that merged into the Puget Sound's restless cold water. A small family seated at a nearby table caught her attention and she watched them for a while. The woman looked about her own age. The two children playing checkers beside her were about six or seven, around the age of the kids she taught. For the first time, she seriously wondered what it would be like to have children of her own. With their striking black hair and pretty faces, both the girls could easily be Jack's daughters.

Her daughters.

She smiled at the whimsy and leaned against Jack as fatigue from their interrupted night caught up with her. She actually nodded off, waking only when the ferry pulled against the pier of the first island and more than half the passengers got off, a line of their departing vehicles wending away from the docks as the ferry continued its journey.

"About last night," Jack said as he put away his phone.

That got her attention. She was about to tell him that maybe this conversation should wait for another time when he added, "I know it must seem to you that I've never gotten over loving Lisa."

Not what she expected, but as that's exactly how it did seem to her, she nodded.

"My feelings for her are frozen in time," he continued as he took her hand in his, "but I don't harbor fantasies that she and I would have ever lived happily-ever-after. Our profound differences were already driving us apart. That last fight wasn't the first one we'd had, believe me. I've let that part of my past with her go. What remains is the what-if part, my guilt, my failures."

"I can see how that is," Sophie responded. "If Danny had gone slower, if he'd understood the issues between my mother and myself instead of trying to use her to influence me, I might have talked myself into marrying him and if that had happened, it wouldn't have been long before I came to the same realizations that you did."

"The person you choose to love shouldn't be a compromise," he said.

"No, you're right, they shouldn't."

"Love has to come from your heart."

She stared at his lips as he spoke, then glanced to see the mother and her children seated a few feet away. The kids had moved on to a computer game.

"You told me to tell you when I was ready to make love," she whispered.

He laughed softly. "Right here, right now?"

"Well, you assured me I wouldn't need any sexy lingerie, so yep, I'm good to go."

He put an arm around her and kissed her forehead. "In front of those little kids?"

"Oh, I see, you're nothing but a big tease. All talk and no action."

He chuckled as he pulled her head close and kissed her nose. "How about we compromise just this once. You're freezing. There's a sign right over there that promises a snack bar. What'll it be? Hot chocolate or coffee."

"Instead of sex? Better make it the hot chocolate," she said with a big phony sigh. "With marshmallows."

He looked straight into her eyes, opened his mouth and closed it.

"What?" she asked.

"Nothing," he said. "Stay here, I'll be right back."

His phone rang as he stood and he looked at the screen. "Detective Reece," he mouthed to her and, answering the phone in a voice totally at odds with the one he used to speak to her, headed toward the snack bar that was apparently located around the corner amidships.

She leaned her head back against the bulkhead and thought about what he'd said and what he hadn't said. The strange thing was how appalled she'd been by Danny's marriage proposal and vows of undying love after only five weeks. But she'd known Jack for only two days. Two days! The thought of falling in love with him did nothing but cast a rosy glow on her future.

And then a horrible feeling came over her. Danny had used her for some reason she still didn't understand but the truth was she'd used him, too. He'd rescued her, in a way, from herself, given her a diversion. She'd met Jack right smack on the heels of escaping her delusions and latched onto the mystery of Sabrina's absence in order to keep from thinking about her own life. And now she was ready to lose herself in an affair with a man who lived one and a half states away, a man she'd known less than forty-eight hours.

What was wrong with her?

She didn't know what kind of cereal he liked, whom he voted for, if he went to the movies, if he wanted children or liked pancakes or long walks or piña coladas…

She felt the wooden bench vibrate and turned her head as she opened her eyes. "Do you—"

The look on his face stilled her.

He stood up and extended his hand, pulling her to her feet when she took it. "Come on, let's walk," he said.

They took a turn around the interior deck. Sophie could feel Jack's anxiety in his stride and the way his gaze took in every detail of their surroundings, including their fellow passengers. He finally paused before a door leading to the outside deck. "Care to brave the elements?"

"Lead on," she said, shivering at the thought of it.

The outside was as cold and icy as she'd known it would be. He turned into the biting wind and they took a few steps. The water rushing by the moving boat was as flat and gray as the skies overhead. Icy gusts flattened her hair and snaked under the hem of her jacket and up her sleeves.

"I talked to Detective Reece," he said, gripping her arm as they slowly made headway. She positioned her head not only to hear him better but to protect her face. Her nose felt as if it was about to snap off. "He heard from Sergeant Jones down in Seaport." When she glanced up at him, the expression in his eyes warned her there was bad news in the offing. "Two beachcombers found a dead body last night—"

She gasped as her knees buckled.

He caught her. "No, honey, I'm sorry. Not Sabrina. It was a man. They've identified him as Hank Tyson."

Once she was able to speak again, she mumbled, "Who is Hank Tyson?"

"The hotel maintenance guy, the one who didn't come

into work this weekend. Reece says he's been dead a couple of days."

"The poor guy," Sophie said, recovered now from her scare. "Did he get trapped by a wave or fall?"

"Reece says it appears he was strangled. It's still unclear if he died from that or the subsequent fall. They'll know more after the autopsy."

Sophie stared at him. "Murdered?"

"Yeah. Sophie, think about it. Hank didn't show up for work Saturday morning. What if someone killed him with the intention of taking his place? Then the hotel got their own employee to cover and he called in Brad Withers and his man Adam something... The thing is maybe the guy who stole Sabrina killed Hank."

"Or maybe Hank's brother-in-law or bookie or estranged wife settled a grudge," Sophie offered.

"True, but I don't like coincidences."

They'd reached the blunt-nosed end of the ferry. In the near distance, Sophie saw the lights and shapes of Weather Island drawing closer. Jack steered them around the corner where the wind was mercifully at their backs. "Why would this 'someone' choose Sabrina out of all the other women in the hotel, and more importantly, why would he kill a guy just on the chance he could snatch a victim in such a public place?" Sophie mused aloud.

"His target was Sabrina and no one else," Jack said, his voice tight. He ran his hand through his hair. "Remember that Sabrina saw someone painting her neighbor's porch. The next day she came home to the impression her house had been violated."

"Jack, what are you saying?"

"In addition to presumably Danny's half brother apparently leaving origami foxes outside her door, never indoors, by the way, there was also another man. This one took pictures of her while she was cooking." His eyes grew bright for a moment and Sophie knew all this was relating right back to Lisa, at least in his mind and his heart. "If he went inside her house and looked through her belongings, he could have seen she had reservations at the Seaport hotel."

Sophie's heart skipped a beat. "I saw scraps of papers on her desk. It appeared she'd jotted down pertinent information about her plans, including hotels and things like that." She stared at him a moment before adding, "You're talking two separate men with the same goal."

"No," he said quietly. "I'm talking two men with two different agendas. One—Danny's half brother, whose aim is to silence Sabrina for some unknown reason. His possible MO is leaving little foxes to intimidate her, throwing rocks in the attempt she'll fall off a cliff and it will look like an accident, trying to run her down. He's not very proficient. Even pointing a gun at you didn't work out. He's dangerous because he's desperate, again for some unknown reason, and his attempts are escalating in violence."

"And the other man?" she asked.

"This guy is different. This guy is a hunter and he's got Sabrina in his sights. For some reason, he fixated on her, spied on her with his camera, came into her house, looked at her things but didn't touch them, made her shudder when she couldn't even see him. And he killed to get to her."

"Jack, that's awful."

"Yeah. But the worst part is we know the half brother doesn't have her or he wouldn't be trying to do in her look-alike—you. That means that this second guy—"

"Don't say it," Sophie blurted out, the ice shards racing through her body having nothing to do with the blustering weather. "You're talking about a cold-blooded killer, a beast, a man like the one who killed Lisa." Warm tears rolled down her frigid face. "You have to be wrong."

The ferry horn blast caught them both by surprise. Jack wrapped an arm tightly around her shoulders as the boat maneuvered its way to the pier.

Chapter Eight

"Being on this island seems like a giant waste of time," Sophie said as Jack followed his phone's voice directions to the Cannon estate. "We should be back in Oregon looking for Sabrina."

"We have three hours before the ferry returns for the trip back to Seattle," Jack reminded her. "And please, don't forget we're looking for the guy who tried to kill you—twice. Who knows, when questioned it might turn out he saw something that will help the police find Sabrina."

"Yeah, I know," Sophie said. "I'm just scared. You know, for her."

He squeezed her hand. "This morning," he said to distract her, "I asked Reece about both Danny's brother and this Cannon guy. He told me Danny's brother's legal name is Paul Rey. He just got out after serving three years for assault. Oh, and they're picking up Danny for questioning. As for Cannon, he's the force behind a lumber empire. It seems he's too rich for his own good."

"And Danny's mother works for him."

"Yep. Her name is Nora Rey. Fifty-five years old, has worked as his assistant slash gopher for umpteen years, trusted employee, etcetera."

"Raised two sons," Sophie added. "One criminal, one attorney with questionable ethics and motives."

"Yeah, well, what Danny told you about his father was only half-true. He did work on a ferry but not as the captain. He was a deckhand and he got fired from that job when he was caught stealing valuables out of passengers' vehicles. After that, he left the family and traveled to Alaska, where he was killed during a bar fight. Meanwhile, Nora married another loser, this one named George Reynard, and gave birth to son Paul. George killed two men in an alley during a robbery a year later. Apparently, she shortened her surname after his death, maybe so her young son wouldn't grow up with the stigma of his father's crimes."

He paused for a second, wanting to protect her feelings but knowing eventually she would learn the truth and it might be kinder coming from him. "Danny also lied to you about quitting his job in Seattle in order to move to Portland to marry you. He was actually terminated months ago because of suspected ethics violations. He's got a kind of…checkered…relationship with things like truth and honesty."

"So he wasn't a practicing attorney when he 'bumped into me' at the grocery store?"

"Nope."

"Boy, I sure want to know what he was up to. I hope his mom can tell me."

"We should find that out very soon," Jack said as the phone announced they'd reached their destination. Jack slowed in front of open wrought iron gates flanking an uphill drive. He drove straight through and eventually they found themselves at the highest point on the island next to a large house that stood against the icy, gray skies like a Gothic nightmare.

"Yikes," Sophie said.

"No kidding." He stopped the car in front of the stairs

leading to a flagstone porch and an arched doorway. As they hurried through the sleet to cover, it was impossible not to notice the 360-degree view that took in everything from the ferry landing far below, to Seattle's obscured skyline to the east.

Their knock was answered almost at once, making Jack wonder if there were surveillance cameras on the gates or warning sensors along the steep driveway.

The woman they faced looked worn-out. Gray hair cut blunt framed a heavily lined face decorated by a pair of bifocals.

The woman gaped at Sophie. "What are *you* doing here?" she all but whispered.

"You recognize me," Sophie said.

"No. Of course not." The absurdity of this response seemed to occur to her and she shook her head. "You're one of them."

"One of who?" Jack asked.

"Those damn twins. You have to be Sabrina."

"Why do you think I'm Sabrina?" Sophie asked.

"Because Sophia's with Dan—" She stopped abruptly and looked from one of them to the other. "Why *are* you here? How do you know—"

"Please," Jack said. "It's cold and wet. Let's not stand here talking in circles, okay? You're Nora, right?"

"Nora Rey, yes." The woman bit her pale bottom lip before standing aside and holding the door open. "You'd better come in."

The entry was two stories tall, dimly lit and oppressive. Steep stairs climbed to the next floor while a crystal-and-gilt unlit chandelier hung suspended from the ceiling. "Follow me," Nora said as she crossed to the threshold of a much smaller and more intimate room. She gestured for them to enter. Once they had, she followed them inside, closing the door behind her, her movements smooth and silent as though she'd spent her life gliding around this very large house like a wraith.

She turned to face Sophie. "Which one are you?"

"I'm Sophia Sparrow."

"I missed a call from Daniel last night. Was that about… you?"

"Probably. Mrs. Rey, Sabrina is missing. Jack and I are here because two days ago your son Danny asked me to be his wife. That same day, your son Paul tried to kill me. The police are actively seeking Paul for questioning concerning my attempted murder and the possible kidnapping of Sabrina."

"Murder! What in the world?"

"Paul tried to kill me," Sophie repeated. "He's still trying for that matter. We believe his intended victim is Sabrina but when she disappeared he mistook me for her."

"Oh, for heaven's sake," Nora interrupted, her thin hand fluttering near her throat. "That boy! How did he find out about all this? What about Daniel? Are you two getting married? I mean, how could you resist such a fine man?"

"Easily!" Sophie said with enough horror in her voice to make Jack feel better about life. "Mrs. Rey, please explain all this to us."

"There's nothing to explain," she said, her lips compressed.

"Don't forget the police will be here sooner or later," Jack said.

"Oh, your damn grandfather," she said wearily with another glance at Sophie. "He's the one I blame."

"Both my grandfathers are dead," Sophie said.

"Not your genuine one, he's not dead, leastwise, not yet, though his time is running out, poor soul." Nora said this with a heavenward glance that Jack took to mean the old guy was tucked away somewhere upstairs.

Sophie backed up to a chair and sat down heavily. "He's here? In this house?" Nora's brief nod brought a groan from Sophie. "I've known something like this was coming since the moment I saw Sabrina's picture on your camera," she told Jack. Her dark eyes were round and stunned. "I don't know why I'm surprised."

"God, you look just like her," Nora said. "You even sound like her."

"Who?"

"Your mother. If the old man had just left things as they were."

"Stop talking in riddles," Jack said with a glance at his watch. "We're running out of time here. By 'old man,' you mean R. H. Cannon?"

"The one in the same," Nora said as she sat down in a chair close to Sophie's. Jack remained standing, too impatient to get back to Oregon to even think about sitting. He could feel Sophie's nerves from three feet away as she leaned forward in her chair, her hands gripped between her knees.

The housekeeper smoothed a few wrinkles from her gray dress as she avoided looking at either one of them.

"Nora?" Jack prompted. "Tell Sophie about her mother and her grandfather. Help her understand."

"Please," Sophie added.

Nora looked up and sighed loudly. "I never wanted anybody to get hurt, I just wanted Danny to have what I couldn't give him on my own. But you deserve the truth. It started with his daughter, your mother. Her name was Shelly and she was as stubborn and headstrong as Mr. Cannon. When she turned up pregnant at sixteen, he threw her out. She showed up again a few months later, just about ready to pop and sick as a dog. He relented and she gave birth upstairs, right here in this house. She died the next day."

Nora shook her gray head. "What was he supposed to do with two infants? He didn't even want to see them so he had his attorney arrange private adoptions. He demanded all the papers be given to him, and those he destroyed because he never wanted to see those kids again, he wanted no path to lead back to him. Over the years, he hinted that me and my boys would inherit his wealth when he died. Who else did he have?"

"So Danny grew up thinking he would be well-off one day," Sophie said quietly. Jack could all but see the gears spinning in her head as she tried to merge the Danny she'd thought she knew with the actual man he was.

"Well-off? Ha. Rich is more like it. This house, the island, the millions in his bank account, everything. And Mr. Cannon liked the boys whenever they came with me to work. In those days I came back and forth to the island. Now I just live here full-time. Anyway, you know how little boys can be. Loud, clumsy, taking things that amuse them… Mr. Cannon had something of a short fuse. Things kind of went downhill as they got older."

"In what way?" Jack asked.

"The university Mr. Cannon helped Daniel get into threatened to expel him over another boy's claim that Daniel cheated on his exams. At first Mr. Cannon said he wouldn't help, but in the end he made a big grant and Daniel graduated. What's a couple of million to the old guy compared to my son's reputation? But Daniel had… issues…in law school. He was too clever for those dullards and they resented him. Right after that, Paul was arrested for some little thing he swears he didn't do. Mr. Cannon bailed them both out but he said he'd had enough, he wasn't going to help them again."

"Mrs. Rey," Jack said when she fell into thought, "it's getting late and we have a ferry to catch. Please get to the point."

"Oh, very well. Last fall, when Mr. Cannon's doctor told him he didn't have much time left, Mr. Cannon decided he wanted to see what had become of his granddaughters, so he hired a private detective to find them. After learning about how each had made something of themselves, at least in his book, he decided he wanted to see their faces, so he ordered photographs."

She looked at Sophie and shook her head. "You and your sister are spitting images of your mother. That got to the old man. He called his lawyer. I kind of overhead them discussing changing his will, you know, before the door was closed all the way. The end result was he cut both of my boys off, and left me a modest endowment. And after all I've done for him, the years I've dedicated—"

"He commissioned photographs," Jack said with a quickening pulse and a glance at Sophie. "That means someone took pictures of you and Sabrina."

"I never noticed anything," Sophie said.

"But Sabrina did. She caught the man on the neighbor's porch." He forced himself not to jump to conclusions. *Gather facts.* "How do you know what's in his will?" he asked Nora.

"He told me."

Sure, Jack thought. He'd bet that none of the old guy's mail got to him without first going through her. How many envelopes had she steamed open? Most likely she found the will and read it without anyone's knowledge. "What about the results of his investigation into his granddaughters' identities? Did he tell you about that, too?"

"The file was just lying around. I…happened to see it one day."

"And you told your sons," Sophie said.

"I told Daniel. It was his future at stake."

"And Paul?"

"I never said a word to Paul," she vowed.

"Why not? It's his future, too, isn't it?"

Nora produced a folded tissue that she used to dab at her dry eyes. Jack knew a delaying tactic when he saw one. "Nora?"

"Paul was…is…a problem. At first he was in jail and then when he got out he was so wired and unpredictable. Who could talk to him about anything—important? I mean, he took his father's full last name again like it was some badge of honor. Paul Reynard, big whoop. I even heard him refer to himself as 'The Fox.' That's what his dad called himself umpteen years before. Some fox. More like a chicken, killing those men by stabbing them in the back. Daniel always said his brother was a loose cannon and that's just how he was acting."

"Reynard is similar to the French word for *fox*, *renard*," Sophie said with a long glance at Jack. "As in those origami foxes he fashioned to threaten Sabrina."

"That fits what we know about him," Jack said.

"If Paul knows about you and Sabrina, then he learned it elsewhere," Nora volunteered. "After all, there was only one available girl." She added this last part with a sweeping glance at Sophie.

"So Danny told Paul and they cooked this scheme up between the two of them," Sophie said.

Nora looked aghast. "No. Daniel wouldn't say a word to his brother. But Paul could have snooped around here while I was busy caring for Mr. Cannon."

"Do you know where Paul is now?" Jack asked.

She sniffed and shook her head. "No."

"You need to call him off."

"I have no way of doing that. He was here last week when the doctor told us that Mr. Cannon had taken a turn for the worse. The old geezer is dying, sooner rather than later. If Paul got it in his mind that he has to get rid of the other girl, well, that's what he'll try to do."

"What about the name and location of the investigator Mr. Cannon employed."

"How would I know?"

"Nora, I swear—"

"Okay, keep your pants on. Something Taylor. In Portland. That's all I know." She studied Sophie again. "I suppose you want to meet your grandfather. Let him see you in the flesh, cement your inheritance."

Sophie shook her head. "When this is all over, maybe Sabrina and I will come here and meet him—together."

"It might be too late by then," the housekeeper said.

For Jack, the words had an ominous ring to them on several fronts.

"So, Danny figured if he married me he would get at least half of my share of my grandfather's inheritance," Sophie said as they drew closer to her house in Portland. They'd each been wrapped in their own thoughts during the ferry ride back to Seattle and the subsequent drive south. Sophie knew that dealing with Danny was the easiest part of what was to come. It was her pending conversation with her mother that she dreaded.

"It looks that way."

"I wonder how he ever convinced himself that I wouldn't eventually see his true motives," she continued. "I mean, his family's connection to my grandfather is obvious—how could he not know I would figure it out? Didn't he learn anything in law school about grounds for annulment or divorce? How dumb and naive did he think I was?"

Jack shrugged, which considering his options seemed like the better part of valor, even to Sophie. Instead he offered an observation of his own. "I think Paul decided that since Sabrina was already married and therefore unlikely to marry someone new before your grandfather died that killing her would mean everything would go to you and thus Danny. Then Paul could show up and have a private chat with his half brother where he could point out how helpful he'd been and claim his share."

"What a couple of morons," Sophie said. "And we're still no closer to finding Sabrina."

Jack reached across the gearshift and took her hand. "Sophie, you know I called Detective Reece on the ferry ride back to Seattle, right?"

"I overheard you," she admitted. "I take it Danny got himself all lawyered-up and that Paul is still on the run."

"Reece also contacted Kyle Woods's grandfather up in Canada. The man swears his grandson hasn't been up there to see him since Christmas and that he's not expecting him until his birthday bash in March. They also checked with Homeland Security. Woods's car hasn't crossed the border. In other words, Kyle is also missing."

"Are the police connecting Sabrina and him?"

"Unofficially, yes. Since Sabrina's car hasn't been seen since Saturday, they're pretty sure she's off with Kyle somewhere on a lover's tryst. And they're very happy with Paul Rey, aka Reynard as the man behind everything else, including Hank Tyson's murder down in Seaport."

"Did they find Mr. Tyson's vehicle?"

"Yeah, at his house. Apparently he was killed there and dumped on that beach."

"So they're not operating on the theory Sabrina has been kidnapped."

"Reece says the chief needs proof before he starts messing with Sabrina's Fourth Amendment right against unreasonable search and seizure. We need something to demonstrate she's in some sort of danger."

"And gut feelings aren't enough."

"No. Especially since I don't know her well and you've never met her at all. But don't worry, I'm going to find your grandfather's detective tonight and get the names of the people who photographed you and Sabrina. If the chief needs proof, I'll get it for him. Do you want to come with me?"

What she wanted was Sabrina, and the desire to meet her, to see her, to touch her was so overwhelming that it took her breath away. But with the very next breath, something else happened. One minute she was riding along in a warm car. The next she was running for her life, plunging through the dark, desperate and terrified.

And then a roar like a mountain lion thundered through her head. Giant teeth closed over her leg, pierced her skin, pulled her to the ground, dragged her back into the underbrush, into oblivion. The putrid smell of rot filled her nostrils as dirty cold water splashed over her face.

The despair was as unbearable as the pain.

Sophie opened her mouth to scream but as suddenly as these sensations had dominated her mind and body they were gone.

Jack's hand brushed hers. "Are you okay?"

"Yeah. Fine," she said with a shaky voice. If what she'd just experienced was a glimpse into Sabrina's soul it meant she was alive, but only just. With a surge of passion, Sophie wished she could join her sister wherever she was, for how did a person fight such desperation alone?

"You got awfully quiet."

"Maybe we've got this all wrong," she said slowly. "Maybe Sabrina drove off the road and is lying in a ditch somewhere out of sight." Trapped and hurt in a mangled car would certainly account for the cold, the water, the hopelessness, especially after two nights alone.

"The police searched the highways."

"Which highways? North, south, east? The only direction she couldn't have driven was west into the ocean. They can't possibly have searched every single side road. For heaven's sake, she's a firefighter. Why don't we get her coworkers all up and down the coast to help look for her? Isn't that what they do, save people?"

"Good idea."

"We need to go back to Astoria."

"I know. But I have to talk to the PI first. I need the names of the photographers. I can't operate solely on the supposition she's been in a car crash."

"I know you can't," Sophie said. "You go do the detective thing, I'll do the mom thing, then we can drive to Astoria together."

Warmth spread up her arm as he took her hand. "That sounds good. I don't want to be far away from you."

"I don't want that either," she said, and an understanding of some sort traveled between them.

"I'll let you off at your house and then come back for you." He added, "And, Sophie, if you feel the need to stay in Portland for the night, we can do that."

She raised his hand to her face, held his knuckles against her cheek and kissed his fingers. Maybe she'd known him less than three days, but they'd been three pretty intense days and no matter what her head said about falling in love, she suspected her heart had a mind of its own. "I'll be ready when you come back for me," she said as she got out of the car and watched him drive away.

"You're back," Margaret Sparrow said as Sophie walked into the house. Her mother sat on her recliner as always. Oscar lay on her lap but he sprang to his feet when he saw Sophie and scampered to her side. She knelt down to scoop the cat into her arms, sparing a second to wonder if Sabrina's tabby, Gabby, was okay. Tomorrow, she'd go get the cat from the vet's. Tomorrow, with any luck, they would find Sabrina and she would finally meet her twin sister.

"I haven't heard from Danny," her mother said with pursed lips. "I think you blew it."

Sophie sat down on the sofa. "Never mind Danny." She took a deep breath, aware that she might not have very long before Jack returned. "I know what happened," she added.

"You know what exactly?" her mother scoffed and Sophie stared hard at her a second. Had she always been this antagonistic and sour? Pretty much, Sophie realized. She wasn't sure what had triggered such negativity—for most of her life she'd assumed she'd been the cause, that disappointment in her only child or even the fact that she hadn't wanted a child in the first place had made Sophie an unbearable burden.

But now, looking at the woman who had raised her, who had nurtured her in her own way…well, she wasn't sure about anything.

Maybe that was where to start this conversation. "I know I'm adopted," she said. "I know I have a twin sister and I know who my biological grandfather is. What I'd like to know from you is how it all began, for you and Dad, I mean." She took a deep breath. How could she ask her mother to be honest if she couldn't do the same, even with herself? "What I'm asking you, Mom, is this—was there ever a point where *you* loved me?"

Her mother looked at her defiantly.

I'm wasting my time, Sophie thought as Oscar jumped off her lap and headed to the kitchen.

Sophie looked from the cat's retreating form to her mother's face. Were those tears glittering in the older woman's eyes?

IT WAS LATE afternoon by the time Jack found Dominick Taylor Investigations. The downtown building he entered was a converted three-story house divided into separate offices. A sign directed Jack to the basement.

At the bottom of the stairs he found a glass door printed with the investigator's name and he tried the knob, hoping it would turn, hoping the guy hadn't gone home for the day.

It was locked. He rapped his knuckles against the glass. "Anyone here?" he called.

It took a second, but then he heard approaching footsteps. The door was opened by a man twice his age whose once dark hair was now threaded with white. He wore thick glasses, but behind the lenses, the eyes were bright and curious. Suspenders held up faded jeans and he was in the process of shrugging on a tweed sports coat. "I'm just on my way out," he said. "Think you can come back tomorrow?"

"I'm afraid not," Jack said and showed him his own license, explaining in as succinct of terms as possible who he was. He threw in Cannon's name as an incentive for cooperation. "I hate to sound dramatic, but it could very well be a matter of life and death," he ended.

The man stepped aside. "Dominick Taylor, call me Dom," the man said, gesturing to his desk, where he indicated Jack should take a seat in the visitor's chair. He settled himself in his own worn swivel chair, the seat sagging, the armrest wrapped in duct tape. A large computer sat off to one side, much as it did on Jack's own desk back in California.

"I've never actually met Cannon," Dom said. "His attorneys contacted me."

"He wanted to find out the identity of his granddaughters," Jack said.

Dom nodded but with obvious hesitation. Jack understood the old guy was determined to protect his client and his coworkers and he respected that. "That investigation had to be tricky," he said. "I was told by Cannon's housekeeper of many years that he had destroyed all the records of his granddaughters' adoptions. In fact, I got the impression he'd never even known the adopted family's names."

"That's what I was told," Dom said. "Hard to believe, isn't it? I have three little grandkids of my own—well, everyone is different. Anyway the lawyer he used was long dead, his office long gone. But we finally found a secretary who remembered the event because…well, suffice to say she remembered it."

"Because it separated identical twin babies," Jack stated, "and I bet that got to her."

Dom smiled. "You're right, it did. She confessed she'd thought many times over the years that she'd like to tell them about each other. In the end, she kept her word and didn't say anything."

"The cat is out of the bag now," Jack said. "Sophia knows about Sabrina and, if at all possible, she will soon tell Sabrina their story. That's why I'm here, to make sure they have a chance at long last to meet."

"Did their grandfather tell them about each other or did they find out through their pending inheritance?"

"Neither. Sabrina is my buddy's wife and she asked for help because she felt threatened. Her twin sister, Sophie, happened to show up at the same hotel. I mistook her for

Sabrina. Together, we discovered Sabrina is missing. The police think they have it all wrapped up but I have a horrible suspicion they're set on the wrong man."

"What do you need from me?" Dom asked as he picked up a pencil and started doodling eyes on a piece of paper.

"I was told the dossier was to include photographs taken on the sly of each woman."

"I took Sophia's myself," Dom said and, swiveling the chair, opened the bottom drawer of a tall cabinet and withdrew a fat file. He took out two photographs. The top one was of Sophie taken as she left a school, obviously, the one at which she taught. Her hair was lighter, longer, and one hand was raised as if to sweep it away from her face. She wore boots and a brown coat buttoned up to her chin. She looked downtrodden somehow, timid, not much like the woman he'd gotten to know the last few days and nothing like the image he carried of her in his heart.

Sophia. His Sophie. Face it, that's how he thought of her, as his. Crazy.

"This one was taken by a guy in Astoria," Dom said, shuffling the photographs around. "I met him once at a friend's place. Funny guy. Anyway, when I couldn't leave town to go to Astoria myself, I sent him directions." He slid a photograph forward.

Sabrina's photo was a three sixty from Sophia's. It had been taken through what appeared to be her kitchen window, the lens zoomed into her face. He could see the steam rising around her, even a few moist droplets on her brow and sticking to the dark tendrils of her hair.

"Arty, isn't it?" Dom said.

"She told me about this," Jack told him. "She felt violated by the photographer."

"She saw him?"

"Yes. He posed as a painter."

Dom's lips disappeared as he frowned. "I wondered how he got something so…personal. The instructions were to get a shot like that of the other girl, a head-to-toe, but this is all he sent me."

"I need his name," Jack said.

"I feel funny giving it to you," Dom said quietly.

"Look, he probably has nothing to do with nothing. But maybe he saw someone else when he was looking at her, who knows? I'm not the cops. They don't even seem to think she's in trouble. I'll make sure he doesn't connect you with me but I have to talk to him and I don't have time to interview every photographer in Astoria."

"Be that as it may…" Dom said with obvious hesitation.

Jack cleared his throat, ever aware of the time ticking away and the urgency of the situation. "Let me put it this way, Dom. Cannon wanted to leave his granddaughters his fortune because somewhere in his heart he knew he hadn't done right by them. The last thing in the world he'd want is to harm them because of something he instigated. From what I hear he's on his deathbed. I don't have time to go back to Weather Island and get him to sign a release form or whatever. It's up to you and me to use our heads."

Dom folded his hands under his chin and narrowed his eyes. At last he said, "Louis. Louis Nash. I don't know how much work he does, what with that limp of his. I don't know where he lives—we did everything over the internet."

"Limp?" Jack asked as alarm stepped up his heartbeat.

"Yeah."

"Which leg?"

"Let me think. The right. Maybe. I only met him once and then I only saw him take a step or two. Yeah, right. I think. Sorry. Does it matter?"

"Probably not," Jack said, but he was already calling

up Lisa's file that he kept on his phone. He found the composite sketch he was looking for and showed it to Dom. "Is this him?"

Dom made a cursory glance. "Nah, Louis is over forty. This guy is what? Twentysomething?"

"It's a ten-year-old drawing," Jack pointed out and felt foolish. There was no way Lisa's killer and this man could be one and the same. Lots of people limped and not all limps were chronic.

Dom took the phone and studied the screen, then handed it back. "Sorry. I mean, it could be. Louis is tall, thinner than that sketch, older—I can't tell. But sketches—I mean, really, they all kind of look alike. Who is this guy?"

"A killer," Jack said quickly.

"Nah, not Louis. He's not the type."

"Chances are good you're right," Jack said as he met Dom's gaze head-on. He knew he'd jumped to conclusions when he heard about the photographer's limp and was already regretting casting aspersions on a man who might very well be as innocent as the driven snow. "That said," he added, "you and I both know there's no way to look inside another man's soul."

"No," Dom said with a weary sigh. "No, there's not."

Chapter Nine

"How long did Lisa live after she was abducted?" Sophie asked Jack as they drove the dark twisting road to the coast. Her question was met with silence but she had to know. "Jack?"

"The condition of her burned body made it difficult to tell for sure," he finally said.

"It's been three days for Sabrina," Sophie whispered almost to herself.

"Remember the cases aren't related," Jack said. "Even if Sabrina's been abducted, it's extremely unlikely it's by the same guy. The odds are astronomical."

"But you showed the investigator Lisa's killer's composite sketch. Doesn't that mean you've connected the two men?"

"Not in any concrete way," he said. "Lots of people limp. No one knows whether the guy who took Lisa had a chronic limp or an injury or maybe no limp at all. Maybe he just used it as a decoy thing. It just hit me hard when Dom mentioned his Astoria photographer limped. I let it get to me."

"Did you have a chance to talk to Detective Reece again? Have they apprehended Paul Rey?"

"I did talk to him briefly. He said they found Rey's car abandoned up in the woods. It's assumed he somehow got another. And that means you're still not safe, damn it. Oh, and Reece said he's talked to the fire department, who have decided to launch a thorough search of side roads starting tomorrow morning. Of course, Sabrina could still be in the Seaport area or have driven south, so those areas need to be searched, too. Search parties are being formed even as we speak."

"Now if we can just get the police to come around. Did you tell Reece about the photographer?"

"No," he said quickly. "I'll go talk to the guy first thing tomorrow. I don't want to cause Louis Nash trouble if he hasn't earned it."

"But how will you know?"

He shook his head. "You make a point. But we need Reece to take Sabrina's situation seriously. I can't afford to put him off by sounding like I'm hell-bent on revenge for a ten-year-old murder case that happened a thousand miles away."

Sophie sighed. "And the clock just keeps ticking."

"I know."

She drew quiet as she tried to reestablish a connection to Sabrina's psyche—if that's what had happened earlier when she "felt" the raindrops and smelled the dirt—but had no luck.

"Tell me what happened with your mother," Jack said. She was startled out of her thoughts, but she knew he was trying to divert her attention and she appreciated it.

"She started out defensive but eventually opened up," Sophie reported. "In fact, I think it's the only genuine conversation she and I have ever had."

"That's good, right?"

"Yeah, it is. She told me how she and Dad had been turned down by various adoption agencies because of their health. When their friend—who was an attorney—

heard about this private no-questions-asked adoption, they jumped on it. I think most people would have been a little put off by the fact that, technically speaking, it wasn't legal let alone ethical, but they saw it as a last chance for parenthood. Much to my surprise, Mom said she was as anxious as Dad to have a family."

"What happened to her...enthusiasm?" Jack asked.

"According to her, I gravitated toward Dad from the get-go. She also admitted she was nervous, always ready for my 'real' parents to demand me back. See, they had no idea where I came from, whose child I was, knew nothing about my grandfather or another baby. I think she decided it would be easier to lose me if she didn't get too attached."

"So she didn't know your grandfather was Mr. Moneybags."

"No idea. She's thrilled, by the way. In fact, she now says she never liked Danny, claims that I can do better."

"And what do you think?"

She slid him a long glance. "I think she's right, I *can* do better."

"Damn straight," he said with a charming grin that lightened her heart for a moment as they drove into Astoria. Without discussing it, he drove straight to the Cromwell house. They found it as they'd left it: dark and seemingly empty. Just to be sure, Jack darted through the rain to knock. When he got back into the car, he took a deep breath. "I think we might as well have dinner and get a good night's sleep. What do you think?"

"Sounds good."

The hotel Jack checked them into was built on the site of a former fish cannery and boasted a restaurant of its own. They both ordered scallops and shared a bottle of Pinot Gris. All around them, people dining by candlelight seemed engaged in intimate conversations as they enjoyed the good food and fine ambiance. But while there was no one in the world Sophie would rather share a meal with, she couldn't help but be preoccupied and she knew Jack was, too.

Would she ever meet the sister with whom she'd entered the world? The fear she would lose her on the eve of finding her was so strong as to border on a premonition. It was a relief when Jack set aside his napkin. "Let's get out of here," he said, and managed to reassure her with a smile.

They tried taking a walk, but the cold rain just made Sophie more upset. Was Sabrina outside in this and hurt? Both tired and heartsick, they retreated to their room, where Sophie told Jack to take the first shower as she had finally remembered to bring clothes of her own from home and needed to sort what she'd hastily thrown in the suitcase.

When it was her turn to bathe, she soaked in the huge tub before changing into the only silky night garment she owned, a long gown that almost matched the fading lilac streak in her hair.

Jack whistled as she reentered the room. "I thought I would miss seeing you in my oversize plaid flannel pajama top, but wowza, you look gorgeous."

She pirouetted. "Thank you."

He was propped up in bed fooling with his phone. He set it beside the lamp, tossed open the covers and held out an arm. "Come here," he coaxed and she crawled in beside him. He gathered her into his arms and held her so close his heart seemed to beat for her, too.

For a second they stared into each other's eyes.

"You look so sad it's breaking my heart," he whispered as he touched her cheek.

"I'm sorry."

"You don't need to be." He hugged her tighter. "She's

never far away from my mind either, and now I heard from Buzz. He's in New Zealand and he's worried sick because Sabrina isn't responding to his calls or email. I told him she's still off on her own. God, I have to find her before he gets here the day after tomorrow. And not just for him either."

"For Lisa and for yourself," she whispered against his wonderfully bare muscular chest.

"No, Sophie, for you. I have to get her home safely for you." He lifted her chin and met her gaze. "Don't you know that?"

Tears filled her eyes and rolled down her cheeks as she nodded. He held her even tighter. The musky scent of his skin seemed to envelop her, while the physical strength of his arms surged strength of another kind into her bones.

"If she's off romancing fireman Kyle, I'm going to be really pissed off," he added.

"She's not off romancing anyone," Sophie said with 100 percent certainty.

"How can you be so sure?"

She closed her eyes and thought about how to respond. In the end she simply said, "I just am. She needs us."

"You can feel her?" he asked.

"Kind of. I just know that she was alive around five o'clock. But she's hurt and scared and about to give up hope." She cast him an upward glance. "We have to find her tomorrow, Jack, we just have to."

He kissed her lips and her forehead. "We will," he said with confidence ringing in his voice.

She closed her eyes, reaching inward, outward, just trying to stay open to any sensation, but there was nothing there. Just the steady beat of Jack's heart reverberating throughout her body.

And for now, that would have to be enough.

JACK WOKE UP with a start. He thought someone was rattling the door and for a second his body tensed. Sophie still lay in his arms, her lovely face visible thanks to a wash of light that fell across the bed. The sound came again and he realized it was the wind blowing a chair against the outside wall of their balcony.

As if sensing his tenseness, her eyes fluttered open. "Is it morning?" she mumbled.

"It's the middle of the night," he told her, burying his head in her fragrant hair, kissing her petal-soft neck. She turned her head and his lips found hers.

What happened next was like being swept up by a giant wave, tossed around in tumultuous fury until finally being thrown onto a foreign beach. They tore at each other's clothes, desperate for the feel of each other, kissing and exploring as they went until they came together with an inevitable explosion. It was over in a flash and they lay side by side, both breathing heavy, Sophie's lovely gown a heap on the floor along with his pajama bottoms. Everything was the same and yet totally different. He couldn't keep from touching her, enjoying the weight of her breasts in his hands and the dewy softness of her rounded buttocks. She, too, explored his body until at last their caresses awakened the same burning hunger that once again brought them together.

Jack had had lovers over the years, some more serious than others, none since Lisa whom he'd ever seriously contemplated a future with, but this was different. He wasn't positive how. He only knew some meals you ate with relish and walked away from the table, sated. And some meals were so special you lingered and then yearned to indulge yourself again, and again.

"That was like a firestorm," Sophie whispered against his ear as her fingers twined in his hair.

He tightened his arm to bring her closer. "I thought of a tidal wave."

She giggled sleepily, the sound like a trilling brook. A trilling brook? Good heavens, he was obviously under her spell. A smile curved his lips as his consciousness drifted away like a wisp of smoke.

"IT's TOO EARLY for room service," Jack said as he stared at the room's complimentary coffee machine. He lifted a packet of what promised to be a Hawaiian blend of deeply roasted beans—sure, he thought—and added, "I'll just double up the packets."

There was no way in the world Sophie wanted to lift the lid on another room service tray until Paul Rey was behind bars, so she simply nodded. She'd dressed in clean jeans, a thermal undershirt and wool sweater and now laced up a pair of hiking boots. The final touch was a pair of silver earrings that she'd grabbed off her dresser at home. Belatedly she recalled Danny had given them to her, but she put them on anyway. The elongated silver discs caught the light and brightened her face.

"You look great," Jack said and she caught his reflection staring at her image in the mirror. "Nice earrings."

She turned. "Thanks. Danny bought them for me."

He shook his head and approached her, wrapping his hands around her waist and kissing her lips. "I could have gone all day without knowing that."

She laughed. "I picked them out."

"Good."

"Hmm—"

They drank a hurried cup of coffee that was still too weak before leaving the hotel room Sophie knew she would always remember. They emerged into a dry morning, holding hands.

And therein lay the conundrum. Sophie felt as if her soul was torn in two. On one hand, she'd never been this happy in her life. Jack was a fantastic lover, generous and thoughtful, yet powerful and assertive. Being special to him made her heart burst. But Sabrina was going on four days of missing and that same joyous heart knew with certainty that time was running out.

They stuffed their things into the trunk before Jack clicked the doors open. Sophie was about to open the passenger door when she saw a small plastic opaque bag tied to the handle.

"Someone was out late or up early distributing something or the other," she said, glancing at the cars parked close by, looking for similar yellow bags. There were none. Jack showed up at her side, and for a second they both stared at the cheerful bag, feeling anything but cheerful.

"Do you want me to open it?" he asked.

"No, I'll do it. I even have gloves in my pocket." She pulled on her gloves and opened the string. They both peered inside and, to no one's surprise, found themselves looking at an origami fox folded from a dollar bill.

"He's back," Sophie said.

. Jack grabbed the bag from her hand. "Get in the car, honey. We're going to go visit Detective Reece."

"WE'VE GOT EVERY available man working on finding that nutcase," Reece reported as he sent the yellow bag with its contents off to the lab. He poured them each a cup of coffee from his personal pot. The brew was so strong it reminded Jack of the stuff they used to drink back when he was a cop in LA. Some of the guys had complained it took the enamel off their teeth. Jack had liked it just fine.

"Paul Rey must have been here the whole time, watching Sabrina's house," Jack said. "We drove there right after arriving back in Astoria last night, then went to the hotel, where we parked in their lot. As you know, it's unfenced."

Reece's cherubic smile faded. "I'll set up a watch on the Cromwell house." He dug in his cabinet and withdrew a file that he laid on his desk and opened. "This is what the loser looks like," he said, turning the photo so they could see it. Paul Rey was about thirty in his prison mug shot and like every other man Jack had seen in an orange jumpsuit, the color didn't become him. His blondish-red hair was cut very short, his mouth was set in a grim line and his eyes looked small and mean.

"He looks like Danny, only younger and a lot nastier," Sophie said.

"You're talking about Danny Privet," the detective said. "I talked to a friend in the Portland bureau. He says Danny is a slick piece of work."

"Yeah, but he's not as smart as he thinks he is," Jack said and Sophie nodded.

Reece turned the file back around. "By the way, Seattle police have questioned their mother, Nora Rey. She admits she told her older son Daniel about the inheritance but not Paul. More important, she claims she doesn't know how to reach him to call off his continued attacks on you, Ms. Sparrow."

"Well, so far he hasn't been real successful and now thanks to his latest origami fox, we know he's in town. Not the most subtle of stalkers." She got to her feet. "I want to join the hunt for Sabrina's car," she said with a glance at the wall clock.

"They've divided into several small groups with each unit tackling a road that leads out of town. It's a long shot they'll find anything but I understand your concern. Try driving out to River Bend. They're combing the verges of a road that connects over to Highway 30 and from there to Interstate 5 and just about anywhere else you want to go. You'll be relieved to know the firehouse in Seaport and all points south for that matter are organizing similar searches."

"Great. Come on, Jack."

Before he could respond, the detective spoke up. "Just a minute now, I have another request of you two. I was wondering if you would mind going through Sabrina's house again. The chief says if we can rule out a clandestine tryst with Kyle Woods we can rev up the search. Maybe you can find something in that house that will give us a definitive clue about her relationship with the guy and this time look for anything that might suggest Sabrina came back home after you saw her in Seaport."

"Have you been checking to see if her phone or credit cards are being used or if she made an inordinate number of calls to Kyle before last weekend?" Sophie asked.

"We can't subpoena records without an investigation," Reece said. "But rest assured we're keeping an eye out for Woods, too. You have to admit it's odd for two 'friends' and coworkers to disappear at the same time, one with a false story about visiting a grandfather and the other while her husband is out of the country and neither of them using their phones or credit cards, neither one's vehicle being noticed…nothing."

"Then why would she call me?" Jack said.

"Who better to alibi whatever story she concocts than her hubby's best friend?"

"You've got this all wrong," Jack insisted.

"And all that aside, you have to keep in mind if she's been abducted she's in mortal danger," Sophie added. "Tell him about Lisa, Jack. Tell him about the photographer."

Sophie sat back down and the detective leaned his forearms on his desk, poised to listen. "Who's Lisa?" he asked.

"An old friend, abducted and subsequently murdered ten years ago down in LA," he said. He explained the situation as he had to Sophie a day or so before.

"So what's the tie-in with Sabrina Cromwell? You didn't even know her then, did you?"

"No. Buzz hadn't met her yet. The only tie-in is the way she disappeared so suddenly and the fact that she was photographed cooking." He explained about Sophie's grandfather's hiring a private detective to assemble dossiers on each of his granddaughters and to include photographs of them. "Sophie's photo was taken by a guy in Portland. It's a standard head-to-toe shot of her leaving the school where she teaches. Sabrina's picture is sensual in nature." Jack paused to hand the detective Dominick's card with his name and address printed on it. "This is the investigator R. H. Cannon hired. He mentioned the photographer he engaged here in Astoria had a noticeable limp."

"Wait a second," the detective said as he studied Dom's card. "Are you talking about Louis?"

"Louis Nash," Jack said. "Do you know him?"

"He takes photographs here in town. Took my son's graduation picture, my daughter's, too. Nice guy. Pays his bills, supports his homebound mother, meets his obligations…never had one complaint against him."

"Then you know him?"

"I've met him. You're barking up the wrong tree."

"How long has he lived here?"

"Near as I can figure, his whole life."

"Was he ever in California?"

"I don't know, Jack."

"Have you had any missing women here in the last ten or fifteen years, maybe longer?"

"Are you accusing Louis Nash of—"

"I'm not accusing him of anything. I'm just asking."

"Well, the answer is the only unsolved murder of a young woman I know of happened years ago. Popular consensus is her boyfriend killed her and no, he wasn't Louis Nash. Listen, I see the guy around town all the time. He's not real chatty, but he's always polite."

Jack brought up the composite sketch of Lisa's suspected killer on his phone. "Does he look anything like this given the fact that the sketch was made ten years ago?"

The detective studied it just as Dom had. "Kind of. So do a hundred other guys. Is this the—"

"The man police suspect killed Lisa and at least one other woman. No one has ever identified him."

Reece shook his head. "You're on a crusade."

"I was afraid you'd think that but the truth is, I'm just trying to find Sabrina. Won't you at least ask Nash about taking her photograph? We know he trespassed on a neighbor's porch pretending to be a painter in order to get the shot he ultimately sent Dominick Taylor. Isn't trespassing enough cause to question him, even unofficially if that's as far as you're willing to go?"

"If the neighbor comes in here and files a complaint—"

"Detective, come on. Can't you just talk with him?"

Reece sighed, glanced at Sophie and ran a hand through his gray hair. "Yeah, okay, I can do that but it's not going to do you any good. I don't for a minute think a guy making a living by taking someone's photograph has a thing to do with anything—I think Paul Rey is the culprit. I think he killed the janitor down in Seaport to get at Sabrina. She must have run off to meet up with her boyfriend when he wasn't looking, but then Sophie shows up out of the blue. He mistakes her for her twin sister. And here we are."

"You're basing this whole thing on Sabrina willingly leaving Seaport of her own volition. But what if she didn't?" Jack argued. "We agree Paul Rey's motive for targeting Sabrina is to eliminate her before her grandfather dies and leaves her half a fortune, right?"

"Right."

"If he has her, if heaven forbid he's already killed her, then why go after Sophie? He'd have to know she isn't Sabrina."

"But he knows there are twins," Reece said. "Maybe he figures if both of the girls are dead, Cannon will leave all his dough to his loyal housekeeper and her two loser sons."

Jack had to admit that was a remote possibility. Rey wasn't the sharpest tool in the shed. "I appreciate the fact that you're willing to talk to Nash," he said with a reluctant nod. "I'll call you later and find out what you learn."

Sophie got to her feet. "After I finish the search I'll go through the house again as you requested. By the way, did you get the test results back on the food off the tray?"

"The lab hasn't responded yet," Reece said. "What with it being a holiday weekend, I don't expect we'll hear back before Friday."

Jack knew what Sophie was thinking because he thought it, too.

By Friday, Sabrina would either be safe in her house with her cat and her husband or she would be dead.

Chapter Ten

Much of the land surrounding Astoria consisted of rivers and coastal plains, but it quickly changed as you traveled inland. Jack and Sophie soon found themselves driving steep, twisty country roads abutted with forests. Occasionally a dirt driveway fronted with a mailbox would announce a home existed somewhere out of sight but mainly it was lonely, desolate-looking countryside that was probably quite beautiful if not seen through the lens of unbearable worry.

They finally found the search already in progress and parked. Before they were completely out of the car, Sue jogged up to them. She was dressed in jeans and boots, like Sophie. Red frizz escaped from under the cap of a Portland Trailblazers cap.

"I saw you drive up," she said by way of greeting. "I wanted to talk to you."

"Sure," Sophie said. "What's up?"

It took Sue a second to speak, during which she stared at her feet and then at them. "I think I was a little flippant concerning Sabrina the other day," she finally said.

Sophie shook her head. "I wouldn't worry about it. You were just telling us things as you saw them."

"Yeah, well, the ugly truth is that after Barbara left Kyle I thought he and I might get together."

"Barbara is Kyle's wife?" Jack asked.

"Yeah. Anyway, it turns out Kyle only wanted to be around Sabrina. They had this bond… I guess they knew each other in high school. Face it, I got jealous. I mean she's got a smart, gorgeous husband and she looks like a movie star—why does she need Kyle, too? Anyway, when the police questioned me and I thought about what I'd insinuated about the two of them to you guys, well, I regretted it. I'm really sorry I was so snotty about the possibility Sabrina would walk away from a friend. I want to do whatever I can to help her."

"Then you don't think she's off with Kyle?"

"I guess it's possible but it seems unlikely she'd ask for your help and then abandon you like that."

"I agree," Jack said.

"I'm glad you told us," Sophie told Sue with a gentle squeeze of her arm.

Sue peered closely at her. "You look so much like Sabrina, but you're different, too."

"She's working on developing an edge," Jack said, nudging Sophie's side.

Sophie laughed. "He's right, I am. Anyway, Sabrina and I are identical twins but we were raised apart. We're bound to have our differences."

Sue nodded. "Come join our side of the road. All we've found so far, thank goodness, are a few unfortunate smashed critters and enough garbage to fill a swimming pool."

The terrain was heavily wooded and steep. On one side of the narrow road a shallow ravine climbed uphill and on the other the land dropped precipitously to a tributary river below that was all but invisible given the density of the foliage. In full winter rainy season, the sound of rushing water rumbled in the background.

The odd thing for Sophie was that she knew from about the second step she took along the south side of the road that they were close. Sabrina was near, she could almost feel it in her bones… What she couldn't feel was in what state her twin might be. Hurt, scared, alive, heaven forbid, dead… Sophie had no idea but the feeling that she was close was as real as the dirt beneath her feet.

A ticking bomb replaced her heartbeat.

"Jack, listen, I have to tell you something," she said, and whispered in his ear. "I sense Sabrina is close by."

"Are you sure?"

"It's just a feeling. Not the first I've had and maybe not real at all."

"Then we'll keep looking, okay?"

She nodded and matched him step for step, studying the roadside for tire tracks and broken branches—anything that would suggest a vehicle had left the road and tumbled out of sight.

"Here, over here!" someone called and along with everyone else, Sophie and Jack darted ahead to join a group staring downhill at the disturbed terrain running down toward the river before vanishing into a tangle of underbrush. Tire prints in the mud beside the road were indistinct at best.

"Okay, folks, listen up," a burly guy of about thirty said as he joined them. "You all know me, I'm Captain Philips with the Astoria division. We all know this is an informal search but just in case…fan out at arm's length and go down the slope, but not directly on this path. We don't want to destroy any evidence. If you see anything, mark it with one of the flags I gave you, and for good measure, stay there with whatever it is you found. Move slowly and watch where you step."

Sophie stood between Sue and Jack, nerves skittering

over her skin like a thousand little ant bites as they started their descent. What if Sabrina's car was down here and Sabrina was beyond saving?

But there was another fear and that was that someone might have dumped Sabrina's body down here after torturing her and murdering her. They might even have burned her remains like Lisa's. How did you steel yourself for such a possibility?

She searched her mind and heart for some reassuring feeling that this wasn't the case, but whatever brief connection she thought she'd felt to her sister would not come back and she was as much in the dark as everyone else.

She glanced up in time to see Jack studying her. He took her hand and held it tightly in his.

The smell reached them halfway down the slope. Rotting flesh, she thought, and her stomach lurched. Jack's hand turned into the only thing keeping her from floating away, from escaping this moment.

"It looks like a four-wheel-drive vehicle came down here and backed up or something," Jack said softly. "The ground is all torn up."

"Jack, the smell—"

"Hold on, don't go imagining things," he said. They all stopped when the thicket in front of them became the last barrier to what was beyond.

"Yikes, what's that smell?" someone asked.

Someone else produced a machete and began whacking at the thicket, pushing it aside. Sophie saw a large shape emerging, rust and white paint. Her heart caught in her throat as Jack whispered, "Oh, God, is that Buzz's old Blazer?" She held her breath as the first of the branches fell.

It was not a Blazer and while Buzz's car might be old, this one was far older. It was also not alone. An old washing machine lying on its side and various car parts along with a rusty roll of chicken wire and an old toilet sporting a bowl full of weeds accompanied it.

And the cause of the smell was explained by a freshly butchered carcass.

"Oh, man, somebody poached a deer and cleaned it out here," Sue said.

"Everybody return to the road," the deputy said. "Same rules, watch where you step. I'm going to make sure a dead deer is all we got going on down here."

Jack grabbed Sophie's arms and turned her to face him. "I'll help the deputy. Go back up to the road with Sue, okay?"

"Yeah," Sophie said, glad to be told to leave this spot. "Okay."

Having found nothing else at the dump site, they returned to the search, but after another fruitless hour in which they discovered more cast-off debris but nothing to suggest Sabrina had ever come this way, Jack and Sophie left.

"I'm driving to Seaport," Jack said.

Sophie glanced at the dashboard clock, then in her rearview mirror. It would be so easy if she still felt that sensation of Sabrina's closeness. Then she could insist they return. As it was, there was no point, no feeling, no nothing.

"Shouldn't we search Buzz and Sabrina's house like the detective asked?"

"If we have time," he said. "I think he was giving us busywork. He's got a whole squad of people who can do that job. His mind may be made up or his hands tied, but mine aren't and neither are yours. I want to talk to the people at the hotel again."

"I could go to Sabrina's house while you do that," Sophie said.

"We stick together," he interrupted. "Okay?"

"Yeah, okay."

As they drove down the coast, Sophie gazed out at the sea. When the road took them inland for a while, she turned to Jack. His profile was just as interesting as the scenery and much more dear, at least to her.

"So you became a cop because of what happened with Lisa?" she ventured.

"Yeah," he said, sparing her a glance.

"Why did you quit?"

"Oddly enough, because of Lisa. Her unsolved murder got me into law enforcement, but the way every case seemed to echo hers drove me out of it."

"And here you are again," Sophie said.

"Yes, here I am again, but damn, this feels different. This isn't just a case of bad memories. This is déjà vu. I'd never forgive myself if I let Sabrina and Buzz down, but it's a slippery slope. On the one hand, I can't assume that just because there are similarities that it's the same kind of case. On the other hand, I can't assume because I'm sensitive to overreacting that I'm misreading things. So in the end, I have to trust what my eyes see and what my gut tells me."

"And it tells you to go back to the hotel?"

"And show the composite sketch around. I should have gotten a picture of Louis Nash to show around, too. Damn, why didn't I think of that?"

"I'll look on the internet and see if he has one."

She did just that while the miles sped by but in the end had to admit defeat. "Lots of pictures attributed to him but none of him."

"Is he a good photographer?"

Sophie looked at a couple of examples of his work. "Not bad. Some of the girls look a little…provocative, but that may just be the way they wanted to look."

As they drove into the hotel parking lot a few minutes later, Jack threw her a grin. "Well, here we are again." He found a parking spot up close to the front doors.

"I wonder if Paul Rey followed us," she asked. "For that matter, I wonder if he followed us out to the search area up in Astoria, too? What's he making of all this?"

"Who knows, but I have a feeling he's around here somewhere. I tried watching for a tail but this guy is apparently pretty good at disappearing and until we know what he's driving—"

"You'd think his mother and brother would have called him off by now and told him the gig is up."

"I don't think he's communicating with anyone," Jack said, holding the front door open for her. "He might be obsessive, his head set on one goal—kill Sabrina, then hit his brother up for half of what you get once she's dead. His family refers to him as a loose cannon. Maybe he's crazy enough to work in a void of his own making."

They bypassed the front desk and went downstairs, where the hubbub of the conference was over. Tuesday at noon seemed quiet at the hotel, perfect for Jack's intention of showing the sketch around.

Finding someone to show it to seemed to be the issue, however. Many of the people they'd grown accustomed to seeing were at home as the hotel had cut back hours once the rush was over. Still, they persevered, starting down in the kitchen and housekeeping, working their way up as they tried to find Jerry or Brad or Adam.

They finally found a guy painting the trim around a large window at the end of a hall on the third floor. As if sensing their interest in him, he paused in his task and looked over his shoulder as they approached. For some reason, his measuring gaze made Sophie extremely uncomfortable.

He was a tall, thin man with intense black eyes and longish black hair.

"Are you Adam?" Jack asked.

The guy kept his paintbrush poised on the wall as he leveled a steely stare at Jack. "I'm Adam."

"You're sure handy with that paintbrush," Jack said.

"What can I do for you? It's just me here right now. Give me your room number or better yet, call the front desk and get on the list. It may be morning before someone gets to you, though."

Jack showed him the composite sketch captured on his phone.

Adam stared at it and as he did so, Sophie looked from the sketch to the man gazing at it and almost fell over. They looked so much alike it was uncanny.

"Who is this?" he asked.

Sophie spoke up. "A man we need to ask a few questions," she said.

"Does he limp by any chance?"

They hadn't mentioned the limp, keeping that back in case someone recognized the sketch. Sophie could sense Jack fighting to rein in his excitement. "Yeah. He limps."

"I saw him Saturday. Up here, as a matter of fact. He was wheeling a cart with a couple of suitcases and a trunk on it."

"How big was the trunk?" Jack asked and Sophie could hear the edge in his voice.

Adam held out his arms. "Sizable."

"Did you see him unload the baggage or have any idea to whom it belonged or by chance see what he was driving?"

Adam shook his head. "I saw him for about thirty seconds on my way to snake a plugged toilet. I didn't see no tags or nothing else. He was just pushing the cart into the service elevator and then he was gone and I was off."

"I'm calling Reece," Jack told Sophie.

"Ask him to get a picture of Louis Nash."

"I will."

As Jack took a few steps to use his phone in privacy, Adam asked why they wanted to know about the guy.

"A woman who looks a lot like me went missing from this hotel last Saturday," she said. "Police will want to question this man if we can find him. They'll probably want to ask you some questions, as well."

"Me?"

"About what you saw."

He shook his head. "Well, they have until five, 'cause that's when I'm leaving here. I have a lot to do on my new place."

"Is it here in town?"

He narrowed his eyes. "No. Why do you ask?"

She shrugged. "Well, you know, if the police want to talk to you—"

"I can talk to 'em here as well as there. Anyway, it's getting late. You got nothing else you want from me, I need to finish this job."

"Sure, only did you know Hank Tyson, the maintenance man who was killed last weekend?"

"Not really," he said. "Brad knows him. Knew him."

"How do you know Brad?"

"We worked together in Idaho a few years back. What's with all the questions?"

Jack's return saved her a response. "Reece is calling Sergeant Jones down here in Seaport," he said. "Time for us to get back to Astoria."

As they hurried back to the car, Jack added, "Reece

said he went over to Nash's house after we left. He said the guy was totally cooperative. He remembered taking the photo of Sabrina, thought it was one of his better efforts. Reece also said Nash has an alibi for the weekend but that he invited Reece to search his house claiming he has nothing to hide."

"Did Reece conduct a search?"

"No. It's easy to tell he thinks we're barking up the wrong tree."

"Maybe we are," Sophie said. "Didn't you notice Adam Cook looks like the sketch?"

"I did notice that but he doesn't limp."

"You were never sure the limp was real, remember? You said it could have been a temporary injury or even a faked diversion. Notice how quick Adam was to point out that the man he said he saw had a limp. Did he do that to avert suspicion from himself?"

"Sophie, I don't know. If that guy took Sabrina would he be painting window trim three days later?"

"I don't know—you're the expert. But I have to remind you of one thing. We're not looking for Lisa's murderer, we're looking for the guy who abducted Sabrina, and in that mind-set, a limp doesn't matter."

"Neither does looking like a guy in a ten-year-old sketch," Jack said.

She sighed. "It seems almost impossible without the police reviewing surveillance tapes and questioning people more stringently. But can we afford not to consider everything and everyone? Remember when we talked to Brad Sunday morning? He said that Adam left here to go get a part. If he'd already stuffed Sabrina into a trunk and rolled her downstairs into a van, what better time to get her away from the hotel and Brad's prying eyes than to fake an errand? Or maybe he had Hank in the van, too. Maybe that's when he dumped the poor man's body."

"A hardware store would have a record of a sale. And damn it all, someone needs to check the hotel's security cameras."

"Oh, and, Jack, Adam said he was leaving town after work to go work on his new house. He was defensive and nervous and he looked at me like—I don't know, he just gave me the creeps."

THEY DROVE BY the Cromwell house and were reassured when Jack recognized an unmarked police car parked down the street. A second later, a taxicab drove by. Was that Sabrina returning from wherever the hell she'd been? The cab kept going and once again disappointment took a giant bite out of Jack's gut.

And that right there was the trouble with this whole thing. He might criticize Reece for not damning the torpedoes and investigating Sabrina's disappearance as a criminal act and yet he himself could go from thinking she'd been carted off in a trunk to holding his breath that she might miraculously emerge from a taxicab.

Jack had a sudden whim. "There's somewhere I want to go before we settle in to search the house again. Mind coming with me?"

"Are you kidding? There's nowhere I'd rather be than with you."

He grinned at her. "The feeling is mutual."

"So, where to now?"

He glanced over at her again, inordinately glad she wanted to be with him and very aware of how patient she was. They'd had coffee for breakfast, and a drive-through chicken sandwich for lunch. Not much of a romantic day after their first sexual encounter. She deserved dozens of red roses and champagne and boxes of chocolates—he wanted to shower her with attention. He wanted to be the man who erased the despicable Danny from her memory forever and showed her what a relationship could be like with someone who loved her.

Because he did love her. A half dozen times that day he'd wanted to tell her so. That morning when they awoke and she smiled up at him and kissed his lips. Later, in the shower, then when she reassured Sue—such a kind thing to do. And during all this, he knew her insides were twisted into a terrible knot as she worried about her sister. She was growing more vibrant by the day, an unselfish and generous woman with a huge heart. He loved her.

He lifted her hand from her lap. "Sophie, I have to tell you something."

"Uh-oh," she said. "That sounds ominous."

"No, it's nothing bad, at least I don't think so. I just want to tell you that I'm aware we've known each other a lot less time than you knew Danny and you thought he moved too fast, but I know how I feel—"

"Shh," she said softly. "Don't say anything. I feel the same way about you, like I want to announce to the world that you're it, that you're the only one for me. But we've known each other just a handful of days and they haven't been typical days for either of us." She laughed softly. "The horrible truth, my darling, is that I am the most boring woman you are ever going to meet. After this is over, you'll see I'll put you to sleep every time I open my mouth. You'll want to run for the hills."

"Oh, Sophie, that's not true and I think you know it."

"This is true. I don't even know if you like oatmeal or walks on the beach or what kind of movies—"

"Who cares about that stuff? Those are the things people find out about each other over time."

"Well, then, how about the fact that you live six hours south of me?"

"More like nine. I'll move, you'll move, we'll work it out. That's what people who care about each other do."

"And then there's Sabrina and Buzz and the immediate future and the potential wreckage—it's too much to think about right now. Let's just be in the moment, okay? Tell me where we're going."

"I just hope by the time you're ready to hear me out, I haven't forgotten what I was going to say," he teased her.

She punched him in the side and laughed.

"We're going to Louis Nash's house. I looked it up on the internet. It's not far from here."

"What do you hope to find out?"

"I just want to get a feel for the guy, see where he lives, what he's like."

They found Nash's residence on a steep street two blocks off the main avenue. Jack parked a couple of doors down and they both spent five minutes sitting in the car watching to see if anyone else parked nearby or drove by suspiciously. They both had an image of Paul Rey in their head now and that should help if Paul got close to Sophie again.

"I have a gun in the trunk," he said.

"Why is it in the trunk?"

"It's back there with the handcuffs, a rifle, the stun gun—all the usual accruements. But I'm not a cop, I'm a private citizen, especially up here in Oregon where my license doesn't even mean as much as it does in California. The stakes go way up when you introduce a lethal weapon. If you carry it, you'd better be prepared to use deadly force. All that said, I'm going to go get it out of the trunk and you're going to use it if Paul Rey approaches this car. Okay?"

"I've never shot a gun."

"I'll show you how." He retrieved the gun, once again scanning the peaceful street that had no new cars parked on it and no pedestrians lingering on the sidewalks. He got back in the car and quickly acquainted her with the weapon. "It's all set to shoot. Just take off the safety, aim and pull the trigger. Got it?"

"I got it. But I don't want to kill Paul. He might know something about Sabrina."

"If he's walking up to this car he's got one thing on his mind, honey, and it isn't a chat. Protect yourself. Promise me."

"Okay, yeah, I will. I promise."

He leaned across the seat and touched her lips with his. "Are you as scared as you look?" he whispered.

"Yes, but mostly because I don't want to shoot anyone."

"I'll be back in ten minutes."

"Make it nine."

"You got it." He kissed her again, then walked quickly down the street toward Nash's house.

A small sign on the door read: Nash Photography. Please Knock. He knocked.

The door was answered by a tall, dark man in his mid-forties. Longish dark hair framed a lean, almost gaunt face dominated by large, heavily lidded eyes.

"Are you Louis Nash?" Jack asked pleasantly, but the truth was the dude raised his hackles on sight. Did he look like the sketch of Lisa's killer? About as much as Adam Cook did. The fact was that Jack had seen dozens of tall, drawn-looking guys over the years who resembled the sketch. This man had more angles in his face, was certainly older. There were surface similarities, but having never actually seen Lisa's killer in the flesh, he couldn't go so far as to say this was the guy.

And there was that conundrum again, that concern that his subconscious was hell-bent on merging Lisa's killer and Sabrina's abductor no matter how unlikely the possibility.

"I heard you were the best photographer in town," Jack said, deciding on the spot not to mention Sabrina.

"One of them, yeah."

"My fiancée and I are getting married this summer. I was hoping you could show me some of your work."

Jack sensed Louis's reluctance. It could mean he had something to hide or he could just be in the middle of something. Maybe the detective's visit earlier that day had put him on his guard. Or here was a thought: maybe he sensed that Jack wasn't being honest.

"I have a few minutes," he said at last. "Come on in."

Jack stepped inside. A steep flight of stairs led upward to his left. The house was messy and cluttered, the walls covered with blown-up photos of kids and trees and oceanscapes.

"Have a seat at the table," Louis said as he swept aside what looked like lunch dishes to make space. "I'll go get the book."

He limped out of sight into a room whose door he closed behind him. He limped—right leg. Could mean something, could mean nothing. Jack used the opportunity to check out what he could see of the house. A closed door off the kitchen could be a pantry. It could also be access to a basement. It took all his willpower not to dash up the stairs or open every closed door, but he could hear Nash's returning footsteps. There wasn't time. If he wanted to poke around, he'd have to get Louis out of the room again.

Nash showed up with two books, one small and one album size. "This is a wedding I did last summer," he said, handing Jack the album.

Jack set it on the table and opened it. "Thanks. How many years have you been taking pictures?"

"Most of my life," Louis said.

"You must really enjoy it."

"Yeah, I do."

"This close-up picture of the bride eating cake is really nice."

"Thanks. Standard photo op."

"I was just thinking it must be hard photographing outdoor events around unpredictable Oregon coast weather. It would have to be easier in someplace more reliable. Like Southern California, for instance, where it's sunny most of the time."

"I suppose."

"Ever been down there?"

"In California?"

Jack flashed a smile. "Yeah."

Louis Nash's expression turned into a scowl. "Maybe. What's it to you?"

Jack shrugged. It was impossible not to notice that Louis had gone from cautious to angry. "Just curious—"

"Damn it all. Marie sent you, didn't she!"

"Marie?" Jack didn't have to pretend to be thrown off balance. "Who's Marie?"

"Are you another one of her private dicks?"

"I don't know—"

"'Cause, yeah, I know I'm in arrears with alimony. This business barely supports me. I have a mother, too, you know, and she needs stuff—Marie has a great job. For eleven years that woman has been making my life a living hell. I'm going to get a lawyer and put an end to this. You tell her that!"

Jack shook his head. "I don't know anyone named

Marie. I'm not here for anything like that. I just need a photographer this summer, that's all."

Louis's balled fists relaxed a little. "She didn't send you?"

"No."

"Oh, man," Louis said, rubbing his face. "Sorry."

"It's okay. Exes can drive a man nuts."

"Ain't that the truth?"

Was Nash a sociopathic killer or a man hounded by an ex-wife? A list of questions to be answered built in Jack's head. "These pictures are of a beach wedding. My girl is traditional. She wants a church. Do you have photos of a wedding like that?"

Louis took a calming breath. "I'm doing one tomorrow morning right down the street. Come back on the weekend and you can see the pictures."

"How about tomorrow night?"

"They won't be ready. Besides, I'm closed tomorrow night."

"Don't you have other church weddings you could show me?"

"As a matter of fact," Nash said as he snapped the appointment book shut. "It doesn't much matter. I'm booked every weekend in July. Afraid I can't help you."

"Maybe we could reschedule—"

"I'm booked clear through the summer," Nash interrupted. They stared at each other again. A noise coming from outside caught both their attention. Jack scrambled to his feet and took off for the front door. He knew the sound of a gunshot when he heard one. He tore the door open and exited onto the wooden porch in time to see a green taxicab with a black diamond on the door pull away from the curb. His heart almost stopped in his chest as he took in the rest of the scene.

The passenger door of his car was open and Sophie lay on the sidewalk clutching some kind of colorful paper in her right hand. Blood soaked her left sleeve. His feet pounded the cement as he ran to kneel beside her.

She was almost as ashen as the cement on which she lay, eyes glassy. His heart started beating again when a dark tendril of hair fluttered against her cheek with an exhaled breath.

She looked up at him as though trying to place him, her gaze traveling between him and Nash, who had followed Jack outside at a slower pace and now stood looking over Jack's shoulder.

"Call an ambulance," Jack said, his voice cracking. Louis turned on his heels and limped back to his house.

How many victims had he knelt over in his life? Dozens. And not one of them had caused this blind panic building in his gut. "Sweetheart," he said softly as he lifted her right hand and pried her fingers from a stranglehold on what he now saw was a city map. "Sophie?"

"I don't need an ambulance," she finally mumbled.

"The hell you don't," Jack said, hoping Louis had phoned for help. He dug in his pocket for his phone. "Hang in there, honey."

"I… I," she whispered as she gazed up at his eyes.

He squeezed her hand. "Don't worry, everything will be—"

"I didn't recognize him."

Jack paused from entering the emergency number just in case Louis hadn't. "Paul Rey?"

"He had a beard…"

"Shh," he said. "Stay still."

"A taxi… Oh, Jack, I…hurt."

"I know, baby," he said, stroking her hair away from her face. She'd hit her forehead when she fell and now

172 Identical Stranger

blood trickled toward her eyes. He found a bandanna in his pocket and dabbed at it as he studied her. Had there ever been a moment in his life when he hadn't known every single detail of her gently arched eyebrows, that lovely little mole on her cheek, the shape of her lips? He knew there had been but it seemed a lifetime ago.

"I hear a siren," he said when the high-pitched wail registered in his brain. He looked back toward Nash's house but the front door was firmly shut. "Here's the ambulance. Try to be still."

The emergency crew swarmed around her and Jack stepped away. While they stabilized her, he deposited the map into the empty paper bag from their lunch stop so he could give it to the police. He couldn't imagine Rey would have finally left prints but procedures were procedures. He looked for his gun, hoping Danny's brother hadn't taken it—wouldn't a stolen firearm be a fun thing to explain to Reece? But he quickly found it in the center console, where Sophie must have slipped it out of sight.

He answered the ambulance driver's questions and watched as they loaded Sophie into the narrow ambulance. Before he got in his car to follow her to the hospital, he called Detective Reece and reported what had happened.

"That damn fool," Reece groaned. "Why can't we catch him? I'll get a crew out to the scene to gather evidence and meet you at the hospital. If they keep her there overnight, we'll protect her room."

"You and me both," Jack responded.

Chapter Eleven

"How do you feel?" Jack asked her several hours later.

Sophie had been sedated through the process of cleansing, stitching and bandaging her arm and had awoken to hear the doctor tell her that she was going to spend the night for observation. Ensconced in a room she had all to herself, she watched as a woman wearing a pink smock covered with frolicking kittens came through the door wheeling a blood pressure machine.

"Hi, my name is Joy," the woman said, addressing Sophie. "I'll be your nurse until midnight. Right now I need to get your vitals and things."

Detective Reece started to leave the room.

"You don't have to go yet," Joy said. She reminded Sophie of a cupcake: round, smiling, rosy cheeked, dark brown curls bunched on top of her head like a dollop of chocolate frosting. "I can work around you."

"So how do you feel?" Jack repeated.

How Sophie felt was shot up, washed out and sleepy. "I feel stupid," she said because that's what she felt the most of.

"So Paul Rey was wearing some sort of disguise?"

"He had a beard and his eyes were dark instead of blue. He didn't look anything at all like Danny's brother." With that comment, she included a glance at Detective Reece, who stood at the foot of her bed. "Nothing like the picture you showed us."

"What exactly happened?" Reece asked.

Sophie took a steadying breath. Joy had finished with the blood pressure and now stood by with a thermometer poised for insertion in her mouth. "I was sitting there with Jack's gun in my hand ready to shoot Paul Rey if he dared show up. Then this cab pulled to the curb in front of the car. The driver got out, smiled at me and waved a map. His body language said he was lost and needed help. I put Jack's gun in the glove compartment so he wouldn't see it and I got out of the car to help the guy." She looked from one man to the other and added, "Let me reemphasize that he didn't look anything like Danny's brother."

"Then what?"

"He spread the map out on the hood of Jack's car and I leaned over to look at it. The next thing I knew, I detected movement out of the corner of my eye and in that moment, I knew what a fool I'd been, that he was Paul Rey and he had a gun. I turned toward him and grabbed it."

"The gun?" Reece asked, eyebrows raised.

"Yes. I grabbed it and he fired. For a second I didn't understand why my left arm went numb when I'd grabbed the muzzle with my right hand and then I realized the bullet had entered that arm. I looked in his eyes before I guess I fainted. The next thing I knew, Jack was kneeling by my side and Paul was gone."

"Good heavens," Reece said, his cherubic face now wearing a stunned expression. "You are one very lucky young woman. I have a CSI team out there right now. They'll find the bullet… We can match it to the one he fired over at the Cromwell house."

"If you ever catch him, you'll have a good case," Jack

said not without irony. "Were there any results from the other foot searches this afternoon?"

"Not a thing," Reece said.

Jack gently touched Sophie's shoulder and she rested her cheek against his warm hand. The nurse took the opportunity to stick the thermometer in her mouth.

Reece continued. "Thanks to your description of the taxi we were able to narrow it down to Green Diamond Cabs. They're a small enterprise that operates a grand total of four units. They figure one of the cars was stolen off their unmonitored lot last night. They hadn't even missed it yet. We found it abandoned out near a rock quarry."

"We drove by Buzz's house when we got back after talking to Adam Cook down in Seaport," Jack said. "Rey must have picked us up there."

As Joy withdrew the thermometer and started entering data into a computer affixed to the wall, Sophie spoke. "We saw a green cab, remember?"

"That's right," Jack said. "Damn. I should have stayed away from the Cromwell house. I figured even Rey wouldn't show up with an unmarked car out front."

"He's either a lot smarter than we think he is or a lot luckier than he has a right to be," Reece said.

"What did you think of Adam Cook's story?" Jack asked Reece. "For that matter, what have you found out about the man himself? And what about getting the hotel's surveillance tapes?"

"Gentlemen," Joy said. "Perhaps you would be so kind as to continue your conversation in the hall while I ask Ms. Sparrow a few questions?"

Jack raised Sophie's hand to his lips and kissed her knuckles. "I'll be right back," he said.

"And I'm posting a guard on your door," Reece added as both men exited the room.

Sophie answered a dozen questions about her health in general and her pain level in particular. Despite Jack's protective streak and Reece's assurances of a guard at her door, she had no desire to be drugged out on pain meds so she said she felt fine. Still, she'd been given something for the procedure where they worked on her arm and the truth was she was having trouble keeping her eyes open.

"I couldn't help overhearing you talking to the detective," Joy said.

"Oh. Well, everyone is trying to catch the nutcase who shot me."

"Of course. My husband is a firefighter and two of his best friends are with the sheriff's office. I know all about shop talk and questions, Lordy, do I."

"I bet you do. Does your husband work here in Astoria?"

"Yep. See, that's what I overheard. You talked about the Cromwell house and I know Buzz is in Antarctica and Charlie, that's my husband, said something about searching for Sabrina... Is she okay, do you know? I keep waiting to hear something on the news..." She narrowed her eyes and gave Sophie a closer look. "I didn't notice this before what with the bandage on your forehead and you lying down and all. You bear a striking resemblance to Sabrina Cromwell, don't you?"

"I'm her twin sister," Sophie said and managed not to burst into tears.

"I didn't even know she had a twin."

"It's a long story," Sophie said.

"Oh, gosh, when Charlie mentioned an informal search, my heart just about dropped. I hope she's okay. She's the nicest person. Charlie was away at training when my last baby came early—it was Sabrina who came over to the house to drive me to the hospital and watch my three-year-old until my mother could get here. And we're not even close friends. And what she did for Charlie's buddy and coworker, well, it was great. If she hadn't gone out of her way to talk to him… Anyway, I saw his wife last week and she was smiling for the first time in weeks and gushed about a trip… Well, Sabrina is a doll."

Sophie just stared at the woman. Something she'd just said rang a distant bell but the words had begun to all run together. She fought to stay awake but it was a losing battle.

Sometime later she opened her eyes to find Jack asleep in a chair at the foot of her bed. "Jack?" she whispered and he instantly opened his eyes and joined her.

His kiss was sensual but brief. "This isn't how I planned on spending our second night together," he said.

"Me neither."

"How are you feeling?"

"Chilled. Is it cold in here?"

"Not really," he said, and kissed her forehead. "You feel warm to me," he added as he laid the back of his fingers against her cheek.

"Never mind that. Jack, I need to call my mother and let her know I was hurt but that I'm okay."

"Your mother," he said as if surprised.

"Yes. My mother. I don't want to shut her out of my life and that includes the bad things, too."

"I'll get your phone. It's in your purse—"

"No, that's okay, it's too late to call her tonight. I'll wait till morning." She blinked her eyes a couple of times.

Jack felt her forehead again. "I'm calling the nurse," he said but before he could press the call button, the curtain parted and Joy walked in. "Last vitals for my shift," she chirped.

"I was just about to call you," Jack said. "Sophie feels warm."

Joy produced a thermometer. A moment later she read

the results. "It's not too bad but I'll get the doctor on call, just to be on the safe side. Don't worry, this isn't uncommon."

Sophie endured an exam that ruled out all serious causes and was started on an antibiotic to be on the safe side. By the time things had settled down, Joy had left for the night and Jack looked as tired as she was.

"Why don't you go back to Buzz's house and get some sleep," she said as he pulled a chair up to the head of her bed.

"I don't want to leave you."

"I know, but I just need sleep. There's a guard on the door."

"But—"

"Sabrina is still missing," Sophie reminded him.

"I know that."

"It's past midnight. Buzz will be home today, right?"

"Tonight, yeah, I see what you're saying. Okay, I'll continue the search." He stared down into her eyes as he added, "Whether you're ready to hear it or not, the fact is, I love you, Sophia Sparrow."

She smiled into his eyes. She'd never said those three words to anyone but assorted pets, stuffed animals and her parents but she whispered them now without hesitation. "I love you, too, Jack Travers."

He kissed her again and she closed her eyes as he left the room.

WIDE AWAKE AFTER the drive back to the Cromwell house, Jack spent an hour searching Sabrina's office for anything to do with Kyle or anyone else for that matter. He checked the emails on her computer—nothing abnormal. She communicated with Kyle and Sue and Buzz and dozens of other people, including the woman Sophie had mentioned, Bunny. He read through everything that was recent but there was nothing to suggest any clandestine romance or that she'd so much as entertained the idea of running off to meet anyone let alone actually done it. It didn't surprise him that a thorough search didn't reveal any indication Sabrina had returned to the house after talking to Jack.

The conversation he'd had that evening at the hospital with Reece hadn't been very productive. While Reece was apologetic about his department's inability to find Paul Rey, they were still dragging their feet on Louis Nash. He learned that Reece wasn't aware Louis had an ex-wife but then he'd laughed and said, "Who doesn't?"

As for Adam Cook, Jack learned he currently lived in Brad Withers's basement in a relatively small house. Where did he get the money to buy a new place? While it was true he had a criminal record in another state, his nose had been clean for several years. The Seaport police promised to look into him more closely in the days to come and Reece assured Jack that the police had requested and tomorrow would review the hotel's security tapes.

And meanwhile, time ticked away.

Jack felt like throwing something across the room. How was it possible Sophie had been shot by that bozo Paul Rey when every law enforcement type in the county was looking for him? How was it possible Sabrina had been missing for days without anyone but him and Sophie and her friends at the firehouse taking it seriously? How was it going to be possible to face Buzz tonight without any news about his cherished wife?

He poured himself a finger of his friend's whiskey and sat in a chair in front of the unlit fireplace. He had far less than twenty-four hours. The mantel clock struck three. He set the booze aside and went to bed.

HE AWOKE THE next morning to a phone call and answered it as he rubbed the sleep out of his eyes.

"Hey, lover boy, you sound like someone who slept in." Hearing Sophie's voice was the best way to wake up. Well, second best.

"Who me? I've been up for hours," he said with a laugh. "Do you miss me?"

"Like crazy. But you're never going to believe who's coming to visit me today."

"Don't tell me it's Danny Privet."

"Funny you should mention *his* name. I called him this morning to tell him to call off his sicko brother."

"And what did he say?"

"He said his lawyer told him not to talk to me. He also said even if he knew how, he wouldn't."

"Wow. I'm guessing it's not Danny coming to visit you."

"It's my mother. She's getting a lady from her church to drive her over after lunch."

"Will you still be in the hospital?" Jack asked.

"Yeah, afraid so. The fever came back. They're being cautious because I don't live locally. Did you find anything in Sabrina's house?"

"Nothing."

"I keep thinking I'm missing something," Sophie said.

"Like what?"

"I don't know. I need to talk to Joy. She comes on at noon."

"Joy?"

"The nurse. I think she said something yesterday that I was too groggy to pick up on. All we need is something to convince the police that Sabrina isn't off on her own free will, right?"

"Or under Paul Rey's control. They still think he might be responsible for everything. It doesn't seem to matter how many times I try to explain about him confusing her for you. I think they're so focused on catching him that nothing else matters."

"You'll work this out, honey," Sophie said. "I know you will."

He hoped she was right. "I'll be at the hospital after I do a few things like talk to Adam Cook and search Louis Nash's place."

"Sounds like fun. Be careful."

Jack's first priority was to talk to Adam Cook but the man didn't answer his phone. He recalled Sophie's telling him Adam had said he was going to work on a house. Vowing not to involve Reece or any other cop unless necessary, he tried looking up Brad Withers's telephone number.

"Yeah, Adam can be hard to get ahold of when he goes up to Glenville to work on his house. Some cousin left him the place but it was a real wreck. He's desperate to get out of my basement, though, so he works on it every chance he gets. He claims he doesn't get good cell service because of all the forest around the place. You said it's important you talk to him so I'll give you his address but don't expect a real warm welcome."

"I'm not sure where Glenville is," Jack said. So that's how the man had gotten a new house—he'd inherited it.

"It's a few miles southeast of Astoria. There's nothing but a sign on Highway 101. Adam's new place is off the road, 33401 Madrone. Real remote."

How handy for illegal activity, Jack thought but all he said was, "Thanks."

He drove by three churches before he saw one being readied for a wedding. Dashing inside, he found a florist setting a single spray by the altar, and created a story about being the bride's brother and asking if the woman knew what time the wedding started.

"In fifteen minutes. Where is everybody?"

"I'm not sure," Jack said.

"It's a crazy time for a wedding, isn't it? Who gets married at eleven thirty on a Wednesday morning? I mean even though it's a really small wedding…" The woman seemed to recall she was talking to a supposed member of the family and smiled. "Of course, love does as love wants."

"Right," he said. "I'll just go outside and wait."

He drove off instead, finding Nash's van—obvious because of the photography sign on its side—parked in the alley behind the man's house. He found a spot at the throat of the alley where he could see when the van left. He'd tucked his revolver into his shoulder holster before leaving the house that morning and checked now to make sure it was invisible. What he'd told Sophie was true. A gun could escalate a confrontation into a life-or-death battle. On the other hand, he didn't know what was inside Nash's house—or who. If Louis had nabbed Sabrina, then the stakes were already through the roof.

At last, Nash limped with purpose to the van carrying a bag of equipment and a tripod. He threw his gear into the back of the van and roared off. Jack left his car where he'd parked it and approached the back of Nash's house on foot. Pausing at the door, he looked for the telltale signs of an alarm system and saw nothing, but that didn't mean there wasn't one. Throwing caution to the wind, he picked the lock and entered the house.

Profound silence greeted his entry into the kitchen that was cluttered with unwashed dishes and bags and boxes of food. As he locked the outside door, he got his bearings. The door he'd noticed the afternoon before turned out to be unlocked and that came as a disappointment. If he was going to hide someone, he'd sure as heck lock the door. The landing behind the door was actually a small pantry with a few shelves covered with what looked like surplus food items. He walked past those until he came across a flight of stairs. He flicked a light to illuminate them and descended with his heart beating overtime.

What he found was an elaborate studio. Photos Nash must have taken himself hung on the walls. Curtained-off areas looked like changing rooms while hooks held different robes and hats maybe for use as props or costumes. A small stage with adjustable lighting took up a corner while an assortment of chairs lined yet another wall.

He lifted area rugs looking for hidden spaces, tapped walls and peeked under paintings and curtains all to no avail. This was obviously the public face of Nash's business and a dead end for Jack.

He immediately made his way to the living room and went up the stairs. He did a quick search of each room, behind mirrors, under drawers, searching for a trunk or some clue the guy had been down in Seaport a couple of days before. Satisfied there was nothing to find, he went back downstairs and picked the lock on the room Nash had disappeared into the day before. It turned out to be a small office. The closet was secured with a serious lock. Ignoring that for the moment, he zeroed in on a locked file cabinet. He found the keys to that in the desk drawer under the felt liner.

It looked like business as usual to him as he thumbed through the files without much enthusiasm until he saw a folder labeled Cases. The file contained several head shots of women including the one of Sabrina. Each had a number on them between one and three. He took a photo of everything. Another file labeled Betty Nash/Mother drew his attention. It contained a mass of forms and old insurance papers along with a recently issued uncashed social security check made out to Betty Nash. He quickly scanned a stapled compilation of her recent bank statements and the deed to a house in her name located on 40105 Manzanita Drive. Maybe the woman would have insights into her son. He needed a map of the area both to locate this house and to find Adam Cook's new property.

He continued taking photos of anything that looked pertinent. Over an hour had gone by since he entered the house. Wedding photos could take forever, but he didn't have forever to spend. It was well after noon now. Buzz's plane landed in Portland at 7:05 this evening. Give him three hours to claim his luggage, rent a car and drive here. That meant he'd be back by ten and that meant that by then, Jack either had to be sitting beside Sabrina on her sofa or know exactly where she was and why.

Was he spinning his wheels, trying so hard to stay busy that it was all for show? For all he knew, Louis Nash had abducted Sabrina days ago, killed her and disposed of her body. He could be looking for a ghost.

A steely reserve flooded his body. Buzz needed to come home to facts, not haunting maybes. Sophie, if denied her sister, had to at least have the truth of her death. No one could move forward without understanding the past, so in that way, whether Sabrina was alive or not did nothing to negate the importance of finding her.

He heard a sound at the back door and froze. Footsteps echoed in the old house. Jack quietly closed the file drawer and locked it again. He replaced the cabinet key. A closet beckoned to him from across the room but there wasn't time to get there—he took the only option he could see:

he dived under the desk but it didn't have a solid back and if Nash happened to look at the desk from the right angle, there was going to be an issue.

A second later he heard a key in the door and that's when he recalled he hadn't locked it after himself. There was a pause and then the door opened. Jack's view was of six inches of brown trouser leg and two worn-looking loafers that didn't move as Nash must have surveyed the room for signs of an intruder. Jack made himself as small as possible, holding his breath. At last, Nash moved—perhaps he decided he must have forgotten to lock the door before leaving the house. Another key in another lock and the closet door swung open. Nash rifled through the contents, grunting when he apparently found what he wanted. He finally limped to the desk and dropped a gray duffel bag with black straps on the floor. It hit with a metallic clang. Jack drew in his legs as Nash sat down and swiveled the chair toward the file cabinet.

What was in that bag? Tripods, maybe? Lighting trees? And what was Nash doing back here so soon anyway?

Nash apparently retrieved the key from the desk drawer, then opened the file cabinet. The drawer rolled out, papers rustled, the drawer slammed shut and, once again, Jack heard the sound of a key in a lock. Nash got to his feet, hefted the bag with a grunt and walked out of the office.

Jack stayed where he was until he heard the outside door slam shut. Curious about what Nash had taken from the file cabinet, he immediately searched the desk drawer, but the key was no longer under the felt.

The closet that had been locked before now stood open. Did that mean that whatever Nash took from here in a duffel bag was the only thing he safeguarded? Jack's quick perusal of the rest of the closet found nothing but photograpy equipment. He glanced at his watch. It was time to cut his losses and leave this house.

Once in his car he drove past the church. The lot was empty, which suggested the wedding party was gone. Maybe Nash dropped by his house to get something he needed for the reception photos.

Jack kept driving, unable to stop, knowing that time continued marching on like a determined soldier. He finally pulled to a stop in front of a small convenience store, where he made himself grab a premade sandwich because he'd skipped breakfast. As he ate the sandwich, he found Adam Cook's general location on the map on his phone and almost choked on salami and cheese.

Cook's new house and the town of Glenville were only a mile and a half from the search he and Sophie had participated in the day before. In fact, they'd driven by the road he lived on. What's more, Nash's mother's place was close to Cook's but separated by the river that had serenaded them as they looked for Sabrina. In other words, the search location, the Cook house and Nash's mother's place were all within a half mile of each other as the crow flies. Sophie's ominous statement came back to him: *I sense Sabrina is close by.*

And now his gut told him she'd been right.

With no bridge to cross the river, one had to go back out to the highway and travel north a quarter of a mile, turning onto a parallel road to travel east again, in effect making a giant U-turn. The three locations all but lined up on the GPS.

Jack immediately tossed the sandwich aside and headed out of town.

The skies were dark and foreboding. Driving through a part of town he wasn't familiar with, he made any number of wrong turns in his quest to find the main road. They all either emptied into other streets or dead-ended against the side of a mountain. Anxiety and frustration had him gripping the wheel so tight his knuckles turned white. Finally plugging the address into his phone's navigation, he followed the instructions, hoping he had enough service to get accurate directions. The synthesized voice actually calmed him and directed him south of town over the bridge crossing the Columbia River. A mile farther and it instructed him to turn east.

After ten more minutes of twists and hills, he turned onto Manzanita. As if exhausted by her diligent service his phone almost immediately lost service.

Living abodes this far out of the city were apparently built off on wandering driveways behind tall fences or acres of forest. The driveway leading to Betty Nash's place was overgrown with underbrush at first but soon cleared to what must be a beautiful meadow when the sun was out and the fields weren't muddy. Those fields held nothing now but a handful of wet cows.

The house itself was a stately looking gray two-story Victorian-influenced building. A dozen or more barns and outbuildings had sprung up around it over the years. Between the outbuildings and the tangle of old roads crisscrossing the land, he thought the place must have been a dairy farm once upon a time. Everything looked old, dejected and worn-out. He parked near the house and stepped onto a porch in serious need of repair. A knock on the door and a ring of the bell produced no results.

He tried yelling.

Nothing. Hadn't Reece said the woman was housebound? If that were the case, she might very well be inside. Maybe she hadn't heard his knock. He tried the knob, his intention to open it a crack and call her name, but it was locked.

He stepped off the porch and walked to a nearby open building that looked as if it might be the garage. All it held was an old sedan circa 1960 up on blocks.

So, she might be inside, too disabled to answer the door. She might have had a friend give her a ride to an appointment. Hell, she might be looking out a window right now holding a shotgun, deciding she wasn't about to open the door to a stranger—he didn't blame her if that was the case.

Did he try to search all the buildings? Several were out in the open, others abutted distant forests, and still others were nothing but dim shapes barely visible through the misty skies. It would take hours.

Something was off about Nash, he just knew it. It all came back to proof and he had zip. If he wanted Betty Nash's insights into her son, he'd simply have to come back later with Reece.

He retraced his route, traveled south until he found Madrone and turned east again. It took a while, but he eventually ferreted out a sign nailed to a tree with the numbers 33401 painted in fading white paint. The drive was muddy from all the recent rain and very dark as the towering evergreens cut out the relative light in the sky. He expected to find a house under the process of renovation at the end of the drive, not the rickety-looking tan building that greeted him. If Adam was working here, it had to be on the interior.

There was no vehicle in sight or any sign that anyone was home. He knocked on the door and peeked through the window. The room he glimpsed was even darker than outside, sparsely furnished and very still. He wasn't surprised when no one responded to his knock or his voice calling out Adam's name.

A detached garage held a van. No trunks, no suitcases. Several big batteries stacked against a wall and, oddly enough, what appeared to be a new golf cart. Adam checked to make sure no one had appeared out of thin air before he opened the double back doors of the vehicle. He found a dozen boxes all sealed and randomly opened one of them to check the contents. It looked like the guy had visited a hardware store and stocked up on lantern fuel in case the electricity went out. Probably not an uncommon event out this far. There was no indication a dead handyman or an abducted woman had ever been in the van; indeed, as it now sat, there wasn't room for a human being back there.

Big fat raindrops started falling from the heavy clouds as he started a foot search of the land, following a fence as he moved while listening for the sound of an approaching engine. Just about convinced there was nothing to find, he ran across what appeared to be a worn path disappearing into the woods and followed it until it ended at a new building set out of sight from the house and sheltered by undergrowth.

The ruts in the path suggested Cook's shiny new golf cart had made this trip with a heavy cargo...

This building had to be where Cook was putting in his time. Overhead, he saw electricity lines connecting the building to the power pole and a spigot near the foundation promised water. Perhaps he was creating a whole other house back here. Jack walked around the entire structure. There were no windows. Odd. That precluded its use for human occupation. But it could be the shop. His father, a retired contractor, had often created a building similar to this one prior to construction. The single door was secured with a heavy chain and two different padlocks.

He studied the locks—no way could he pick them. If there was the slightest indication that Sabrina was being held here, he'd shoot the locks, but there just wasn't. In fact, face it, there was no indication at the Nash house or this one that anyone did anything wrong. Still, he pounded on the door and listened with his ear against the wood after calling Sabrina's name.

Striking out twice in a row and this late in the day was infuriating as well as heartbreaking. He headed back to town, determined to use what little time he had left to turn things around. Both Betty Nash's house and Adam's Cook place were well outside the city limits… He decided he'd stop and talk to the sheriff.

He drove back to Astoria with a bitter taste in his mouth.

AGAINST DOCTOR'S ORDERS, Sophie checked herself out of the hospital. The fever had been gone for hours and she was restless. While the visit with her mother had been stilted and thankfully short, it was one of the few times in Sophie's life where she could recall her mom trying hard to make a connection and she deeply appreciated the effort it took.

But what really drove her was the conversation with nurse Joy that had taken place after her mother's visit. She finally thought she could prove to Detective Reece that Sabrina had not run off with Kyle Woods.

As for Jack? He was hopefully doing what he knew how to do best and that was locating Sabrina, and there was no way she was going to get in the middle of that. She'd change places with her sister in a blink if she could, but the depressing fact was that there'd been no further sense of contact. Sabrina had disappeared, it seemed, from the earth and from Sophie's psyche.

She took a taxi—not a green one—back to the Cromwell house and used the back door key she'd taken from the hook in the kitchen the last time she was there. She was careful to relock the door before making her way to Sabrina's computer. The light was blinking on the desk answering machine and Sophie decided to listen to the messages. How ironic would it be if Sabrina had called home on the off chance someone was there to answer her call and no one knew it.

But the calls were from Jack, people at work, people Sophie didn't know, the vet's office and Buzz, all begging her to respond. And these were just the calls to the home phone—who knew how many had been made to Sabrina's cell wherever that was?

She'd heard them all and learned zilch. She pressed the save button, just in case...

Just in case this all wasn't as hopeless as it seemed. She switched on a lamp to combat the darkness, plugged in her cell to recharge the battery that had gone dead hours before and booted up the computer, where she looked for and found the email she recalled reading a couple of days ago.

Guess what? He asked me again. This time, I don't know, it was different. It was as though he was finally seeing me the way he used to... It made me remember what we once had. I know he's been confiding in you and I want you to know that your advice has been invaluable to both of us. I still love him and if we can make this marriage work, well, that would be wonderful. So, no calls, no email or texting, no internet or television. Just him and me in a friend's cabin, alone, together for five days. Maybe we can recapture what we lost.

Thanks for being his friend and mine. You're an angel. Have a great time on your hiking trip. Bunny.

On the night Sophie was shot, Joy had told her about her husband's friend with the broken marriage and the way Sabrina had helped. The friend's husband was a fireman just like Joy's husband was. Somewhere in her medicated mind, Sophie had connected some of these dots with this email she'd read days before, an email signed by Bunny, which today Joy confirmed was Barbara Woods's nickname.

Sabrina was Kyle's friend, not his lover. Kyle was off with Bunny in an apparently secluded location, purposely shutting out the world in a battle to win back his wife.

As Sophie picked up the desk phone to call Reece, the computer went dark and the lights went off, plunging the bedroom into near blackness. The sounds of the storm—the creaking, the rain pounding on the metal roof and the wind banging limbs against the windows—now escalated, making the unfamiliar house feel scary. She carefully found her way to the bedroom door from which, through the front window, she could see falling rain highlighted by the sidewalk lamps outside. A porch light flicked on down the block. And that upped the spook factor.

Hairs on the back of her neck rose for no reason. She had to get out of this house. She turned on her heels to run to the kitchen but an explosion of shattering glass drove her to the floor, where she instinctively covered her face. She heard a thud as something heavy landed inside the room with her, then crunching sounds. Glass pieces fell from her shoulders and hair as she scrambled to her feet. She glanced at what was left of the front window, where the dark hulking shape of a man approached through the rubble. She took off again, desperate to reach the back door, where she could escape into the neighbor's yard. She hadn't taken more than a half a dozen steps when two hands grabbed her from behind. A cloth covered her lower face, killing a scream before it could escape her throat. She sank into unconsciousness.

Chapter Twelve

It took a while to jump through the hoops but Jack finally found himself seated in Sheriff Leroy Donner's office. "You see, son, Reece," he said in what sounded like a Deep South drawl, "has to please Chief Holt and Holt has to please the commissioner—plus we're just getting over a holiday weekend. I swear, this whole city stops on a holiday, any holiday. Plus Reece is a cautious man. I am not. No siree. My calling card is blazing guns and everyone knows it."

Well, Jack had wanted someone who would act and it looked as though he'd found his man. Still, the guy was over the top. Big, florid, stuffed into his tan uniform and bursting with self-importance, he made a hard pill to swallow.

"I actually remember old Alastair Becket," Donner added. "He's the geezer who left Adam Cook that nice little piece of hillside up there near Glenville. Quiet guy. Traveled all over the countryside taking pictures and developing them in his basement darkroom. The library and courthouse are full of his work. Personally, I think it's boring."

Unlike, Jack supposed, the painting of a tiger hauling its prey off into the jungle that hung above the sheriff's desk. "There's a darkroom in the basement of that old house?" Jack asked.

"Yeah. Nice one, or at least it used to be."

He mentally slapped himself. Adam Cook had a link to photography, too. What if he'd also been taking pictures of Sabrina? Why hadn't Adam gone inside that dumpy tan house and looked for a basement?

"Anyway," the sheriff continued, "I wouldn't mind going up there and introducing myself to Adam, have a look around, push a few buttons. First thing tomorrow, that's what I'll do. If anything makes me suspect the guy is involved in Mrs. Cromwell's disappearance, I'll tear the place apart. You have my word."

"Your word is good enough for me," Jack said, and endured a bone-crushing handshake. He had hoped things would start happening tonight but maybe it was better this way. The sheriff was a bulldozer—pushing too hard in the wrong places might drive things forward with awful consequences.

One way or another, he'd finesse Cook into showing him the basement before the sheriff got there.

He left the station with big plans. First Cook's basement and, if that didn't produce any results, on to Betty Nash's place. If she'd been off to an appointment surely she'd be home by now. Back in the car, he checked his phone again and found that though he still hadn't received any calls, he had been sent a text from someone he didn't know two hours before.

Hi, it's me, Sophie, he read. I'm using Joy's phone because my battery is dead. The thing is, I need to look at something at Sabrina's house so I'm taking a taxi over there (not with Paul Rey at the wheel, I promise). I don't want you to drop everything and come running, okay?

Just wanted you to know that's where I am. I'll meet you there whenever. Love you.

His lips curved. She loved him.

He immediately punched in her number and once again, it went to voice mail. Must still be out of juice.

All the same, he decided to go to the Cromwell house before driving back out into the country to check Cook's and Nash's places. The car's wipers fought the deluge while an annoying bumper-hugging orange subcompact rode his tailpipe. He wasn't positive why he felt anxious unless he was worried Sophie might be in danger. Hell, as long as Paul Rey was running around loose, of course she was in danger! He took a wrong turn, twice, and gritted his teeth.

The sight of Buzz and Sabrina's utterly dark house on a block of illuminated homes took a big old bite out of his gut. He grabbed a flashlight out of the console and ran up the front walk to come to a dead halt on the porch. The front window was gone, broken, glass both inside and out. He glimpsed something at his feet and bent to pick up one of the hated origami foxes. He climbed into the living room, where glass covered almost every surface. He conducted a hasty search of the house and found Sophie's phone plugged in next to Sabrina's computer. The flashlight died as he searched the backyard. Dripping wet again, he called the police.

He gave Dispatch the address. "A woman has been attacked and is now missing. Paul Rey may be chasing her. Get people out here to search the neighborhood. Her name is Sophia Sparrow. Have Reece call Jack Travers ASAP."

He ran outside and looked up and down the street, then he got in his car and unfolded his fist to reveal the crumpled dollar bill. Had they all underestimated Rey's determination and adaptability? He had been escalating his attempts—was this blatant in-your-face destruction his last step?

Jack's phone rang and his heart leaped but it was only Reece. "I've been trying to reach you," the detective said. "We finally heard from the fireman, Kyle Woods. He was off with his estranged wife. That leaves Sabrina Cromwell's safety an issue. The chief is finally willing to take this seriously."

"That's great," Jack said with all the patience he could muster. "But—"

"That's not all," Reece continued. "We got a call about fifteen minutes ago. Someone saw a man fitting Rey's description out by the state park. He's driving north in an older-model black Chevy with stolen plates. There was a dark-haired woman with him. My officers are keeping their distance while we work out the best way to go about stopping the car. There's no way of knowing if the woman is Sabrina—"

"Or Sophie," Jack interrupted. "She's been taken from the Cromwell house. I found her phone. I also found one of those origami foxes."

"That places Rey at the scene. Know when this all happened?"

"Not exactly but I called it in and I can hear sirens approaching. Your guys can question the neighbors. I'm on my way to join you," Jack said. He hung up as Reece told him to stay put. Sure.

He tore out of the subdivision right as two police cars rolled in. He kept going. It wasn't until he was a mile along that he noticed a car tagging him. Not again. He drove under a streetlight and glanced in his rearview mirror in time to see an orange subcompact that looked just like the one that had followed him from the hospital to Sabrina's house.

The only person he knew who liked to follow people was Paul Rey. On the other hand, Paul Rey was, first, supposedly driving north in a stolen car, not southeast. Secondly, the man had proved pretty damned accomplished at remaining out of sight.

No rock unturned, he decided. Somewhere up here was one of those annoying unposted no-outlet streets that he'd run into earlier that day. He turned onto the first one that looked vaguely familiar. After a block or two, he realized this was the one that back-ended a forest preserve with a seasonal day park. He drove past the closed-for-the-season sign and hit a sawhorse barricade before circling the small parking lot, the orange car following. Then he immediately turned his bigger car to block the exit and got out. A man popped out of the orange compact, fired a round of shots that went wild and took off at a run down a heavily wooded path, his own headlights illuminating his retreating figure. Jack took off after him.

The helpful headlights extended until the path curved and they were plunged into a dripping, dark world of massive ferns and towering trees. Jack chased the guy's shadowy silhouette and the hollow sound of his footsteps until the timbre of those steps changed. His quarry had to be on a bridge—wood by the sound of it. He heard a scrambling sound and an oath followed by a thud as his prey apparently lost footing and skated on mossy, slippery boards. There was the sound of a splash into the stream running under the bridge, then more oaths as Jack raced to get to the guy before he took off again. He reached for the writhing shape as it tried to slither from his grasp. With adrenaline pumping through his veins, he yanked the man to his feet.

He was too short to be Cook or Nash. Jack frisked him and found no weapon. "Where's your gun?" he demanded.

"I dropped it when I fell," the guy said. "Why are you chasing me?"

"Why am I chasing you?" Jack said. "Nice try." He marched his complaining catch back to the parking lot, where the headlights once again proved their worth.

The guy was covered in wet moss and slime. "Paul Rey," Jack said. "Why am I not surprised?"

"Reynard. My name is Paul Reynard."

"Your mother shortened the name two decades ago."

"I'll make her respect it again, you wait and see," Rey blustered. "When she and my precious brother find out what I've done for them, for all of us, they'll change their tune. They'll know who they owe, you watch. I won't be the screwup anymore, I'll be the one with vision."

"You've been chasing the wrong woman, you moron," Jack interrupted. "Sabrina Cromwell was taken from her hotel room days ago."

"Don't give me that," Rey protested. "I saw you and her standing at her hotel door. I saw her in the parking garage and outside her house."

"Who you saw is Sabrina's twin sister. You've been shooting at Sophia Sparrow, your older brother's former ticket to riches. Now she's missing, too. Guess who the cops want for both women's abductions?"

"Me?" Paul choked out, the bravado slipping from his voice.

"Yeah, and for a murder down in Seaport, too. You're a real popular guy right now." Jack walked him to his own car, where he opened the trunk and took out his bag of supplies. His gun was still in his shoulder holster but he dug out handcuffs and used them and a lot of threats to secure a swearing, kicking Rey's arms around a small but substantial tree.

"What time today did you leave the origami on Sabrina's porch?" he asked.

"Wait a second," Rey said, his face buried in bark. He tried to look back over his shoulder at Jack. "I have nothing to do with either girl's disappearance."

"Answer my question."

He sputtered moss and bark from his lips. "This morning. I left it this morning. Then I went to the hospital. Honest. When she left, I followed her to the house but she went in the back door and didn't even see the fox. That's my calling card, you know, because Reynard is pronounced like *renard*, which is—"

"French for *fox*. Yeah, I know."

"The dollar bill signifies her only value in the world."

Jack's jaw knotted. "What else did you see?"

"Nothing. I decided to wait and get her when she came back outside but then this dude showed up in a van. He disappeared around the side."

"Was there anything funny about the way he walked?"

"I wasn't watching him walk. I was watching the front door for the girl. Instead, all the lights go off in the house, then he comes back to the front and knocks out the window. In he goes. The next thing I know, out he comes with the girl over his shoulder. He threw her in the back of a van and off they went."

"You must have seen him then. Did he limp?"

"I don't know, I swear. It was dark and raining and I was—"

"Did you follow him?"

"Yeah. But I lost him. I decided to go back to the hospital but then your car drove right past me so I followed you back to the house. Take these handcuffs off," he begged. "My arms are killing me."

"Too bad." Jack thrust the muzzle of his gun against

Rey's spine to emphasize his point. "Exactly where did you lose the van? I swear if you lie to me, come spring, the park rangers are going find your rotting corpse still hugging this tree."

"I'll tell you the truth, I swear," Paul Rey shouted. "Just stop poking me with that gun!"

"Start talking," Jack said.

SOPHIE AWOKE IN a twilight space surrounded by cinder block walls. She groaned when she moved her head. A tsunami of nausea rose in her throat and she rolled over on hands and knees to throw up.

Where was she?

She remembered a man coming through the broken glass, remembered big hands, a cloth—

She hadn't seen the guy's face. She wasn't sure if he was Adam Cook or Louis Nash or someone else entirely, just that it wasn't Paul Rey.

A nearby moan drew her attention. It seemed to come from what appeared to be a pile of cast-off clothes in the corner. She found she was not restrained and crawled the distance to discover the rags covered the body of another woman.

Sophie turned the woman's face toward the light coming through the two inches between the bottom of the door and the threshold. Even in the murky light, even with the woman's bloody split lip, her face streaked with dirt and caked with blood from an angry red slash down one cheek, Sophie recognized her. She'd seen that face every day for the past twenty-six years when she caught her own reflection in a mirror.

"Sabrina?" she whispered. *At last.*

Sabrina's trembling lips were her only response. Sophie discovered her sister was naked beneath the pile of clothes, her body bruised, her left leg swollen with what appeared to be a bullet wound in her thigh. The wound was infected. Alarmed, she touched Sabrina's forehead and found it dry and hot. "Oh, Sabrina," she said.

"Water," Sabrina moaned. Sophie's gaze traveled in every direction. The room itself was small, empty, dank, cold. Besides herself and Sabrina, the only object she could see was an overturned metal bucket with an attached length of chain as though it had been yanked from a well. She walked first to the door to pull on the knob. Surprise, the door didn't budge. She picked up the bucket, wincing at the clattering sound the chain made as it hit metal on metal, stilling it by grasping the links.

The bucket smelled horrible but she extended her fingers into the murky depths until she touched a substance near the bottom that felt almost as thick as mud. She took the bucket back to her sister's side and sat down.

"Water," Sabrina moaned again.

"Hang on," Sophie said as she pulled out the hem of her thermal shirt from beneath her sweater and scooped a handful of the muddy substance onto the box weave of the garment. She tightened the cloth around it and squeezed. Moisture dripped out. She held the gooey wad over Sabrina's face and directed a few precious drops onto her sister's dry lips. Undoubtedly it was filthy and germ laden but that seemed like the least of their problems at the moment. Sabrina's dry lips parted and she swallowed. Sophie repeated the process until at last Sabrina opened her eyes.

"Hello," Sophie whispered, taking her sister's hand.

"It's true," Sabrina gasped softly as she examined Sophie's face. Her voice was hoarse as though she'd screamed for days. Of course she'd screamed for days. Five days to be exact. "He told me he saw *me*. Not here but somewhere else. I thought he was crazy. I—I didn't believe him."

"Who is he?" Sophie asked.

"I don't know," she said, her words slow in coming and because of the split lip, hard to understand. "Sometimes he says the word *darkroom*. I don't know if he means himself or this...this place."

She started trembling then and her grip on Sophie's hand tightened.

"We're going to get out of here," Sophie said.

"I tried to escape—a day or two ago, I tried. But he shot me and dragged me back here... Oh, I'm so sorry you're here, too. How is this possible?"

"Jack Travers and I have been looking for you."

"Jack?"

"Yes. We met because of you, and we fell in love because of you. Buzz is on his way home—"

"Buzz!" Sabrina cried as tears welled in her eyes. She raised a shaky hand to wipe them away. "My Buzz?"

My Buzz. The hope in those two words flooded Sophie's heart and in that instant she faced the fact that rescuing Sabrina and herself was the only way she would ever see Jack again. *Her Jack.*

"Buzz is coming," she repeated. "And you know what Jack is like. He'll never give up looking for us. But we have to do our part. Can you sit up?"

With Sophie's help, Sabrina struggled into a sitting position where at last Sophie could drape her with some of the discarded clothes to ward off the cold. "How did you escape before?" she asked.

"I jumped him." She licked her lips and frowned. "He comes with a rifle now and locks the door."

"What's on the other side of that door?"

"A small room...a horrible room...then another one filled with old appliances and junk. The exit leads into a forest." She touched Sophie's hair. "What's your name?"

"Sophia. I go by Sophie."

"We're identical twins?"

"Yes."

"My mother told me she heard a rumor after she adopted me that there were two babies but she was told the records had been destroyed. She tried but she could never find out anything else."

"The rumor was true."

Sabrina reached up and touched Sophie's hair. "I dye mine to get it as dark as yours."

"I dye mine, too," Sophie said.

Sabrina smiled. "You couldn't stand the mousy brown either?"

"I did for years but suddenly, I just couldn't."

Sabrina's free hand fell to her lap. "I always wanted a twin. I used to think what fun it would be to trick my parents into mistaking one of us for the other."

"We'll make up for lost time after we escape," Sophie said, her voice distracted, the wheels in her head suddenly turning.

"Escape? How?"

"It's going to require a lot out of you," Sophie said slowly as she looked her sister in the eye. Was the poor woman up to it?

"Anything, anything to see Buzz again."

What other choice did they have? "Good." Sophie pulled her sweater over her head and then her thermal shirt. She took off her bra and shivered in the cold. "We're going to trade places," she said.

"No. No," Sabrina protested. "You don't know what he's like, what he'll do. I can't let you—"

"Shh," Sophie said. "He'll do all that anyway if we don't stop him. This is our chance and we're going to take it." She tore the clean hospital bandages off her arm and stuffed them out of sight. The cold room got even colder as she pulled off her boots and socks, then jeans…everything. If Sabrina had endured this man stark naked, so would she. It was what he expected to find and she would give it to him.

Dressing Sabrina was tricky. Between the injuries, the fear and the fever from her infection, she hurt everywhere. At last Sophie took off the pearl necklace her father had given her and fastened it around Sabrina's neck.

"This isn't going to fool him," Sabrina whispered. "He'll never let it happen. He's excited about having two of us. He has terrible plans."

"So do I," Sophie said with as much confidence as she could muster. She took off the silver earrings Danny had given her a lifetime ago.

"My ears aren't pierced," Sabrina muttered.

"That's okay. I need a cut on my face and I can't think of any other way to get it." She gripped one of the silver disks and scoured its edge back and forth against a protruding cinder block in the wall.

"You're making a blade," Sabrina said through chattering teeth.

"Yeah. But you're going to have to help me."

She ground the silver until the edge looked ragged enough to tear skin and then handed it to Sabrina, whose hand shook as she grasped it. Sophie touched her own face from the top of her right cheekbone down to her jaw near the bottom of her ear. "Put some muscle in it and remember you're saving my life, okay? That's what you firefighters do, right?"

Sabrina took the earring and held it to Sophie's cheek. Her hand fell. "I can't," she said after a moment.

"Yes, you can. I'll help you." She put her stronger hand over Sabrina's. Together, they managed to cut deep enough to spill warm blood down Sophie's cheek and throat. The pain was almost unbearable and it took every ounce of courage Sophie had not to tear the makeshift blade away from her skin. When it was done, she scooped up a handful of the mud in the bucket, then rubbed it over her face to approximate Sabrina's condition and in her hair to disguise the lilac streak. She wrapped a bloody piece of the clothing around her thigh as though she'd bandaged the gunshot wound. Next she added mud to cover the stitches in her arm. She was going to be on antibiotics for a month after this.

If there was an *after this*…

One of the hardest things she'd ever done was not put on every rag lying at her feet. Instead, she helped Sabrina to stand and slowly walked her to the place she'd woken up minutes before. After helping her sit, she finger-combed Sabrina's hair. "Keep the cut side of your face against the knee you can bend so he doesn't see it," she cautioned. "With any luck he'll think you're still out. I'm still out, I mean."

She went back to the pile of rags and hid her newly made blade. If it tore her skin it would tear his. Then she picked up the bucket to go replace it but at that moment the not-so-distant sound of a banging door and heavy footsteps drove her heart into her throat. She glanced at Sabrina, who sagged against the wall toward the floor.

The footsteps grew closer as Sophie huddled under the heap of rags.

THE RAINY, MOONLESS night was as dark as the inside of an abandoned well. The only saving grace was the fact that Jack had been here once already today. He kept his headlights off and his foot soft on the accelerator, willing the car to creep up the long driveway without making a sound. While there was no moonlight to expose him as he got to the clearing, there was also no light to help him find his way. Better to be on foot than in a big machine if he crashed into anything. He shut off the interior lights and opened the door to merge into the rainy night like a shadow.

What killed him was the uncertainty that came with taking the word of a delusional sleaze like Paul Rey. He was here at this house on this night with nothing but the word of a convicted man, a man who had tried to kill Sophie multiple times, a man without a conscience or a moral compass. For all he knew, Paul Rey had made up this story to cover his own tracks. He might have already shot Sophie.

He couldn't think like that. He'd heard on the radio that the guy with the stolen plates was leading half the police on a merry chase into Washington. Now the Washington police were involved, as well. Sabrina or Sophie could be in that car, not with Rey because that loser was still hand-cuffed to a tree, but maybe with Nash or Cook or even a faceless, nameless fourth man. Jack didn't want police to drop that ball to chase this one. It all came back as it did every time—how did you trust a guy like Paul Rey to tell you the truth?

You didn't. You checked it out yourself and called for backup when you had facts. That in this case backup meant "blazing gun" Leroy Donner, well, that was a sobering thought.

The house was as dark and foreboding as the night. He paused as he stood beside the car listening, trying to hear anything but the sound of the rain. Should he break in and search the place?

A light suddenly went on in the distance behind the cover of a few trees. He'd already taken the rifle out of his trunk and grabbed that now before silently closing the driver's door and starting toward the light.

The first thing he managed to do was trip over an invisible boulder that lined the drive—he'd forgotten they were there. He made his way toward the barn, his eyes on the light in case it was extinguished and he had to go from memory.

The building was open, unlocked, the interior light flooding a small patch of muddy ground outside. Jack took his time approaching the door, making sure no one was waiting for him. The hair on the back of his neck stood on end and he reminded himself it wasn't just Rey who sent him here, it was his own gut. He'd made a promise to himself after Lisa—he would listen to his instincts.

Once he was pretty sure he wasn't walking into an ambush, he entered what looked like a twelve-by-twelve room. Three upright freezers were lined up against two of the walls. A table used for butchering, if the floor drain and rusty-looking stains were any indication, sat against a third. A dangling unlit lamp hung over the table.

Gruesome.

And ominous, made more so by the gray-and-black duffel bag sitting atop the table. Louis Nash's bag, last seen in his office, retrieved from behind a locked door. Jack walked silently to the bag and found it unzipped. Inside he saw a picture that momentarily stunned him. Obviously taken through a window, a bloodied Sophie lay on the sidewalk, Jack hovering over her. And under her picture, he found the head shot of Sabrina and all the other women he'd last seen in Louis Nash's file cabinet along with the list of names under the heading Cases.

Paul Rey hadn't been lying. Louis Nash had taken Sophie and Sabrina, too.

He moved the papers and discovered the reason the duffel bag had clanked when Nash dropped it. The bag was filled with tools, including long serrated knives, saws, clamps and what appeared to be surgical implements. Some of it looked like things he remembered from the one and only time he'd helped a friend clean and dress a deer. They all sent chills down his spine.

The sound of a lock opening farther inside the structure caught his attention. He needed to hurry but there was no way he was leaving this room without checking out those freezers. He quickly opened the nearest and found it empty. He opened the one standing next to it and stared at its frozen contents for an interminable moment without breathing.

Shock and repulsion made him slam the door without consideration of noise. Holding the rifle in front of himself, he moved through the doorway toward the sound of the lock and into a dimly lit room dominated by a filthy mattress. Manacles were chained to the walls. Photographs of women in obvious agony loomed over the mattress like tortured souls caught in limbo. A camera sat on the mattress as if ready for use.

There was another door on the far side of the room.

From behind that door, he heard the low grumblings of a man's voice. He raised the rifle and moved to the door. He could see that it was locked. The only quick way through the lock was with a bullet but he didn't want that bullet to hit someone on the other side because there wasn't a doubt in his mind that Sophie was back there and maybe, maybe, Sabrina, too.

The matter was settled when a heart-wrenching scream cut through his heart.

SOPHIE SAW THE dark shape of two feet as they arrived on the other side of the door. She heard the jangle of the lock and then the creak of the wood as the door swung inward. Too late she wondered if she should have positioned herself right there by the door. No, no, he would have anticipated that. It was probably why it was taking him so long to enter.

What she had hoped was that this might be the one time he wouldn't lock the door behind him but that was not to be the case.

She heard his limp as he approached, but instead of coming to her, he walked over to Sabrina. She could see him through one eye if she squinted. He stopped before her sister's sitting form, grabbed her hair and pulled her face up to look at it. Surely he would see the cut on Sabrina's cheek. Her heart sank down to the depths of hell.

"Wake up," he said and kicked what Sophie realized was Sabrina's injured leg. Sabrina didn't respond. She had to have passed out. He moved toward Sophie. She steeled herself.

"Okay, bitch," he whispered as he stood over her. "I'll start with you."

He leaned down to grab her. She made herself go limp as he pulled her to her feet, a rifle in one hand, his other hand clamped around her arm. She held the makeshift blade so firmly she was pretty sure it was cutting through her own skin. She made a few appropriately weak-sounding noises and sagged as though too hurt to move on her own. He ran his hands over her body like he owned her. Then he leaned down and hoisted her over his shoulder and took a struggled step toward the door.

And that's when she dug the blade into the side of his neck, aiming for his jugular vein or his carotid artery—she didn't care just as long as it stopped him.

He flung her away from himself. She hit the floor with a bone-cracking thud. A moment later he was on top of her, blood dripping unheeded down his neck and into his clothes. She fought him but he was unimaginably strong. He pinned her to the floor and sat atop her, the rifle still gripped in his hand, a smile now toying with his lips.

From over his shoulder she saw Sabrina's face. She'd somehow managed to stand on her own and grab the bucket. She held a length of its attached chain between her hands. Nash seemed hell-bent on dominating Sophie and to keep it that way she spit up into his face. The spit didn't quite make it but the gesture infuriated him. As he raised a hand to pummel her, Sabrina threw the chain around his neck. In her weakened condition, she was no match for this monster. He rose in one fluid motion to his feet, shaking Sabrina off his back like a piece of lint. She hit the wall with a piercing scream.

Sophie took the second he was distracted by Sabrina to grab the abandoned bucket. She flung the chain over his head again and managed to get it around his neck but he was too tall and the chain too thick for her to tighten it into a stranglehold. He roared as he freed himself, his face crimson as he shook her away. She searched the floor for her makeshift blade but couldn't see it. A string of oaths filled the room as he grabbed Sophie's leg and dragged her toward the door. Her muddy foot slipped from his grasp and she crawled back to Sabrina's side. He was going to kill both of them in this hellhole if she didn't do something to stop it but she was out of tricks and opportunities...

A shot thundered in the small room and for a second, Sophie thought Louis Nash had fired it. But neither she nor Sabrina had been hit and Nash had frozen in place. As he turned toward the door, she once again grabbed the bucket and found the chain. Another shot boomed. As Nash fell backward, she threw the bucket aside and scuttled to pull Sabrina out of his way.

Footsteps broke the almost deafening silence and Sophie looked up to find Jack framed in the doorway. A sob of relief choked her as he crossed quickly to Louis Nash's downed body, kicked the rifle away and knelt.

The big man lay as still as stone. Jack stood.

"Sophie," he whispered as he crossed to her. He fell to his knees, his gun still trained on Nash. With a glance at Sabrina, he whispered, "How is she?"

"Alive," Sophie said through the tears rolling down her cheeks. "Alive."

"Thank goodness."

He gently touched Sophie's bloodied cheek before shrugging off his wet but blessedly warm jacket and draping it over her bare shoulders. His arm enfolded her as he pressed her against his chest and for a second, his grip was so tight she couldn't breathe.

Well, who needed to breathe when they'd been yanked from the yawning pit of the devil's throat to find themselves magically delivered to heaven? And wrapped in Jack's arms, that's exactly where she was.

"Let's get you both out of here," he whispered into her hair.

IT WAS ALMOST dawn and Jack sat in the hospital waiting room talking to Detective Reece. Sheriff Donner had come and gone like a boisterous windstorm, Sabrina was in recovery after surgery, Sophie was being treated and Buzz was stuck on the wrong side of a mudslide in his journey to the coast from the airport.

"Nash is going to make it," Reece said.

Jack, not trusting his voice or choice of words, just nodded.

"He got chatty. I think Sabrina is alive because of her car. Nash apparently stashed her in his van after he got her to open that hotel room door, drugged her and stuffed her in a trunk. Then he drove her car to a spot where he hid it. Next he drove his van up here with a slight detour to dump the handyman's body. He hitchhiked back to Seaport. He retrieved her car and drove the back roads to Astoria and that took a while. By then two days had gone by. She tried to escape and he shot her. When he saw Sophie lying on the sidewalk, his warped mind built a lovely little scenario—well, you know what was in those freezers."

"Heads," Jack said woodenly, wishing the image would magically disappear and knowing it never would. "Women's severed heads."

Reece nodded. "He's been nabbing women for years and bringing them back to that horrible, horrible place."

"What about his mother?"

"She's in the freezer, too. Nash has been cashing her social security checks."

"And Adam Cook's big secret," Jack said, "according to Sheriff Donner, who got a wild hair and went up to Cook's land tonight, is the meth lab he built on the back of his property. I should have guessed what he was up to when I saw that box of lantern fuel in his van."

Reece shook his head, met Jack's gaze and sighed deeply. "And I should have listened to you, Jack. I could have gotten both Sabrina and Sophie killed. If you want a job, by the way, it's yours."

Jack half smiled. "Thanks. Who knows, I may take you up on it. I don't think Sophie is going to want Sabrina out of her sight for a long time. They have some major catching up to do. But there's one more thing and that's Lisa. Nash said he lived in California years ago. He mentioned an ex-wife—"

"After you told me about that, I checked it out," Reece said. "The ex-wife lives in San Diego now and Nash was telling the truth, she did hound him for money that was rightfully hers. I don't know if we'll ever be able to trace Nash back to Lisa, but we'll do our best."

Jack nodded. As far as the law was concerned, their best would have to do. As for him—he *knew*. Not with proof but with his gut.

May Lisa finally rest in peace.

A figure appeared in the doorway, as tall as Jack, a little heavier, bearded and sunburned and wearing a parka that looked like it had become a second skin. Buzz Cromwell's gaze went directly to Jack, his gray eyes filled with worry. "Where is she?"

Jack got to his feet. "She's in recovery," he said as he went to hug his friend. "She was banged up pretty good, Buzz."

"I need to see her."

"Come sit down. Let me tell you what her doctor said."

The man came reluctantly, nodding a greeting at Reece, who muttered his farewells and left.

Buzz sat down heavily. "What did that creep do to her?"

"I don't know the details, but I do know she's had a harrowing time. The biggest physical problem was the shot to her leg, but that's going to mend. If anyone can get through this, she can, you know that."

A nurse motioned to them from the door. "Gentlemen," she said. "You can follow me."

As they got to Sabrina's room, Buzz paused, and Jack saw his gaze travel from Sophie, who stood holding Sabrina's hand, to Sabrina, whose swollen cracked lips curved when she saw him. Even through their individual scars and bandages there was no mistaking their likeness. Buzz rushed to Sabrina's side and leaned over her.

"I didn't want to worry you," she whispered.

He kissed her forehead. "I'm here now, sweetie. No

one's going to hurt you again, I promise." He laid his cheek against her forehead and closed his eyes.

Jack's gaze moved to Sophie, whom he found staring at him. She settled her sister's hand by her side and moved from around the bed. The nurses had helped her shower and lent her blue sweats. Her forehead and right cheek were bandaged and her skin was as white as ivory. By now he'd heard her story, what she'd done, and he wasn't sure if the glow that seemed to pour from her eyes came from the outside or the inside. Both, he decided.

He met her halfway and put his arms around her.

"Thank you for saving us," she whispered after a few moments.

"I love you, Sophie Sparrow," he said as he searched for a place to kiss her that wasn't bandaged. "I can't imagine a life without you."

"You don't have to," she said, and touched her lips to his. "I'm not going anywhere."

BEFORE A WEDDING could be accomplished, they decided Jack needed to return to California to tie up loose ends and Sabrina had to get well enough to act as Sophie's maid of honor. On the day Sabrina was finally being released from the hospital, the two sisters found themselves sitting side by side on the bed. Sophie had been on the phone and now she clicked it off and turned to her twin. "Grandpa is expecting us next weekend," she said. "Jack will be home by then so maybe all four of us could drive up there together to see him."

Sabrina nodded. "I could use a short road trip. What does our grandfather want?"

"He's anxious to discuss our inheritance and the house and the island—all of that."

Sabrina's smile was wistful. "That's nice. What I really want to know from him is what our birth mother was like, if he knows who our father is, if we have any other family—that kind of stuff."

"Me, too," Sophie said. Then she added, "Whether or not we do we both have something we didn't have before."

"Each other," they said in unison.

* * * * *

SPECIAL FORCES:
THE SPY

CINDY DEES

Chapter One

Relishing the morning sunshine pouring through her cozy bungalow's kitchen window, Piper Ford poured herself a cup of coffee and sat down at the table to catch up on current events. Of course, she didn't bother with newspapers. Instead, she browsed the classified briefing she and her teammates got each day covering every hot spot in the world.

It was one of the best perks of being a Medusa. She loved knowing the dirt that few besides her all-female Special Forces team had access to. But then, she always had been a poli-sci geek. Even at West Point, she'd reveled in getting into political debates with her classmates and instructors.

Her cell phone rang and she picked it up. Her next-door neighbor was calling. Susan and her six-year-old son, Jack, had welcomed her warmly to the neighborhood when she bought this place a few months back.

Piper had a particular fondness for the little boy, and he for her. Jack was a cool kid—funny, curious and smart as heck.

"Hi, Sus. What's up?"

"Hey, Piper. I'm stuck at the hospital. My day replacement called in sick at the last minute, and they can't find a nurse to sub in. I'm stuck in the ICU pulling a double shift. But my babysitter can't stay late this morning. Is there any chance you could run Jack over to his school on your way to work?"

"When does he need to be there?"

"Eight fifteen."

The Medusas had training at nine, but it was only about a twenty-minute drive from the town of Houma, Louisiana, to their classified facility, Training Site Vanessa, usually referred to as the TSV. It was tucked next to the Mandalay National Wildlife Refuge, deep in the bayous of southern Louisiana.

"Yeah, sure. I can drop him off on my way to work. Will he be ready to go around eight?"

"He should be. Rosie feeds him breakfast, gets him dressed and packs his lunch. I really am sorry about the last-minute notice. You're an angel. I owe you one."

Piper laughed, "I'm hardly an angel."

"Shrimp étouffée? My place, this weekend?" Susan offered.

"Deal. I'll bring the wine."

Piper dressed in jeans and a casual white oxford shirt, befitting her cover story of being a civilian historian researching pirate activity in this part of southern Louisiana.

She stuffed the daily intel brief into her backpack, along with her pistol, some basic survival gear she felt naked without and a uniform for running around in the woods with the Medusas. Vietnamese Special Forces instructors were in town this week teaching her and her teammates advanced jungle camouflage and ambush tactics—key skills for Special Forces operators like the Medusas.

Piper backed her little sports car out of the garage and pulled into the driveway next door. Susie's salmon pink front door opened and Jack darted out, all restless energy. Piper pushed the passenger door open for him and waved at Rosie, the babysitter, who followed him out the door at a more sedate pace, locking it behind her.

"Thanks for taking Jack to school!" Rosie called. "I have a doctor's appointment today in New Orleans, and I'm gonna be late as it is."

"No problem!" Piper called back. As Jack tumbled into the car beside her, she admonished, "Buckle your seat belt, squirt."

A bolt of envy for Susan and regret for opportunities lost shot through Piper's gut at the sight of Jack. Longing for a child tugged at her—longing for a family of her own. She'd have thought she would be over the sense of hollow emptiness for the children she would never have by now, given the career she'd picked. But it turned out biological clocks were powerful little bastards.

It had been a trade-off, and she'd made her choice. She had arguably one of the coolest jobs on the planet. But the sacrifice in return was no time for a private life.

In point of technical fact, she supposed a personal life was possible. But that would entail finding a man who didn't mind his partner being a lethally trained special operator, prone to running off at a moment's notice to who knew where to face who knew what danger.

The only man besides her boss who even knew the Medusas existed at this point was Captain Beau Lambert, the Medusas' operations officer. And her teammate, Tessa Wilkes, had that man locked down tight. The two of them were engaged and had set a wedding date next year. They made a great couple. Goo-goo eyes flew thick and fast whenever they were in the same room.

But that left her without any eligible prospects in the love department.

"I like riding in your car, Miss Piper."

"Why's that?"

"'Cuz your car doesn't have a back seat, and I get to sit in front."

"When you get bigger, your mom will let you sit in front with her."

"That's what she says. I'm eatin' as much as I can so I'll get big really fast."

"Patience, grasshopper. You'll be all grown-up before you know it. Enjoy being a kid while you can."

"Don't you like being a grown-up?"

"I do most of the time. But it's a lot easier being a kid. And more fun."

"My mama says you have a super boring job."

Piper mentally snorted. If Susan only knew the truth. The poor woman would run screaming from Piper. She smiled serenely. "I like my job."

"Lucky dog. I hate school. I suck at it."

"You do not. I happen to know you rock at all your subjects."

"School's boring."

"Maybe you're just too smart for the first grade."

"Mama says I'm smarter than my teacher."

Piper laughed, "I can believe it."

They pulled up in front of Southdown Elementary School, a dark redbrick building that Piper privately thought looked more like a prison than a school. As Jack jumped out, she called after him, "Have a good day. And behave yourself!"

He flashed her an impudent grin and dashed inside.

She made it nearly halfway to the TSV before she happened to glance down and spied a brown paper bag on the floor of the passenger side of the car.

Rats. Jack had forgotten his lunch.

If she hit the stoplights exactly right, she had just enough time to zip back to his school, run his lunch inside and make it to the training site on time. The Medusas' commanding officer, Major Gunnar Torsten, had no sense of humor whatsoever when it came to tardiness.

Classes had started by the time she got back to the elementary school, and the drop-off area was deserted. Parking quickly, she grabbed Jack's lunch and hurried inside. To the left of the front door was a large glassed-in office that looked like a reception area lined with institutional, Formica-topped desks. Several women sat at them. A little girl who looked about eight years old stood beside one, shifting her weight from one foot to the other.

Piper stepped inside. "Is this where I drop off a lunch a student has forgotten?"

"Yes, ma'am. Just a minute." The gray-haired woman who answered her went back to talking with the child. "Your mom says she'll be here in ten minutes with your inhaler—" The woman broke off, staring at something behind Piper.

A flurry of movement in the hallway outside caught Piper's attention out the corner of her eye. Something—someone—adult-sized had just run past.

Was there a problem?

As she turned to take a better look, a man dressed all in black with a black ski mask over his face burst into the office. Piper flipped into combat mode in a millisecond, her senses going on high alert and adrenaline rushing to all her muscles.

She noted several things at once. The weapon, held across the man's body, was an AK-47 with an extended mag, and he handled it like he was familiar with it. He was a shade over six feet tall. Athletic in build. Moved fast and silently, rolling from heel to toe with each step. *Like a Special Forces operator.*

"Everybody down!" he shouted.

The three women at their desks started to scream, and the little girl awaiting the inhaler froze, staring up at the man in openmouthed terror, like a rabbit in front of a wolf.

Stunned, Piper dropped to the floor with the other women. She was unarmed, alone and had no idea how many more men like this there were already inside the school. Terror and panic exploded in her gut in spite of all her Special Forces training.

God. Not a school shooting. A worst-case scenario on all counts. Nonexpendables everywhere—*children*—completely unequipped to defend themselves from harm. Targets handily clustered together in classrooms. Limited egress points. Even more limited sight lines. Chaos guaranteed.

Tragedy guaranteed.

By force of will and outstanding training, she pushed back all the paralyzing feelings and focused on acting.

Surreptitiously, she eased her cell phone out of her jeans pocket and dialed 9-1-1 by feel. She stuffed the phone under her hip lest the armed man brandishing the AK-47 hear the operator ask what the nature of her emergency was and kill her before she could answer.

She eased her hip off the phone and shouted, "What do you want, barging into an elementary school with an automatic weapon like that?"

"Quiet, or I'll kill you!" the man shouted back. "Where's Mrs. Black?"

"She's out sick today," one of the other women quavered from the floor.

Piper eased back on top of the phone, praying the emergency operator had gotten the idea and called for the SWAT team. And the FBI and the National Guard and whoever else could be called.

Standoffs with kids caught in the middle were no picnic, but maybe when law enforcement got here, they could negotiate some sort of hostage release.

She calculated her options at the speed of light. She could probably take out the lone armed man—she did have all the necessary unarmed-combat training and the element of surprise on her side.

Question was, where were the other men she'd peripherally seen racing past, and how many of them were there? If she got the weapon away from this one, she could go hunting for the others…although hunting in a building full of children and teachers would be a dreadful environment for taking out bad guys. The odds of shooting an innocent bystander were far too high to risk.

As those thoughts darted through her mind, the armed man did an odd thing. He strode over to the little girl, grabbed her by her upper arm, glanced around, then led her over to a tall wooden coat cabinet against the wall.

He opened the door, pushed her inside and said low, "Stay in there until the police come for you and don't make a sound until then."

Piper stared, so confused she momentarily forgot her terror. Did the intruder just save that little girl? Why on earth would an armed assailant do something like that?

He shut the closet door just before two more men raced into the office, dressed like him and similarly armed. Terrorist the First nodded tersely at his buddies.

What in the hell was this about? What did a bunch of men, attired and armed like bank robbers, want with a freaking elementary school?

"Where is she?" one of the newcomers demanded in Farsi. Piper's Farsi wasn't fluent, but that was definitely what she'd heard. These guys were Iranian? What on earth did they want *here*?

The terrorists commenced walking around the room,

examining each of the women cowering on the floor. One screamed as an assailant grabbed her shoulder and lifted her up enough to see her face. These guys were looking for somebody? This was a hell of a violent and aggressive way of finding whoever they wanted.

The terrorists reached Piper, and she stared fixedly at their combat boots. Steel toes, nylon uppers, flexible rubber soles, quick-don zippers. Special operators' footwear.

Was this some sort of exercise aimed at her? The Medusas did some wild stuff in the name of training, but surely they wouldn't scare the hell out of a bunch of kids and teachers. Nah. This was the real deal.

A hand grabbed her shoulder roughly and threw her over onto her back. She rolled with the shove, not resisting. Unfortunately, the roll exposed her cell phone, and one of them kicked it away from her with his foot. Reflexively, her hand went out to retrieve it, but she froze as she made eye contact with the kicker.

Clear amber eyes stared down at her, the color of a fine cognac. They were hard eyes, but they didn't contain the rage or fanaticism she'd expected.

He glanced at her outstretched hand splayed on the floor and did a double take. She swore mentally. Clearly visible on her fourth finger was her West Point class ring. In her guise as a civilian historian, she told people it had been her father's, but it was actually hers.

The man's eyes lit with recognition as he spied the chunky ring and its dark green central stone.

Dammit.

"Here she is!" he called out to the others in Farsi.

What? These men were here for *her*? How on earth did they know who she was? *Nobody* knew about the Medusa Project. It had been resurrected from ashes less than a year ago, for crying out loud.

Everyone had been led to believe the program was defunct and the military had abandoned the idea of training and equipping a team of female Special Forces operatives after the second Medusa team was wiped out in a mission gone terribly wrong.

The other two masked men grabbed her by her arms and hauled her upright. Adrenaline roared through her body, and it took all the discipline she had not to lash out and fight for her life against these men. She was hopelessly outgunned, and three on one was not the kind of odds she wanted to take into a fistfight.

She was a good hand-to-hand fighter, but she wasn't invincible. Martial artists won against three attackers only in the movies. Carefully choreographed and scripted movies. Not real life. Not in an elementary school full of children.

"You're sure this is her?" one of the other men asked the terrorist who'd hidden the little girl.

He stared at her indecisively. His gaze strayed to a telephone sitting on the desk beside her, to the exit door and then back to her face. He exhaled hard. Regret glinted in his stare. "Yes. That's her." His voice was a rough baritone and sounded stressed.

Who in the *hell* did they think she was? Who *were* they? Her only play was to delay these guys as long as she could. Give the police time to respond to her call.

"Who are you?" she demanded in English. No way was she giving away that she understood anything they were saying to one another. "What do you want with me?"

She didn't see the blow coming. A fist plowed into her jaw from the right side, snapping her head hard to the left and making her see stars. Dazed, she stared at the first man—the one with golden eyes—wincing silently in front of her.

Gingerly, she poked her right cheek with her tongue. No

teeth felt loose, but the inside of her cheek was shredded. She opened her mouth, flexing her jaw experimentally. It didn't feel broken.

Well. That didn't go as planned. Dazed, she stared at her attackers. Real fear for her life flowed through her. She registered it, cataloged the emotion and forcibly pushed it down. She had no time for fear. Not if she wanted to live. And not if she wanted to protect the kids in this building.

She had to get these men outside, into the range of armed law enforcement officials, but slowly enough that said officials could get here before these guys fled.

"You're sure it's her?" the third man asked doubtfully in Farsi. "She doesn't look much like her picture."

"Yes, yes," Goldeneyes snapped back in Farsi. "Blonde. Tall. Thirty years old. And she does match the picture. These Western women wear a lot of makeup and it changes how they look. I'm used to that, and you're not. I'm telling you it's her."

With that declaration, Goldeneyes apparently sealed some sort of fate for her. The other two men nodded, accepting his word.

What picture? Part of becoming a Medusa was having her life scrubbed completely off the internet. *Completely* off. A team of cybersecurity experts did the initial wipe and then maintained continuous scans for any new images that might pop up. Even official public records were scrubbed. She did not exist in cyberspace.

So, how did these guys know her, let alone have a picture of her? She certainly had no idea who they were.

Belatedly, her mind working a couple steps slower than normal, she mentally corrected him. She was twenty-seven years old, not thirty, thank you very much.

In the distance, sirens became audible. God bless the 9-1-1 operator. She'd called in the cavalry, after all.

"Time's up. Let's go," Jaw Puncher bit out.

The men hustled her out into the hallway. She briefly considered making a stand right there in the entrance, but they had AK-47s, and one blow from the butt of one of those would knock her out cold. She would just as soon stay conscious if she could. Also, there were all those kids just down the hall. She had no way of knowing if there were any more armed men in the building, and she dared not provoke these guys to start shooting.

She did her best to slow the men down, though, shortening her steps and resisting moving forward between them in the guise of being too zoned out to do anything but shuffle along drunkenly.

Irritably, they overpowered her and shoved her outside into the parking lot. More sirens were audible now. Lots of them. Unfortunately, they still sounded a half-dozen blocks away.

Goldeneyes stepped up close behind her and body-checked her hard but not painfully, shoving his hip into her lower back, helping the other two men throw her into a white step van. She tumbled to the floor, slamming hard into its metal ribs. Gasping for air, she noted a fourth man darting out of the building to join them. A fifth man drove, pulling away from the front door with a hard lurch of the van.

One of the men snapped at the driver not to leave tire tracks, and the vehicle lurched again as he slowed down abruptly.

Fear bubbled up again in her throat, momentarily choking her.

She did the four-step breathing technique she'd been taught. *In. Hold breath and count to four. Out. Count to four. In...*

It took several breaths, but calm prevailed once more over her panic.

Okay. She was being kidnapped. Major suckage.

But there had been multiple witnesses. Law enforcement would put out an APB for this van in a few minutes. Houma was a small town deep in the bayou country, which meant there were only so many roads these men could travel in between the copious waterways.

This would be okay. An hour. Maybe two. A standoff, perhaps. With her, a trained Special Forces operative, on the inside. She would be the police's secret weapon when it came time for a rescue. All she had to do was stay conscious and keep her wits about her. Trust her training.

The van pulled out of the parking lot and turned right. That would be south on Maple Street. They went straight for what she estimated to be five minutes, and then they turned left. A few minutes, another right turn and then they accelerated to highway speed. Maybe Bayou Black Drive heading west out of town?

Which would be ironic. That road would take them right past the unmarked turnoff to the Medusas' secret facility, where her teammates were gathering for today's training.

A sense of unreality washed over her. Surely, she was not being kidnapped by Iranian terrorists. This *had* to be a bad dream. It couldn't be happening to her. Was that shock lowering its protective fog over her brain? It felt just the way her instructors had described it. Everything was happening at a distance. Muted. Not really touching her.

One of the men admonished the driver in Farsi, but she didn't understand the command. In a second, she felt the vehicle slow down to a more sedate speed. Piper frowned. What on earth did Iranians want with her? She'd never had anything to do with that part of the world before— had never served or even traveled there and had no particular expertise on the region beyond reading her daily intelligence brief. What was going on here? She had to be missing something critical—

Something heavy smashed painfully into the back of her head, and she toppled forward as everything went dark.

Chapter Two

Zane Cosworth swore silently, wincing involuntarily as the terrorist calling himself Yousef clocked the woman prisoner on the back of the head with the butt of his AK-47. "Don't kill her," he snapped at the guy, the most volatile of the bunch.

"Shut up, Amir. I didn't like how she was looking at me," Yousef snarled back.

An urge to return the favor and clock the bastard upside the head made his hands twitch. Zane balled them into fists at his sides.

Amir was the name he'd used to infiltrate these SOBs' sleeper cell. Not that they were sleeping after this morning's little stunt.

They were a frustrating bunch, closemouthed and stingy with information for him, the new guy on the team. He was the only actual American among them, and he was convinced it was the sole reason he'd been brought on board. They called upon him to interact with other Americans and used him as their errand boy in any public situation where their accents might draw attention.

But that also meant he was completely expendable if he offended these guys or got in their way of whatever the hell their actual end goal was.

The team's leader, Mahmoud, was definitely taking instructions from someone who communicated via encrypted cell phone, or occasionally via a Dark Web site that was even more heavily encrypted.

Rolling his eyes at Yousef, Zane leaned over the woman, ostensibly to check her pulse. He grabbed her right wrist with his left hand while surreptitiously slipping the ring off her fourth finger with his other hand and palming the piece. No way in hell could he let his compatriots discover that this woman was a West Pointer. If he was gauging Mahmoud correctly, the guy would kill her instantly.

Mahmoud said practically nothing about his personal beliefs, but he made no secret of despising Americans, particularly military members.

Zane slipped the ring into his pocket. He was seriously grateful that chance had thrown a female soldier in his path this morning. What she was doing at some elementary school in a small town in southern Louisiana, nowhere near an active military base, he had no idea. Call it a small act of God that had gone his way.

Not that he was a whole lot happier about throwing a soldier to the lions than he would be about doing it to some random civilian woman.

But he'd been forced to make the best of an impossible situation.

Of the four women cowering on the floor in the school's front office, she'd looked to be by far the youngest and fittest of the bunch. Naming her as the target had been the least awful choice under the circumstances. Which wasn't saying much.

Honestly, he'd feared that if he told the others he didn't see their target in the office, where she normally worked as an assistant principal, they would start shooting kids to get the woman to reveal herself.

Mahmoud was a cagey bastard and had barely shared

any information with any of his men about this fiasco. He'd briefed the cell members only about an anonymous woman they were supposed to find and kidnap.

Zane hadn't thought it was enough detail to pass on to his superiors. He'd assumed Mahmoud and his boys would spend days or weeks finding the target, doing surveillance on her, picking the perfect spot to abduct her and then launching an operation to kidnap the woman.

Zane *thought* he had plenty of time to find out who the woman was, slip away from the other men and send a message to his superiors about this little operation. It galled him to have been outmaneuvered by a freaking terrorist like this.

Mahmoud also hadn't given the team any indication whatsoever that today would be the actual snatch.

Zane had been nearly as shocked as the teachers and kids of Southdown Elementary School when they'd piled out of the van for real, armed with actual weapons and ammunition.

Mahmoud had passed around a picture and name of the target, Persephone Black—whoever the hell she was—in the van as they turned into the school parking lot. Zane hadn't even had time to send an emergency text to his handlers to let them know who the target was and that an attack was imminent before Mahmoud had ordered them out of the van and barged into a flipping elementary school, armed to kill.

The picture itself had been informative. It was fuzzy and taken from a distance. The woman had been with a man on a crowded street that looked like some place in Europe. She was looking over her shoulder at something, and the shot of her face had been snapped in that moment. For all the world, it looked like a surveillance photo taken by someone following the couple.

Did that mean Mahmoud and his men were in the US on behalf of some foreign government with an intelligence service of its own? Iran was the obvious candidate, given that they sounded like native Farsi speakers.

Regardless, they were some sort of black-ops team, and they'd proved this morning that they were not averse to using violence.

As soon as he'd heard that the real target was out sick, he'd known he had a big problem. Mahmoud and his boys wouldn't hesitate to shoot up a school full of little kids in retaliation for their victim being absent.

He felt really bad for this woman he'd inaccurately fingered as the target. He glanced down at her, crumpled on the floor of the van at his feet, and silently vowed to make it up to her somehow.

One thing Zane hated worse than just about anything else was being forced into a no-win choice. And God knew he'd faced one of those already today. He could either go along with assaulting a school, snatching a woman and scaring the hell out of a bunch of kids…or he could blow his cover, and throw away months' worth of work gaining Mahmoud's trust and worming his way inside what Zane's superiors believed to be a dangerous and violent sleeper cell.

He'd very nearly gone ahead and turned his weapon on his coconspirators to take them out this morning. The one thing that had stopped him was being in an elementary school. The possibility of an innocent child being hit in the cross fire was the *only* reason any of these bastards were still alive.

If he just knew who they were, he would end this farce right now.

He did know one thing about them. They would *never* say anything under interrogation. They were all fanatic enough to die before giving up even their names.

He'd lived and worked with Mahmoud and his fellow psychopaths for months, and he *still* didn't have any idea who they worked for or what their ultimate goal was. That was how closemouthed these men were.

Normally, Zane would pull the plug on an undercover op like this immediately and get the civilian victim out. Hell, he was on the verge of doing that very thing right now.

The only thing stopping him was that ring in his pocket. If the kidnapped woman was a West Pointer, maybe he could let this thing play out just a bit more—a few minutes or a few hours—and get his answers before he called in the big guns to take these jerks down.

Thing was, if Mahmoud and company did work for Iran, they would only be replaced by another sleeper cell of trained killers when US authorities took these guys down.

Hence the urgent need to know who they worked for and what their end goal was. He didn't for a minute believe that kidnapping some woman from an elementary school was the primary reason this cell had infiltrated the United States.

They posed some much-greater national security threat. But *what*?

Nope, he'd had no choice today. He had to throw this woman he'd never seen before under the bus and maintain his cover a little longer. He hated it, and he would do whatever he had to do to protect her.

Just a little while, he mentally promised her.

The unconscious woman beside him moved faintly and then subsided again. Yousef had hit her way too damned hard if she was still out cold. Zane knew from long experience in the field that if she was unconscious more than a few minutes, she would likely be out for the next couple hours.

Patience, Zane. Now was not the time to make his move

to rescue her. He was probably her only chance of survival. But he would get one shot—and no more than one shot—at rescuing her. He had to wait until she was conscious, able to move fast and willing to cooperate with him.

He hoped to God she understood his choice and one day forgave him for it.

Did it make him a dreadful human being that he'd forced her into helping him figure out what these terrorists were up to? That he'd potentially sacrificed this woman's emotional well-being, and maybe her life, to save many more lives down the road?

Hell, he was already a dreadful human being. As an undercover agent, he deceived people and lied for a living. He'd even done criminal acts in the name of keeping his covers. He drew the line at hurting or killing innocent victims, although he was skirting dangerously close to that line today. Hell, sometimes he wondered if he was even one of the good guys anymore.

He owed this woman huge. When the time was right, he silently promised her he would find a way to save her from these men.

But how…and when…he had no idea.

Scowling, he leaned back beside her slumped body. He propped an elbow casually on his upraised knee. "Anyone following us?" he asked Bijan, the youngest of the crew, who crouched at the dirty rear window of the van.

"No. We're clear," the kid answered.

Zane had to give these guys credit. They'd run the grab-and-go to perfection, managing their time on scene to the second and getting away moments before the first police car arrived. His certainty that they were military trained—more specifically, Special Forces trained—intensified.

His concern for the woman intensified, as well. Men like

this wouldn't hesitate to kill her if and when they figured out they had grabbed the wrong person.

He studied her face. She was pretty. Her hair was dark blond and her skin was smooth and slightly olive complexioned. The combination was unusual and striking. Her legs were lean in her blue jeans, and her shirt was currently twisted tight against some nice curves. Her fingers were long and slender with short, cracked fingernails.

Those fingernails surprised him. She looked put together enough to be the kind of woman to always have a perfect manicure. What did she do to beat up her hands like that?

"Pull over at the next gas station," Mahmoud, the team leader, ordered Hassan, the driver.

It took a few minutes, but Zane felt the van decelerate. They pulled around to the side of a tiny rural gas station advertising with a hand-painted sign that it also sold beer, fishing bait and, more alarmingly, gator bait.

After a quick check to verify that the gas station had no surveillance cameras, Mahmoud and Yousef piled outside. Zane followed more slowly. The other men were already peeling off temporary decals on the side of the vehicle announcing it to be an air-conditioning service van. Meanwhile, Bijan used a screwdriver to change the rear license plate. *When had these guys set up this van as a slick getaway vehicle?*

Alarm slammed through him. Had they done it before he'd joined the team? *Or had they done it behind his back?*

Odds were they'd done it recently. Which was freaking scary. It meant they *still* didn't trust him.

Which also meant that not only was his life in mortal danger, but the woman's, as well.

The underlying tension that always hummed in his gut when he was undercover ratcheted up violently. He didn't like this. Not one bit. Was he a prisoner in this van, too?

How fine a tightrope was he walking with Mahmoud and his men? He'd been useful to them as long as they were trying to keep a low profile and not be noticed by the locals. But if they'd completed their mission, these men would go to ground or flee the country and not need his services any longer.

His intuition screamed that he was blown. That it was time to bug out.

Normally, he never went against his gut feelings. Over and over through the years, his gut had proved to be right. And right now, it was telling him in no uncertain terms to abandon this operation *immediately*. The feds had plenty of ammunition to arrest these men and put them away for a very long time after this morning's stunt in the elementary school.

The authorities might never figure out what Mahmoud's primary goal had been, but at least this particular terror cell would be off the street.

However, the woman changed everything. Zane couldn't possibly bail out now. Not as long as these men held an innocent woman captive. An innocent women *he* had put into these violent men's hands.

He mentally swore. He mustn't do *anything* to arouse these guys' suspicions. The danger of staying in this undercover assignment drove home hard, a punch in the gut that left him gasping.

Too tense to be still one more second, Zane walked around behind the van, pretending to stretch his legs. "Can I help with the signs?" he asked casually.

Mahmoud wadded up the last of the adhesive vinyl and tossed it in a trash can. He shoved a cigarette lighter down into the barrel, and a thin stream of smoke commenced rising from its contents. "No. We're finished. As soon as Osted gets out of the bathroom, we'll go."

Zane nodded slowly, trying to look impressed. "You guys are good. I'm grateful you let me learn from you, *al-muelim alhakim*." He dropped in the Arabic phrase meaning "wise teacher" to gauge Mahmoud's reaction.

The guy nodded shortly and looked vaguely less irascible than usual, acknowledging the compliment.

Zane guessed they were assets of VAJA—the Iranian Ministry of Intelligence. But they never talked politics, not even in the most general of terms. They talked about European soccer and the weather for the most part. And such a degree of operational discipline scared the living hell out of him.

He strolled to the corner of the cinder-block building and, with a glance over his shoulder to make sure no one saw him, surreptitiously dropped the woman's class ring on the ground. There. One piece of evidence showing her to be a soldier erased. Now he just had to make sure she didn't have some other form of ID on her—dog tags, or maybe a wallet with a military ID in it.

For that matter, he needed to get rid of *any* identification she had on her. He had to keep up the ruse of her being Persephone Black for as long as he possibly could. Until both he and the woman could escape. Everything depended on it.

Including his life. And hers.

TESSA WILKES EYED her boss cautiously. Major Gunnar Torsten was not a happy camper this morning. He barked, "Still no answer on Piper's phone?"

"No, sir," Rebel McQueen replied from her post at the ops center's communications panel. "I pinged her phone's locator function, and it puts her in Houma." Which was the nearest actual town to their secret training facility.

"Where in Houma?" Torsten demanded.

"Um, at an elementary school."

"What in the hell is she doing there?" he snapped.

Rebel didn't answer and instead threw Tessa a distressed look. She felt Rebel's pain. Torsten was usually a stern guy and all business, but this morning he really had a burr up his butt. Catching the silent plea for help, Tessa sighed and spoke up. "Do you want me to go fetch her, sir?"

"No! But I damned well want to know why one of my highly trained, supposedly responsible operatives has gone AWOL."

Rebel spoke from her console again, muttering, "That's odd."

Everyone looked at her. She glanced up and started. "Oh. Um, I just pinged her backup locator. The one in her class ring from West Point. It's not in Houma."

"It had better be headed this way at a high rate of speed," Torsten ground out.

Man, the boss had seriously woken up on the wrong side of the bed today. Not that he was ever tolerant of screwups. He was fond of saying that seconds were the difference between life and death. He wasn't wrong, of course.

Rebel reported, "Her secondary locator is moving away from us on Bayou Black Road, heading northwest. It's about fifteen miles west of here."

Tessa, the first member of their new Medusa team and more at ease with Torsten than Rebel, leaned forward. "Something's wrong. Piper would have called one of us if she had a problem and couldn't get here on time. And she would *never* go AWOL."

Torsten huffed in irritation. "We can't wait any longer. Our Vietnamese instructors are only here for a few days, and I need you to learn as much as you can while you have access to them. Fall out, ladies."

Rebel and Tessa stood, trading worried glances with

one another. It was supremely unlike Piper to blow off required training, and even more unlike her not to check in with someone. A note of worry started to vibrate low in Tessa's gut.

The major led the way to the reinforced steel door disguised to look like weathered wood siding, unsealing it and stepping out into the morning's steamy heat. Tessa fell into step beside Major Torsten.

She said soberly, "Sir, I'm worried something has happened to Piper. You taught us to listen to our intuitions, and mine says she's in some sort of trouble. I think one of us should go look for her."

He frowned, but at least he didn't rip her head off. "I'll take your intuition under advisement. If Piper doesn't show up in the next hour or so, I'll go looking for her myself."

Yikes. Piper was in a heap of trouble.

Chapter Three

Piper regained consciousness slowly. Her head throbbed painfully, and it didn't help matters that every time the van hit a bump in the road, the metal floor bounced underneath her temple, whacking her head again.

Her lips were dry, and her bladder was full, which meant she'd been out for a while. A couple hours, possibly. Dang it! They could've changed directions a dozen times without her knowing. She had no way of knowing where she was now!

A sense of disorientation swirled around her. As if she was completely disconnected from the real world. It was scary as hell, and she had to force herself to lie perfectly still until her breathing settled back down and the panic attack passed.

Questions peppered her mind almost too fast to catalog. Where was she? Who were these guys? What did they want with her? How much danger was she in? Where were they taking her? Would she have a shot at escaping them? Did they plan to kill her? Was this even real?

Cautiously, she cracked her eyes open and saw black pants and black combat boots. It hadn't been a terrible dream. She really had been kidnapped. The weight of panic landed on her chest again, and she struggled to control her breathing.

She could just lie here pretending to be unconscious…
but just then the van hit a big bump and slammed her head
hard into the floor.

Ow.

She probably had a concussion already from the blow
that had knocked her out. No need to exacerbate the stupid thing. Piper pushed against the floor with both hands,
sitting up groggily. At least none of the men stopped her
from doing so.

The ski masks had come off, replaced by baseball
caps pulled down low and dark sunglasses. Drat. She still
wouldn't be able to identify her kidnappers in a lineup. She
felt the weight of their stares upon her and did her best not
to freak out and start screaming hysterically.

Whatever this was, whoever they were, she had to keep
her wits about her, watch, wait and seize the opportunity
to escape when it presented itself. And surely one would.
She *had* to believe she would have a chance to get away,
eventually.

Be calm. Breathe. Relax.

She did her level best to settle into the state of loose
readiness that Major Torsten stressed over and over was
absolutely necessary to peak performance.

At least they hadn't tied her up. It was a small victory,
but she knew from her POW training that those were all a
hostage could hope to achieve.

Choking fear bubbled up in her throat unbidden, and
she stomped it down hard. She had no time for that. This
was a battle of wits and wills, and she needed all of hers. In
the meantime, maybe she could figure out who these guys
were, why they'd grabbed her and where they were going.

Pitching her voice to be polite and diffident, she asked,
"Who are you?" A little rapport with her kidnappers could
never hurt.

They stared back at her in stony silence. One of the men was seated beside her, between her and the driver. Which ruled out her making a dive for the steering wheel and maybe putting the van in a ditch.

"Why did you kidnap me?" she added.

Still nothing.

She debated starting up a one-sided conversation with these men to provoke them to talk, but ultimately decided she would be better served acting scared to death and letting them lead the conversation wherever they wanted to.

She craned her head to peer out the front window and saw a ribbon of interstate highway stretching away in front of the van. The sun seemed to be overhead, so she had no means of working out what direction they were going. But it confirmed she'd been unconscious for a while.

She realized her elbow was lightly rubbing the arm of one of the bad guys. Based on his build, she thought it might be Goldeneyes. Subtly, she shifted away from him. If she wasn't mistaken, she heard him exhale in irritation. What did he have to be irritated about? She wasn't his freaking girlfriend. And she wasn't about to cozy up to some homicidal terrorist.

Except, when they finally stopped at a rest area near a truck stop, that same homicidal terrorist was the one who helped her out of the van and steadied her elbow for a second while blood flow returned to her legs. Yup. Definitely Goldeneyes. He was the tallest and broadest of shoulder of the whole bunch.

He muttered in unaccented English, "Don't try anything, or my companions will shoot this place up and kill everyone here." Oddly enough, he sounded almost apologetic when he made his threat. What was the deal with this guy?

He also was the one who guided her over to the ladies'

restroom, parked outside the door and said gruffly, "Two minutes, and then I'm coming in after you."

She went inside and checked quickly to see if there were any other women in there whom she could ask for help. The place was empty except for her. Damn.

But there was a window on the far end of the long bay of toilet stalls. She eyed it critically. It was small and high, but she might be able to squeeze through it. At least it was worth a try.

She climbed up on the nearest sink to the window and punched her fist through the screen covering it. The actual window was mounted on a hinge that swung out, and she forced it wide-open. It was awkward aiming her arms through the small opening while jumping up, but she managed to land her waist on the sill. Pushing against the outside wall with her hands and kicking her legs, she wriggled through.

She fell headfirst and caught herself with her arms, rolling into a somersault.

Yes. Free.

She jumped up and took off running as fast as she could. A large field of mowed grass separated her from the truck stop—and other people—perhaps a quarter mile away.

She sprinted for all she was worth. Her breath came in huge gulps, and pounding blood roared in her ears. *Must. Get. Away.* Her thighs burned and her lungs screamed for air, but she pumped her arms hard and kept on going for all she was worth.

She was about halfway across the field when, without warning, something huge and heavy tackled her from behind, landing on top of her and knocking the breath out of her. She gasped frantically for air, but none came.

Dammit. She'd never even heard him coming.

A hard hand plastered over her mouth, which did nothing to help her regain her breath.

A male voice snarled low in her ear, "You and I are going to stand up. Then you're going to turn around and walk back to the van and climb in, all nice-like and cooperative." Hot breath wafted over her ear as her captor leaned close to add, "And if you don't, I'll knock you out and carry you back to the damned van."

A detached voice in a far corner of her mind registered that he hadn't threatened to kill her. But in the abrupt rush of adrenaline that accompanied the return of her ability to breathe, she ignored the voice and thrashed wildly beneath him.

She managed to get turned over on her back, but he was significantly bigger and stronger than she was, and apparently a trained wrestler. He flattened her with demoralizing ease. Their bodies pressed together in what would be a blatantly sexual fashion under any other circumstances.

As it was, she held herself rigid beneath him and did her best to ignore the way his thighs pressed against hers, the bulge of his crotch against the junction of her legs, the way his hard stomach pressed into hers and how her breasts smashed against his chest.

Goldeneyes, indeed.

She stared up at him in shock. Either his tackle or their struggle had knocked his baseball cap and sunglasses off, and she got her first good look at him.

If one human being could look any less like a violent criminal, this guy was it. His hair was a sun-tossed mix of brown and gold, nearly the same color as his eyes. His skin was tanned, his jaw chiseled, his features classy. All in all, he looked like he belonged on Martha's Vineyard, wearing chinos, a polo shirt and a white cricket sweater, sailing a boat on a crisp summer day.

Her brows twitched into a frown. She'd pegged all of these guys as Iranians from their use of Farsi. But this one didn't look even remotely Persian.

"Who are you?" she breathed.

"Get up." With a quick flex of powerful biceps, he popped to his feet. He had a crushing grip on her hand and gave a hard yank on it now, dragging her upright.

He frisked all her pockets and then did a weird thing. He checked her neck for jewelry. "What are you doing?" she demanded.

"Making sure you don't have a wallet with any identification in it or dog tags on you," he muttered.

Realization smacked into her, like a slap across the face. He didn't want any of the other terrorists to figure out her real name. If that was the case, then this wasn't about her being a Medusa at all. That was a relief, at least. Although it still left behind the glaring question of what in the world these guys wanted with some woman who worked with little kids.

With a quick jerk, he twisted her arm up and back behind her, shoving her along in front of him, back toward the rest stop building. The van was out of sight on the other side of the structure.

"What's your name?" she gasped.

"Amir."

"Baloney," she blurted. "That's not your name. You're named something preppy like Chad or Blaine."

He gave a warning tug on her twisted arm that was just shy of painful.

"You really should set me free," she tried. "I guarantee you don't want to face the criminal penalties when you guys get caught. *All* the law enforcement authorities will already be out looking for me. You'll never get away with this. If you let me go right now, by the time I can get over to the truck stop, call the police and wait for them to respond, you guys can be long gone. A clean getaway."

"The others will come out of the van any second to see what's taking so long. They have long-range rifles and know how to use them. You'd never make it across that field alive."

He almost sounded regretful about that. Weird.

"Be quiet," he bit out as they approached the building she'd broken out of.

He shocked her by walking her into the ladies' room and shoving her toward a toilet stall. He was still going to let her go to the bathroom? By rights, he should haul her back to the van, toss her in and let her suffer—or soil herself—after her attempted escape.

She used the facilities fast and was not surprised when she opened the stall door to see him looming just outside. He grabbed her elbow and steered her toward the van.

He growled low, "If my partners find out about your little stunt, they'll kill you—or worse. However, if you'll promise not to say anything about your failed escape attempt, I won't, either."

"Um, okay," she responded in confusion. Now, why on earth did he make that offer? Surely it was only because he would get in trouble for her nearly getting away. Still. Something was off about this guy.

He hustled her back to the van and started to hoist her inside. "I've got this," she snapped, yanking her arm out of his grip. She got the distinct impression he chose to let go of her. His hand felt plenty strong enough to have resisted her tug.

"That took a long time," one of the other men complained in Farsi.

"Women," her strange captor responded, rolling his eyes. The other man grunted in commiseration.

A frisson of satisfaction coursed through her. If they wanted to underestimate her because she was a woman, she was totally fine with that. Wait till they figured out she was a trained Special Forces operative. They weren't going to know what had hit them. Anticipation of the moment when she kicked butts and took names coursed through her.

Patience, Piper. Patience.

Not to worry. She would show them, all in due time.

She considered her captor's name. She supposed it was possible his name really was Amir, but it had rung false when he said it. He just didn't seem to own the name the way he would have if it had been his actual name. No, Goldeneyes fitted him better.

They drove for perhaps two more hours, taking back roads exclusively. The next time they stopped, she spied through the windows a tiny town boasting a single flashing red light, one gas station/convenience store/Laundromat and a Baptist church. Goldeneyes was the only man to exit the van. Which made sense if he was the only American in the bunch. He would draw a lot less attention than the others in this rural part of the country where few foreigners visited. He went outside to pump and pay for gas, and escorted her to the restroom again.

She didn't have a peanut-sized bladder, and in the absence of anything to drink didn't particularly have to use the restroom, but she still took the chance when offered. Who knew when they would stop again? And it felt good to get up and move around, get some circulation back in her legs. Wary of her captors killing the cashier, she didn't cause a fuss as Goldeneyes marched her inside.

She did, however, make a point of saying hello to the teen girl behind the counter and making direct eye contact with her. Maybe if this girl saw some sort of news story on a kidnapped woman, she would remember seeing Piper and call the authorities.

Goldeneyes had a painfully tight grip on her elbow as they walked past the store attendant, and Piper didn't test his unspoken warning to behave herself. There was no telling how far his goodwill would extend, and she'd pushed it pretty hard already.

He deposited her back in the van and went inside once more, returning after a few minutes carrying several grocery bags full of sandwiches and snacks.

Oh, no. That looked like road-trip food. Which meant they still had a ways to go before reaching their final destination.

"Where are we headed?" she tried.

Her captors just stared at her stonily.

The van pulled back out onto the road, and despair washed through her. The next time they stopped, she needed to let someone know she was in trouble and to call the police. But how? With Goldeneyes hovering over her every move and the threat that his teammates would kill innocent bystanders ringing in her ears, it wasn't like she had a lot of options.

He passed her a bottle of water. Silently, she took it and downed the whole thing. She had to give him credit; he was taking pretty decent care of her, all things considered. For the moment, at least, these men seemed interested in keeping her alive. Thank God.

At least she was able to tell by the setting sun that they were traveling more or less toward the north, and maybe slightly west. By now they had to have left Louisiana, which put them possibly in Arkansas.

They started to go up and down hills—which made sense if they were in the western portion of Arkansas, entering the Ozark Plateau. Which was both good and bad news. Good because it was lush country with plenty of food, water, shelter and cover for her eventual escape. The bad news was that it was isolated country with areas of very sparse population. She might have to evade her captors for days before she found help.

Why in the world had these men gone to all the trouble of kidnapping her just to haul her off on this extended road trip? Why not kill her in or near Houma? Did they plan to ransom her back to the Medusas? Surely they knew the US government adhered to a strict pay-no-ransom policy. And it wasn't like she had a rich family that would cough up money for her return. Her dad owned a small auto-repair shop and her mom was a preschool teacher.

Her captors took turns napping and driving into the evening, all except for Goldeneyes. He seemed to have appointed himself her personal guard, and the other men seemed to have silently agreed to let him assume all baby-sitting duties.

A small blessing for which she was grateful. He seemed generally concerned about her comfort and well-being, while the other men looked at her with open contempt as if she were of no more worth or interest than a bug crawling across the floor of the van. Their dismissive attitude would be their undoing if she had anything to say about it.

It had gotten dark outside when she noticed most of the men were dozing. Only the driver and Goldeneyes were awake. His disturbingly beautiful stare was locked on her like it had been for most of the past twelve hours.

"What's your real name?" she asked in a low voice.

"Amir."

"Fine. Be that way. I'll just stick to calling you Goldeneyes in my mind."

His right eyebrow lifted faintly, but he didn't show any other reaction.

"My name is Piper."

He replied firmly, "Your name is Persephone Black."

"I beg your pardon?" she blurted. He'd asked about a Mrs. Black when he'd first stormed into the school office. Was she a teacher? Why would these men kidnap an elementary school teacher?

"Your name. It's Persephone Black. You can pretend to be anyone you want. But we know who you really are."

What on God's green earth was he talking about? Had they kidnapped the wrong person?

"But…you looked right at me… You said you'd seen my picture…that you knew I was the right person—"

"Quiet," he bit out low, cutting her off.

She looked away from him and realized that the man who acted like the leader was awake, his eyes barely slitted open. How had "Amir" known the boss was awake? She hadn't gotten the slightest indication of it—not even a hint of intuition that she was being watched. Wow. Her powers of observation were messed up worse than she'd realized. And his—they were sharp and on point.

"May I please have some more water?" she asked meekly.

Goldeneyes passed her a bottle of water without comment.

She downed it and added the bottle to the pile of trash growing in the back of the van: food wrappers and soda cans. These men's discipline clearly did not extend to picking up after themselves. Either that or they planned to ditch the van at some point. Still. There would be fingerprints and DNA all over that trash.

With darkness, the team had taken off their sunglasses and hats, and she'd seen all their faces now. She'd watched them all evening, learning each man's features from many different angles. The bump on the bridge of a nose, the angle of a jaw, the shape and fullness of lips, even the timbre of their voices.

She was confident she could pick out any of these men from a lineup if it ever came to that. Now she just had to make sure she stayed alive and got away so it could.

All of them except Goldeneyes were black haired, dark eyed, and their skin was caramel toned, in keeping with a Middle Eastern heritage. Two of them looked quite young, in their early twenties.

The other three looked hard as nails and closer to their midthirties in age. The older men reminded her of Gunnar Torsten. They all had the same hardness and cool, lethal confidence as her boss. She made a mental note not to mess with any of the older men.

As for Goldeneyes, he was the odd man out. Besides his fair coloring, he looked about thirty years old, and he carried himself differently than the others. At least, he did now.

When he'd stormed into the school office, he'd exhibited all the deadly confidence of the older men. But now, he slouched in the back of the van, eyes down, shoulders hunched. As if he was trying to make himself invisible to the other men. Odd. He didn't strike her as the submissive-follower type. At all. But he was clearly acting like the low man in the pecking order.

The van slowed and turned off the winding two-lane road they'd been following up and down mountainsides for the past hour. It commenced bumping and banging over what was obviously some sort of bad dirt road.

They spent two or three more minutes getting tossed all over the back of the van, and then, just like that, the vehicle stopped. The driver turned off the ignition.

They'd arrived. Wherever that might be.

The silence and stillness were a shock to her system

after spending the last twelve hours or so in the rumbling, vibrating van.

"Out," the one called Mahmoud ordered.

Bijan, one of the young ones, opened the double back doors, and Piper glimpsed the dark silhouette of a decent-sized log cabin with a long porch across its front. Trees—deciduous, she noted—crowded close, and there was no ambient light in the sky to indicate a city of any kind nearby. Yup. These guys had brought her out into the middle of nowhere to hold for whatever dastardly purpose they had in mind for her.

Goldeneyes hopped out of the van in front of her and turned around to help her out. She was tempted to shake off his hand, but her legs were numb, and as she stood on them, they tingled so badly she wasn't sure they would hold her full weight. She clung to his powerful forearm while circulation returned to her aching limbs. After a few seconds, she let go of his arm.

"Better?" he murmured under his breath.

"Uh-huh," she muttered back.

He stepped behind her, efficiently twisting her arm behind her, but putting no pressure on it that would be painful. His intention was clear: if she didn't fight him, he wouldn't hurt her.

For now, at least. As long as their silent truce held.

She didn't for a second believe these terrorists had brought her out here solely to enjoy the fresh air. They had some agenda up their sleeves. She just couldn't fathom what it was.

Which led her back to the same question that had been preoccupying her all day. Why her?

Chapter Four

It didn't take long after the report of armed men at Southdown Elementary School in Houma hit the news for the Medusas to put two and two together. They were taking a water break in the woods when Rebel, glancing at her cell phone, exclaimed.

Tessa piped up, asking, "Whatcha got, Reb?"

The communications specialist looked up from her phone grimly. "I just got a breaking-news alert. Armed men burst into Southdown Elementary School in Houma this morning and kidnapped an unnamed woman. She's described as tall, blonde and in her mid-to late twenties."

Tessa lurched upright from where she'd been lounging on a patch of moss. "That's got to be Piper!"

Major Torsten cut in. "Where are Captain Ford's cell phone and class ring locations now?"

Rebel answered, "I'd have to go back to the ops center to answer that, sir."

"What are you waiting for, then?" Torsten snapped.

Tessa got that he was worried about Piper. But he didn't have to bite their heads off!

Her train of thought derailed abruptly. Torsten was always tough, but he'd never been this snappish before. She traded worried looks with her fiancé, Beau, and his thoughts clearly mirrored hers. He was worried about the boss, too. Beau had worked for Gunnar Torsten for several years before being asked to help train the new Medusa team. If even Beau was worried about him, something was definitely wrong with Torsten.

When they hustled back to the vehicles to drive back to base, she made a point of climbing in the front passenger seat of the Hummer Torsten was driving.

"What's up, sir?"

He glanced over at her and bit out, "I've got a missing and possibly kidnapped team member."

"Besides that," she replied carefully.

"Isn't that enough?"

"You were way more tense than usual even before we thought anything was wrong with Piper…sir."

He exhaled hard and turned his eyes back to the road. "I got an intel report last night."

"And?"

"It indicates that Abu Haddad may not be dead."

"What?" she and Beau squawked simultaneously. The two of them had by a hair escaped dying in the explosion that had killed Haddad last year. The international, and very illegal, arms dealer, had to be dead! His entire yacht—and everyone on it—had been blown into bits not much larger than her finger. Beau had set the charges himself.

Torsten replied heavily, "We never did get a confirmation of death."

Beau leaned forward from the back seat and ground out, "That's because nothing but matchsticks and the occasional chunk of meat were left when I was done blowing up that bastard's yacht."

Tessa frowned at their boss. "Why does someone think Haddad may be alive?"

Torsten huffed, clearly as unhappy as she and Beau were. "A rumor has surfaced that the Haddad network may be doing some sort of big secret deal with a Middle Eastern nation. The source apparently has it on good authority that Haddad himself is expected to close the deal. It's possible that one of his flunkies has taken over the business. But there's also a very small chance that the bastard is back."

"What country is this deal with?" she asked.

"Rumor places the deal in Iran."

"For what kind of weapons?" Beau asked quickly.

Tessa wasn't sure that mattered. The Iranians were dangerous enough with the weaponry they already had. Although she supposed the last thing anyone needed was for that country's leaders to get their hands on something high-tech and truly deadly.

"No idea," Torsten replied.

"It's not like we have a ton of human information sources on the ground in Tehran," she commented. "If someone outside its borders could figure out who's making the sale and what the cargo is, we'd have a better chance of finding out what the Iranians are getting their hands on."

Appearing to give himself a mental shake, the major replied, "Not our problem, today. Right now, I need us to focus on finding Piper."

"Of course, sir." But curiosity about what a dead arms dealer was selling to a country like Iran continued to niggle at the back of Tessa's mind.

They parked in front of the one-story building that was their communications facility and operational headquarters for Training Site Vanessa, named for Brigadier General Vanessa Blake, the founder of the Medusas over a decade ago.

Their headquarters squatted on stilts and looked like every other ramshackle fishing shack in this part of Terrebonne Parish. Notable only was the building's lack of windows, and the unusually bulky storage shed under the center of the building.

In reality, that shed disguised the elevator shaft down into the underground/underwater bunker that housed the heart of their ops center. The aboveground building mainly disguised antennae and receivers for the equipment below.

They piled into the elevator and stood in silence as it whooshed them down into the bunker. The door opened into the perpetual twilight of a room crammed with computers and monitors.

Rebel sat at her communication console and typed quickly. In just a few seconds, she reported without looking up from her screen, "Piper's phone is still at the elementary school where it was this morning."

"And her backup locator signal?" Torsten asked.

"It appears stationary about fifty miles west of here," she reported. "Reporters are saying a group of masked men were seen coming out of a white air-conditioning company van and heading into the elementary school. They left in the same vehicle. Presumably with Piper in tow."

Major Torsten left Rebel to man the ops center in case Piper called in, and loaded Tessa and Beau into his Hummer. They drove west, paralleling the murky waters of Bayou Black to the GPS coordinates Rebel had given them for Piper's backup locator signal. It turned out to be coming from a crappy little 1950s-era gas station in the middle of nowhere.

The gray-haired Cajun man inside the station swore he hadn't seen any woman fitting Piper's description all day. When Tessa showed him a picture of Piper on her cell phone, the attendant declared her hot, but again denied having seen her. Tessa was inclined to believe him.

Torsten called Rebel to confirm they were at the right

place, and she was adamant that their position locators were literally on top of Piper's. And it was still pinging.

They fanned out to search the area, and after a minute or so, Tessa spotted a glint in the gravel at the corner of the building. She bent down and picked up Piper's West Point class ring. The one with the locator in it.

"I found her ring!" she called out.

"Don't move!" Torsten ordered immediately. He knelt down, examining the dirt between himself and Tessa. After a moment, he moved off to his right, toward the side of the building. Using his finger, he drew a rectangle on the ground. "Tire track. Recent," he commented, continuing to stare at the dusty clay.

Beau moved forward to join him in staring at the ground. He had a sniper's outstanding eyesight and was the best tracker of all of them.

"Looks like three men," he murmured. "They milled around beside the vehicle."

Torsten nodded. "And one walked over there to the corner of the building and back, close to where the ring was."

"Did he drop it, maybe?" Tessa asked.

Beau answered grimly, "I don't see any tracks small or narrow enough to be Piper's. These are all men in boots."

"Agreed," Torsten muttered. "I don't think she dropped it as a bread crumb for us."

"Either way," Tessa commented, "we know she was headed west a couple hours ago."

Beau crouched and studied the dirt a bit more, adding, "It looks like some of the tracks lead over to this burn barrel."

Tessa detoured around the footprints to stare into the rusty container at the pile of light gray ashes inside. It didn't look like it would hold any clues to Piper's whereabouts.

Torsten moved over beside her to gaze into the trash barrel, the contents of which were smoking lazily and stank of burnt plastic. He gingerly poked around in them.

"Do you see anything, sir?" she asked hopefully.

"Nope. Just ashes. If the guys in the van dropped anything in here, it's gone."

Damn.

Torsten moved away from her and pulled out his cell phone.

"Where's Piper now?" Tessa asked logically.

Beau looked up grimly from snapping pictures of the tracks. "I think it's safe to say she was kidnapped. Which leads to the even more salient question. Why her?"

They stared at one another grimly. Were the Medusas compromised?

How? Practically no one knew of their existence, let alone what their real mission was supposed to be. The only—deeply buried—paper trail that led to the team vaguely referred to it as an environmental research group.

"Back in the Hummer," Torsten ordered briskly. "We're going to New Orleans."

"What's in New Orleans?" Tessa ventured.

"An NCIS field office. It's time to bring in the big guns to track down Piper and figure out what in the hell is going on."

She wasn't about to voice the idea that, if Torsten had listened to her and Rebel earlier, Piper's kidnappers wouldn't have such a big head start on them. Torsten looked like he was probably having that thought all on his own, without her having to say it.

They climbed back into the Hummer in silence, and Torsten stomped on the accelerator, blatantly ignoring any notion of speed limits as they raced toward New Orleans at nearly a hundred miles per hour. No doubt about it, the boss was definitely more worried than he was expressing aloud.

They all were.

ZANE GOOSE-STEPPED the woman into the cabin as gently as he could. "Piper," she'd called herself. After a brief stop in the bathroom, he followed Mahmoud's order to take her downstairs into the basement and secure her.

The cellar was dirt walled and windowless, cool and dank smelling. He led her over to a four-inch steel pipe running vertically up one wall and pulled out the pair of handcuffs Mahmoud had handed him.

He looped them around the pole and then carefully snapped her wrists into the cuffs. He made sure they were tight enough that she couldn't slip out of them, but not so tight that they hurt her.

Zane brought over an armload of blankets and spread them out on the ground beside her. "It won't be the most comfortable place you've ever slept, but it's dry and you'll be warm enough."

"Why are you doing this for me?" she asked under her breath.

Why indeed? If he was one of the bad guys, he ought to be roughing her up, scaring the living daylights out of her and terrorizing her into unquestioning cooperation with him and the other men. But she was the innocent victim in this scenario, and he was the criminal who'd put her here.

He had already considered telling her who he was in hopes of gaining her trust and cooperation. But he'd reluctantly ruled out revealing his true identity to her.

If—when—Mahmoud and Yousef got around to torturing her, which Zane had no doubt both men were sadistic enough to enjoy doing, he really needed her not to blurt out that he was an undercover CIA agent. People in the midst of torture would say or do just about anything to make the pain stop. He dared not give her a grenade that she could lob to save herself.

As much as Zane would like to put her mind at ease

and tell her he was one of the good guys, he couldn't. Not yet. Not until the two of them were out of here and clear of Mahmoud and company.

Her eyes were big and dark as she stared at him, revealing for a moment the fear that she was valiantly holding at bay. God, she was brave. Admiration for her coursed through him.

"Get some rest," he said gruffly.

Her brows furrowed in confusion.

"I'll take you upstairs to use the bathroom in the morning. If you have an emergency before then, let me know." He bent down and deposited a bottle of water and a protein bar on the floor next to the pole. "There's a drink and a snack right here, where you can reach them."

He headed toward the stairs and his hand lifted toward the light switch.

"Could you please leave the light on?" she asked.

"Of course." His hand fell to his side. He hated leaving her alone down here with her fear and uncertainty, but Mahmoud and the other men would be suspicious as hell if he hovered over her like a worried mother hen.

He hurried up the steps before he could lose his resolve.

"She tied up?" Hassan asked when he emerged into the kitchen.

"Yup. Not going anywhere."

Hassan nodded and set a TV dinner on the table for him. Turkey and gravy. Not his favorite, but he wasn't about to complain. Not with so much on the line.

Zane ate about half the bland meal before asking around a mouthful of pasty mashed potatoes, "What does Mahmoud want with the woman?"

Hassan shocked him by actually answering. Whether it was because the man already knew that Mahmoud planned to kill Zane, or because Zane had actually earned some trust today by participating in the kidnapping, he had no idea. "She's the wife of some guy that our employer needs to do something."

"So she's being held as leverage, then," Zane commented neutrally, leaping all over Hassan's rare chatty mood. "Got it. Keep her alive. Reasonably healthy. Just maintain control of her."

Hassan grunted in what Zane took as an affirmative.

"Do we know who her husband is?" Zane asked.

"Above my pay grade."

"And who exactly ordered the kidnapping?" Zane pressed.

"Above your pay grade."

He grinned and shrugged at Hassan. "Sorry. It's hard for me to keep operating in the dark all the time. At some point you guys are going to have to learn to trust me."

"I think you're okay. Don't take it personally. Mahmoud always plays everything close to his chest."

"Thanks, man." Zane got up and carried his empty dinner tray over to the trash can and tossed it in. "Tomorrow, you gotta let me go to a store and get us some real food if we're gonna be here awhile. That crap tasted like cardboard."

"No lie," Hassan laughed. "I'll ask Mahmoud in the morning."

"You want me to guard the prisoner overnight?" Zane offered.

"Don't you want to take shifts or something?" Hassan blurted.

"I don't mind doing it tonight. You drove most of the day and could use some rest. I can sleep at the foot of the stairs. It's not like she can get loose and go anywhere."

"You show admirable dedication to the work, my friend."

He shrugged and made eye contact with Hassan. "Just

trying to prove myself to you guys. But you're tough nuts to crack."

Hassan grinned and merely dipped his chin at the compliment, reverting to his usual taciturn self.

By the time Zane went back down to the basement, the woman was curled up on her side next to the steel pole, nested in the blankets like a puppy. She was out cold. Exhausting day she'd had. He pulled one of the blankets over her gently.

Rough day for him, too. He unrolled the sleeping bag he'd carried down here and spread it at the bottom of the steps. His offer to stay with her was a two-edged sword, of course. Not only did it keep Piper from escaping, but it kept the other men from paying any extracurricular visits to her, as well.

Confident that she would be out cold for hours to come, he closed his eyes, knowing that sleep would claim him immediately. It was a combat trick he'd learned during his stint in the army, fresh out of college. When he'd never known when or where his next chance to sleep would come, he'd become expert at napping anywhere on a moment's notice.

A PAINFUL KICK in his ribs woke Zane up sometime later. He tensed to do violence before he remembered where he was. He threw off the sleeping bag and rose, silent and fast, to his feet. Yousef was grinning at him and looking pleased with himself.

"Boss wants to see you," the man announced.

Zane suppressed an urge to bury his fist in the guy's face and merely gestured for Yousef to go first up the stairs. A quick glance at Piper confirmed that she was still dead to the world.

Yousef led him to the living room, where Mahmoud and Hassan already sat. These three were the senior members of this cell. The other two guys, Bijan and Osted, acted mostly as muscle.

Mahmoud held out a cell phone and a national newspaper to Zane, who stared at them suspiciously. After months without him having access to any kind of news or electronic communications, why in the world was the guy offering him both now?

"I need photographs of the woman," Mahmoud announced. "Clear ones where her face is easy to see. And she needs to be visibly tied up. We want her husband to understand in no uncertain terms that she is a captive."

"Of course," Zane responded. "Do you want them right now?"

"Yes."

"Back in five minutes."

Zane jogged down the basement stairs loudly, announcing his coming to the woman. Sure enough, when he looked across the space at her, she was awake and watching him.

In the middle of the cellar, he set down the wooden chair he'd carried from the kitchen, then moved over to her to unlock the handcuffs.

"What's happening?" she asked quickly.

"Picture time, Mrs. Black."

"You need proof of possession of me? To show whom?"

"Your husband, of course."

"Are you asking for a ransom? Blackmail? What's the play here?" she demanded.

An interesting, and decidedly military, turn of phrase. He responded, "The play is you're going to sit in that chair with your hands tied behind your back. You're going to look properly terrified, and I'm going to take a picture of you to send to him so he'll do what we want him to."

"Which is what?" she snapped.

God, he'd love to know that very thing. But he also

wasn't about to admit to her that he didn't have the slightest idea what any of this was about. He propped the newspaper against her chest, being careful not to touch anything personal while he did so. When he was satisfied that the headline was prominently visible, he stepped back from her.

"Say *cheese*," he muttered as he pointed the camera at her.

"Are we doing just stills, or do I get a video, too?" she asked.

"So you can blink out an SOS or something clever like that?" he asked dryly. "Trust me. Your husband will know you're in trouble without you having to tell him."

"Jerk," she muttered.

"You have no idea," he muttered back.

"Do tell."

"Look scared, Persephone."

The end result was her scowling at the camera, looking more defiant than frightened. But her features were clear and readily recognizable.

Which was, of course, a gigantic problem for him. As soon as Mr. Black saw the photos and declared them not to be of his wife, and that information was relayed back to Mahmoud, this woman would be dead. How long did Zane have until all that happened? A day? Two, maybe?

Urgency to get this woman out of here and run far, far away from these bastards pounded through his gut. The only thing keeping him here with her was the fact that he still had no idea why she'd been kidnapped. That, and so far, the men upstairs had shown no inclination to harm her. If he kept his cool for just a bit longer, hopefully whatever Mahmoud had planned for this woman would be revealed.

He briskly led her back over to her pole and cuffed her to it once more. "Don't go anywhere," he said wryly.

"Are you kidding?" she retorted. "I love what you've done with the place. Why would I leave this cozy little dungeon?"

One corner of his mouth turned up in sardonic humor. She was a sharp one, all right. "Don't try that sarcasm on any of the others. They'll kill you for showing them such disrespect."

"But not you?" she asked quietly.

"I'm the one with the sense of humor. Just don't push your luck."

She subsided, silenced by the admonition. Dammit. He much preferred her sassy and mouthing off to him over this silent, apprehensive version of her. If only he could tell her who he really was, what his mission was here.

"Look," he muttered under his breath, "I don't know what the boss has planned for you. I'm going to do my best to protect you from harm. But I need you to hang in there for a little while longer."

Her brow twitched into a perplexed frown. "Who *are* you?"

"I'm the guy giving you a wad of cotton balls. Keep them in your pocket for now, but if it looks like we're coming back down here en masse to rough you up, slip them in your mouth between your molars and cheeks. They'll protect the inside of your mouth, cushion any blows and help keep us from knocking any of your teeth out."

Her frown deepened sharply as he tucked several cotton balls into the front pocket of her jeans. The pocket was snug and warm against her body, and he jerked his fingers out quickly. Must not allow himself to feel anything for this woman. No attraction. No interest. No affection.

He scooped up the fluffiest of the blankets and breathed, "Lift your shirt."

"I beg your pardon?" she squawked.

"Keep your voice down," he admonished sharply. Using the knife out of his ankle sheath—a big fighting blade he kept razor sharp—he sliced the edge of the fleece and then tore off a strip of the soft, thick cloth as quietly as he could.

He reached for her, and she flinched away from him. He couldn't blame her for the reflex, but it cut at his soul and made his heart bleed a little. Reaching up under her shirt, he wrapped the length of fleece around her torso. His palms smoothed across her body, and it was slim and warm…and surprisingly muscular. This woman was in hella good shape. Thank God. She might just survive the worst of whatever Mahmoud and company threw at her.

He tucked the top edge of the blanket under the sides and back of her bra, then tugged the shirt down over the padding. He stepped back to examine his work.

"You can take another strip," he muttered half to himself. "You're leaner through the middle than I realized." He tore off another strip of the blanket and wrapped it over the first one.

"Sorry about this," he warned her, before tucking the second piece beneath the underwires of her bra. The backs of his knuckles momentarily rubbed against soft, resilient flesh, and his entire body tensed at the feminine feel of her.

Nope, nope, nope. Not going there.

Quickly, he tucked the blanket around the sides and back of her bra, too. "If Mahmoud gets any crazy ideas, that'll absorb the worst of the impact from his fists. It'll still hurt like hell, mind you, but maybe you won't bruise so badly or break any ribs."

"Why are you doing this for me?" she mumbled as he tugged her shirt into place once more and stood back to observe his handiwork.

She looked a little thicker than before, but he didn't think the other men had been paying all that close attention to her, based on how they'd treated her so far. She'd been a target to them. An object to be seized and stolen. Not an actual human being.

"Do you by any chance know how to take a punch?" he asked in a low voice.

"As a matter of fact, I do."

This time it was his brow that twitched into a frown. How on earth did she know how to get punched? That wasn't the sort of thing many people had practical experience with. Not even graduates of West Point. He prayed she'd tried boxing at some point in her past, and not any less savory possible sources of the knowledge.

"Try not to dislodge that padding. I may not get a chance to fix it before you need it."

"Thanks," she mumbled. She looked up at him without warning, and their gazes locked. It was all right there in her eyes. Naked fear, confusion, questions.

She whispered, almost as if she wasn't even aware of saying the words aloud, "Am I going to die?"

"Not if I can help it," he answered, before he could stop to think about the words. An urge to wrap her in his arms, to surround her in safety and comfort, nearly overcame him. His arms even started to lift toward her.

No! He mustn't give himself away to her! Both their lives depended on him, and he had to keep his cover intact until they got out of here. He looked at her in silent apology, willing her to understand. To trust him a little bit longer.

She frowned faintly as if she sensed his unspoken message but was confused by it. "Why would you help me?" she whispered.

He stared at her, frustrated at his inability to answer her truthfully. God knew, she deserved a straight answer. "I can't tell you. But I promise you this—I will do everything in my power to get you out of this alive and unharmed."

She weighed his words, his sincerity—heck, him—for a long time. Then she nodded, apparently accepting him at his word. "Okay, then," she breathed. "Thanks again."

"No problem. I'm gonna be sleeping down here with you tonight. If you need anything, let me know. Quietly. Honestly, the quieter and less trouble you can be, the better."

"Don't draw attention to myself, in other words?" she asked.

"Exactly. I've learned that Out of Sight, Out of Mind is a good motto around these guys."

She stared hard at him, and mentally he cursed at himself for having been too revealing with that comment. He spun away from her and jogged upstairs to deliver the camera to Mahmoud.

Mission complete, he came back down and wrapped up in his bedroll at the foot of the stairs. He mustn't give away to her who he was. Not yet.

He tried to sleep, but it eluded him. Instead, he spent the time wondering who on earth she was. How did an army officer, obviously in fighting physical shape, end up in Houma, Louisiana? There wasn't an active military base anywhere near that town. Was she on leave, maybe? Visiting family in the area?

He could only be grateful for whatever twist of fate had thrown Piper in his path. She'd been braver and calmer than any woman should be about being kidnapped at gunpoint, thrown in a van and driven hundreds of miles into the wilderness. He just needed her to be brave for a little while longer. Just until Mahmoud revealed his orders, now that the sleeper cell had been activated.

Chapter Five

Piper was immeasurably grateful for the padding and cotton balls her friendly captor had given her, but she also was overwhelmed with dread at what it signified for her near future. As she lay in the quiet, dimly lit cellar, unable to sleep, she listened to the light, slow sound of Goldeneyes's breathing, and mentally braced herself for the torture to come.

In her POW training, the trainees had been slapped around some, and they'd all pretended it was an approximation of the pain they might experience as prisoners of war. But as she lay here now, she settled into the grim realization that nothing could prepare her for what was going to happen to her soon. She was going to suffer a real beating—or worse—at the hands of men who wouldn't hesitate to break her.

Her instructors had told the POW trainees that their endorphins would kick in and the pain would lessen. That women had an advantage over men because their bodies threw out more endorphins faster than men's, as a result of being biologically designed to withstand childbirth.

But she was still scared to death.

Goldeneyes had made it clear to her that the other men thought she was some woman called Persephone Black. Should she pretend to be that person, or was she better off denying being Mrs. Black? Would she piss off her kidnappers if she insisted she wasn't the woman they'd meant to kidnap?

But she had no idea who this other woman was. She couldn't correctly answer *any* questions about her. Her kidnappers would figure out soon enough that she couldn't possibly be the woman in question. Maybe she should just go ahead and stand by not being Persephone Black.

Of course, then her kidnappers would demand to know who she really was. And it wasn't like she was eager to spill her true identity or the fact that she was part of a highly classified Special Forces team.

The best bet was probably to go along with being Mrs. Black for now.

Working quickly, she built up a fake identity for herself. Originally from Minnesota, she decided to pretend she was from Wisconsin. Not that she expected any of the men except Goldeneyes would know a Midwestern accent when they heard one.

She would stick with the historian cover she already used in Houma: she was researching pirates in the early days of American history, particularly those who'd run through and hidden in the bayous of Louisiana.

She knew her captors thought she was thirty years old. How long had she been married? Three years seemed like a safe enough number. If only she knew what Mr. Black did. Since these people were obviously trying to coerce him into doing something, she probably had better avoid the topic of his work. If she was lucky, her captors already knew what work Mr. Black did and wouldn't bother to confirm it with her.

Since sleep was totally not happening in the face of impending pain, she opted to rest and meditate, practicing centering herself and separating her mind from her body. And she prayed for strength.

The long hours of the night passed, and eventually, she heard stirring overhead. Apprehension tightened across her skin, and she checked her padding awkwardly. Still in place, thank goodness.

She stood up and maneuvered the cotton balls into her palm just in case.

The door at the top of the stairs opened and daylight flooded downward. Goldeneyes stood quickly, just in time to meet three of her captors at the foot of the stairs. They held a quick, quiet conversation in Farsi, most of which she missed.

Goldeneyes threw her a single warning glance, touching his cheek briefly with his finger.

Damn. It was time for the cotton balls. Turning her back to the men, she quickly slipped them into her mouth and used her tongue to push them into place between her molars and cheeks.

"Bring her over to the chair," Mahmoud ordered.

Goldeneyes moved over to her and released one of her handcuffs. Using them like a leash, he dragged her toward the middle of the cellar. She resisted, unable to stop herself. She simply couldn't go meekly into whatever was coming.

She wouldn't say Goldeneyes was exactly gentle with her, but he wasn't rough as he forced her over to the chair and pushed her down onto it. Quickly, he threaded the handcuffs through the chair's back slats and pulled her free hand behind her back to recuff it.

Panic ripped through her and she looked up at him in anguish.

"Courage," he muttered without moving his lips.

Right. Courage. She was a Medusa and would acquit herself like one.

She hoped.

Mahmoud moved over to stand in front of her. He passed what looked like a video camera to Goldeneyes. "Film this."

Great. If this was going to be theater, then she could expect big dramatic punches. Blood. Pain. Lots of pain. She was all over giving these guys the best show she could. Maybe they would stop sooner if she did a lot of screaming and wailing.

Goldeneyes took the video camera, opened the foldout screen on its side and nodded. He didn't look up at her. Rather, he stared fixedly at the tiny monitor. Almost as if he couldn't bear to look directly at her.

The one called Yousef stepped up in front of her. He drew his arm across his body and backhanded her across the face. Hard. She let her head snap to the side with the slap, doing her best to move with the blow and minimize its impact.

But her entire right side of her face exploded with stinging fire. *Crap, that hurts.*

She glared at Mahmoud, standing behind and slightly to one side of Yousef. "Aren't you going to ask me any questions before you start slapping me around?"

The bastard's only response was, "Again."

Yousef struck from the opposite direction this time, smacking the other side of her face painfully. That was the same side that he'd punched yesterday at the school, and the inside of her mouth was already cut up. She was immensely grateful for the cotton ball to cushion the blow. Her eyes watered copiously, though.

She gritted her teeth, partially to keep the cotton balls hidden and partially because she was getting mad. Past her tight jaws, she ground out, "You guys are freaking cowards, hitting a woman who's tied up and can't defend herself. Does it make you feel like men? Because it makes you look like scared little boys."

Yousef punched her this time, burying his fist in her left side, at belly button height. She let her body pivot in the chair as the blow landed, tensing her abdominal muscles to protect her internal organs.

She yelled a curse as pain exploded in her gut, relieved not to have passed out from a drop in blood pressure from being hit in that location.

After that, she did her best to absorb each blow with a minimum of damage, but the toll started to add up. One of her eyes swelled nearly shut, and blood ran down her chin from her nose and mouth. Soon her entire body felt like hamburger, and the pain was so loud and steady now that more blows almost failed to register.

That must be the endorphins kicking in. Thank God.

Yet again, her attacker came back with a fist aimed at her face. She closed her jaw and kept her tongue well away from her teeth, prepared to let her head snap to the side, rolling with the punch.

"Stop!" Goldeneyes yelled.

Her eyes snapped open, and she stared at him, along with everyone else.

"What?" Mahmoud demanded.

"Unless our orders are to kill her right now," Goldeneyes ground out, "you need to stop making a punching bag out of her. As it is, you may have already seriously injured her. If she's got internal bleeding, hitting her again could kill her. What did your handlers tell you to do, Mahmoud? Are we here to kill her now or not?"

She looked at the leader of the cell. Fury was obvious in his eyes, but his jaw worked like he was struggling with some decision.

Goldeneyes added less belligerently, "She's plenty softened up. She'll answer your questions if you just give her a chance to." He threw her a significant look as if to say, *Answer his questions, for God's sake.*

Mahmoud turned to glare down at her. "What's your name?" he asked sharply.

She might need to help out her would-be rescuer and answer questions, but she didn't have to be nice about it. "You know my name," she snapped at Mahmoud.

"Say it for the camera."

She scowled at him, and only when Yousef drew back his fist, a glint of almost-sexual pleasure in his eyes, did she spit out, "My name is Persephone Black."

Goldeneyes's head snapped up from the video camera. She didn't spare him more than a glance because she had to keep her eyes on Yousef and prepare as best she could for a possible blow from him.

"Who's your husband?" Mahmoud demanded.

"Jack Black," she replied sarcastically.

Nobody said anything. They must not know the pop culture reference to the celebrity by that name. Goldeneyes looked up again, and after a glance at his cronies to make sure none of them were looking at him, shook his head slightly at her in warning.

Mahmoud demanded, "Where is your husband now?"

"I have no idea."

"What country is he in?"

What *country*? He wasn't in America? Huh. Who was this guy, Mr. Black? Aloud, she responded, "I said I don't know where he is."

"What work does your husband do?"

She snorted. "Not enough, I can tell you that. I end up paying most of the bills, thank you very much. You'd think a man like him could bring home a decent living, but no.

He sits around pretending to work when I'm slaving away like a dog—"

This time Yousef's fist caught her in the left eye. There was only so much she could do to protect herself from the blow and it snapped her head back hard.

She yelled a curse at the top of her lungs and took a certain small satisfaction from her loud outburst making the men jump.

"What do you want from me?" she shouted.

Goldeneyes jumped forward and grabbed Yousef by the shoulder. "You idiot. You're going to kill her, and then Mahmoud will be royally screwed. He'll be lucky if they only kill him. And it'll be all your fault."

Yousef's glare shifted to Mahmoud, who growled, "Stand down, brother."

This time, Mahmoud actually moved to stand between Yousef and her before asking, "Your husband is overseas right now, is he not?"

She blinked hard, her eyes watering like crazy as. blood from a cut over her brow dripped into them. She was going to get a hell of a shiner out of this.

"Well, um, yeah, he's overseas," she mumbled.

Mahmoud nodded in satisfaction. "And did he tell you where he was going this time?"

"He never tells me anything," she said bitterly. "I'm just the wife at home. I'm supposed to cook and clean and not ask any questions about his work."

Apparently, that was the right answer, for Mahmoud nodded slightly as if that information jibed with what he already knew. He did surprise her by following up with, "What is your husband willing to do to keep you alive?"

So, this was a hostage situation, after all. She was supposed to be used as leverage against her "husband" to get him to do something. "What do you want him to do?" she asked.

"None of your business."

She looked back and forth between Mahmoud and the video camera. "Tell me what you want him to do, and I'll tell him to do it. You're filming me to show this video to him, aren't you? Let me help you convince him."

"Shut up," the man snapped, making a slashing gesture across his throat as a signal to Goldeneyes.

Mahmoud headed for the stairs, snatching the video camera out of Goldeneyes's hands as he passed. "We'll have to edit out that last part." He devolved into Farsi cursing. Something about women who couldn't keep their mouths shut. Maybe that they were a curse to men?

God, she hoped so. She would love to be a curse to him.

Yousef and the third guy, the one who'd driven the van most of yesterday, disappeared upstairs. Goldeneyes waited a minute, staring at the closed door at the top of the steps, before rushing over to her, swearing a blue storm under his breath.

"My God, I'm sorry," he muttered. "I had no idea they would go that far… My fault… Miscalculated terribly… You paid the price… Sorry, so damned sorry… Have to get you out of here…"

Her handcuffs popped free. Gently, he chafed her wrists, helping circulation return to her hands.

"That's it. I'm going up there right now and killing them all," he gritted out through clenched teeth.

Alarmed, she grabbed the front of his shirt to stop him from barging out of the basement then and there. She asked quickly, "Do you have a gun? An automatic weapon? You'll need it to put down four men before they can jump you and take you out. And that's assuming you're fast as hell and surprise them."

"No. But there are knives in the kitchen." He tugged at her grip on his shirt, but she tightened her hold frantically. She couldn't afford for her only protector to lose his cool and get himself killed.

"You won't win with a knife," she said urgently.

"But—"

She cut him off sharply. "You're no good to me dead. As furious as you are right now, I need you to calm down. Think. Keep your wits about you and be patient. It's the only way either one of us will make it out of this situation alive."

He stared at her in rage that very, very slowly faded to anguish. "But look what they've done to you."

"I'm alive. I was trained to survive stuff like that, and I did."

"You shouldn't have had to go through that—"

"Stop." He was starting to work himself up again, and she cut off that train of thought before it could leave the station.

He exhaled hard. Closed his eyes tightly. And when he opened them again, sanity had returned.

She let out the breath she'd been holding. Thank God. He'd come down off the precipice of breaking.

"How is it you're the one talking sense into me?" he muttered. "You're the one who should be hysterical."

"Oh, I am underneath. I just don't have time to let it out right now. I have to think about staying alive first and foremost."

He pushed her tangled hair back from her face gently. "God, you're extraordinary."

Their gazes met for a moment of naked honesty. She let her fear show for a second, and he let his guilt show. Then, together, they forced down the emotions in an unspoken agreement that now was not the time for either feeling.

Eventually, when their stares had both hardened into determination, he nodded once at her. She nodded back.

From here on out, they were in this together.

"Are you okay?" he asked under his breath. "Can you breathe all right? Did that bastard crack any ribs?"

"No broken ribs."

"Teeth? Any loose? New cuts in your mouth?"

"Cotton balls worked," she sighed, suddenly feeling so exhausted she could barely focus. That was the adrenaline draining away after a near-death experience.

"What can I do for you? Name it. Anything. My God, I can't tell you how sorry I am you had to go through that. I had no idea Mahmoud would turn that sadistic bastard loose on you. I'm gonna kill them both one day soon—"

She cut him off gently. "I'll live. I could use some ice for my eye."

"I don't think there's any ice in the cabin." He wiped the blood off her face gently and then dabbed at her eye with the hem of his shirt.

Once the blood was cleared away, he examined the cut again. "Under normal circumstances, I'd tell you to get a few stitches in that. Or I'd sew it up myself. But I don't have any sutures. I think there's a butterfly bandage in the first-aid kit upstairs. I'll bring it down."

"And maybe a styptic stick to stop the bleeding?" she asked hopefully.

"Sorry. Don't have one."

He jogged upstairs and returned with a tube of antibiotic cream and the butterfly bandage. Very gently, he treated the cut and taped it together carefully.

"That's the best I can do. I wish it was more."

"Thanks."

"Don't thank me. You should never have been here. Never gone through that."

She stared at him intently. Was he admitting that he'd intentionally misidentified her? That it was his fault she was here?

"Why did you—" she started.

He cut her off, muttering quickly, "Not now. Not here with them upstairs where they could hear something,"

"Who are you?"

"How's your jaw?" he countered quietly.

"Sore."

"Your side?"

"Same."

"Any serious injuries you're aware of?" he inquired.

"Why do you care?"

"Because I'm freaking trying to keep you alive and in one piece to the best of my ability," he snapped.

"Why?" she demanded from between clenched teeth. She was really getting frustrated with not knowing what his deal was.

"I really wish I could tell you. Does it help to at least know that there *is* a reason?"

"How good a reason?" she retorted.

Without answering, he led her over to the steel post and latched her handcuffs around it once more. Once she was secured, he went back to applying pressure to her eyebrow.

"I thought it was a vitally important reason until I saw you getting beat up. Now, I don't give a crap for reasons. My only goal now is to get you out of here alive and safe."

What in the *hell* was he up to? She desperately wanted to trust him. But did she dare?

"Do you need to go to the bathroom?" he asked.

She glared at him. "Yes, but I'm damned well not walking upstairs into the midst of your friends so they can rough me up some more."

"Good point. I'll bring a bucket down to you."

"Oh, joy."

A faint smile bent his lips for a moment. "There's my brave and bold girl," he muttered as if to himself.

"I'm not your girl!"

He looked down at her bleakly. As he did so, his eyes gradually became harder and colder than she'd ever seen them before. His hand fell away from her eyebrow. "Right," he bit out. "I forgot. In your world, we're enemies."

Well, hell. She didn't mean to alienate the one person who was taking care of her and showing a modicum of kindness toward her. "I'm sorry," she sighed. "I'm not exactly at my best right now."

He stared at her a moment longer, and his expression softened. He fell to his knees in front of her, bringing their gazes to the same level. "I will never be able to make this up to you. I know that. I can only say I'm so damned sorry and that I'll do my level best to get you out of here unharmed. Well, not harmed any further. You're going to have to trust me. I don't deserve it, and you have no reason whatsoever to believe me. But I'm asking you to all the same."

He rose, turned and left the basement without saying another word.

How was she supposed to trust him when he wouldn't even tell her his name, let alone anything else about who he was, why he was here among these animals or why he'd dragged her into the middle of this? Whatever *this* was.

She sagged against her pole, hugging it forlornly, feeling utterly alone in a never-ending nightmare. This time the tears that slipped out of her eyes and down her cheeks weren't solely about pain.

Chapter Six

Tessa fretted while the NCIS agents in New Orleans were briefed on who Piper Ford really was and who the Medusas really were. Major Torsten also explained the importance of maintaining operational security around the Medusa Project and of getting Piper back as soon as possible before she was forced to reveal anything about the Medusas' training and capabilities.

When the agents made it clear they understood both the sensitivity and urgency of retrieving Piper, Torsten, Beau and Tessa climbed into a helicopter that would fly them to Barksdale Air Force Base near Shreveport, Louisiana, to await news. The FBI had received a tip from a convenience store clerk who she had seen a woman matching Piper's description with a man in that area.

As soon as they got to Barksdale, Torsten set up shop in the intelligence office there, and he put his team to work combing through intel reports from the past few weeks, in search of any clue to who might have snatched Piper.

"Keep an eye out for any references to Abu Haddad," he ordered them.

Beau and Tessa both scowled. Beau commented, "Hell, Gun. You saw the explosion. Do you think anyone made it out alive?"

Torsten shrugged. "You two did."

"Yeah, but we were on the deck and in the midst of jumping overboard when we blew the charges. The helicopter that was taking off went down, too. No way did Haddad get away."

Torsten replied grimly, "And yet I have a report that Haddad's organization is setting up some super secret deal with the Iranians and that Haddad himself is expected to close the deal."

"Does Piper's kidnapping have something to do with that?" Tessa asked. "Is there any way Haddad found out about us and spread word that the Medusas are back?"

The men looked at her grimly. Torsten eventually answered, "We can't take the possibility off the table. Back to work, people. The clock's ticking."

ZANE DROPPED THE grocery bags on the cabin's kitchen table in disgust. He'd hoped to go alone to get food and make a quick call to his superiors, asking for an extraction for himself and Piper, but Yousef had gone with him, and the bastard had kept an eagle eye on him. Which was a departure from the usual protocol. Mahmoud almost always used Zane as the lone white-bread American for any required public interactions by his team. The fact that Yousef had come along this time was alarming in the extreme.

It looked for all the world like Mahmoud didn't trust him, and had sent his number two man along to babysit. Which worried the hell out of Zane. He hadn't even had a moment to scribble out a fast note and pass it to the cashier at the grocery store.

Which meant he and Piper were still on their own in the middle of freaking nowhere. It had taken nearly an hour for Yousef to drive to the nearest grocery store, and that had been a tiny, run-down shop about a quarter of the size of a regular supermarket.

"Amir!" Mahmoud bellowed from the living room.

Bracing himself mentally and putting on his best subordinate face, Zane went as summoned. "We'll have decent food for supper tonight. I'm cooking," he announced.

"Praise Allah," Hassan commented.

Mahmoud announced, "I sent the pictures of the woman and the video you shot of her. They want more video."

It was on the tip of Zane's tongue to ask "They, who?" but he knew better. And given the apparent precariousness of his status, he dared not show undue curiosity. "What kind of video?" he inquired.

"We need to put her under more duress so they can raise the pressure on her husband, in case he doesn't give in immediately when we speak with him."

Thank God. The husband hadn't been approached yet. That meant he and Piper had at least another day or so to find a way out of here. "How much more duress?" Zane asked.

Yousef smiled aggressively from beside Zane. "It's not a sin to rape an infidel. They're not human, after all."

Zane's entire being froze. Rape? A little voice in the back of his head started screaming, *No, no, no, no, no!* No woman should endure that for any reason. Mentally swearing up a blue storm, he thought fast.

He said as casually as he could manage, "The problem with doing something like that is the forensic evidence it leaves behind. The FBI can lift DNA from a woman weeks after the fact—whether or not she's alive or dead. Right now, we're in the clear. No one can identify us. But after doing something that…" He trailed off and shrugged.

"You'll do it," Mahmoud declared. "And film it."

Abject relief pounded through him. No way was he assaulting Piper. But if this attack was up to him to perpetrate, maybe he could find a way to spare her.

But on the heels of that came indecision. Should he protest being chosen to do it? He probably should, given that he'd just declared it a bad idea. "Why me?" he whined.

Mahmoud snapped, "You weren't born Muslim. You've already lain with unclean females and are soiled in God's eyes."

Not to mention he would be the one to leave DNA evidence behind. Although there was no way he was actually going through with it. "Where's the damned camera?" he groused.

Hassan handed the video camera over.

"Make her scream," Yousef said, far too eagerly for Zane's taste.

"You wanna watch?" Zane snapped.

Yousef actually hesitated before declining.

Sick bastard.

"Do I get to watch some porn or something to get in the mood?" Zane asked hopefully.

Mahmoud snorted. "As if there would be Wi-Fi reception out here. Ha."

"Maybe on a cell phone?" he asked.

"We don't even have cell coverage in this godforsaken hole," Hassan muttered. "I had to use a satellite phone to send the images of the woman."

Well, hell. There went his plan to pilfer one of the senior men's cell phones and call for help.

"Fine," he huffed. Zane trudged out of the living room and through the kitchen. When he closed the basement door, he wedged a step stool across the door frame and under the latch. No way did he want any of the others to get a bright idea to watch, or heaven forbid, join in the "fun."

A faint smell of urine pervaded the basement now. Honestly, he hoped it would help keep the other men away.

Piper was awake and alert, sitting on the floor by her

pole. "What now?" she asked quickly. She must've seen the grim expression on his face as he mounted the video camera on its tripod and pointed it at her nest of blankets.

She stood up as he approached her.

He leaned in close to her, putting his mouth near her ear. "We've got a problem," he said very low, vividly aware of the other men overhead.

"How bad?" she whispered.

"Bad. They want me to rape you and film it to coerce your husband to cooperate."

Her eyes went wide with fear, but to her credit, her voice remained steady. "I expected something like this."

He breathed, "I have *no* intention of actually attacking you. Period. But we're going to have to put on a good show. Will you help me do that?"

"As opposed to the alternative? Hell, yes."

"Okay, then. I'll go turn on the camera. And I'm sorry in advance." He pushed away from the wall, hating this with every step he took toward the tripod.

He switched on the camera and turned toward her, his back to the lens. He gestured at his face, where he was miming fear, indicating that she should look afraid.

She cowered convincingly enough that a real spear of guilt stabbed his gut as he stalked toward her, considering how he was going to do this. He unlocked her right hand, but looped the handcuffs around the pipe, leaving her left hand chained to it.

"Take off your clothes," he ordered her loudly enough for the camera to pick up.

"No!"

Scowling, he grabbed the front of her shirt. He gave it a yank and buttons went flying. Piper's eyes widened in fear for real then. Her bra was a plain white cotton affair, but damned if it wasn't sexy as hell. Her chest wasn't huge but had lovely curves above the cups of her bra that begged a guy to cup them in his hands.

A guy whom she trusted and wanted to share her body with. Not him. Zane had no right to even think about touching her like that. God, he hated this.

"I'm sorry, I'm sorry, I'm sorry," he chanted over and over under his breath.

"Just get it over with," she muttered back from behind unmoving lips.

He reached for the zipper of her jeans, and she used her free hand to bat his hand away.

He wound up for a backhand slap, giving her plenty of time to see the blow coming. When she met his stare and nodded infinitesimally, he swept his arm dramatically across his body. He relaxed his hand as much as possible and mostly brushed it across her face. The slap still made a reasonably satisfying smacking sound, and Piper's head snapped to the side.

When she looked at him again, he slapped back the other way. "Whimper," he whispered.

She complied, and his skin literally crawled at the sound. Thank God his back was to the camera because no way could he keep the apology out of his eyes.

She made eye contact with him, and forgiveness shone in her gaze.

He was humbled by it. Nearly driven to his knees by it. Only the sure and certain knowledge that Yousef would happily rape her for real if he didn't go through with this pretend travesty kept him on his feet.

"God, I hate this," he muttered as he reached for her shoulders, shoving her up against the dirt wall, pinning her against it with his body. A host of sensations registered all at once. Her body was soft and warm through the cotton of his T-shirt, and it fitted against his just right.

He had no right to enjoy *anything* about this. His gut roiled with nausea at the mere idea of finding anything about this appealing.

"I'm so damned sorry," he murmured.

"It's okay. I know you won't hurt me."

Her trust came within a hair of breaking him. He didn't deserve it. She didn't deserve any of this. It was his fault she was in this position at all. All. His. Fault.

Protectiveness surged through him as he covered her from the prying eye of the camera. "I won't let them hurt you again," he breathed. "I'll find a way to kill them all if I have to."

"Don't bother. Let's just get out of here."

"Working on it."

She stared up at him, and he stared down at her, silently begging her to see the truth in his words.

She nodded once. Slowly. And then she did the damnedest thing. She relaxed against him, her body going sleek and soft and warm against him. She believed him. Thank God.

She burrowed closer against his chest as if relishing the human contact and safety that he represented. He lowered his mouth very slowly, slowly enough not to startle her in the least, to the junction of her neck and shoulder, relishing the silkiness of her skin against his lips. She tasted faintly of salt but was all woman.

"Fight me," he breathed against her neck.

"What?"

"The camera," he reminded her.

"Right."

She used her free hand to shove at his left shoulder, and he was shocked at how strong she was. She managed to push him back, throwing him off balance.

He stumbled back, wiped his hands across his mouth and snarled, "That's better. I like it when my whores fight."

Her gaze was momentarily stricken when she stared at him as if she'd forgotten for a second what they were supposed to be doing. This was acting. This was just acting.

Forgive me, he mouthed.

He stepped forward more aggressively, grabbing her by both shoulders and holding her against the wall as he kissed her too hard. Aww, hell. Her lips were as silky and soft as the rest of her. He ought to smash her lips against her teeth. *Bite her lip. Make her bleed.*

But damned if he didn't do the opposite, gentling the kiss, inviting her to open for him. He simply couldn't brutalize this woman, who'd already been so brave through so much.

Her mouth opened beneath his, and without thinking, he tilted his head to fit their mouths together better.

She kissed him back eagerly. Hungrily. Poor woman was so desperate for some safety, a pretense of normalcy, that she'd lost herself in this kiss. Not that he blamed her for a second. But when she found out who he really was, that he'd chosen to put her in this terrible situation, she was going to hate him forever. And for good reason.

Her hand, which had been shoving at his chest, fisted against his T-shirt, twisting the soft fabric in her fingers, tugging him closer. Thankfully, her hand was out of sight of the camera.

He moved his mouth across hers leisurely, enjoying the way she rose to meet him, lifting her mouth to his and kissing him back.

He shouldn't enjoy this. Shouldn't love the feel of her mouth against his, the scent of her feminine musk filling his nostrils, the resilient strength of her body sliding beneath his palms. Nope, he shouldn't love any of it.

And yet he did.

She was an amazing woman, and her mental fortitude astounded him.

As they continued to kiss, passion built between them, not a wild explosion all at once, but rather a gradual falling away of everything else that had led up to this moment. It left just the two of them kissing each other, sharing their stress and worry with each other, commiserating in their mutual danger and losing themselves in this new and unexpected attraction to each other.

Her free arm crept around his neck, her fingers twining in his hair, and abruptly, he remembered where they were and what they were supposed to be doing.

"Pull my hair," he muttered against her mouth.

She kissed him once more and then complied, giving a painful yank that made him yelp. He jumped back and made a fist, pretending to bury it in her solar plexus. She did a credible job of jumping up slightly and grunting hard as if he'd clobbered her for real.

He grabbed her jeans then and tore the button open. She thrashed from side to side, but he used his superior weight to force her back against the wall. It was surprising how much effort it took to keep her pinned against that wall. Reaching between their straining bodies, he managed to snag her jeans zipper and pull it down.

She let out a scream then, a primal sound of frustration. But hopefully Yousef would interpret it as something more akin to fear.

Zane shoved her jeans down around her knees and was privately relieved when the sturdy fabric tangled around her legs and slowed down her thrashing. He couldn't help but notice she wore bikini underwear—also white cotton, but with a sassy little pink bow and white lace panels on each side that took the panties from utilitarian to freaking sexy.

Piper's torso was golden and gorgeous. Her waist nipped

in to a beautiful and feminine hourglass, and her stomach was flat and toned. Her thighs were muscular against his and as toned as the rest of her. He shoved his still-clothed thigh between hers and she froze reflexively, obviously galvanized by the sensation of sensually riding his thigh.

In *any* other circumstances, he would be so turned on he would hurt. But as it was, there wasn't the least thing sexy about forcing himself on any woman. And positively not this woman.

An urge to just get this over with washed over him. He reached between their bodies and violently shoved her panties down her thighs. She jolted against him, letting out a gasp of shock and protest that sounded entirely real.

"It's almost over," he whispered in desperation. "I hate this as much as you. Just a little bit more to make it look real." He swore under his breath.

"Do what you have to," she was magnanimous enough to whisper back.

"I'm sorry. A thousand times sorry—"

"No more apologies. Just finish the damned video."

He reached for his own zipper and shoved his jeans down to the tops of his thighs. Silently, he prayed that his T-shirt was long enough to cover up most of his bare ass hanging out in the breeze for the camera.

Piper's eyes glazed over with real panic then. She fought like a wildcat, and he was sincerely grateful he'd kept one of her hands chained to that blasted pole. He'd met some strong, fast, fit women in his day, but Piper was in another class of athletes altogether.

Her fist caught him painfully on the side of his jaw, and he forcefully grabbed her wrist, yanking it up over her head. He had to use his height and strength to full effect to even stand a chance at subduing Piper. It took a couple hard-fought minutes, and he was breathing hard before she finally appeared to exhaust herself enough to stop flinging herself around wildly.

He noted a trickle of blood running down her handcuffed forearm. God, he hoped the camera caught that. Because no way was he doing anything else to harm her.

He shoved his crotch against her lower belly over and over, mimicking sex. His jaw clenched against a scream of fury at being forced into this travesty of what should be a beautiful, gentle and respectful sharing of souls.

He ground out, "Scream, Piper. Scream as loud as you can."

Man, she had a set of lungs on her. His ears rang from the piercing shriek she let out about four inches from his right ear. Grimly, he pumped his hips, bumping and grinding against her belly.

How long did he have to keep this up for it to look like a realistic rape, anyway? He had no idea.

The good news was that Piper dissolved into tears—real tears—just then. He felt physically ill for upsetting her that badly, but dammit, for her own safety it had to look believable. It wasn't like he had any choice about this, either. They were both victims this time.

He sped up his hip pumps and made grunting noises that disgusted him, hearing them coming from his own throat. He gave a shout and then collapsed against her.

He muttered against her sweaty neck, "May God forgive me. Not that I'll ever deserve it from Him or from you."

And then he stepped away from her. Keeping his back to the camera, he pulled up his pants and fastened them. Still blocking the camera, and without looking down at her unclothed body, he tugged up her underwear and jeans and pulled her shirt closed over her bra. The buttons were long gone, of course. But at least he could preserve a bit of her modesty for her.

Last, but not least, he reluctantly lifted his gaze to hers. Her good eye was huge and terrified, brimming with tears and accusation. The other eye was puffy and swollen from yesterday's video beating, but it still leaked a stream of tears that streaked her cheek.

Swearing at himself in a continuous mental stream of castigation, he stepped behind the camera and zoomed in on her face, catching all the betrayal and hurt in her expression in one last, intensely cinematic shot before he turned off the camera.

"Thanks for your help with that," he said quietly. "Can I get you anything?"

"Get out of here. I need to be alone. I don't want to look at you right now."

Yeah. He deserved that.

Feeling about as crummy as he'd ever felt in his life, he nodded miserably and unscrewed the video camera from the tripod. He turned to leave, then paused and turned back to her one last time.

"I am more sorry than words can convey. From the bottom of my heart. But I swear to you, there was no other way. It was them or me."

Chapter Seven

In her rational mind, Piper knew she'd dodged a horrendous bullet. But in her emotional heart, feeling Golden-eyes's flaccid man parts thrusting against her belly over and over and over had been invasive, humiliating and degrading. It might not have been rape, but it certainly qualified as sexual assault.

She was intensely grateful to him for not actually raping her. But foremost in her mind, she was appalled that he'd been big enough and strong enough to overpower her like that. She'd deluded herself into believing that, with her specialized training, no man could do that to her ever. But he'd proved her wrong.

It wasn't his fault, of course, that he'd been picked to attack her. And it wasn't even particularly his fault that he was the man to puncture her false assumptions about her invincibility.

Granted, she'd been handcuffed to a pole, which gave him a distinct advantage. But still. She prided herself on being as strong as most men and better trained to fight. The fact that she was still that vulnerable to an assault was beyond appalling. It was terrifying.

What if next time one of the other men decided to have a go at her? What if it wasn't a simulated assault? Her mind shied away from even trying to imagine what that would be like. As it was, a protective fog of shock was lowering around her like a blanket.

She slid down the pole to huddle on the floor beside it. Using her as yet untethered right hand, she reached out and pulled one of the blankets around her shoulders. Then, hugging her legs, she dropped her forehead to her knees and sobbed out her fear and exhaustion.

A completely irrational sense of betrayal filled her that her one champion had put her through that. Rationally, she acknowledged that in some ways, he was also a victim in the scenario. He'd apologized profusely, over and over, clearly horrified by the whole situation, too.

He'd been as considerate as he could possibly be, given what they'd both been forced into pretending to do. But when he'd dropped his pants, all the reasonable explanations for being okay with any of it had fled her mind. It had become too real. Too personal.

She'd squeezed her eyes shut and refused to look at him. She couldn't bear to see him enjoy any part of what they'd done together.

As she forced herself to replay it in her head, something dawned on her. He hadn't been turned on by the encounter. At all.

His male parts had been completely unaroused against her belly as he'd shoved his pelvis at hers over and over. Thank God for that, at least.

Gradually, the initial shock of the simulated attack wore off, and she registered other small details that she'd failed to notice when the assault was happening. He'd never hurt her once, not the whole time she'd been fighting against him. And she'd landed a few pretty good punches on him.

He'd also carefully used his body to block her from the camera. The most anyone would ever see on that film was her face and maybe some of her legs.

She did note ruefully that he'd done a number on her shirt, though. It was ruined. Still, rather than give her captors the pleasure of taunting her with them, she collected the buttons she could reach off the floor and stuffed them in the back pocket of her jeans.

Her captors probably wouldn't cough up a needle and thread for her to sew the buttons back on. The garment had effectively become a jacket. Which meant she couldn't wear her blanket armor anymore, either. Not without a shirt to hide it.

She didn't relish parading around in her bra in front of these jerks, and she resorted to tying the tails of her shirt together to form a makeshift crop top. It exposed a strip of her stomach—which God knew would be plenty of temptation for a crew of terrorists. But her bra and most of her cleavage were safely covered up now.

Major Torsten would undoubtedly tell her in this situation to learn from it. To focus on taking care of herself and being ready to exploit any openings that came her way. Speaking of which, Goldeneyes had mentioned at the beginning of that awful encounter that he was working on an escape for both of them. Did she dare hope he was telling the truth?

If he indeed ran away with her, she would go with him initially, and then break away and strike out on her own. She didn't dare trust him, and honestly, her survival skills were probably vastly superior to his. He would be nothing but dead weight to her…

Okay. Fine. She was lying to herself. She mostly didn't want to be alone with any man right now, especially not the man who'd just convincingly made a video of assaulting her.

Mentally exhausted and emotionally wiped out by the

encounter, she rested her head against the pole, closed her eyes in genuine exhaustion and went to sleep.

ZANE HANDED OVER the video camera without comment and made sure to give it directly to Mahmoud. It occurred to him yet again to wonder if, now that Mahmoud's superiors had this video, they might not need Piper alive any longer to act as leverage to force her supposed husband into action.

Ready or not, he was out of time to get her away from these men. The two of them had to disappear before this cell of violent thugs received orders to kill her and hide the body.

Mahmoud had the gall to ask, "Was she any good?"

Bastard. "Of course not," Zane replied scornfully. "She fought almost until the very end."

"Excellent," Mahmoud commented.

"Do you need anything else from me, or can I go cook us a decent supper now?"

"Go."

Zane mechanically went through the motions of making his grandmother's world-famous spaghetti sauce. Thankfully, he'd seen her make it a thousand times and he'd made it a hundred times himself because his mind was completely occupied with the woman downstairs.

He had to get her out of here sooner rather than later, identifying Mahmoud's real target be damned. Now that the taboo of raping the hostage had been broken, he didn't doubt that Yousef or one of the others would get the bright idea to have a go at Piper for themselves.

That, and he was certain that Mahmoud's superiors would give the green light to get rid of Piper any minute.

Man. If only he had some Rohypnol. He would totally roofie these bastards' food and knock them all out. He eyed the bottle of wine he'd bought to flavor the sauce with. Muslims technically weren't supposed to drink. But he'd found over the years that some of them would indulge from time to time. And this crew had not shown itself to be particularly religious.

Why would they be religious? After all, if they casually killed people without remorse, what was a glass of wine among friends? If nothing else, maybe a glass of wine would relax these guys and get them to sleep a little more deeply tonight.

He set the kitchen table for dinner and made a point of pouring glasses of wine at each place. He also made sure to give himself the smallest wineglass and to put only a splash of wine in it—just enough to make it look like he'd been drinking while he prepared the meal.

He piled big mounds of spaghetti on each plate and slathered them with sauce. What wine couldn't accomplish, maybe a carbohydrate coma could. He'd toasted a huge basketful of garlic bread as well, and put that in the middle of the table.

Then he called out, "Dinner's served."

The other men piled into the kitchen and dug into the meal with gusto. He made a point of refilling their plates over and over, stuffing them as much as he could.

Eventually, the men pushed back from the table, bellies overfull and their moods expansive. Zane got up and started carrying dishes over to the sink. "You guys go chill out and I'll clean up this mess," he said casually.

Bijan, the youngest of the bunch, commented, "Having you around is almost like being home with my mother."

He grinned at the kid. "I'm about to start yelling at you about it being past your bedtime, little boy."

The other men laughed and jumped in, ribbing Bijan about being a baby as they sauntered out of the kitchen in good humor. It was one of the few times he'd ever seen them let down their hair and relax. Maybe the wine was having the effect he'd hoped for.

He'd done all he could to ensure they crashed early and slept hard tonight. When the dishes were done, he carried a plate of spaghetti down to Piper. She was asleep, so he set it beside her quietly and retreated without waking her up. She'd earned some rest after her earlier trauma.

God willing, she would need to be rested before the night was out.

He joined the men upstairs and was delighted when Yousef produced the case of beer he'd added to the grocery cart earlier. They all lounged on the furniture and floor, drinking and watching an American preseason football game on the crappy box-style television hooked to an old-fashioned satellite dish.

Zane carried his beer with him when he went to the bathroom, and poured it into the toilet. He passed out fresh beers whenever someone emptied theirs, and just as important, he made sure everyone indulged about equally. He needed them *all* to pass out.

The game ended, and Mahmoud stood up, asking, "Who's taking first watch tonight?"

Nobody volunteered, and Zane sighed loudly, "Fine. I'll do it. Who's second?"

Mahmoud pointed at Osted, the quietest of the bunch.

Zane nodded at the young man. "I'll wake you up in, say, two hours?"

"Make it four," Mahmoud objected. "That way only two of us have to stand watch tonight."

Osted grinned and Zane flipped the kid off.

As the others headed for their beds, Zane stepped outside into the bracing chill of a mountain evening and took a lap around the cabin. Ideally, he would get the van keys and drive away from here with Piper. But Mahmoud kept the keys on his person at all times, and Zane wasn't interested in accidentally waking the guy up while trying to steal the stupid things.

He'd checked out the van yesterday, and it wasn't an ideal vehicle to hot-wire, either. Not to mention hot-wiring could get noisy as an engine tried and failed to ignite a few times before it caught and actually started. He couldn't afford to risk any sound waking up the other men.

Nope, the best bet was going to be for him and Piper to sneak away on foot. To disappear into the mountains. Thankfully, she was a soldier. Even though she was beaten up, she should be half-decent at hiking over rough terrain.

He made another circuit of the cabin, scouting for patches of loud leaves on the ground and noting logs and other obstacles to a silent departure. He also forayed out into the woods in several different directions, being sure to make obvious tracks each time. No sense making it easy for the bastards to track him and Piper.

Preparations complete, he went back inside the house to wait for the others to get fully to sleep. He noted that the kitchen door, which he used to enter, squeaked a bit.

While he waited, he quietly packed a rucksack with all the survival gear he'd secretly collected over the past few days in anticipation of bugging out with the hostage. He also dabbed a bit of olive oil on the door hinges to quiet them. There. Ready to go. Now he just had to let the others have plenty of time to fall into a deep slumber.

He timed it on his watch, waiting two full hours before he eased into the kitchen. And then he headed down into the basement.

Here went nothing.

PIPER WOKE ABRUPTLY as a hand closed over her mouth. Her eyes flew open, and she stared up at Goldeneyes. Without ncovering her mouth, he leaned close to whisper in her ear, 'You and I need to leave now. If you stay here any longer, hey'll kill you. Or worse. Do you understand?"

Oh, she understood, all right. But did she dare trust him?

Frowning, she nodded up at him. If she could get him alone in the woods, away from here, she could at least sneak away or overpower him and make her own escape. But vivid in her mind was the memory of how easily he'd wrestled her into submission earlier.

He gripped her handcuffs to keep them from rattling against the steel pole, then unlatched them quietly, easing them off her wrists and tucking them in his back pocket.

She rubbed her left wrist gently, checking to see how bad the abrasions were from when she'd fought against the fake attack earlier. Two thin red rings of raw flesh encircled most of her wrist.

A hand appeared in front of her, palm up in offer, and she took it, letting Goldeneyes help her to her feet. He held out a sweatshirt to her, and she glanced at him, making eye contact for the first time.

"Leave your shirt on and put this on top," he whispered. "It's cold outside."

She nodded and donned the sweatshirt. As it passed over her head, she recognized the scent. It was the smell of him. A little bit spicy, a little bit musky. All man. She'd gotten a good whiff of it when his body had been mashed against hers from neck to knee.

Residual panic flashed through her at the scent trigger.

Swearing silently, she tugged the soft fabric over her face and pulled it down her torso angrily. She was all right. She hadn't been raped for real. It had all been fake. She was lucky as hell that he'd been willing to merely simulate sexually assaulting her.

He grabbed the two thickest blankets and stuffed them

into a rucksack. It wouldn't zip all the way up with the bulky blankets in it, but he slung it over his shoulder and gestured for her to follow him.

She trailed after him up the stairs, rolling from heel to toe with each step the way she'd been trained to move silently. He pointed at one of the stairs and then stepped over it, and she did the same. She'd already noted from his various trips up and down that it squeaked.

He held up a closed fist at the top, telling her to stop, and she did so. Huh. How did he know that she would know that hand signal? Oh. Right. He'd spotted her West Point class ring. He must presume—correctly—that she was a soldier.

He eased over to the back door and opened it gently.

Unbidden, a rush of adrenaline slammed through her. She was getting out of here. Away from her captors. The nightmare was over.

Well, not quite over. She and Goldeneyes still had to get away from here safely and get to help. But she was confident in her field training. Once they hit the woods, she would be in her native element. They would be fine.

She hoped.

Praying this escape was exactly what it looked like it was, she stepped outside and into the clean, cold, fresh night air.

Goldeneyes eased the door shut and then stepped around her, gesturing for her to follow him. She was impressed that he moved away from the porch at a snail's pace, placing each step with care not to disturb the leaves or make a footprint in any soft dirt. He, too, rolled from heel to toe with every step. Now, where had he learned that? Only Special Forces types routinely practiced walking like that.

She walked the same way, of course, additionally making sure to place her feet in the exact same spots he was stepping with his. No sense making it any easier to trail

the two of them. Her footprints would be unique and noticeable to a decent tracker. Hence her disguising her steps
within his.

They reached the shadow of a giant oak tree, and he signaled for her to stop. She did, and he squatted to examine
their trail back to the cabin, checking to make sure they'd
left no tracks. While his back was turned and his concentration elsewhere, she could totally take off into the woods
and flee from him.

But she tamped down the urge. The thinking soldier's
response to this situation was to play it out a little longer.
Use him to get farther from the cabin. Far enough away
that he couldn't easily rouse the others and put them all on
the hunt for her.

He stood up, nodded the all clear and headed into the
woods. She had no idea what direction they were heading.
Under the heavy canopy of trees, it was impossible to see
any stars overhead and get her bearings. She would just
have to trust him for now.

They moved with cautious stealth for ten minutes or so,
gliding away from the cabin in complete silence disturbed
only by the occasional swish of a leaf against their clothing.
His silhouette was big and black in front of her, blending
into the night as if he was a natural part of it. The guy totally had some sort of military training in his background
to be moving so smoothly over the rough terrain.

Over the next half hour or so, her eyes fully adjusted to
the darkness, and she began to pick out more features of
the forest they passed through.

It was mostly big old oak trees. Which was good. The
tannin from their roots had a tendency to retard the growth
of brush under them, and the going was relatively easy. It
wasn't exactly a stroll through a park, since dead branches

and holes lurked under the carpet of leaves, invisible until stepped upon.

She estimated they'd been walking the better part of an hour when Goldeneyes finally stopped in the lee of a vertical outcropping of layered sandstone. He sat down on a boulder and eased the rucksack off his shoulders. He held out a plastic bottle of water to her, which she took and downed gratefully.

"Since we were never officially introduced… Hello, Piper. I'm an undercover operative for the CIA. And I'm truly, deeply sorry for everything that has happened to you."

Chapter Eight

Zane held his breath. This was the moment of truth. Would she believe him—and trust him? Or would she continue to fight against him and make this a battle between them? Escaping and evading the men back at the cabin while fighting with her was going to be a bitch if she chose not to believe him.

He dared not tell her much about himself in case they didn't successfully get away from Mahmoud and gang. Although, if the two of them were caught, he suspected there would be only torture and pain before they were both killed. Mahmoud probably wouldn't bother to interrogate either one of them extensively. Still, Zane had to be cautious and keep his wits about him.

"Do you have some sort of government ID on you to prove who you are?" she challenged.

"Are you kidding?" he blurted. "Have you seen how dangerous those men are back at the cabin? No way would I carry something that damning on me. I only carry identification that goes along with my deep cover legend."

"What should I call you?" she asked dryly. Dryly enough that she obviously realized any name he gave her would be an alias.

He shrugged. "I am conditioned to respond to Amir. Or

your nickname for me—what was it? Goldeneyes?—will do for now."

"Why did you kidnap me in the first place? And why did you tell them I'm Persephone Black when you knew darned good and well that I'm not her?"

He sighed, "Like I said. I really am sorry about that. Mahmoud told us Mrs. Black was the assistant principal of that elementary school—and our target—about one hour before we barged through the front doors of the school, guns blazing. They weren't going to leave that place without Mrs. Black, and I was afraid that when they didn't find her, they'd shoot the place up. If you'll recall, one of the secretaries told me Mrs. Black was out sick that morning."

"So you told them I was her?"

"You seemed like the best substitute out of the available women in the front office. You were also the only person there who even remotely looked like the surveillance photo we were shown of the real Mrs. Black."

"Who is this Persephone Black woman?" Piper asked curiously. "Why would a bunch of terrorists be interested in the assistant principal of an elementary school in south Louisiana?"

He shrugged. "As far as I can tell, she's the wife of someone important. Her only value to Mahmoud's superiors appeared to be as leverage to get her husband to do something."

"What do you know about Mr. Black?" she pressed.

"Nothing. As soon as we get back to civilization, though, I'll damned well be looking into who he is and what's so special about him."

"You seriously don't have a cell phone to call for an extraction?"

He blinked. *Extraction* was a distinctly military term. That West Point ring had obviously been the real deal.

"Mahmoud doesn't allow any electronics besides his, which are heavily encrypted. No phones, no tablets, no laptops. Nothing that can be tracked by the authorities."

She looked around at the trees. "How far are we from a phone or a human being with a phone? As soon as we reach one, I can call in considerable resources to come pull us out."

"So can I," he replied dryly. "Who are you, anyway?"

She frowned heavily enough that he was able to see the expression in the dim starlight filtering through the trees. She said cautiously, "As you saw from my college class ring, I went to West Point. I'm in the army."

"That reminds me," he said. "I've been dying to know how you ended up in Houma, Louisiana, in an elementary school."

"Bad luck, I guess."

Hmm. An evasive answer. He responded, "Well, it was great luck for me." Silence fell between them as they rested. He added, "How are your injuries? Do you need first aid? I have a small kit with antibiotic cream and some bandages. I can put a new butterfly on that cut over your eye—"

She cut him off. "I'm fine. Shouldn't we be moving on?"

"You're not too tired?" he asked.

She snorted. "I can hike all night, all day tomorrow and all of tomorrow night before I start feeling tired. Just get me away from those men and to the nearest phone as fast as you can."

"I'm actually not heading for the nearest town. That's where they'll expect us to go."

"Are we headed in the opposite direction?" she asked sharply.

"Actually, the nearest town is to the north. We're headed more or less east."

She subsided beside him, muttering only, "All right, then."

He would take that as approval for his choice of direction. He stood up, shouldering the pack once more. "If you get cold, let me know and you can wrap one of the blankets around you."

That garnered another snort out of her. "Once you pick up the pace to something decent, I'll be plenty warm."

"Would you like to lead the way and set the pace?"

He made the offer sarcastically, so was shocked when she nodded and said briskly, "Show me the last landmark you were headed toward, and I'll take point for a while. Let me know if I'm going too fast for you."

Her going too fast for him? Right.

Except when she did head out, she stunned him by setting a killer pace that had him huffing and puffing behind her to keep up. Cripes. He'd known she was in good shape, but he had no idea she was *this* fit. He would hate to see her pace when she wasn't bruised and battered.

She led the way toward a distant mountain peak for a solid hour before stopping again. She even had the gall to murmur, "Do you need a rest?"

"I'm fine, thanks," he replied. "Where did you get so buff? Do you run marathons for fun or something like that?"

"Something like that."

"Color me impressed," he commented.

"Do you want to take point for a while, or should I continue leading the way?" she asked matter-of-factly.

"I'll take over the lead." He knew it to be the more tiring role, and they would both have to pace themselves physically and mentally to make their escape.

"Who are those guys, anyway?" she asked as he passed her one of the last two bottles of water and downed the other himself.

"I'm not sure."

"But you lived and worked with them."

"They were incredibly closemouthed. The intel briefings that led me to infiltrate their group indicated they might be a terrorist cell. Whether they're state actors or freelancing, I couldn't tell you. I know they speak Farsi as their primary language, which pegs them as likely Iranian in origin."

"And?" she asked expectantly.

"And that's roughly all I know about them. Mahmoud, the leader, is taking orders from someone. He's the only one in the group who routinely uses a cell phone or the internet, and the encryption on both his cell phone and laptop is top-notch. Trust me. I've checked both."

"He and the two older guys—Yousef, and I never heard the other one's name—"

"Hassan."

"—and Hassan—struck me as military," she offered.

"Agreed. I actually think all of them have military training. Mahmoud, Yousef and Hassan also appear to have some sort of advanced training. Special Forces, maybe. And training in covert intelligence operations."

"Well, that's just special," she commented. "How much danger are we in of them finding us out here? Do they have infrared or heat-seeking gear for tracking us?"

He considered her question. "I don't know. Mahmoud kept tight control of a couple large duffel bags full of gear. It's possible they have night-optical devices and other tracking paraphernalia."

"What I wouldn't give for a nice pair of NODs right now," Piper said wistfully.

NODs, huh? That was definitely military jargon for *night-optical devices*. Special Forces types, in particular, made frequent use of them. But it wasn't like he could up and ask her about where she'd learned the terminology. She was still refusing to tell him her full name, and he guessed he couldn't blame her. Not after all she'd been through.

And after all, he hadn't told her his name, either.

He had to assume that at least one of Mahmoud's guys was a skilled tracker and would be able to follow them. He didn't want to stress out Piper any more than necessary, but they really did need to keep moving. Quickly.

After the water break, he stood up and moved out, taking the lead and setting fully as fast a pace as she had. Thankfully, she kept up without complaint.

For now. At some point, fatigue would override her fear, and then he would have a hard decision to make. Did he push her to continue on, or let her rest and risk Mahmoud and company catching up with them?

He would cross that bridge later. In the meantime, he kept an eye on the ground in front of him and frequently scanned the forest behind them for signs that they were being followed—movement, sudden silence from the night creatures, anything to indicate that Mahmoud's men had found them.

He and Piper were dead if that happened. Between the two of them, they had his Ka-Bar knife strapped to his ankle and a pocketknife. Mahmoud's men had AK-47s. Their only hope was to outrun and evade the other men.

Around daybreak, it started to rain.

He'd managed to salvage a single large trash bag from the kitchen, and he slit its seams now to create a small makeshift tarp. They huddled together under it, doing their best to stay as dry as possible. But it was a losing battle.

They were both cold and wet, and he was tired, his eyes gritty.

Piper surprised him yet again by saying, "Take a fifteen-minute power nap. I'll keep a lookout while you rest."

It wasn't a bad idea. "Only if you'll do the same when I'm done," he replied.

"Deal."

He didn't exactly feel better after the catnap, but he knew intellectually that it had helped a little.

With daylight came ease of seeing their footing, and the rain made it silent going. But they also faced a whole new set of dangers. They had to be careful not to make themselves visible while topping ridges, and they were forced to stick to the heaviest tree cover they could find, which slowed them down somewhat. Not to mention it was nearly impossible not to leave muddy tracks. He could only pray the rain would erase the prints before Mahmoud's tracker found them.

Mahmoud and the others were surely awake by now and knew that he'd absconded with their hostage. He wasn't absolutely sure they would actually come after him and Piper. But if they did, it would be with the intent to kill both of them. Urgency to reach civilization and call for help ripped through him.

Cold and miserable, they pressed onward.

About midmorning, Piper asked, "Where are we with food and water?"

"I wasn't able to carry out much of either," he answered. "By my estimate, the nearest town in this direction is at least thirty miles from the cabin."

She responded, "In virgin forest, we can only expect to make, at most, something like five or six miles a day. So that means at least five days out here. Let's round that up to a solid week for caution's sake. I gather, then, that we'll have to forage for food and water while we hike."

"That's correct."

She nodded, seemingly not alarmed by that prospect.

He asked curiously, "Why isn't the idea of eating bugs and weeds freaking you out?"

"I've done a fair bit of wilderness camping," she replied evasively.

"How's that? Not many people can say that."

She glanced over her shoulder at him, her gaze giving away nothing. "I like the outdoors."

He frowned at her back. Man, she was being cagey with him. He got that he had no right to expect her trust after he'd put her in this situation to begin with. But it still stung. He'd blown a long-term operation for her, and he'd risked his own life to stick around to pull her out. But he wasn't in any position to explain that to her.

Hmm. Did she have secrets of her own that prevented her from being honest with him? If so, what could those be? He occupied himself for the next few hours turning over possibilities in his head. Was she AWOL from the military? Maybe she'd been discharged under less-than-honorable conditions.

The good news with the rain was that it created plentiful rivulets of runoff water. They found a good one running fast and clear, and he passed Piper a plastic bottle to fill while he filled one of his own.

He had managed to slip a bottle of water-purification tablets into his pocket in the grocery store yesterday without Yousef appearing to see him. He pulled that out now and passed it to Piper. As an experiment, he intentionally didn't say anything to her about how to use them.

She casually broke the wax seal, popped one tablet in the water and gave it a good shake. She stuck the bottle in the makeshift sling she'd made of one of the blankets across her body.

Huh. She definitely knew how to use the tablets. She knew to give them a little while to kill any bacteria in the water. He did the same, and they filled the two remaining water bottles and treated that water, as well. They commenced walking again.

They entered a valley with relatively heavy underbrush and pushed through it carefully, trying not to snag clothing or break branches in such a way as to leave a trail. It was slow going and hard work.

When he judged it to be midday—it was too cloudy to know for sure—he called a halt and offered Piper one of their precious protein bars.

"Are you going to have one, too?" she asked.

"I'll be okay for now. I had a big supper last night," he replied.

"Don't be a hero on me. You need to keep up your strength if you're not going to become a liability to me out here."

He managed not to stare, but just barely. *Him* a liability to *her*? Was that just her army training showing, or did she seriously see herself as more capable out here than him? Fascinating. Who in the hell *was* she?

The far side of the valley was very steep and rocky. It wasn't exactly a sheer cliff, but wasn't far from it.

"How are you at free-climbing rocks?" she asked him as they stared left and right at the long stone wall in either direction.

"I've done it before," he answered. "And it looks like a time-consuming detour to go around this."

"Up it is, then," she declared. "I'll go first. I've done a lot of rock climbing."

Of course she had.

She backed up and studied the face for several minutes, planning her route. Then she stepped up to the wall, reached for the first handholds and winced.

"What hurts?" he asked instantly.

"Ribs. Your buddy worked me over pretty good."

"He isn't my buddy. Yousef is a psychopath and a terrorist." He added, "If you've got broken ribs, we shouldn't try this climb."

"Your makeshift padding worked, as far as I can tell," she grunted as she hauled herself upward. "My ribs are just bruised."

"Still. If this climb is going to hurt too much, we can go around."

"Pain is weakness leaving the body," she commented absently as she eyed the next handholds above her.

He snorted. "The rest of that saying is, 'Unless you've served in the military. Then it's probably arthritis.'"

A burst of laughter escaped her. "Don't make me laugh. I'll lose focus and fall."

Grinning, he continued climbing behind her, privately enjoying the view of her tush and long, lean legs.

They were mostly silent during the climb, communicating only to warn each other of loose rocks, or to point out a possible change to their route up the wall. It took nearly a half hour to make the climb, and as they flopped on their bellies on the flat ground above, they were both breathing hard.

"Well. That should slow down Mahmoud and company a bit," he commented.

He climbed to his feet and helped Piper to hers. He noticed that she was moving distinctly more creakily than before. "Do you need to stop and rest for a while?" he asked quietly.

"No. Let's press on."

As impressed as he was by her fortitude in the face of pain and exhaustion, he said, "Look, we can't walk straight through for the next week. You're going to have to rest sometime."

"They're following us by now, right?"

"I expect so."

"Then now is the time to press on. Our tactical advantage will come from moving farther and faster than they can possibly expect us to. When they don't find us right away, they'll get frustrated. The rigors of tracking us will start to weigh on their minds, and we'll have won."

"Okay. Who are you?" he blurted. "That's seriously military-trained thinking."

"I told you. I'm in the army."

"Well, yeah. There's army and then there's *army*. Not that many women run around with field infantry units."

"There are plenty of women in the infantry, thank you very much. And we keep up with the boys just fine."

He threw up his hands. "I meant no offense. Suffice it to say I'm impressed by your training."

"I'll be sure to pass that on to my instructors."

He shook his head. "Fine. We'll press on a little while longer. But tonight, we stop, find or build a shelter, and get some proper rest."

"Fair enough."

She met his gaze, smiling a little as she did so. Hark. Was the ice queen's wall of suspicion actually beginning to thaw?

Chapter Nine

Pain, exhaustion, relief and fear pulled at Piper in about equal amounts. The idea of building a nice fire, getting dry and warm, and curling up for a long nap sounded better than just about anything on earth. But she wasn't wrong. Now was the exact time to press on and push the hardest. When other people would stop and rest, this was the moment to put distance between herself and her captors.

The Medusas had a long history of capitalizing on their foes underestimating the capabilities of women, and this was definitely one of those times.

Thankfully, Goldeneyes was insanely fit himself and able to keep up with her as she pushed herself to her prodigious physical limits.

A CIA officer, huh? That certainly explained a lot. She was inclined to believe him. After all, he'd been unflaggingly protective of her from the very beginning, and he, too, had kept his cool in multiple high-stress situations.

It started to rain again as darkness fell. The rain became a downpour, and the temperature dropped precipitously.

She knew it didn't have to get colder than about sixty-five degrees for hypothermia to become a threat, and it was definitely colder than that now. Neither she nor her companion had proper clothing for cold, and their blankets were soaked, too.

Vaguely, it occurred to her that they should probably consider stopping and trying to find shelter. But where? She looked around and saw only trees and more trees. If they had a parachute they could build a great shelter. She couldn't remember what she was supposed to do if she didn't have one.

Alarm shot through her. Something was wrong with her.

She stumbled just then, and barely managed to right herself without face planting. Hmm. That was unlike her. She wasn't usually clumsy.

"Are you okay?" Goldeneyes asked from behind her.

"Uh, yeah. Fine."

"What's eight times nine?"

"What?" She turned around to peer at him in the thick darkness. The heavy cloud cover made it nearly impossible to see out here.

"What's eight times nine? Quick. Just tell me the answer."

"No fair. I suck at math."

"Answer me. Right now."

"Um…fifty-six—no. Seventy-two."

"Too slow. We're stopping," he announced.

"No! We have to keep going!"

"You're either exhausted or hypothermic or both. We're stopping. Now," he said firmly.

"Speak for yourself. I'm keeping going." She turned to face forward and disorientation swirled around her as she stared at the thick trees in every direction. Where was she supposed to go?

A hand closed on her upper arm. It was gentle but strong enough that she couldn't ignore it. "Listen to me, Piper. You need to take care of yourself now if you're going to be able to keep going tomorrow."

"But Mahmoud—"

"Mahmoud is no hero. He'll call it quits if the weather gets this nasty. He's just a guy doing a job. But his number one priority is saving his own hide and his own comfort and well-being. We've got some time to rest."

Should she believe him? As she considered that, it gradually dawned on her that her brain was fuzzier than it ought to be. A lot fuzzier. "I don't know…" she mumbled.

"There's a rock face about a hundred meters in front of us. Maybe we can find an overhang that's reasonably dry. Come on. Let's go have a look."

For lack of any better ideas, she fell in behind him. He followed the line of the cliff for a little while and stopped in front of a long, narrow ledge about waist high. It jutted out, forming a flat roof over an indentation caused by long-term erosion of the layers of sandstone below.

He announced, "It's not great, but this will have to do."

They crawled under the narrow overhang, which was only about eight feet deep. The good news was the dead leaves and debris collected at the back of the space were more or less dry. Which meant the ground beneath was dry.

He made her go in first, and then he stretched out beside her with the garbage bag draped over his back to buffer the worst of the rain that blew in under the ledge.

As soon as they quit moving, the chill and the wet caught up with her, and she started to shiver. Over the next few minutes, the shivering worsened until her teeth chattered and her entire body shook violently.

Goldeneyes put his arms around her, but he didn't feel much warmer than her. After a couple minutes, he announced, "This isn't working. We're both getting more hypothermic. We'll be in serious trouble soon if we don't do something."

Hypothermia. That was bad. Deadly if not dealt with.

She'd memorized something having to do with it some-where before, a lifetime away from this moment.

She recited, "Dry clothing. Hot food and drink. Heat source. Share body heat."

"Did you get a merit badge in scouting for survival?" he asked humorously.

"Scouting? No. Medusas."

"Medusas? What?"

"Never mind," she mumbled.

He ticked off her list. "We have no dry clothing, and it'll take a fire to heat up drinks or food. For that matter, we could use a fire for the heat ourselves."

"Fire's a beacon," she mumbled.

"True. But we could die if we don't build one," he re-plied. "I don't think we have any choice."

"Shield it," she responded.

"Gotta build it first," he replied humorously. "And ev-erything out here is wet."

"Not everything." She reached into her front jeans pocket and pulled out a handful of cattail fuzz.

He peered between their bodies for a moment, obvi-ously working to figure out what she was holding in her fist. "Where did you get that?" he finally asked.

"Crossing one of the streams this morning. I grabbed some in case we needed a fire starter. My body heat dried it through the day."

He shocked her by dropping a fast, hard kiss on her mouth. "You are a goddess. You may have just saved us both."

She blinked, startled.

"Stay here while I go gather the driest wood I can find for a fire. I won't be long."

"Don't go far," she said quickly as fear of being alone

out here roared through her. Weird. She didn't fear forests, and she certainly didn't fear being by herself.

"I won't."

And then he was gone. Only the sound of rain batting at leaves and water dripping nearby broke the heavy silence. She huddled inside the damp blanket, her fingers and toes numb with cold, and her brain at least as numb.

She had to move. Do something to increase her circulation. Otherwise, she was going to drift off to sleep and her core body temperature would drop even more. Gritting her teeth, she threw off the blanket and crawled out of what little warmth the thing had provided.

She cleared a wide space on the ground under one end of the overhang, collecting the relatively dry leaves and debris for starting their fire. In the center of the space, she used a stout stick and her hands to dig a hole. When it was knee-deep, she worked on widening it.

If they built the fire in the bottom of the hole, the worst of its light would be hidden from distant eyes.

To additionally protect the flame from being spotted, she draped one of the blankets over bushes just beyond the firepit. She left a small gap between the top of the blanket and the rock face so smoke and heat could escape without setting the blanket on fire.

Not only would it act as a light shield, but it would also protect the fire from wind and the worst of the rain. They'd sacrifice some warmth from the blanket for themselves, but the payback in heat from the fire should more than make up for the loss.

She was just finishing up when a shadow loomed suddenly, startling her badly. Goldeneyes. Wow, she was seriously off her game.

He dumped a big armload of wood on the ground and nodded in approval at her preparations.

"I've got one more thing to do before we hunker down and get warm," he murmured. He dug in his pack and came up with a plastic grocery bag.

"What's in that?" she asked curiously.

"Fishing line and mousetraps."

"You're going to trap the perimeter?" she blurted in surprise. "Do you need help?"

"Nah. You're too cold. Do you feel comfortable starting the fire by yourself?"

She threw him her best "are you kidding?" look and asked dryly, "Do you have some matches, or am I rubbing sticks together?"

He tossed her a cigarette lighter from his pack, which she snagged neatly in midair.

He grinned. "Good luck."

Smart-ass. She would show him.

She piled up her dry cattail fluff and a few of the dry leaves and small twigs to prepare a fire. Using her body as an additional shield against the wind and rain, she used the cigarette lighter to start it.

She bent close, blowing gently on her fledgling blaze and feeding in more leaves. It smoked heavily, but gradually, the twigs caught fire. She fed it more twigs, and then sticks the diameter of her fingers. It took perhaps ten minutes for the fire to really get established. But eventually, she laid down branches the diameter of her wrists and held out her hands to warm them over the growing flames.

Now and then a gust blew a sheet of rain under the overhang and the fire guttered. But it had established a bed of coals and, tucked down in the bottom of the hole she'd dug, was mostly protected. She broke all the branches she was strong enough to crack into smaller lengths, and ringed the firepit with the wet wood to dry out some before she had to stack it on the blaze.

Heat began to roll off the fire, but it wasn't enough to beat back the violent cold making her shiver uncontrollably.

Gradually, though, her hands dried, warmed and regained feeling. She stripped off her soaked tennis shoes and socks and draped them over logs near the fire. Her toes were white and wrinkled with wet and cold, and she held her feet close to the fire to dry and warm, as well. It hurt like crazy as circulation returned to them, but at least they were thawing and warming.

Goldeneyes was gone a solid half hour before he called out from the woods, "I'm coming in now." Which was kind of him. She would have hated to break his neck in reflexive reaction if he successfully sneaked up on her.

"Wires set?" she asked.

"Yes. The mousetraps won't be very loud, but they should silence all the critters around them. I set some about four hundred yards out and another group about two hundred yards out."

He was correct. Abrupt cessation of sound out here would be as noticeable as a loud noise. Assuming the rain didn't drown out all sound. The good news: Mahmoud and his men had probably hunkered down in some sort of shelter to ride out this downpour.

"Give me your water bottles," Goldeneyes directed her. He set those beside the fire to warm up the water inside.

Good idea.

But then he stripped off his sweatshirt and T-shirt. His bare chest looked primal in the flickering firelight. He reached for the hem of her sweatshirt, as well.

"Whoa, whoa, whoa," she blurted.

"You said it yourself," he said. "We have to get dry. We need to dry out our clothes if we're going to have any chance of warming up."

She frowned at him, trying hard to come up with some reasonable argument to refute his logic.

Damn. She had nothing. She reached for her hem and winced as her ribs gave a mighty protest.

"Let me do that for you," he said quickly. Very gently, he slipped his hands under the wet cotton and pushed it up to her neck. He grabbed the cuffs and tugged while she pulled her arms free of the sleeves. A grunt of pain slipped out of her mouth.

"Easy," he murmured. He stretched the neck of the garment with his hands and lifted it very carefully over her battered face. The cold air hit her bare skin and she gasped.

He sucked in a hard breath as well, but it was probably the sight of the copious bruises across her torso that made him suck wind like that. She gathered the white cotton of her shirt across her middle, clutching it for a second in embarrassment before she steeled herself to shuck it off in turn. Still, after she took it off, she reflexively wadded it in her hands, clutched at her throat, clinging to its meager protection.

Carefully averting his eyes from her bruises and bra, he spread her sweatshirt out next to his on the far side of the fire, and then he held out his bare arm to her in invitation. He never once looked her way.

It was a small courtesy, but it meant a lot to her. She hadn't realized how embarrassed she would be by the evidence of her beating. Maybe it was a reflection of the helplessness she'd felt while she'd been tied to that chair taking punches.

Appreciation that he didn't force himself upon her in any way also registered. He waited patiently, his arm extended, not a muscle in his body moving. She stared at his chest for a long moment. It was muscular. Strong. It shouted of danger to her.

And yet she realized with a start that she trusted him. He had never hurt her before, and he wasn't about to start now. All at once, she shook out the torn cotton shirt and spread it on the ground. Then she scooted over close to him.

He gasped involuntarily as she pressed her side against his. "You're an ice cube, Piper. Why didn't you tell me earlier that you were freezing?"

"W-was t-trying t-to ignore it."

"While I admire your efforts to be tough, we're in this together. Please tell me if you're cold or hungry or thirsty or tired, so I can take care of you."

"I'm all of th-the above," she admitted against his chest.

His arm tightened around her shoulders, protectively but not restrictively. An odd sense of comfort flowed over her, gradually sinking into her. Or maybe that was just his body heat.

"We probably need to take off our jeans, too," he sighed into her hair. "Mine are soaked, and I assume yours are, too. I didn't want to freak you out by suggesting all at once that we strip down."

She considered his words. What he said made sense. At least her mental functions seemed to be returning a little bit.

"You can take your jeans off and I'll leave mine on if you want," he offered.

"But that would mean you'd be sitting around in wet pants, not warming up," she objected.

"I put you through hell the past several days. It's the least I can do for you."

"We'll both take our pants off," she declared.

It was awkward working in the tight confines of the narrow space, and the wet denim clung to their legs stubbornly. They ended up having to take turns lying on their backs and holding their legs up while the other one peeled the jeans off.

Piper giggled as she yanked at his pants and accidentally got a fistful of his tighty-whities. He made a fast grab to preserve his modesty.

"It's not as if I haven't been exposed to all of your… equipment…already," she announced.

"I'm sorry about that."

"You can quit apologizing now. I got the message loud and clear that you deeply regret everything that has happened to me."

He shifted to lie on his side facing the fire, close to the back wall of their little shelter. She still sat upright, and he spooned lightly around her lower torso from behind.

"You'll be warmer if you lie down beside me," he murmured. "Let me block the cold coming off the rocks at our backs from you while the fire warms your front."

"Won't you get colder?"

"Nah. I'm a furnace. Always have been. Once this fire gets a little bigger, you and I will both be toasty in no time."

She stretched out beside him, cuddling back against his body. He was fully as cold as she was. It was kind of him to lie about being all right. If nothing else, the fire could warm her, and her body heat would warm him up a little.

"As soon as the other blanket is dry, you should put it over you," she told him.

"By the time it's dry, most of our clothes should be dry, too."

"Not the jeans, though. Those will take a while," she replied.

Silence fell between them as they spooned next to the fire. She curled around the firepit, as close as she could get without being singed. With him pressed tightly against her back, she actually began to warm up and feel semihuman again.

"I'm doing better," she announced. "Do you want to switch places?"

"Nah. I'm good. You're warming me up."

With dryness and heat came awareness of the man pressed against her back from neck to ankles. His chest was muscular, his belly slabbed in muscle, as well. His legs were hairy, but the hair was soft against her skin. Whisker stubble on his face was rough against her shoulder. His knees tucked up under hers where they bent around the fire, and his arm was heavy across her middle.

She was surrounded by him. By his skin and muscle and sinew.

Not only did she feel almost warm, but she also felt almost safe. Finally.

She let out a big sigh, releasing the crushing fear and relentless stress of the past few days. Not surprisingly, a few tears escaped her eyes and ran sideways over her nose and dripped off her temple.

"Hey," he said in a low voice. "What's wrong?"

"Nothing. This is just relief."

"Ah." A pause. "That's good." Another longer pause. "Although I would be remiss if I didn't tell you we're not out of the woods yet. Literally or figuratively."

She smiled a little. "I hear you. But being chased by bad guys and evading them in the woods is more in my regular wheelhouse. I'm trained to deal with doing that, and it doesn't freak me out."

"Ri-i-ight."

Damn. She'd given away too much again. This guy lulled her into a sense of safety and relaxation where she spoke without thinking and kept tossing him hints about who she really was. She had to stop that!

"For the record," she said reflectively, "I really appreciate everything you did to take care of me and protect me

Everything except that tackle in the field when I tried to escape. That hurt."

He chuckled into her ear. "I would have let you go except one of the guys would have stepped out of the van to look for us any second. I was afraid we would get mowed down by an AK-47 before we got to the truck stop."

"Speak for yourself. I'm pretty fast."

"I know that now," he replied. "But I didn't then."

"Are you really in the CIA?" she asked.

"I really am. And that's classified, by the way. When we get back to the real world, I'll need you not to tell anyone about it."

"Or what? You'll have to shoot me?" she quipped.

"I could never shoot you. I—" He broke off.

"You what?"

"I care too much about you."

She froze in his arms, and he went just as still.

At long last, she mumbled, "You don't know anything about me."

"I know you're braver than just about any woman I've ever met, and you have a great sense of humor, even in the face of terrible, terrible events. You're unbelievably calm in a crisis, and you keep your wits about you under pressure. You tried to protect me by telling Mahmoud you were Persephone Black, and you sure as hell didn't owe me a damned thing in that scenario. Which tells me you have a noble and self-sacrificing streak a mile wide. And, of course, you're freaking beautiful. But that goes without saying."

She didn't know what to say. Eventually, she mumbled, "You still don't know most of the important stuff about me."

"Okay, tell me something important about you," he murmured.

"You first."

He sighed, "When are you going to learn to trust me? I mean, I get why you're cautious, but I promise, we're on the same side."

That might be true, but her secrets weren't the kind she could share with anyone. Her life, and those of her teammates, depended on total secrecy around the Medusa Project.

He surprised her by continuing. "Fine. Something important about me. Let's see. I'm from New Hampshire originally. I was amused when you said my name should be Chad or Blaine. And yes, I have actually been sailing off Martha's Vineyard. I grew up being the preppy you accused me of being."

"Ha. Nailed it."

His arms tightened a bit around her. "Remind me to add being perceptive to your list of virtues."

"Trust me. I have plenty of vices," she retorted.

"Name one."

"I love junk food. If I could get away with it, I would live on pizza, chips and soda. Oh, and ice cream. Lots of ice cream."

"What do you do to stay so fit, then?"

"I do my job. I run around in the woods, do calisthenics and swim and run basically all day long every day."

"What's your job?" he asked, sounding surprised.

She paused. "Here's the thing. My job is classified."

"So I gather. You know what NODs are. You walk and talk like a warrior. Your survival skills are outstanding. Are you an infantry officer?"

"I was one."

He went still, obviously thinking hard.

Dammit, she'd done it again. She'd gone and revealed way too much about herself to him. She didn't need him making the next leap of logic that she'd moved beyond plain-Jane infantry to the Special Forces.

She half turned in his arms so she could look up at him. He stared down at her intently, obviously weighing everything he knew of her and drawing his own conclusions.

"Can you do me a favor?" she murmured up at him.

The thoughtful look in his eyes was abruptly replaced by sharp alertness as he stared back at her. "What's that?"

"Would you kiss me, please?"

Caution leaped into his eyes. "Why do you ask for that? I would have thought that after I, um, attacked you, you would want nothing to do with me."

"In the first place, you didn't attack me. You simulated attacking me, and you were as much of a gentleman as it's possible to be in a situation like that. In the second place, I would like to replace the bad memory of that event with a good one."

"You're sure?" he asked soberly.

"Positive."

His chin dipped, his mouth moving toward hers slowly. Carefully. Like he expected her to change her mind—or maybe attack him. When their lips were no more than a few inches apart, his upper torso pressing her opposite shoulder down into the ground, he murmured, "Are you okay?"

Hell, no. She wasn't okay. The fake attack had been traumatic no matter how nice he'd been about it. It had been a chilling demonstration in what it felt like to be helpless and at the mercy of another human being. What if he hadn't been such a decent guy? What if he hadn't taken care of her and only simulated the attack?

She mumbled aloud, "Yes, I'm okay. And thank you for practicing good consent behavior. But could you kiss me already? The suspense is making me nervous."

Which was to say, she was terrified her courage would

desert her and that she would back out of her request. Worse, if she didn't get back in this saddle right now, with this man, she had a sinking suspicion it would be a very long time before she trusted any other man to kiss her.

"It's only the suspense making you nervous?" He almost sounded disappointed that it wasn't him doing so. News flash: *he* was making her nervous. More than she wanted to acknowledge, in fact. She'd just spent the past half hour more naked than not, pressed against him skin to skin, vividly aware of his body against hers.

Her heart raced and her breath hitched as he closed the final gap.

His lips brushed across hers lightly, a bare caress, so feathery she might not have felt it if she hadn't been looking straight at him.

She froze, and he stopped, apparently waiting for her to gauge her reaction to the bare touch of their mouths.

She lifted her chin to kiss him this time, a little more firmly. A little more actual mouth-on-mouth contact.

It was his turn to freeze. Had her hand not been resting on his chest directly over his heart, she would've missed the abrupt acceleration of his heartbeat, pounding hard against her palm. Well, then.

What *was* she going to do with this man? She certainly knew what she would like to do with him. Did she dare?

If the past few days had taught her nothing else, it was that life was too short to let chances like this pass her by.

She kissed him again, more passionately this time. Was he aware that his hips were rocking a little against hers? Oh, yes. She wanted him, too.

"You okay?" he breathed.

"Getting there…"

Chapter Ten

Getting there, indeed. Zane was way ahead of her, racing toward desires that were surely far, far beyond what she had in mind. He'd spent most of the past few days watching this woman, practically around the clock. He knew every curve of her face, had memorized every angle and curve of her body, the expressions that flashed across her mobile face—

Get a grip, man. This was the woman he'd kidnapped, for crying out loud. Guilt roared through him that he'd put this wonderful, warm, generous woman through hell. The last thing he wanted to do was take advantage of her vulnerable, emotional state. Hell, for all he knew, she was suffering a case of Stockholm syndrome, where the prisoner began to empathize too much with his or her kidnapper in a psychological-defense reaction to extreme duress.

She captured his mouth with her soft, sweet lips. She felt like an angel and tasted like heaven—

His brain reengaged sharply. He had no business kissing her. Yes, he got that she wanted to reassure herself that she was not traumatized. He was willing, happy even, to help her with that.

But no more than that. He owed her complete self-restraint on his part. If he cared about her at all, he would leave her the hell alone.

He went perfectly still, letting her call the shots. But

damned if she didn't continue letting her warm, resilient lips linger against his. Her mouth was fully as warm and pliable as it looked and he loved how her lips molded to his.

She deepened the kiss just a tiny bit.

Mistake, mistake, mistake!

She shifted beside him, rolling more fully onto her back and twining her arms lightly around his neck to take him with her. He propped his left elbow between her and the edge of the firepit. He partially covered her body with his but was careful not to let much of his weight come to rest upon her. No need to scare her when she was just starting to relax.

What are you doing, you idiot?

He answered himself that he was helping her move past the trauma of her near rape. That he was letting her use his body to heal herself.

Liar. You totally want this woman.

The fire was hot on his forearm, but it didn't hold a candle to the heat suddenly pouring off the women beneath him. Her fingers slipped into his hair and tugged his head down to hers once more, pulling him more urgently into their kiss now.

Ignoring the warnings of logic and his better impulses, he obliged her and kissed her even more deeply, opening his mouth a little in invitation, but letting her set the overall pace. Her tongue traced the outline of his lips and then the sharp edges of his teeth. He held himself stock-still, not moving a muscle throughout her explorations.

She tilted her head to one side, fitting their mouths more tightly together, giving herself even deeper access to his mouth. Her chest lifted off the ground slightly, arching up toward his body. Her cotton-covered breasts rubbed lightly against his chest, and his breath hitched. Hard.

Man, that felt good. He silently wished for her to do it

again. But no way would he ask such a thing of her. This was her show. She called the shots tonight. Whatever she wanted, he would give her. No less, and no more.

Their tongues swirled together, mimicking the sex act in a carnal dance that made him wild with desire.

He reined in his urges ruthlessly, refusing to give in to his baser impulses.

Her right hand slid across his shoulder, over the bulge of his biceps, and trailed down his arm. Then her fingers lifted away from him momentarily. Mentally, he howled a protest. But then her hand touched his waist, tracing a path of destruction across his ribs, following their length around the front of his torso toward his sternum.

Her hand dipped lower, her palm coming to rest upon his belly where the muscles were contracted so hard already that they were painful. He wasn't trying to show off—her touch just did that to him. It made him tight and hard all over, in fact. Schooling himself fiercely to be still and let her set the pace of their embrace, he actually shook from the effort of holding himself perfectly still.

At least he wasn't cold anymore. Far from it. Suddenly, he felt as if he was burning up. With need. And lust. For her. So much for hypothermia. One kiss from this woman and he was in danger of going up in flames.

What he really wanted to do was surge up over her, rid them both of their underwear, position himself between her legs and pump mindlessly into her body until the universe went supernova around them.

Instead, he gritted his teeth and suffered in silence, loving and hating the slowness of her explorations as her hand wandered at a snail's pace across his bare skin.

It was torture.

He owed her this.

In a way, it was fair payback for the torture he'd put her through.

But he was getting the better end of that deal by a lot.

His breath caught and then stopped altogether as she slide her hand down his stomach, lower and lower yet. Her fingers slipped inside the waistband of his underwear. They tangled briefly in his pubic hair, and then her hand encircled his engorged erection.

"Oh, thank goodness," she sighed.

"I beg your pardon?" he blurted out.

"I was worried when you didn't get at all aroused during our fake attack that you didn't find me attractive."

He snorted. "I don't find the idea of forcing myself on any woman the least bit attractive. In fact, I can't think of a bigger turnoff than that."

Her fingers gripped his erection firmly, sliding up and down the shaft experimentally. His hips lurched and he inhaled hard.

"I can't tell you how relieved I am to learn that a) you don't relish assaulting women, and b) that you do relish me at least a little."

He buried his face in her hair and mumbled, "This is not me being turned on a little. This is me being turned on like crazy."

"Hmm. What are we going to do about that?" she teased.

"We're doing nothing at all about it. You may do whatever you like to me and with me, Piper. But I refuse to lift a hand to you in any way, lest you feel the least bit threatened." To that end, he rolled onto his back beside her.

She raised up on an elbow to stare down at him. In the firelight, she looked like some primal goddess bathed in warm light, her hair glinting like spun filaments of gold, her eyes darker than the night around them.

"Are you serious?" she breathed. "I can do whatever I want to you?"

Whatever encompassed a very broad range of possibilities. But he owed her more than he could possibly begin to repay. This was the least he could do. He nodded firmly. "Whatever you want. My body is yours."

She rose on her knees beside him. Dry leaves crunched under the blanket he lay on, and the ground was hard and unyielding beneath him. Piper reached for his underwear, and he lifted his hips, helping her strip them off him. His erection jutted up, as hard and hot as newly forged steel. No help for it. And she seemed to want to look at all of him. So be it.

She ran her palms lightly over his torso, and he jumped occasionally as she found ticklish spots. Then she shocked him by stripping off her panties quickly and throwing a leg over his hips to straddle him.

"You'll get cold," he protested.

"The rocks overhead have warmed up and are radiating heat down on me," she countered.

"I don't have any condoms," he ground out from between his clenched teeth. The control it took to stay still beneath her as her lady parts rubbed up and down his shaft was almost more than he could muster.

She murmured, "I have a long-term birth control pellet in my arm. As long as you know you don't have any sexually transmitted diseases and haven't had sex with anyone else in a while, we're good."

"God, I love how prepared you are for every contingency," he muttered.

She laughed a little and then her moist, hot opening was poised at the tip of his penis. He reached up to grab her hips. To stop her.

Lord, man. Have you lost your mind?

Shut up, horny me. I'm trying to do the right thing here.

Aloud, he bit out, "Are you sure about this?"

She reached for his hands and drew them away from her hips. Slowly, she drew his hands up over his head and pressed them to the ground. Her breasts were right there, only inches from his mouth. He would love to suck and lick at them, to make her scream with pleasure—

But this was her night.

"Don't move," she murmured.

Such sweet torture. "I won't move," he ground out.

She sat back up and reached between their bodies. Her fist gripped him strongly and he couldn't stop the groan of pleasure that escaped his throat.

And then she was sliding down onto him, impaling herself by slow degrees. The heat and tightness of her body nearly made his eyes roll back in his head with pleasure.

His hands jerked reflexively, started to reach for her. "Keep your hands over your head, please," she whispered.

He slammed them back down to the ground as she started to move on him, easing herself up and down his erection. Gliding in and out of her tight sheath was almost more than he could stand. A need to explode into her rolled through him, and he clenched his teeth against it.

Long and slow and easy, she rode him. Gradually, her eyes glazed over with pleasure as she angled herself just right for maximum sensation. Her body undulated in the firelight, and was without question the sexiest thing he'd ever seen. Stretched out on a rack of pleasure beneath her, he lost himself in the blissful agony of letting her use his body however she wanted to.

And use it she did. She rode him faster, harder, until he was groaning aloud with the struggle not to come inside her then and there. She took pity on him and slowed her pace, letting him almost, but not quite, recover his composure before she rode him hard again.

Over and over she took him right to the brink of losing it and then backed off. Thankfully, she seemed wired for pleasure and achieved orgasms quickly, shuddering hard around him once. Twice. Three times.

Finally, when her body glistened with perspiration and his literally shook from the effort of holding back his own orgasm, she took pity on him.

Placing her hand in the middle of his chest, she leaned forward a little and rode him like a wild creature, a fey being of the night who'd come to him to take him on a fantasy adventure into a realm beyond humans.

"You can move a little if you want," she panted.

His hips bucked beneath hers as he surged up into her over and over, completely lost in the pleasure she'd created between them.

"Now!" she cried. "Let go now!"

He surged up into her with abandon, and she slammed down onto him, their bodies raging together toward release. His entire body arched up off the ground and she slapped her hand over his mouth hard as he coiled, clenched, and then his entire being exploded up into her. Up into the night. Up, up into the magic spell she'd woven around them both.

The power of it tore away everything, leaving him raw and exposed, his soul bared before her. He fell back upon the blanket and stared up at her as she panted above him. Her muscular legs were relaxed now around his hips.

Both her hands were planted on his chest now as she leaned on him, catching her breath. He knew the feeling. Running a marathon didn't even wipe him out like this.

She stared down at him in what he hoped was a modicum of satisfaction. Maybe even a bit of wonder shone in her clear, serene gaze.

"Warm enough?" he finally managed to gather his scattered thoughts enough to mumble.

She smiled knowingly. "I'm going to have to cool off and let the sweat dry before I dress again."

"That's a better problem to have than freezing half to death."

"I'll take this any day over being cold," she murmured.

He reached up to wrap his arms against her, and she came down to him willingly, sprawling across him bonelessly.

"Am I crushing you?" she murmured.

"Little thing like you? Nah."

"I'm not that little. I'm almost five foot nine. And I'm solid muscle."

"I'm six foot two, which makes you a shrimp in my world. And you may be muscular, but you're still lean. And may I say, beautifully proportioned."

"Thanks."

"Thank you," he replied fervently.

"I'm pretty sure I'm the one who should be thanking you for that," she retorted, pushing up on his chest to stare down at him.

Her hair fell in a curtain around them and he pushed it back and tucked it behind her ears. "Tell you what. I'll stop apologizing for getting you kidnapped and everything that followed if you'll stop thanking me for what we just shared. I assure you, I got at least as much pleasure from it as you did."

"Fair enough. But it was very nice of you to let me do whatever I wanted like that."

He laughed up at her, "I'm definitely adding that to my regular rotation of things to do in bed with beautiful, sexy women."

"Oh, and you have a lot of women in your bed? Your last name isn't Bond, is it?"

"No. My name is Zane." He added reluctantly, "Zane Cosworth."

Very, *very* few people outside of his immediate family knew his name. For him, it was the ultimate signal of trust he could give to anyone.

She stared down at him, looking deep into his eyes. At least she seemed to understand the significance of him giving her his real name.

"Nice to meet you, Zane Cosworth. My name is Piper Ford. Captain, United States Army."

"Nice to meet you, too, Captain Ford." And then he added, "Who are the Medusas?"

Chapter Eleven

She rolled off him and sat up, hugging her knees and staring into the fire. "How high is your security clearance?" she finally asked him.

"High enough that the name of it is classified," he answered quietly, sitting up beside her.

They really did need to get dry again before they thought about getting dressed. Ah, but what a way to get damp. He checked their clothes and turned over the sweatshirts and jeans to let their other sides dry.

Piper surprised him by saying, "The existence of the Medusas is a well-kept secret and needs to stay that way. I actually will have to kill you if you blab about it to anybody."

"You don't have to tell me about it if you don't want to," he responded seriously.

"No. I want to. You shared with me who you are, and if I don't miss my guess, risked your life to do that. I owe you no less."

He shrugged. "You're not wrong that knowing my name gives you a lot of power over me." He threw a couple logs on the fire and then settled beside her again. "This isn't a tit-for-tat relationship, Piper. I don't think in terms of you owing me anything. If you'd like to tell me about it, I would love to hear more about how you acquired your... atypical...skill set."

"The Medusas are a joint military task force, manned— or womanned, as the case may be—by women from all the branches of the military. We're a small all-purpose, all-female Special Forces team."

"All female?" he exclaimed under his breath.

"Correct."

"Well, that certainly explains a lot about you." He fell silently, obviously thinking back to everything he'd observed her do over the past several days. At length, he asked, "What were you doing at an elementary school in Houma, Louisiana?"

She laughed ruefully, "Dropping off my neighbor kid's lunch that he forgot in my car. I gave him a ride to school that day."

"What a stroke of luck that was. I couldn't have asked for a better hostage."

"Thanks, I think?" she replied wryly.

"You know what I mean. If Mahmoud and his guys were going to snatch anyone, you were the best possible person to end up being their prisoner. Have you had enhanced prisoner-of-war training?"

"Oh, yeah. We've had all the training."

"I thought so. When you knew how to take a punch, and you knew just how long to hold out under interrogation, and just how much information to eke out to your interrogator, I wondered where you'd learned that."

"I didn't tell Mahmoud much. I just parroted back stuff you'd already told me and then followed Mahmoud's lead from his questions."

"Like I said. You were the perfect hostage."

She poked at the fire with a stick, and the flames flared. This fire was life to them out here. It was recovery from hypothermia, dry clothing and hot water to drink and bring up their core temperatures.

"What kind of missions do these Medusas of yours run?"

"The previous Medusa teams did all sorts of missions. They guarded high-value female targets, went undercover on rescue missions, even freed a hijacked cruise ship. We mostly go into nations where women are ignored and marginalized, or where we can work under the radar because the locals aren't looking for women operators."

He nodded thoughtfully. "I can think of some situations where you ladies would be handy assets."

"Next time you need a woman, give us a call."

He laughed a little. "Next time I need a woman, I'll give *you* a call."

A blush made her cheeks feel even hotter than the fire did. "You know what I meant. Next time you need a female operations team, call the Medusas."

He grinned at her, and she ducked her head, embarrassed at her slip of the tongue and secretly a little delighted that he would consider calling her again. Most of the men she met were intimidated by her confidence, intelligence and self-possession. That, and her utter failure to be impressed by their macho posturing and mansplaining.

To his vast credit, Zane hadn't done any posturing or talking down to her ever. He had always treated her with complete respect. Even when he was pretending to rape her, for crying out loud.

"We need to get some sleep now that we're out of danger from hypothermia," he said, jerking her thoughts back to the situation at hand.

"We'll need to take turns sleeping and tending the fire," she responded.

"Are you tired now?"

She shook her head. "If you can sleep now, I'll take the first shift on fire-guard duty."

He pulled on his underwear and now-dry T-shirt, then stretched out along the back wall of the crevice on his side, facing her and the fire.

"Here." He held out his Ka-Bar knife to her, hilt first. She took it easily, hefting it in her hand, getting the feel for its balance.

He murmured, "Wake me up if there's any trouble at all."

"I will." She added, "But I can generally take care of myself, and I don't get afraid of the dark. It's my preferred work environment."

One corner of his mouth curved up as he planted his head on his bent elbow for a pillow. "Duly noted."

She added wood to the fire as the night grew colder around them. The rain came and went, sometimes nearly stopping, sometimes coming down hard.

During a lull, she pulled on her sweatshirt, which was mostly dry, and her jeans, which were damp but not sodden, and went out to gather more wood. She dug under the leaves for branches that were less soaked than the stuff lying above the deadfall, and hauled it back to their little camp.

On the way back, she noted with worry that the glow of the fire was still somewhat visible through the blanket they'd hung to screen it. Hopefully, this awful weather would drive Mahmoud and his men back to their cabin.

If they knew what was good for them, Mahmoud and his guys would leave the United States altogether. They had no way of knowing how soon they would be reported to the authorities and when a massive manhunt for them would be launched.

But one thing she'd learned in her Medusa training: there was no accounting for the logic of terrorists. If they were zealots, they might get it in their heads that she and Zane needed killing at all costs.

She spread out the wood to dry around the fire and stripped off her clothes to let them dry again. She passed the time alternating between watching Zane sleep and gazing out over the valley below for any sign of pursuit. Of course, the night was pitch-black with the total cloud cover, and she wasn't likely to see anything out there, let alone a team of stealthy bad guys. But it didn't keep her from staring apprehensively out into the darkness.

When she'd judged that several hours had passed, she reached out to touch Zane's foot. She was glad to feel that it was warm and dry. His eyes opened, and she reveled in their beautiful golden color. She'd nicknamed him well indeed.

"Hey, beautiful," he murmured in a sleep-roughened voice that made her toes curl in delight.

He sat up, stretching lazily and throwing off the blanket he'd been wrapped in. "Feels like it has gotten colder."

"It has. Rain's letting up, though."

"Okay. To sleep with you, Piper. I've got the watch and the fire."

They traded places, with her tucking back under the ledge on the bed of dried leaves, while he took her place huddling by the fire. The ground still held a little of his body heat, and the heat of the fire had collected under the overhang and warmed the rocks. They radiated that heat back gently now. It wasn't exactly a spa hotel room, but on a wet, freezing night, it wasn't half-bad.

And the blanket smelled like Zane with a hint of his male musk. She went to sleep with a smile on her lips.

ZANE REPLENISHED THE fire and settled down beside it, his feet stretched out beside the pit. He leaned back against a big rock, and alternated staring out into the darkness and glancing over at Piper. Her face was relaxed in sleep, and she was beautiful with the firelight glinting off her satin skin.

He couldn't get enough of looking at her. Which was a first for him. He wasn't the type to sit around gazing at any woman. He was all about the job. Always the job. In his line of work, anything less than total concentration spelled a mistake, and a mistake spelled death.

But then Piper had become the job.

The rain trailed off and finally stopped about an hour before dawn, according to his watch. He was glad for the earlier nap, but his eyes were gritty again, and his eyelids heavy. This was the worst time of day to stay awake. His biorhythms were declaring in no uncertain terms that this was sleep time.

He got up to gather more wood and check his trip wires. Moving around would help him stay awake.

He was on his way back to camp, just inside the inner ring of trip wires, when he heard a sharp snap behind him.

He froze. That was one of the outer mousetraps. He had set the wires thigh high specifically so that small and even medium-sized animals wouldn't set them off. It would take a bear—or a man…to hit the fishing line stretched between trees.

Gliding back toward camp on silent feet, he moved swiftly nonetheless. He had the advantage of having walked around out here a fair bit last night, and he knew his way back to Piper well.

He barged into the camp and dropped to his knees beside her, pressing his hand urgently over her mouth. She woke instantly, her eyes alert. He signaled fast, holding up three fingers and pointing in the direction of the tripped mousetrap. She nodded and yanked on her jeans and shoes at lightning speed while he pushed the pile of dirt near the firepit back into the hole, dousing the flames. He packed the water bottles, wadded up the blankets and shoved them in his rucksack, and helped Piper scatter leaves all over their little site.

They had no more time to cover their tracks, for another, closer snap sounded in the woods. Whoever was moving around out there was headed this way. And was now two hundred yards away.

He hand signaled for Piper to take the lead. She took off, heading out of their little camp away from the sound. She moved so fast through the trees that he seriously struggled to keep up with her.

Damn, she was good.

Which might just save their lives out here. He would never in a million years have guessed that a woman could run that silently, that quickly and sure-footedly through terrain like this.

After about fifteen minutes, he was breathing hard. After a half hour at the killer pace, he was sucking wind.

Thankfully, Piper stopped without warning, ducking under the spreading branches of a pine tree and melting into the deep shadows there. The sky was just starting to turn gray in the east.

You okay? she mouthed.

He nodded, concentrating on breathing deeply and exhaling fully. He had to get as much oxygen to his screaming muscles as possible.

In exactly one minute, she breathed, "Ready to go?"

He nodded resolutely. At least when she took off like a bat out of hell this time, he was expecting it. There was no way Mahmoud and his guys could move this fast. Not if they were having to track his and Piper's movements. And to her credit, she was following anything but a straight line out here. At varying intervals, she made direction changes of at least thirty degrees or more. Assuming they were even making a trail that could be followed, she was giving Mahmoud's tracker hell.

They settled into one pattern, though. Every ten minutes, she stopped for about a minute to let both of them catch their breath. They didn't speak. They just breathed deeply and then took off again.

Dawn came and went, and early morning came and went. And still they ran. She slowed the pace a little, to a ground-eating run that allowed them to pass quietly through the forest but put a ton of distance behind them. Hopefully, they were putting a ton of distance between themselves and whoever was behind them, too.

In a perfect world, that had been a bear.

But in a worst-case world, they had to assume Mahmoud and his men were hot on their trail.

On and on they ran, until Zane was so exhausted he could barely see straight. How Piper was continuing to hold this pace, he had no idea. Maybe she was superhuman. They had to have covered four or five miles before she finally stopped again, just shy of a wooded ridgeline.

"I'll top the ridge first and have a look on the other side," she whispered in his ear. "Wait here."

He nodded and turned automatically to keep a lookout behind them, searching for any sign of pursuit or movement back there.

Piper was gone maybe sixty seconds before she came back grinning ear to ear. "C'mon," she murmured.

He followed her across the ridge and stared into the valley. Cleared pastures stretched below, and two long, narrow barns made of galvanized aluminum pointed toward a small house at the far end of the valley.

"Praise the Lord and pass the potatoes," he muttered.

Piper took off down the hillside, fully as fast as she'd run from the campsite initially. He felt it, too. The burst of adrenaline at the idea of this nightmare being over was huge. He rode the wave of renewed energy to fly down the hill beside her. They hit the edge of the pasture and she veered into the trees beside it.

They would have gone faster in the cut grass beyond the barbed wire fencing but would've been out in the open. He had to give Piper credit for proper caution.

It took them almost ten minutes to run the length of the big pasture, parallel the barns and then swerve toward the house. A rusty pickup truck was parked beside it. Please God, let someone be home.

They raced across the front yard and up onto the covered front porch. Piper knocked on the door. The next few seconds were perhaps the longest in Zane's life as he prayed for someone to be in. For there to be a working phone. For him and Piper to be safe.

The front door opened, and a man of about fifty years stood there. "Little early to be out selling stuff, isn't it?" he growled.

"Please forgive us for bothering you," Piper said politely. "My friend and I have been out hiking and got lost. We desperately need to use a telephone and call for help."

The farmer looked her up and down and then did the same to Zane. For his part, Zane smiled and did his best to look nonthreatening. But the truth was, he and Piper probably looked like ax murderers. He had several days' growth of beard going, and both of them were covered in mud and debris from their wild run through the woods.

"You look like you got lost in the woods," the farmer grunted. "Come on in. Phone's in the kitchen."

Piper stopped by the phone and looked at him questioningly. "Who can get here faster—your people or mine?"

"Mine," he answered without hesitation.

She gestured at the old princess-style phone hanging on the wall, and he picked up the receiver and dialed. He chose the emergency number he'd memorized before this mission. It went straight to a CIA crisis-response desk.

He rattled off his identification credentials and waited impatiently while they were verified.

A female voice said, "You are authenticated. Go ahead."

"I'm blown on an undercover assignment and need immediate emergency extraction. Armed hostiles are in close pursuit of me." He looked at the farmer, whose mouth hung open. "What's the street address here?"

The farmer shook himself and answered. Zane relayed the address and then said, "We need a police helicopter here ASAP, along with armed law enforcement response."

"We?" the woman at the other end of the phone asked briskly. "How many people need extraction?"

"I have a civilian female with me. I brought her with me from the undercover operation, and she will also need transport. She's a material witness in the investigation."

"Understood. Is this a good call-back number?"

"Yes."

"Shelter in place. We'll have people out to you as quickly as possible. I show you being in a fairly remote area. Police response may take up to an hour."

"Tell them to hurry," he bit out.

"Will do."

Zane disconnected the call and passed the receiver to Piper. She dialed quickly, and her call was answered immediately, too.

"Hey, Rebel, it's Piper."

Zane heard the exclamation from the other end of the line. But Piper cut off whatever the other woman was saying. "Look, Rebel. We're in trouble. I've got a team of foreign terrorists on my tail. Same guys who kidnapped me. Police response has been called in to this location, but if you could have Major T call in any military assets that are close by, that would be helpful. If he can get a National Guard helicopter scrambled to this location, and maybe a gunship, that would be good."

Zane listened as she relayed the farm's address. There was a pause, and then the person at the other end of the line spoke for several seconds.

Piper's expression went grim as she listened. "Understood. Thanks."

She hung up and surprised Zane by turning to the farmer. "Is there anyone else here besides you, sir?"

"Nope. Wife already left for work."

"Do you happen to have any guns and ammunition here?"

The farmer frowned. "Why do you ask?"

"A satellite looking down at this position reports a team of five humans moving in this direction. They're about a half mile from the ridge at the back end of your pastures. We've got about fifteen minutes until they get here. And my source said they looked armed."

Zane winced. Mahmoud and his guys would come in hot with AK-47s blazing, and possibly more weaponry than that.

The farmer appeared hesitant.

Zane said quietly, "Look. I know you have no reason to trust us. But I'm a federal agent, and she's a military officer. We're running from some very, very bad men. We all need to get in your truck and drive away from here as fast as possible."

"Truck's broken down."

"Can we get it running in fifteen minutes?" Zane asked urgently. "The government will buy you a new truck—hell,

I'll buy you a new truck—if we can at least get it moving and get a few miles away from here."

"Naw, man. It's dead. Won't even turn over, let alone start."

"Tractor?" Piper bit out.

"It's parked behind the chicken sheds—"

"Too far for us to reach before Mahmoud's guys would be within shooting range," Zane responded.

Piper nodded in agreement. "Sir, we need you to bring us any firearms you have in the house. What's your name? Mine's Piper, and this is Zane."

"Irv Smith."

"Nice to meet you, Irv. I'm so sorry we've brought this trouble to your door. My partner is right. The government will compensate you fully for any damage to your property today."

Zane was impressed with the calm, confident, soothing tone of voice Piper used on the man. It had the desired effect, too. The farmer smiled a little and nodded at her.

"Guns?" Zane prompted gently.

The farmer headed for a spare bedroom, and Zane followed close on the guy's heels with Piper close on his. They had to step around and over an elaborate model train set that took up most of the floor.

Irv opened a closet and pulled out a .22 shotgun and a larger Remington rifle. He rummaged on the upper shelf and emerged with four boxes of ammo, two for each weapon.

Zane looked at Piper. "You wanna shoot long range or short?"

"Long. I've had a fair bit of sniper training." She picked up the Remington, and he picked up the .22.

She looked over at the flabbergasted farmer. "How true do these fire?"

"I been huntin' with 'em for nigh on twenty years. Don't miss much."

Piper nodded. "Do you have any more weapons in the house?"

"My wife's got a little peashooter she carries in her purse from time to time. She don't usually carry when she goes to work. Lemme see if it's around."

Zane gave the .22 a quick once-over, checking for rust, familiarizing himself with the trigger action and practicing loading it. Piper did the same with the Remington, handling it with smooth ease.

"Aha!" the farmer exclaimed. From a drawer that looked to be full of ladies' lingerie, he extracted a dinky little handgun.

Zane said, "You keep that. Use it to protect yourself if it comes to that."

"What's in the barns?" Piper asked. "Chickens?"

"Yup. Nearly a thousand laying hens. Raise 'em free-range, I do."

Zane said quickly, "The barns are made of aluminum siding. No protection from gunfire. Might as well be inside a tin can."

Piper nodded tersely. "This house will offer the best cover, then. If you head down to the barns, Irv, you can hide there. We'll draw the gunfire up this way and you'll be safe. The bad guys want us, not you."

"You sure? I'd be a third gun."

Zane smiled warmly and patted the older man's shoulder. "We appreciate the offer, but that little pop gun isn't going to do much good against the firepower these bastards are going to bring to bear on us. Piper's right. You need to head on down to the barns and stay out of this. We don't want you to get hurt. And Uncle Sam will build you a new house and renovate the whole farm after this. So don't panic if you hear stuff getting shot up."

Piper added, "Go look after your hens. We'll take care of the bad guys."

"All right, then." Looking worried, Irv headed out the back door and hurried toward the barns, pistol in hand.

"ETA?" Zane asked Piper as they moved furniture out of the way of windows and created clear pathways from one window to the next.

She looked at the clock on the kitchen stove. "Ten minutes."

He commented, "If they try to search the barns, we'll shoot at them and draw them up here, yes?"

"Yes." She asked, "Will they try to surround us or will they take up protected firing positions and pepper us for a while?"

"Mahmoud will want to kill us both. But he's got several young guys on his team. My guess is they won't be experts at field-of-fire control. I don't see him fully surrounding the house because he won't trust the youngsters not to shoot him or his more experienced guys. I could see him trying to burn us out."

She nodded. "Then we shoot just enough to draw them up here to us and then lie low until they try to close in on the house."

"Fair enough. And then we'll improvise when the plan goes to hell," he added dryly.

She smiled at him. "Exactly."

Her grin was almost wolfish. "Are you enjoying this?" he asked incredulously.

She shrugged. "I want to protect that farmer, and I have to admit I'd like to drop a few of these bastards. Particularly that Yousef guy who took so much pleasure in beating me up. I'm not afraid, if that's what you're asking me. I'm trained for this stuff."

"Thank God," he replied fervently.

She disappeared into the kitchen and emerged with two big, sharp butcher knives. She passed him one, presenting him with the handle. "Mahmoud won't expect me to know what to do in a firefight. He still thinks I'm the assistant principal of an elementary school."

Zane grinned. "He's in for a hell of shock when he sees what you can do." If this came down to hand-to-hand combat, his money was on Piper. He tucked the knife in the back of his belt, checked the load on his weapon one more time and settled down to wait with the extra ammo on the floor beside him.

Piper went into the kitchen and made another phone call. Zane listened as she said quietly, "ETA on our hostiles?"

There was a pause, no doubt for the satellite technician to get a fix on their position and look for warm bodies. Piper listened for a minute and then stayed on the line.

She called to him in the living room, "ETA three to four minutes. They're about halfway down the side of the pasture. Five incoming."

They had tipped the refrigerator over on its side across the back door, and they'd pulled a bulky wood stereo console across the front door to barricade it. Piper knelt behind the refrigerator now, watching the approach to the house from that direction.

She called, "My eyes in the sky say they appear to be circling wide of the barns to approach the house from the west side."

That would put Mahmoud and company facing the living room's side wall. "Will you have a shot at them from the kitchen?" he called back.

"Yes. I can shoot out the window over the sink."

They had already opened every window in the house a few inches so they could put the barrels of their weapons on the sills to steady them. He moved to the living room window on the west wall of the house and scanned the tree line a little over a hundred yards away.

From that distance, the AK-47s should shred the house's siding and quickly start putting rounds into the living room. Zane glanced about and spied a hefty coffee table in front of the television. He jumped up, grabbed it and dumped it on its side in front of the window for extra protection. It was made of oak planks a good two inches thick. That sucker would stop bullets for a good long time.

"Have you got decent cover in there?" he called.

"The kitchen sink is enameled cast iron. I've got my shooting nest all set up. You?"

"My nest is built. I've got a two-inch thick oak table in front of me," he replied.

"Check. I'll let you know when they emerge from the trees. If they head for the barns, I'll call the shots."

God, it was nice working with a highly trained Special Forces operative. He couldn't think of anyone he would rather have beside him in a gunfight.

There was one last thing he needed to do before this show went down. He propped his rifle at the ready and went into the kitchen, where Piper was looking out the back door.

"Eyes in the sky have us covered," he murmured. "They'll see our hostiles well before you will."

"I know," she sighed. "Looking for them just gives me something to do." She turned away from the door to gaze at him questioningly. "Are you really as calm as you look, Zane?"

He stepped forward and drew her into his arms. "I am. I've done everything in my life that I ever wanted to, and

I found you. My life is complete. If today's my day to die, I'm at peace with that."

He dipped his chin and kissed her reverently, doing his best to convey just how genuinely extraordinary she was to him. Her arms went around his neck and he swept her body up against his, holding her tight as she kissed him back desperately.

Her intensity sucked him in, wrapping him in the scent and feel of her, drawing him into that special magic the two of them created between them. It was a place of trust and safety, where nothing could touch either one of them.

As their mouths joined, so did their bodies, pressed together from chest to knee. Even though they were fully clothed, he felt every contour of her, remembered the feel of her skin against his, her heat embracing his, her arms and legs wrapped around him in the throes of passion. It was all right there again. Everything they'd shared between them last night.

It hadn't been a dream. It was real, and it was here, right now.

"I won't let anything hurt you," he murmured against her sweet lips.

"Same," she breathed into his mouth. "I've got your back."

He plunged his hand into her thick, soft hair, washed clean by the rain. "Don't be a hero on me. I need you to come out of this alive. Promise me, Piper."

"I will if you will."

"I promise. No heroics," he said as sincerely as he could. It was a total lie. He would do whatever it took to get her out of this day safely. Including sacrificing himself.

The phone rang, jarring both of them out of the moment.

She grabbed for the phone and he spun away, moving quickly back to his shooting nest and settling in for whatever happened next. *C'mon, Mahmoud. Show your face. Give me a clean shot so I can blow your head off.*

He had never been more eager to end a mission with a kill than this one.

The house went silent as he and Piper waited, mentally preparing themselves for the chaos to come. He focused on draining all emotion from his mind and becoming cold and calm. A killing machine. He had no doubt whatsoever she was doing the same.

"One minute out," she announced.

Thank God. Her voice was calm, cool as a cucumber. She was mentally ready to rock and roll.

So was he…almost. Only one emotion refused to go away. Fear. Specifically, fear for Piper's safety. Dammit.

He concentrated fiercely on transforming it into utter determination to do what was necessary to keep her safe. When it had become a hard kernel in the middle of his chest, he took one last deep breath. He was ready, come what might. Even if that included sacrificing himself for her.

Piper spoke quietly from the kitchen, her voice pure ice. "Here they come."

Chapter Twelve

Piper saw the men emerge from the woods at almost the exact same moment that Beau Lambert murmured through the telephone receiver, "Hostiles moving into the open. Inbound to your position. Contact imminent."

"Roger, I have visual contact. How's that gunship coming?" she muttered into the receiver.

"Airborne. ETA your position, eighteen minutes."

"Tell them to firewall it."

Beau murmured, "You should've heard Torsten bully them into launching. They know to get to you ASAP."

"I'll keep the line open, but I'm gonna have to put down the phone now and get ready to fire," she reported to her operations officer.

"I'll shout if I need to relay information. Good shooting, Piper."

"Will do."

She laid the phone receiver in the kitchen sink and took up a firing position, kneeling on a chair in front of it. Mahmoud's men were moving cautiously, fanning out as they approached the farm. Dammit. Two of the men peeled off to head toward the barns.

The whole game now was to engage in a delaying action until reinforcements could arrive. To that end, she watched and waited as Mahmoud, Hassan and Yousef went out of sight behind a shed.

"Have you got eyes on Mahmoud plus two?" she called quietly.

"Affirmative," Zane replied.

"I'm watching the young guys. When they've almost reached the barns, I'll fire and draw them back here. If your three move before then, you fire first."

"Ammo's very thin," he warned. "Only take kill shots if able."

She smiled against the stock of her rifle. She was fully versed in ammo management. He was worried about her. "Roger. Will do," she replied quietly.

She settled back into emotionless concentration on the scenario unfolding in front of her. She picked the spot where, when the young guys reached it, she would fire at them. She probably wouldn't hit them at this distance, but she hoped to use the shot to check the accuracy of the weapon's sights.

All those endless hours on the firing range rolled through her, with neural pathways and habit patterns built over hundreds of shooting sessions and thousands of rounds fired clicking into place. *Relax completely. Breathe long and slow. Exhale and hold.* One last gun sight correction; her finger touched the trigger…

The pair reached the spot, and she squeezed smoothly through the trigger. The sound of her rifle firing was deafening, shattering the morning's silence shockingly.

The young men reacted violently, flinching and ducking and then racing back toward Mahmoud's position behind the shed. She took note of the hole that appeared in the side of the barn. Slightly high and right of where she'd aimed. Duly noted. She would adjust her aim a tiny bit low and left.

She swung her rifle toward the shed, following the zigzagging path of the two terrorists until they disappeared from sight. She would love to be a fly on the wall to hear the discussion happening behind that shed right now. The terrorists had lost the element of surprise, and now they knew their prey was not entirely without teeth. That had to be a nasty shock to poor Mahmoud.

She waited with detached interest to see what he did next. She and Zane were badly outgunned, but they had excellent cover inside this house, and Mahmoud and his guys would have to come out in the open to use their assault weapons.

He and his guys would also be running around with only the ammunition they could carry. And ammo was heavy, which meant they had a finite supply of it and would have to be careful with their firing habits, too.

A drawback of a weapon like an AK-47 was that it could chow through a whole lot of rounds very fast. If Mahmoud's guys didn't control their fire tightly, they would spray a few impressive fusillades against the side of the house and then be clicking on empty.

From her and Zane's end, this was purely a delaying action, buying time for that gunship to get here. Which gave them the tactical advantage.

If any of Mahmoud's guys weren't particularly experienced with combat, they were very likely to be excitable and fire off all their ammunition too quickly. She figured Mahmoud, Yousef and Hassan probably would keep their cool. But the younger two…they might be convinced to behave stupidly and unload their weapons all at once.

In Mahmoud's position, she might order the worst shot of the young guys to go ahead and empty his AK-47 magazines against the side of the house just to gauge what kind of reaction she and Zane had to offer.

Sure enough, one of the young guys jumped out from

behind the shed with his weapon held at waist height, one hand on top of the barrel to hold it down as it tried to climb.

"Incoming," Zane bit out. "Take cover."

She crouched on her chair behind the sink, making as small a ball as possible. The weapon cut loose, roaring like a dragon as the side of the house was peppered with dozens of rounds. Some of them penetrated the wood siding and missed wall studs, zinging past her to bury themselves in the far wall.

"They're rushing from behind the shed to your left!" a voice shouted over the phone.

"Incoming!" she called out to Zane. "Left side of the shed!"

Two more men rushed around the corner just as the first round of fire ceased. Piper took quick aim, fully exhaled and pulled off a single shot.

Hassan, the driver, spun back behind the shed. The other guy, one of the young ones, lurched, obviously hit. He spun for cover more slowly than Hassan. But she knew as well as anyone that a single gunshot wound rarely took a combatant completely out of a fight. The other men would be tying a strip of cloth over the wound and telling him to get back in the fight right about now. Shock and adrenaline would mask any pain the kid felt.

"Hostiles on the move again," Beau reported over the phone. "Looks like they're spreading out."

"I've got no visual," she called back, loudly enough for Beau to hear. More quietly, to Zane, she asked, "Any visual?"

"Negative."

They must be crawling around in some sort of swale that provided them with cover from the house.

"Position report?" Zane asked quietly from the living room.

"Where are they, Lambo?" she called.

"Straight line. About ten yards apart. Thirty yards from your position. They look to be taking up prone firing positions," Beau replied.

She relayed the information to Zane, relieved that he was as disciplined as he was and prepared to wait out the bad guys with her. Amateurs would be firing away like crazy by now, panicked and burning through their ammo.

All at once, Mahmoud and his men started firing at them. They were, indeed, conserving ammunition, firing single shots and taking turns, keeping up a fairly steady barrage, one shot every fifteen seconds or so. Still, they were going to burn through their ammo quickly that way.

"ETA on that chopper?" she asked Beau.

"Thirteen minutes."

"Still too long," she replied tersely.

Beau announced, "Hostiles are advancing, but appear to be prone. Do you have visual to fire?"

"Negative," she bit out. "Once they hit the front yard, though, the only cover they'll have is the pickup truck."

Another voice came on the line. Major Torsten's. "That truck is only about twenty feet from the house. When they charge you from behind the truck, you'll only have a few seconds to neutralize all of them, or your position will be overrun. Do you have an egress route?"

"Not really."

"Can you create one in the next minute or two?" he asked. "Look for chemicals. Can you blow a hole in the back wall of the house?"

"I'm no MacGyver, but I'll try."

A quick inventory of the cupboards in the kitchen yielded enough chemicals to create a low-order explosion, but nothing that would punch through a wall.

"Wait a minute," she exclaimed under her breath. "The

guy who owns this house has a model train set. Don't they use something fairly nasty as fuel?"

Rebel interjected, "Some model trains use nitromethane."

"Now we're talking," Torsten said sharply. "Can you disengage to go look?"

"Zane. I'm leaving my position for a minute. Call if you see movement."

"Roger. What's up?" he asked without looking away from the window as she raced through the living room.

"Boss thinks we need an emergency exit. I'm gonna set up an explosion to create an impromptu door on the other side of the house."

"Um, okay."

She smiled a little at his apparent confusion. *Welcome to working with the Medusas.* They were trained to think and operate outside the box. And he—along with the jerks outside—was about to get a taste of what that really meant.

She ducked into the spare bedroom and found a gallon jug of model-engine fuel. Sure enough, it was volatile nitromethane. She carried it and the chemicals she'd brought from the kitchen into the bathroom. Working fast, she unscrewed the toilet tank from the seat and lifted it quickly. Water cascaded all over her feet and the floor as the tank emptied.

Working quickly, she plugged the bottom drain hole with duct tape she'd found in the kitchen, then ran a rag through the taped plug to act as a fuse. She tucked the other end of the rag in a bottle of flammable cleaning solvent and set the other containers of chemicals beside it inside the ceramic vessel. She pointed the open tank top directly at the wall. It was a crude-shaped charge at best and might not even work, but it was worth a try.

Worst case, she and Zane could jump out the bedroom

windows. But that was a harder maneuver than it looked when armed, trying not to get hurt and needing to land, fall, roll and come up running. Particularly when one or more of Mahmoud's guys were likely to be waiting for them to come out the windows.

"They're closing in!" Zane called from the living room.

She raced back to the kitchen and resumed her position in the window. And just in time, too. The long grass on the far side of the yard was moving; five trails of moving grass were headed straight at the house.

"ETA?" she bit out into the phone.

"Hostiles? Twenty seconds. Gunship? Eight minutes."

"We don't have eight minutes. We've got maybe three," she snapped.

"Roger. You know what to do. Just relax and let your training take over," Torsten said calmly. All the faith in the world was packed into his voice, and it steadied her. Focused her on the job at hand.

She called to Zane, "You good?"

"I'm good."

"Ops thinks they'll cluster behind the truck and rush us from there. We'll have a few seconds to take out whoever we can, then we need to retreat to the bathroom, blow the wall and run like hell for the trees. We'll need to evade until the gunship arrives. Rendezvous when able even with the chicken barns, a hundred yards into the trees."

"Got it," he muttered absently. "I've got the right-hand field of fire. You've got the left."

"Roger, I'm left," she replied, making the reflexively ingrained response. She would shoot at whoever came around the left end of the truck. And if all the bad guys came from the same side of the vehicle, she would take the left-hand targets in the cluster.

She watched in total concentration as the trails of swaying grass converged and disappeared behind the truck. The show was about to get real.

Any second now.

She was glad she was in this with Zane. He'd been her rock through everything, and even now he made her feel safe. Protected. The bubble of caring and concern he'd surrounded her with in that kiss a few minutes ago still cocooned her. She still felt his arms around her, the bulwark of his big body shielding her from harm.

She trusted him. With her life.

And then she emptied her mind of even that thought. It was go time.

"They're gathering themselves to charge," Beau announced.

"Get ready," she relayed to Zane.

Without warning, all hell broke loose. Two men rushed from behind the truck and two rushed around the front. Showing as little of herself as humanly possible, she fired at will at the rushing men. She knew without a shadow of doubt that she hit with multiple shots on multiple targets. But the bastards kept on coming.

When they'd almost reached the house and she and Zane were losing any sort of decent angle to fire without showing too much of themselves, he yelled, "Go now!"

She ran for the bathroom and used the cigarette lighter she'd found in a kitchen drawer to light the fuse. She spun into the hall, estimating that she had ten seconds—

It was more like three seconds. A tremendous explosion deafened her, slamming into her body like a physical blow. The whole house rocked violently, and she peeked around the corner. Debris was everywhere, and there was a ragged man-sized hole in the wall.

"Come to me!" she shouted.

Zane spun away from the living room window and

sprinted toward her, waving her through the hole ahead of him.

"I've got the left," she called as she jumped outside. Her sweatshirt caught on something and tore, but she yanked violently and pulled free, spinning left to clear that corner of the house.

She felt Zane land beside her and spin right.

They took off running at top speed, crossing the fifty feet or so of lawn in a few seconds and diving into the trees.

They separated to make harder targets of themselves and divide the force brought to bear against them. She dodged and zigzagged, using as many trees for cover as she could. She worked her way up the hill and then cut right, toward the prearranged rendezvous point.

A shot rang out on her right, but she thought it wasn't aimed at her. She pressed on grimly, not bothering to look over her shoulder. Doing so would only slow her down, and seeing who was behind her wouldn't make him go away or change where she was headed.

As she neared the rendezvous point, she slowed and veered left, higher up the slope into some heavy brush. The going was very slow through brambles and bushes, but the cover was excellent. Confident she wouldn't be seen by her pursuers, she eased forward to approach the spot from above.

Peering out from the bushes, she scanned the forest around her both for Zane and for hostiles. Knowing he was out there, she would refrain from shooting at any movement she saw until she had a positive ID on the person.

She hunkered down to wait for Zane to show up, scanning all the while. Her brain raced, replaying the events of the past few minutes quickly, seeking information or mistakes by Mahmoud.

Why had only four men rushed around the truck to attack them? It wasn't like Mahmoud had come around be-hind the house to lie in wait for them as they'd blasted their way out. Where had he gone? Had he headed for the barns…and Irv?

Crap. If Zane didn't show up soon, she would have to head down to the barns to make sure Irv was all right. How much longer should she give Zane before she had to assume he was hurt or pinned down? Did she need to go rescue him?

Who to rescue first? The innocent civilian, or the man who'd saved her life and, not to mention, was her lover?

Her duty was to Irv. But her heart belonged with Zane. And Zane could help her rescue Irv. They would be more than twice as effective working as a team than her alone.

Dammit, she was trying to rationalize going after Zane first.

She wrestled with the decision a few more seconds, pray-ing that he would show up and erase the dilemma, and then spotted movement below her. A man, creeping forward stealthily. Wearing a dark sweatshirt with the hood up—no help. She couldn't see hair color.

Crouching, she eased around the bushes, heading off to her left. She'd moved maybe twenty feet when she spot-ted another man. This one stood still in the lee of a large oak tree.

And his hair was light brown touched with gold. Zane.

As she looked on from her perch above, the second man—the first one she'd seen—crept toward Zane.

She lay prone on the ground, propped her rifle on a downed log in front of her and took careful aim. The tar-get, the height and build of Hassan, would pass in front of her about fifty feet away. His profile didn't make for the world's biggest target, but she was going for a head shot, anyway. A body shot wouldn't stop a man like him. It would have to be an outright kill.

She tracked him until he was directly in front of her and paused for a moment, appearing to listen for movement around him. She pulled the trigger.

The shot rang out, and Hassan dropped. She couldn't see if she'd hit him or not, for Zane took off running to her left, abandoning the rendezvous point. He had no way of knowing it was her who'd fired, of course. She leaped to her feet and paralleled his position, doing her damnedest to keep sight of him as he raced through the trees.

Whenever she could, she angled to her right, down the hill, closer to his path. If someone besides Hassan had been on Zane's tail, it brought her into danger, too, making a single target of both her and Zane. But she dared not lose him out here. She might never find him again.

She put on a burst of speed as she crossed a tiny clearing, jumping for the brush on the other side, the back of her neck twitching at being exposed like this.

She dived into the thicket and jolted as an arm snagged her waist, yanking her down violently. She reached for the knife in the back of her jeans, and her hand had just closed on the hilt when Zane's face appeared in front of hers.

Oh, thank God. Relief that he wasn't one of Mahmoud's men made her knees weak for a moment. But in the next breath, her tension ratcheted back up. They were still being hunted out here.

And frankly, she'd had just about enough of that. She didn't like being the rabbit. She much preferred being the tiger. And given how shot up Mahmoud's men had to be, she figured this had to be close to an even fight by now.

Zane hand signaled that he'd heard one hostile behind them, farther down the hill.

She leaned forward, putting her mouth directly on his ear. "Time for us to go hunting."

He nodded, and they moved out together.

Chapter Thirteen

Zane liked the way Piper was thinking. He was pretty much over skulking around in the woods getting shot at.

Moving slowly, they circled back toward the barns and whoever might be behind them. Stealth was on their side now. Piper did something odd in front of him. She moved up the hillside purposefully, gazing from side to side as if she was looking for something.

After about three minutes, she tensed, then stalked forward slowly, her cheek pressed to the Remington rifle in a ready position. He did the same.

She stopped and he spared a glance down at the ground in front of her. Hassan's sightless eyes stared up at the sky. A large kidney-red hole in the side of his head announced that he was very, very dead.

One down. Four to go. Although Mahmoud and his guys couldn't possibly be at full strength. As they'd closed in on the house, the men he'd seen had all been bloody and injured.

Piper leaned close to whisper to him, "Is this who you heard behind you, or is there another one tracking you?"

"I don't know."

"Did they use earpieces?" she asked.

He glanced down quickly and realized that in what remained of Hassan's ear there was no earbud. Piper used the tip of the rifle to turn his head. There was no listening device in the other ear, either.

"They trained with earpieces and mikes," he replied under his breath.

She nodded. "One of the others may have already found Hassan and taken his earpiece so we can't eavesdrop on them. He would have headed back toward the others rather than be out here alone with both of us."

"Barn?" Zane asked tersely. Poor Irv must be losing his mind hiding out with his chickens and hearing all the gunfire.

"Roger that," she breathed.

Piper took off ahead of Zane. He probably ought to offer to take point, but she was the Special Forces soldier who trained in armed combat every day. As an undercover operative, he had the training, but he didn't use it often. He ran around in the woods like this at his recurrent field ops training only every other year. He wasn't ashamed to let the better soldier lead the way.

They met no opposition at all as they headed for the barns. They'd almost reached them when Piper froze in front of him. The two of them were right at the edge of the woods, where it came within about a hundred feet of the nearest long barn. Close enough to smell the odor of a thousand chickens.

THREE ARMED MEN came around the far side of the barn. Zane recognized Yousef, Bijan and Osted. All three looked bloody and battered. Twigs and leaves stuck to their clothes, and Bijan was limping badly. Yousef was holding his weapon weirdly, like he had an injured arm or hand.

Yousef raised his AK-47 and fired a short burst through the end of the barn, peppering the big metal sliding door with bullet holes.

Piper eased down to a crouch, rifle ready, and Zane mimicked her. When Yousef loosed another burst, Piper fired her weapon at him, and Zane did the same an instant later.

All three men pivoted and shot wildly at the woods. Spooked, were they?

Behind them, the big sliding door opened without warning, squeaking violently. The men started to turn toward it, then pivoted back as Zane and Piper fired again at them.

And then a cloud of frantic chickens swarmed out of the barn, some running, most flapping and flying, all of them panicked.

Osted screamed and took off running back around the barn, and Yousef wasn't far behind. Bijan followed more slowly because of his limp, but appeared no less freaked out by the attack of the flying chickens.

In the distance, Zane heard the thwacking of a helicopter. It got louder rapidly as he and Piper advanced toward the now open barn door.

"It's me, Irv!" Piper called before approaching any more closely. "Are you okay in there?"

"Bastards shot at my chickens!" Irv bellowed.

It sounded as if he was headed toward the other end of the barn, and Zane risked peering around the door. Sure enough, the farmer was charging down a long concrete aisle, brandishing the teeny handgun threateningly in front of him.

Zane sprinted after the farmer and Piper spun into the barn behind him, pausing only long enough to shove the big door shut again.

Zane caught up with Irv a dozen feet from the front door and grabbed the farmer in a horse-collar tackle, throwing his arm around the big man's neck to stop him. Urgently, he whispered in Irv's ear, "Don't go out there! That's an army gunship and it'll kill anyone who moves outside with a weapon in hand."

Piper caught up with them, panting hard. "Have you got a cell phone on you, Irv?"

"Yeah, but coverage is spotty out here. Middle of the barn's your best bet."

She grabbed the phone he held out and took off running. When she reached the middle of the barn, she placed a quick call and talked into the device urgently for a few seconds. She ran back to them.

"Gunship's been told we're in here. They passed a message to come out with our hands over our heads. They've killed two targets on the ground and the third one has fled into the woods on the other side of the road. They were instructed not to pursue him, but rather to stay here and provide support to us."

"Thank God," Zane said fervently.

He laid down the shotgun and made sure Irv did the same with the pistol. Piper put the Remington beside the other two weapons, and then all three of them stepped outside. They were met with violent downwash from the chopper that all but knocked them off their feet. Irv's baseball cap flew off his head. The farmer started to grab for it, but Zane barked, "Let it go."

"Oh. Right," Irv grumbled.

The chopper hovered over them for perhaps two minutes before moving off to hover over the woods across the road from Irv's destroyed house. A second helicopter, this one a Huey with a police paint job on it, landed between the house and the barns.

A man in full body armor raced out of it and over to the three of them. "Your names?" he demanded, weapon trained on them.

"Piper Ford, Zane Cosworth and Irv Smith," she shouted over the noise of the choppers.

"I wasn't told about Irv Smith!" the cop yelled back.

The farmer bellowed, "I own this place! Or what's left of it!"

"He's with us!" Zane shouted.

The cop waved all three of them over to the helicopter and loaded them aboard. Three other fully armored and armed police were inside, and it was a tight squeeze. Piper ended up sitting on Zane's lap, and Irv sat on the floor. The aircraft lifted off the ground and swooped away from the house quickly.

THEY LANDED AT a state police barracks about fifty miles away, and Zane grinned as Irv declared, "Well, hell's bells, that was a fun ride! Can I get a ride home that way?"

The police led the farmer off to take his statement, and tried to separate Zane and Piper to get statements from them, too.

But Zane objected. "Sorry, gentlemen. This mess is above your pay grades. I'll be happy to give you my supervisor's phone number in Washington to confirm that, of course."

"Same with me," Piper said regretfully. "Although I'll have to give you a different phone number."

The police still insisted on putting Zane in an interrogation room and Piper in another until their identities were confirmed, which actually pissed Zane off to no end. He hadn't been apart from Piper for days now, and he hated not being with her.

What was up with that? He never got attached to people. Never mind that they'd made love last night and he felt closer to her than he had to anyone in years.

Cripes. When had he fallen for his hostage?

While he sat there staring at himself in the two-way glass, he had plenty of time to wonder about it. That, and what in the hell he was going to do, now that he had fallen for Piper.

His grim reflection gave him only one entirely unhelpful answer. He was screwed.

PIPER HATED BEING away from Zane. He'd been her only source of support and safety for days, and she felt naked and vulnerable with him gone to who knew where. He was probably sitting in another interrogation room like this one, thanking his lucky stars this mission was over and he could get back to his regular life.

Now that they were both safe, where did that leave them? Did they still have a relationship? Or was everything that had happened between them purely a reaction to the crisis they'd been caught in? Had any of it been real?

Doubt speared through her.

Major Torsten had been blunt in their classroom instruction for advanced prisoner-of-war training; weird things happened to people under that extreme amount of pressure. The brain did all sorts of bizarre things to protect itself from the unimaginable, including normalizing crap that was no way normal.

Was that what she and Zane had done? Had they been attracted to each other and formed a relationship rather than face the horror of what they were both experiencing?

For she had no doubt that being undercover with violent terrorists had been fully as stressful as being their prisoner had been. Except he'd lived in that environment for months. She'd been under that kind of pressure only for a few days, and it had pushed her to the breaking point and beyond. What would it have been like not to have been rescued for *months*?

Her mind shied away from even thinking about it.

So where did that leave her and Zane?

Had they shared a one-night stand of pure relief? Had their connection been based only on fear and mutual survival?

A police officer poked his head in the door, interrupting her mental spiral. "You're still refusing to write up a report for us?"

"I'm sorry, but I can't. The information in it would be classified if I wrote it down. I'm sure the military will give you a redacted version of my formal report if you ask for it. Can I go now? Or can I at least make a phone call?"

"Some dude's here to pick you up, anyway. Wearing a military uniform and scaring the hell out of the rookie cops. C'mon."

She leaped to her feet and followed the cop eagerly down the hall. "Big blond guy? Eyes like ice?"

"That's the one."

"That's Major Torsten. And he doesn't scare *you*?"

The cop grinned at her. "Semper fi, ma'am. Once a marine, always a marine. Guys like him and me get along just fine."

They rounded the corner into the squad room and Rebel and Tessa raced over to hug her tightly. She might or might not have shed a few tears of relief in the midst of the hugs at seeing her teammates again.

Major Torsten came over at a more measured pace. "Welcome back, Captain Ford. I hear you acquitted yourself well."

She shrugged modestly and started to speak, but then caught sight of Zane coming around the corner. His gaze riveted on her immediately, and she nodded slightly at him. A smile lit his eyes but didn't escape to the rest of his face.

Thank God. He cared about her at least a little. Or at

least he was prepared to be civil to her. That was better than nothing. Right?

God. If only she knew him better. Then maybe she could guess where his head was at.

She made the introductions quickly, using no last names, given that a bunch of police without security clearances surrounded them.

Torsten said to Zane, "Can I give you a lift to the nearest secure telephone?"

Zane nodded. "That would be helpful."

Piper piled outside with the others and jumped in a big Hummer Torsten had obviously commandeered from someone local. Zane ended up in the front passenger seat, and she ended up stuffed in the back of the vehicle as far from him as it was possible to get. Had Zane engineered that? Or maybe Tessa and Rebel had tacitly arranged it.

Either way, it felt strange to be this close to him and yet feel so far away.

"Any chance we could get something to eat?" Piper asked. "We ran out of food a while ago."

Without comment, Torsten drove them to a diner and loaded them both up with tall stacks of pancakes, and then they headed to a regional airport and boarded a small business jet.

"Where to, sir?" the pilot asked Torsten as they approached the plane.

Major Torsten turned to look at Zane. "If you don't mind, I'll get my debrief from you two first, and then you can give your full debrief to your people, Zane. I expect yours will take some time, since you were embedded with those men for the long term."

Piper interjected. "We have a more pressing problem than debriefs."

Everyone turned to stare at her.

"The real Persephone Black is still out there, somewhere. And by now, it's entirely possible that Mahmoud and his boys have been informed that the woman they kidnapped was not her. Forgive me for feeling a special connection to her after experiencing what was meant for her, but I think we need to go find her with all due haste and secure her safety."

Torsten nodded tersely. "What about you, Zane? Do you want to come with us, or do you need to get back to your people?"

Piper's gaze shot to Zane's face. She saw it. The moment of hesitation.

Her heart fell, thudding to the ground somewhere in the vicinity of her feet.

He said emotionlessly, "I'd better come with you. I'll feel responsible for Mrs. Black if something bad happens to her."

Right. Responsibility. That was all he'd felt toward Piper, after all. He was a naturally protective guy. Which made him a decent human being but also meant what they'd shared had been nothing more than general compassion. Nothing personal. He'd just been comforting the exhausted, cold female and making up for any trauma he'd caused her.

The knife twisting in her gut served one purpose, at least. It told her she'd actually had some real feelings for him that extended beyond mutual survival or clinging to safety in the midst of terror. Not that those feelings meant a damned thing now that the two of them were back in the real world.

Well, hell.

An urge to cry made her eyes burn and the back of her throat tight.

She was not going to break down!

She fought back the urge. *I'm just overwrought—whatever that actually means.*

"Captain Ford makes a good point," Torsten declared. "Zane, where did your group's surveillance of Mrs. Black indicate that she can usually be found?"

"We did no surveillance at all on her. We just barged into that elementary school to snatch her."

"Then that's where we'll start." To the pilot, he said, "We need to land as close to Houma, Louisiana, as you can take us."

The pilot nodded. "It'll take us a few minutes to write up and file a flight plan, and then we'll be out of here."

It was a cool morning, and they all lounged in the back of the airplane with the door open while they waited to take off.

Piper asked no one in particular, "Where do you suppose Mahmoud and Yousef took off to after they fled the firefight?"

Torsten responded tersely, "They had better be on their way out of the country. The manhunt that's about to go after them will be the end of them if they don't get the hell out of Dodge."

Piper looked over at Zane sharply. "Did you give their identities to the police?"

"Yes. Along with surveillance pictures of them that I uploaded to the cloud before they took my cell phone away. The authorities have the photographs and a list of every fake ID I saw any of them use."

She nodded in satisfaction. "I hope they die horribly."

One corner of Zane's mouth turned up sardonically. "I hope so, too, personally. But professionally, I'd love to get my hands on one of them and force him to tell me exactly what they were in this country to do."

"Kidnapping Piper wasn't their main objective?" Torsten bit out.

Both Piper and Zane shook their heads. Zane added, "She was definitely a side job. They were collecting resources slowly and methodically while training together as a team to hone their skills."

"What sort of training?"

"They ran all kinds of armed-assault scenarios. Along the lines of a hijacking or taking over some space filled with civilians to use as hostages."

That sounded scary.

Piper spent part of the hour-long flight trying to imagine what target she would go after if she were part of an Iranian sleeper cell specializing in taking hostages. The problem was not coming up with targets. The problem was narrowing down the possible list.

Chapter Fourteen

It was early afternoon when they landed at Houma-Terrebonne Airport with a bump onto the runway that woke Piper from a deep, disorienting sleep. Fortunately, her Medusa training had prepared her to go long periods of time with little or no sleep and to wake instantly on full alert even when exhausted. Which she was.

They deplaned and climbed into the Hummer Beau Lambert had driven over to the airport to meet them. He sat in the driver's seat and Tessa and Rebel sat in the back. Obviously, Torsten had spoken with him from the plane, for as soon as they were in the vehicle, Beau took off toward Southdown Elementary School without having to be told where to go.

They arrived at the school and pulled up in front of it. As they approached the front door, the police officer lounging in a chair beside it went tense. His hand drifted toward the revolver at his hip.

But thankfully, when Torsten pulled out his military ID and asked the cop to escort them to the office of the assistant principal, Mrs. Black, the guy relaxed.

A wave of déjà vu rolled over Piper as she turned left into the glass-walled front office. Had it been only a week ago that she'd walked in here with Jack's lunch? It felt like a lifetime.

She didn't look over at Zane. What must this feel like to him? Last time he was here, he'd been brandishing an AK-47 and terrifying women and children.

Torsten told the receptionist, "We're here to see Mrs. Black. It's urgent."

"Um, I'll let her know you're here," the woman said nervously.

A tall, pretty blonde who actually did look a bit like Piper stepped out into the large room. "Who are you?" she asked a tad sharply.

"Major Gunnar Torsten, US Army. We're here in connection with last week's school invasion. Can we speak in private?"

"All of you?"

Torsten shrugged. "If you'd be more comfortable, I can pare it down to, say, three of us."

"Please do."

Torsten nodded at Piper and Zane, who followed him into Persephone Black's office, while the others stayed outside in the main area. Zane closed the door behind them.

Piper sympathized when the woman went around behind her desk and sat down, clearly using it as protection from these threatening strangers. Reading the stress in the woman's eyes, she dived in to speak before the men could.

"Mrs. Black, we know why those men barged into your school last week, and it has to do with you. That's why we're here today. To explain to you what happened, who those men were and what it means for you."

"Really? The police have nothing. No motive and no identities." Then she blurted, "I'd love to hear your theory."

Piper nodded in Zane's direction. "This gentleman here is a federal agent. He has spent some months…observing… a group of men he believes to be Iranian operatives. The same group that invaded your school."

"Iranian? Does this have to do with Mark?"

"Who's Mark?" Piper asked quickly.

"My husband. He's working in Iran right now."

"You are correct," Piper replied gently. "Those men came here to kidnap you."

"One of the secretaries said they were asking about me. But I couldn't believe I was that important to anyone. I mean, I'm an assistant principal at an elementary school in a small town no one's ever heard of."

"The secretary was also correct. Those men planned to kidnap you, take pictures and video of you, and send the images back to Iran, where somebody planned to coerce your husband into doing something. Do you have any idea what they might have wanted from him?"

"Well, yes. He's a nuclear facility inspector on an international team. I imagine the Iranians would want him to falsify a report or maybe pretend to have inspected a facility he hasn't seen."

Piper stared at the woman in shock. Ho. Ly. Cow. She glanced over at Gunnar Torsten, who also stared grimly at the woman. Looking sidelong at Zane, Piper muttered to him, "Does that jibe with what you know of Mahmoud and company?"

"Yes. Perfectly."

"Then maybe she was their main mission, after all."

Zane shook his head. "I don't think so. I still think she was a side gig. If they're hostage-taking specialists, they would be the logical choice to be activated and sent in to kidnap a civilian."

"What are you two talking about?" Persephone interrupted. "How do you know what these men wanted? If they actually wanted to kidnap me, why didn't they come to my home when I wasn't here at school and grab me there?"

Piper answered, "Because they thought they had you. One of the men identified me as being you."

Persephone stared at her. "I don't understand."

"I was here that day. Delivering my neighbor kid's lunch that he forgot in my car. When they barged into the office and saw me, they mistakenly identified me as you and kidnapped me instead."

"Oh, my God!" Persephone exclaimed. "But you're okay? They didn't hurt you?"

Although the worst of the swelling in Piper's black eye had gone down, she still had a cut over her left eyebrow and her eye was turning a rainbow of various colors. It was patently obvious she hadn't gotten out of the experience unscathed. She answered honestly, "They did hurt me, in fact. And they would have done the same to you."

"Oh, my God!" This time when the woman exclaimed, she actually rose out of her chair. "This can't be true! I don't believe it."

Zane leaned forward and spoke grimly. "Believe it, ma'am. I'm one of the men who attacked the school, and I'm the one who identified her as you."

"You're one of the assailants?" Persephone gasped. She reached quickly for the phone on her desk. It was obvious she intended to call the police.

Major Torsten leaned forward and pressed his hand down on top of Persephone's, stopping her from lifting the receiver. "We told you. He's a federal agent. He was undercover, infiltrating the team. He was instrumental in getting those men out of your school without anyone being harmed."

"How can you say that?" Persephone's voice rose toward a screech. "The children are traumatized! My teachers are terrified—"

Torsten cut across her unfolding tirade. "They're alive.

The attack on this school could have gone immeasurably worse. That team was trained killers with no capacity for remorse. They wouldn't have hesitated to mow down everyone in this building if they hadn't found you—or a woman they believed to be you—right away."

Persephone looked unconvinced, and Torsten continued tersely, "My operative, Captain Ford here, was beaten and brutalized on your behalf. Ask her how capable of violence those men were if you don't believe me."

Persephone looked at Piper in horror and woman whispered, "Is that true?"

Piper leaned forward and looked her squarely in the eye. "Yes. It is. Had I not had the highly specialized training that I do, and had I not had the surreptitious help of this agent, I would have suffered even more serious attacks than I did and very likely would have died. *That* was what those men had in store for you."

Clearly appalled, Persephone pressed a hand over her mouth and stared at Piper, her eyes full of silent questions over just how bad it had been.

Piper stared back at her implacably, doing her best to convey that it had been every bit as dreadful as the woman was capable of imagining.

Torsten's voice cut through their silent communication, woman-to-woman. "Where exactly is your husband now, ma'am?"

"Last I heard, he's in Tehran."

"Do you have a direct phone number for him?" the major pressed. "We need to warn him. Tell him to head for the American embassy immediately for his own safety."

"Um, yes. Of course." She pulled her purse out of a drawer, set it on her desk and fumbled inside it. She emerged with a cell phone. Unlocking it, she pushed a few buttons and then listened intently.

She murmured in alarm, "He's not answering."

"It's late evening over there," Torsten replied. "He's probably asleep."

"Yes, but he always picks up my calls."

"Can you leave a message?" Torsten responded.

She nodded and said into the phone, "Mark, it's me. Please call me the second you get this."

Torsten leaned forward. "Tell him to go to the embassy first."

Persephone continued, "Umm, you need to go to the American embassy right now. You're in danger and need protection. I'll explain it when you call. Just get to the embassy and then call me. I love you. Be careful, and be safe."

She laid the phone down, her expression troubled. "Something's wrong. Even if he were asleep, he would wake up and answer a call from me."

Torsten swore under his breath, and Piper silently echoed the sentiment. Her antennae were wiggling wildly. Mark Black was in serious trouble.

Then Torsten said, "Would you consent to entering into protective custody, Mrs. Black? I'll have some of my people stay with you and guard you until FBI agents can come from New Orleans and pick you up."

"My job—"

"It will wait." Torsten cut her off. "Your life is in danger, ma'am. Two of the terrorists got away this morning, and it's possible they're headed here to kidnap you for real."

"What about Mark?" she demanded, sounding near panic.

"We'll locate him and put him under guard, as well. But I can't in good conscience leave you without protection. The sooner you agree to let me take care of you, the sooner I can get on with finding and protecting your husband."

Piper was impressed. It was a low blow by Torsten to

use the woman's husband to manipulate her into agreeing to protective custody, but Piper got why he'd done it. Right now, time was the enemy. The major was only doing what was necessary to move the mission along.

It had been one of the more difficult transitions to special operations thinking for her. Lies and subterfuge were standard tools of the trade.

Of course, Zane must be an expert at wielding both. Which would explain how he'd survived with Mahmoud and his cronies for *months*. She had no business believing anything he'd said to her in the heat of their lovemaking, and she certainly couldn't believe any feelings he'd revealed to her.

Persephone rose from her desk, purse in hand, and nodded at Major Torsten. "If it'll help you protect Mark sooner, let's go right now."

It was decided that Tessa and Rebel would stay with Persephone at Piper's house—a neutral location not connected with Persephone Black's life in any way—until FBI agents arrived to take her into custody. Torsten explained that the FBI would put her in a safe house or a hotel room at an undisclosed location and under guard around the clock until this crisis was over.

When they all arrived at her bungalow, Torsten agreed to let Piper take a quick shower and change into clean clothes while he made the arrangements with the FBI.

She shampooed her hair three times to get out the dirt and grime of that horrible basement and from running around in the woods for days. She scrubbed her body from head to toe with a loofah until her skin was red and tender—

Huh. Maybe she'd been more affected by her captivity than she'd admitted to herself. Go figure. She rinsed off and climbed out of the shower thoughtfully.

It was a little slice of heaven to put on clean clothes, blow-dry her hair and actually put on a bit of makeup. Finally. She felt like herself again.

She emerged from the bathroom and Zane rose to his feet. He'd been waiting for her apparently, sitting on the edge of her bed. Whether he stood out of general politeness or out of shock at seeing her cleaned up, she couldn't tell.

"Feeling better?" he asked quietly.

"Definitely."

He continued to study her intently, and she added, "It's a bit of a shock being here in my house with everything suddenly back to normal."

"I feel that way when I come off a tough undercover assignment," he offered.

"How do you settle back into your real life?" she asked curiously.

"I don't have a real life, so I'm not the guy to answer that."

She stepped closer, gazing up into his sober eyes. He wasn't being flippant. "How do you stay yourself when you spend so much time being somebody else?"

He flinched ever so slightly. She waited him out, though, and at length he answered, "Sometimes I don't know who I am anymore."

"Well, that sucks."

He snorted in what sounded like startled humor. Closing the distance between them, he wrapped his arms around her and buried his nose in her hair. "I feel like myself when I'm with you. I see the man you see when you look at me, and I remember who he is. For a minute or two, I'm back in my own skin."

"You're welcome, I think."

She felt his smile against her temple. Then he murmured, "I'm starting to think you saved me in the nick of time."

"You're the one who saved me," she protested.

"I might have saved you from Mahmoud and his boys, but you saved my soul, Piper."

Her arms tightened around his waist, and they stood like that for a long moment, silently sharing their relief at having made it out alive.

He commented reflectively, "You'd have figured out a way to escape on your own eventually. I just sped up the process."

"I'm not superhuman. They had me handcuffed to a steel pipe. That would have been hard to overcome."

"You'd have found a way," he stated confidently.

"We'll never know." She paused. "The good news is we're both alive and we're both safe."

"For now," he sighed. "I'll go back undercover to identify the bad guys you and your team will chase down and take out. This momentary respite is just that—momentary."

Her stomach plummeted. He was right. If this was the real world, neither of them truly belonged in it. They both lived in the dangerous shadows beyond this shiny, safe place.

She had no business imagining them being together for the long term, imagining them finding some sort of permanent happiness, together or otherwise. This moment, this man, what they'd shared between them—it was nothing more than a sweet illusion.

Their realities bore no resemblance to this whatsoever. Her world was that basement, facing down bad guys. That forest, evading death. That farmhouse, shooting it out with terrorists.

Happiness with Zane had no place in that world.

Silently devastated, she stepped back, pulling away from him, slipping out of his embrace. Unable to look at him, she turned and headed away from him. Anywhere that wasn't the circle of his arms.

"Anyone hungry?" she asked everyone else.

Nobody wanted anything to eat, but she desperately needed to do something to keep busy. Her steps took her to her cheerful yellow kitchen.

It was a lie. All of it. The bright colors and homey touches. They were a big fat lie she told herself—that she could have a home. A picket fence and a dog and 2.1 kids. Maybe a husband. Family and friends. All lies.

When Zane followed her into her kitchen, she still refused to look at him. Instead, she stuck her head in her refrigerator and pulled out the makings for grilled cheese sandwiches.

"Hungry?" she asked Zane reluctantly.

"After the past few days of nothing to eat but bugs and weeds? That would be a yes."

She smiled in his general direction but didn't make eye contact. Her courage deserted her and she put her head down, buttering bread and stacking Swiss, cheddar and provolone cheese slices on the bread. *Damn. Nothing to do now but watch the sandwiches cook.*

Zane grabbed a quick shower while she got the stove heating up, and she was relieved to have the kitchen to herself to regain her composure. Everyone else had settled in the living room to wait for the FBI to arrive and take custody of Persephone.

By the time Zane came back, his hair damp and smelling like her shampoo, she'd managed to shove her feelings into a drawer in her mind and slam the damned thing tightly shut.

She said nothing, concentrating on slicing apples for the two of them.

"How are you doing?" Zane asked quietly.

"I'm glad to be home."

"Yeah, I got that. How are *you* doing?"

"What do you mean?"

"C'mon. It's me you're talking to. Your boss can blow off the past week by saying it was only what you were trained to deal with, but I know what you really went through. That kind of stuff leaves its mark on anyone."

She flipped the sandwiches and busied herself pulling out glasses and filling them with ice. "Something to drink?"

"Sure. Whatever you're having."

She poured sweet tea from the pitcher in her refrigerator. Napkins. They needed napkins—

"Stop, Piper."

He snagged her hands and forced her to come to a halt in front of him. Reluctantly, she lifted her gaze to his. She didn't want to do this!

"How are you doing?"

She huffed. She really, *really* didn't want to talk about it. But apparently Zane was prepared to burn the sandwiches black if she refused to answer him. "I've been better," she admitted.

He let her go when she tugged her hands away and turned to rescue the sandwiches from the stove. She cut them in half diagonally and plated them, along with apple slices and potato chips.

"Sit," he ordered. "And stop fussing."

Zane held her chair for her and she slid past him, so close that she could smell the earth-and-rain scent of him.

He moved his chair from across the table to beside hers and sat down. "I'm not letting you run away from what happened to you. If you don't face it and deal with it, it'll gnaw at you until it eats you up."

"Thanks to you, nothing really bad happened to me."

"I have to disagree."

She shrugged. "So I got slapped around a little. They could have branded me with hot pokers or shoved bamboo spikes under my fingernails. I'm healing, for the most part. And as for a sexual assault, it didn't happen, thanks to you."

He frowned as if he was searching for words. Then he leaned forward and spoke quietly. "Just because I didn't actually attack you doesn't mean that the mental—and emotional—damage wasn't done. You still have to deal with the very real possibility of it happening."

Was he right? She realized she was staring at him, and looked down at her plate hastily.

"Whatever you need from me to aid your recovery—just let me know. If you need me to go to therapy with you, or you need me to go away and to never see me again—"

"No. Not that," she said quickly.

He fell silent, studying her intently. "You're sure?"

"I'm not sure about anything except that it feels supremely weird to think about being apart from you."

He gazed at her for a long time and then quietly said, "So be it."

Chapter Fifteen

Zane always felt underdressed when he visited the Pentagon. A plain civilian suit just didn't impress when everyone else was running around in starched, spit-shined, beribboned-uniform glory.

He must have sighed aloud, for Piper murmured beside him, "What's wrong?" Either that or she was just that closely tuned to his emotional state. Which was entirely possible. Their morning of debriefing at the CIA had been a revelation.

She had an uncanny ability to know what he was going to say next, to finish sentences for him, supply the right word when it failed to come. And to correctly read every moment when he waxed uncomfortable, sometimes subtly touching his foot with hers under the table.

Not that they'd had a minute to themselves to talk in private, of course. The debrief had been thorough to the point of torture, and mentally exhausting. He'd walked through his months with Mahmoud's terror cell, and then through the kidnapping of Piper. She joined in at that point, and they gave their debriefs in parallel. He described a portion of her captivity from his viewpoint, and then she told the same portion of it from hers.

Notably, she left out most of her fear and terror. But then, her boss and her teammates were also sitting in on the debrief. It wasn't like she was going to admit to being panicked and overwhelmed in front of them.

And it wasn't like he'd admitted to his own superiors how freaked out he'd been those last few days undercover, with his gut screaming at him to get the hell away from Mahmoud, but his head insisting he stick around to save Piper.

As for Mark Black, there had been no word from him. His supervisor on the international nuclear inspection team thought it was possible he'd gone on a short vacation over the weekend. In another eight hours or so, it would be Monday morning in Tehran, and they would find out if Black showed up for work or not.

In the meantime, they'd come over to the Pentagon to plan a rescue of the man in case he didn't turn up.

Zane had been included in the mission planning because he was an Iran specialist and fluent in Farsi. Also, he suspected Piper had spoken to her boss on the side and asked for him specifically.

Knowing her, she wasn't above playing the card of her recent trauma to get her way. Smiling a little, he opened the heavy glass-and-brass door for her and followed her into the Pentagon.

They were installed in a secure briefing room with a big-screen monitor on the wall flanked by two large whiteboards. The soundproof doors sealed shut, and Major Torsten turned to look at the three Medusas, his operations officer, who was a sharp guy named Beau Lambert, and Zane.

Torsten spoke briskly. "Okay, kids. The mission is to infiltrate Iran, find and secure Mark Black, and exfiltrate him…"

They brainstormed for a solid hour, and gradually a plan took shape. Personally, Zane thought it was freaking brilliant. He would never have thought of it himself. But then, he'd never had the tactical advantage of working with female Special Forces operators. They did, indeed, open up possibilities he'd never considered.

The whiteboards were carefully erased and washed, the browsing history of the computer attached to the big monitor deleted, and Major Torsten gathered up all his notes and locked them in his briefcase. He finished by saying, "I'll get the plan rolling. If the rest of you would like to stand down for now, I'll let you know when we're green-lighted."

"When will we know whether or not Black shows up for work?" Piper asked.

Torsten glanced at his watch. "Tehran is eight and a half hours ahead of Washington, DC. Black has a briefing at 9:00 a.m. Tehran local, so that'll be 12:30 tonight here."

Zane knew from long experience that a rescue mission could be green-lighted in a matter of minutes, or the decision could get mired in bureaucracy and take days or weeks to gain approval.

The first ride-share car to show up was small, so Zane suggested, "Why don't Tessa, Beau and Rebel take this vehicle? Piper and I will call another one."

To their credit, her teammates didn't rib him—or Piper—but merely sent her quick, questioning looks. She nodded slightly, and the others piled into a car and drove away.

"Thanks," she murmured. "I was getting claustrophobic sitting in that tiny, windowless, sealed room. I wasn't quite ready to get stuffed into a car yet."

Of course. It hadn't occurred to him that a side effect of her captivity might be fear of enclosed spaces, but it made sense.

A car showed up in just a minute or two, and he held the

door for her. As he slid in beside her, he murmured, "Need a window open?"

"No, thanks. I have to get used to small spaces sometime."

"But you don't have to do it all at once, today."

She shrugged. "Actually, I do. If we get the go-ahead tonight, I may be trapped inside an airplane by tomorrow morning."

"Are you sure you want to go on this trip? You've had a rough week. Maybe you should stay home—"

"Don't coddle me. Aren't people supposed to get right back on the horse so they don't develop an irrational fear of riding?"

"They also say not to set yourself on fire to keep other people warm. The—" He broke off and glanced at the back of the head of the driver, then continued, "This party can happen without you."

She shrugged. "We work best together as a team. And I would hate to sit at home, staring at the walls, knowing I'd been left out of all the fun."

He huffed. But truthfully, he couldn't argue with that. Staying home when his teammates went out on a dangerous mission would drive him crazy, too.

They were silent for the remainder of the ride to a hotel in northern Virginia. They checked into rooms Torsten had arranged for them, and Zane stared around the bland, antiseptic space. It felt weird to be alone like this after months living in tight quarters with Mahmoud's men. His room phone rang, and he picked it up.

"Hi. It's Piper. Are you hungry?"

He laughed, "Yes. I'm still not caught up after our involuntary fast in the woods."

"Me, neither. But I don't feel like peopling tonight. Wanna come to my room and order in?"

Thank God. He replied, "I'll be there in two minutes."

They found an online food-delivery service and ordered Chinese from a local restaurant. They each ordered two entrées, and the grocery bag full of white cardboard cartons ended up holding enough to feed six people. They had a picnic, spreading the feast out on the floor by the big glass window in Piper's room and grazing until they were both stuffed.

He started packing up empty containers and Piper groaned, "Now I finally feel caught up on food. But I also think I can't move."

"A food coma is called for," he declared.

They stretched out on her bed, and she rolled over to put her head on his shoulder. He let her.

He should probably establish some sort of professional distance between them if they were going to be working on the rescue op together. But not today. Tomorrow would be soon enough.

For one more night, he was going to hold her in his arms and pretend that the two of them could have a future together. Pretend that he wouldn't head off to one end of the world on an undercover mission and disappear for months, and that she wasn't a commando about to be bombing off to the other end of the world, jumping into hot zones herself.

She snuggled a little closer, and her lush hair rubbed against his chin, soft as kitten fluff.

"Comfortable?" he murmured.

"Best spot in the world to be," she mumbled back. She sounded half-asleep. Did she even realize what she'd just said? Her breath settled into the light, shallow rhythm of sleep, and he followed after her, reveling in letting his eyes drift closed and his mind drift off into dreams of him and Piper doing other things besides napping together.

IT WAS DARK when Piper woke up. She felt safe, which registered as strange. She was very still so her captors wouldn't know she was awake—

Oh. Wait. She was free. She and Zane had successfully escaped. She sagged against her pillow. Then frowned. Her pillow was hot. Hard. Resilient.

She raised up on an elbow and it finally dawned on her she'd been sprawled on top of Zane the whole time.

"Hi, beautiful," he murmured in his deep, raspy voice that never failed to delight her.

"Hi. Sorry I woke you."

"I've been awake for a while."

"Why didn't you wake me up and shove me off of you?" she exclaimed.

"I was enjoying watching you sleep."

"That bad, huh? Do I snore like a freight train? Or drool? Or maybe talk in my sleep? Oh, God. What did I say?"

"You did none of the above. Although you did become restless while you were dreaming."

"I dreamed I was back in that van. And it hit a trip wire on the road and blew up."

"Jeez. That's dark. Was I in the van when it blew?"

"We both were. I was frantic to get the back door open so we could jump out before it—I don't know—hit the ground or something."

He rolled onto his side without removing his arm from under her ear and gathered her against him. "We're safe on the ground now. It's all good."

"Crud," she mumbled against his chest. "I'm a wreck, aren't I?"

"Not at all. Everything you're experiencing is normal after a traumatic event."

"You say that like this isn't your first rodeo with trauma," she commented.

"It's not."

"Tell me about it?"

"I've been undercover for most of my career. First with a couple religious cults, and then with several supremacist groups. Then Mahmoud and company."

"Who was the scariest?"

He thought about that for several seconds. "Depends on the kind of scary you mean. The cults were scary because of how subtle they were. They played on people's minds like nobody's business. Lost, naive people got sucked in like dust bunnies into a vacuum cleaner. The supremacist groups were scary for how violent they were and how truly ugly their beliefs were. Mahmoud's crew was terrifying because of how incredibly disciplined they were. I had no idea who they were or what they were here to do, and I lived with them for *months*. What kind of a fanatic does a person have to be to maintain that level of focus for so long?"

"Are you talking about yourself having to focus not to blow your cover or about them maintaining operational security like that?" she asked.

He stared down at her. "You think I'm a fanatic? I'm doing the same thing you are—serving my country by doing a hard job very few other people could handle."

She frowned thoughtfully. "I don't think of myself as a fanatic, but I guess an outsider might see the Medusas that way. We have to go to some pretty extreme lengths to prepare for the work we do. Particularly since we're women."

"I was startled by the brainstorming session with your team today. Having an entire group of women operatives opens up all kinds of unique possibilities for missions."

"You have no idea. In today's meeting we only scratched the surface of the sort of stuff we can do."

"Tell me more."

She stared down at him from the lofty perch of her

elbow. "Well, we're trained exotic dancers, and we wear fancy gowns with guns strapped to our thighs, drink champagne and play baccarat and seduce heads of state. It's all very glamorous."

"Stop," he chuckled.

"Isn't that what people think you do when they find out you're an undercover operative?" she retorted.

"People don't find that out about me. Ever."

"Really? You told me without having any idea who I was."

He used one finger to gently tuck a strand of her hair behind her ear. "I had a good idea of who you were. I spotted that class ring of yours—"

She glanced down at her West Point class ring, which Tessa had returned to her this morning.

"—and the quality of your character was evident in how well you handled yourself in a crisis. Most women, or men for that matter, would have been completely panicked. You kept your cool and worked with me instead of against me."

"Well, yeah. You were helping me," she replied.

"You let me help you, and that made all the difference. It's why we both made it out alive," he responded soberly.

"Was it that close a call?" she asked reflectively.

"I was told nothing, as in *nothing*, about the attack on the school. They set up the getaway van without my knowing, and when it came time to sexually assault you, I was chosen to do it because they didn't want to leave behind any DNA evidence to incriminate themselves. You tell me what that sounds like."

"They didn't trust you, did they?"

"Nope. Had it not been for you, I would have bugged out and called in the authorities to grab them as soon as I realized we were going to attack the school. Had Mahmoud and Yousef not barged into the office when they did, I was going to ask you to call the FBI while I delayed their getaway."

"Why didn't you?"

"They were focused on finding Persephone Black at all costs. They would have shot everyone in that office, including you, if that was what it took to get her to show herself to them. I hoped they would take longer searching the school room by room before they came back to the office, but they were too fast."

"It's not that big a school. And I imagine the teachers were quick to volunteer the information that she would be in the principal's office and not in any of the classrooms. Their focus would have been on getting those gunmen out of their classes as soon as possible."

"I can't blame them," Zane muttered.

"How close was Mahmoud to killing me when you and I escaped?" she asked curiously.

"My guess was that, as soon as he handed over that fake rape tape, his bosses had everything they needed from you to secure your 'husband's' cooperation. You had become expendable."

"And they had a violent end planned for me?" She knew the answer, but she wanted to hear him say it. She needed to hear Zane say it. After all, she'd killed a man in those woods.

He shrugged. "You were trapped in that farmer's house with me and then hunted through the woods. I think they made their intentions toward both of us crystal clear."

Indeed, they had. Hassan's death had been necessary. It had been a kill-or-be-killed situation. She took no pleasure in killing, but she could live with the necessity of it.

"How did you find Hassan, anyway?" Obviously, Zane's thoughts were paralleling hers as he processed yesterday's events.

She shrugged. "Once we were out in the woods, I flipped the script and hunted the hunters. The Medusas are taught to believe their training is superior to the other guy's, and that we'll be underestimated because of our gender. Often, we're actually the aggressors when people are chasing after us in the mistaken belief that we're the prey."

"Handy, that."

She smiled at him. "Yes, it is."

His hand slipped under her silky hair, cupping the back of her head and very gently urging her down to him. It was more of an invitation than a demand, and she appreciated his continued gentleness and restraint. She leaned forward, propping herself on his chest and kissing him leisurely.

His mouth was warm and gentle, his kisses as lazy as a wide river on a hot summer day. She sank into him, into the lure of his mouth, loving how the attraction between them simmered today, easy and sure.

It was a relief to discover that the attraction between them wasn't solely about fear and survival. And it was doubly a relief to discover that they still wanted each other now that they had returned to the real world.

Missions were fraught with danger and tension, and it was inevitable that the stress would find outlets. She'd been worried their hot sex in the woods had been nothing more than that to him, and nothing more than trauma recovery for her.

But the desire building in her now, filling her belly like magma flowing into an underground chamber, was reassuringly insistent. And frustrating in the best possible way.

This time, Zane took the lead, slowly undressing her, taking time to taste every new bit of skin he uncovered as he peeled off her T-shirt and stripped off her jeans. She returned the favor, savoring the soapy, male scent of his skin and the faint savory-sweet taste of soy sauce lingering on his tongue.

Tonight, they got to know each other's bodies more thoroughly. She learned the textures and tastes of him, and he learned where all her most sensitive spots were and what felt the best to her.

He murmured words of praise and encouragement, and she murmured words of trust and assurance back to him. Eventually, she laughed.

"What?" Zane asked quickly, looking up from her belly button.

"We're both being so careful we're starting to sound like a pair of nervous old ladies."

"Speak for yourself. I am merely sensitive to the trauma you've experienced."

"You can help me get past the trauma by treating me like a flesh-and-blood woman and not a crystal statue."

"Done," he murmured.

He drew her into his arms once more. But he still kissed her lazily as if he didn't have a care in the world, no expectations of anything more from her. Thankfully, his erection was thick and heavy against her hip, or else she might have wondered if he found her attractive at all. The man had the patience of a saint.

Not so herself, however.

"You taste like sweet-and-sour," he murmured.

"You're rocking *moo goo gai pan*," she replied, smiling against his lips. "But can we move this along?"

He laughed quietly, "But I like driving women crazy with desire. Trust me. I have a plan."

"*Crazy* being the operative word," she grumbled.

He eased her onto her back, smiling down at her and murmuring, "Let me have my moment with you. Imagining this kept me going for a lot of our trek from hell."

"How's that?"

"I spent hours thinking about what I was going to do with you once I got you naked. And after that night in the rain, I vowed that someday I would get you into a real bed and do every one of the things I'd imagined."

"What happened by the campfire was premeditated, was it? And this? Do you have every bit of this planned out?" She looped her arms around his neck and pulled him down to her for a long, deep kiss that left her gasping for air and extremely impatient for more.

"I'm open to a little spontaneity," he murmured against her lips.

"I'm relieved to hear you're not *entirely* unable to change your plans," she teased.

"In my line of work? That's all I do." He drew his fingertips down her body slowly, starting at her throat, caressing her neck, stroking down the valley between her breasts, then down her belly, culminating in a delicious stroke between the soft folds of her feminine flesh that had her arching up off the mattress and struggling to remember the thread of their conversation.

With some effort, she managed to say a bit breathlessly, "It would make sense in your private life if you wanted complete control and predictability."

Toying with the hard little pearl of her desire, and stealing at least forty points off her IQ in the process, he commented, "I like control and predictability, but not like how you mean them. It's rare that I get to turn off my internal alarms and be fully at ease. That's what I crave. Safety, so I can relax."

"What do you like to do when you're fully at ease, Mr. Cosworth?"

"I'd rather show you," he whispered as his lips closed on a rosy peak of her breast and laved it into a tight little bud.

"Feel free," she gasped.

"Mmm. I'd like to spend weeks wooing you." A gentle suck and a flick of his tongue made her cry out. He continued, "I would take you out to nice dinners. Some movie nights. Maybe a concert or two."

"You wouldn't want to stay in? Be unseen?"

He didn't answer right away. Instead, he lavished the same attention on her other breast until she was nearly sobbing in need. Then he murmured, "I know this great jazz club in DC that I'd love to show you—"

She interrupted him, tugging his head up to her mouth so she could kiss him, showing him just how desperate she was for him to get on with business. "I appreciate your willingness to put in some time on me—"

He interrupted in turn. "You're not a project to be managed and completed. But I want you to be comfortable with me. To feel safe."

"Me? I feel plenty safe. I could incapacitate or kill you in any number of ways, thank you."

He rolled onto his back beside her and laughed under his breath. "God. I never thought I'd hear a woman in my bed say *that*."

It was her turn to wince. "I'm sorry. I suck at romance."

"Lucky for you, I don't," he replied, humor vibrating in his voice.

"I sincerely appreciate you planning out how you would romance me, but all I really want is you."

"Are you telling me you don't have any interest at all in romance?" he responded, sounding surprised.

"Oh, I love being romanced as much as the next girl. But I have a weird sense of what constitutes romance."

"Like what?"

"I thought you letting me use the restroom after I tried to escape from you that first morning was shockingly chivalrous. And you always fed me and made sure I had plenty of water. You helped me out of the van and checked to make sure my handcuffs didn't chafe my wrists. You covered me with a blanket when I passed out in the basement."

"You caught all that, huh?"

She answered softly, "Yeah. I did. And thank you."

Frustration crept into his voice. "I felt so damned helpless to protect you. I wanted to tell you who I was so you wouldn't feel alone and you would know you were going to make it out of there, but I worried that you would slip up if they put you under enough duress and that you might reveal who I was."

She smiled up at him. "We Medusas are tougher than we look."

"Oh, yeah? And here I was thinking you're so much softer than I expected."

"Hey! I stay in good shape!"

He grinned down at her, stroking his palm across her stomach and up to cup her breast gently. "I dunno. You feel like all woman to me." His mouth hovered barely a millimeter from hers. "And I love the idea of a woman who's strong and fit and capable, too."

"You're just saying that because you want in my panties," she teased.

"Darlin', we're already way past your panties."

"I dunno. You're spending a whole lot of time talking and not getting busy."

He laughed down at her. "You did *not* just challenge my manhood."

"I might have…"

Their laughter mingled as they kissed, gradually transforming into something more serious. More passionate.

But still he moved slowly, treating her with care. She appreciated him taking it slow with her. It gave her plenty of time to check in with herself and make sure nothing along the way freaked her out.

She loved the way his hard body pressed her down into the mattress. His muscular thighs tangling with hers were sexy as hell. And when his hard, hot length filled her ever so slowly, the only thing that went through her mind was a wish that he would go faster and deeper and harder.

She moved against him experimentally, and it was good. Very good. Bordering on outstanding, in fact.

They found a rhythm easily this time, their bodies accustomed to each other and finding synchronicity immediately. She had time to register liking being tall enough that their bodies fitted so nicely and to register liking that he was fully as strong and fit as she was, which made her feel at ease showing her eagerness for more from him. She wrapped her legs around his hips and welcomed him into her strong embrace, and he met her on equal ground.

Gradually, he let go of the caution he was exercising with her and unleashed his full passion into their lovemaking. And that was when it blew right past outstanding into the realm of epic.

They were unabashedly athletic with each other, surging into each other until their bodies were slick with perspiration and they were both gasping for air. Riding a wave they built between them, they rushed all the way to completion, a lovely race with only winners and no losers.

The pleasure built and built until it finally toppled over, crashing down around them in delicious destruction that left her breathless, her limbs languid, and her mind and soul sated.

It was fully as magical as she remembered, maybe even better this time around because they were more comfortable with each other, not to mention they were dry and warm and in a proper bed. Not that she minded sleeping on the ground or sprawled across his chest as the case might be. But this was better.

And falling asleep cuddled up next to Zane, replete with pleasure and relaxed with knowing he would look out for her while she rested, was even better yet.

Chapter Sixteen

Zane woke up gradually, reveling lazily in the happiness that washed over him. That was not a feeling he really ever ascribed to himself. But he was definitely feeling great tonight. It was a weird contrast with his normal wake up, where his mind would turn immediately to the day's work, to the threats at hand, to remembering the identity he was supposed to be living in from the moment he opened his eyes and started his day.

Happiness had no place in his work, and his work had been his life for a decade or more.

But there were no immediate threats at hand, and the only identity he had to assume was the rather unfamiliar one of Zane Cosworth. Even better, the only work at hand was to enjoy the amazing woman sharing his bed.

What had he been missing, denying himself this feeling for so long? Piper brought up a good point. Was doing his duty to the exclusion of all else really worth it? Was there a way to make time for happiness—for her—in his life, too? Could he have his job and a personal life?

It would take exactly the right woman to be sure. One who understood the importance of his work and how much it meant to him. One willing to sacrifice time with him, willing to put up with long silences when he was undercover, willing to worry and wait and have faith that he would survive and make it home once more.

A woman like Piper.

If only she would give him some indication that she was willing to consider a longer-term relationship than just this time together. But she'd never said a single word about what came after this mission.

He got that people like the two of them needed to live in the moment. They both needed to be able to focus completely on the task at hand, on the dangers directly in front of them. It was how they both stayed alive in their respective lines of work.

Her house had been cozy. Clearly a personal and private sanctuary, not set up for anyone else to share. He knew: he'd searched the place for pictures of other men. For hints about her family, about her past, about her life before the kidnapping. The place had been completely bare of any such mementos.

Yup, she was an operator through and through. Her life revolved one hundred percent around her work.

Exactly like his life revolved around his work.

Or more accurately, like it had until he'd met her.

Huh. He'd never expected to fall for a woman who hadn't fallen for him first. He was always the one to break things off, to move on to the next mission, to the next identity, to the next false life.

But Piper made him think about settling down. About resuming life as Zane Cosworth. About home. Family. Love. All the things he'd given up and hadn't realized he missed until this very moment.

"You're thinking pretty hard over there, sailor," Piper interrupted from her pillow beside his.

"Sorry. I didn't mean to wake you up."

"You didn't. I set a silent alarm on my watch to wake

me up, and it's due to vibrate in a few minutes. My mental alarm clock usually beats my watch by five minutes or so."

He glanced over at her quickly. "Why did you set an alarm for half past midnight?"

"Mark Black is supposed to show up for his Monday morning briefing in a few minutes."

Right. The mission.

Obviously, for Piper the mission came first, and Zane came in a distant second.

The realization tasted bitter in his mouth. Not that he could blame her. It was just strange wearing the shoe on the other foot. He was always the one who made the glib excuse, slipped out of the woman's bed and disappeared, never to look back. But tonight, it was her citing the mission to slip out of bed, collect her clothes and efficiently get dressed.

Zane rolled out of bed and pulled on clothes, as well. No way was Mark Black showing up for that meeting. And when the guy was officially declared missing, a manhunt would be initiated. Quietly. Which meant the CIA would probably green-light the op Torsten had proposed to find the guy.

Piper's phone rang, and they both stared at it.

Then she jolted into motion and picked it up, listening for a few seconds. "Roger. On my way," she replied. She disconnected the call.

"Black didn't show up, did he?" Zane asked.

"Nope."

"I'd better get back to my room. My phone's going to blow up in a minute or two."

She nodded, her face set in serious lines, her mind obviously already at work on what came next.

He kissed her quickly and left, striding down the hall and slipping into his room.

Must not look back.

Let her go.

No regrets.

Maybe in another time, another place, they could've been good together for a long time. Maybe a lifetime. But duty called them both.

He'd been in his room perhaps thirty seconds when someone knocked quietly on his door. He opened it cautiously, leaving the chain on and barely cracking it open.

Shit. Gunnar Torsten.

He threw the door open.

"Five minutes. Out front," Gunnar murmured.

"I'll be there."

As Zane closed his door, he heard Gunnar knocking quietly on another door down the hall.

Zane used three of his five minutes to leap into the shower and try to wash Piper off his skin, out of his heart, out of his life.

It didn't work.

He swiped a razor across his cheeks, tossed the razor in his prepacked bag and was out the door with a minute to spare. He jogged down the hall and took the stairs, arriving in the lobby exactly five minutes after Gunnar's knock.

A dark blue government van was just pulling up, and the three Medusas and Torsten nodded to him.

"Where's Beau?" he asked.

Piper murmured, "He's gone home to plan the party from his end."

They piled into the vehicle, and he was surprised when the van didn't head down I-395 toward the Pentagon. Rather, it wound north, ending up on Rock Creek Parkway.

"Are we going to Langley?" he blurted in surprise.

Gunnar nodded. "Your guys are going to be running

this show. They want you and Piper involved, since you have personal knowledge of possible operators involved."

He and Piper? They got to work together on this op? *Yes*. His gut leaped with joy. A little longer to savor what could have been before it was ripped away from them for good. Hell, he was so desperate to be with her that he would take whatever morsels of time he could snatch with her.

It took several minutes to pass all their government IDs through the window to the gate guard and for them to be waved through to the parking area at CIA headquarters. He had only his fake IDs generated for the Amir legend, but those were on file, and he was approved to enter without delay.

He led the way through long corridors to the briefing room the guy at the front desk told them to report to.

It was a bland conference room with bland paneling and bland furniture that belied none of the massive technology and intelligence resources pulsing around them in this, the living brain of the US intelligence apparatus.

A bland-looking man in a suit walked into the room, and Zane recognized one of the senior Iran analysts, a guy several pay grades above him, Dominic Farris.

Dominic nodded at Zane and said in a bland tone, "Welcome back. Good work on your recent mission rescuing Captain Ford."

Zane snorted. "It's entirely possible that she ultimately rescued me."

Piper's gaze snapped to his, and he belatedly realized that his comment could be taken both literally and figuratively. He shrugged, silently owning both interpretations.

Torsten leaned forward, asking Dominic, "What can you tell us about Mark Black?"

The analyst picked up a remote control, and a section of the paneling slid back to reveal a backlit screen. An awkward official portrait of a man in perhaps his midthirties, wearing horn-rimmed glasses and an ill-fitting suit, popped up on the screen. It could've been straight out of a high school yearbook were it not for the guy's age.

"Mark Black. Nuclear physicist and propulsion engineer by education. Senior field inspector for the Global Atomic Inspection Team, or GAIT. He has been in Iran for three months, monitoring and inspecting various facilities there for GAIT. His boss is this man, René Descarnes. French. Long-time Interpol asset. Sharp guy."

Zane leaned forward as a picture of Black walking on the street he recognized to be in Tehran flashed up on screen. "And Black? Is he an asset to anyone?"

"Not officially. Obviously, his GAIT reports come across our desks, compliments of Descarnes. But Black's just a nuclear inspector."

Piper interjected, "Then why was his wife targeted for kidnapping?"

"Black is scheduled to be the first inspector inside a new Iranian scientific facility in a few days. Place is called the Iranian Center for Materials Research. We believe her—your—kidnapping—" he nodded in Piper's direction "—was an attempt to pressure him into not reporting something the Iranians expect him to see at that facility."

"Like what?" Zane asked quickly.

Dominic shrugged. "We can speculate all day long, but until Black gets inside those labs, we'll have no way of knowing."

"Where is Black now?"

"We believe he's a guest of the Iranian government."

"Meaning what?" Torsten snapped.

"Meaning they will hold him in their custody until he has inspected the facility and issued the report they want him to make."

Torsten asked briskly, like the military man he was, "What's our mission?"

"Go to Tehran. Find Mark Black. Let him go to the Center for Materials Research and, after he's out, retrieve him and bring him home. We need to know what he sees in there. While you're at it, make sure he knows his wife is safe. He may not cooperate with you otherwise. Once you've got Black's debrief, at all costs, he must not fall back into the hands of the Iranian government. We do not want a high-value hostage situation to develop."

Zane leaned back hard in his chair. Damn. The powers that be wanted Black dead rather than in Iranian hands? Just what did the CIA think was inside that lab, anyway?

"Any other mission parameters?" Torsten asked briskly.

"Don't get caught."

Torsten threw Dominic a "duh" look. "That's why we're here. The Medusas specialize in being invisible. Speaking of which, do you have your own plan in place to get this team into Iran, or are we on our own to arrange it?"

"Did you have something in mind?" Dominic asked with interest.

Torsten grinned, and Zane was struck by how wolflike an expression it was. The major continued, "Yes, actually we do. An air show is scheduled to start in Tehran the day after tomorrow. Business jets are being flown in by all the big global airplane manufacturers to Mehrabad International Airport downtown and shown off to various government officials. The Iranian government plans to buy a new fleet of small jets and is accepting bids from companies all over the world."

"And?" Dominic asked.

"We'd like to fly in on one of those jets. We'll pose as crew members and corporate representatives, which will give us a reason to be in Tehran and to be doing nothing for most of our time in country while we wait to fly the jet out. We'll use real pilots to fly the plane, of course. They can fly any demonstrations Iranian officials want."

"And you'll bring Mark Black out on that plane with you?" Dominic asked.

Torsten nodded. "Correct. Mehrabad is very close to the city center. It'll be a lot easier to get there than Imam Khomeini International Airport, which is well outside of Tehran."

Zane murmured, "It's about thirty kilometers southwest of Tehran. Good roads. Traffic's not too bad out that way. But plenty of time for security forces to catch up with a person. Security's tight at Mehrabad, though. We'll need a subterfuge to get Black onto the airfield."

Zane's boss nodded thoughtfully. "I'll need a list of equipment and support you'll need to mount the operation, and a time frame for execution."

Torsten replied, "The equipment list is already built. I'll email it to you as soon as we're done here. We can be ready to go as soon as you pull the trigger."

Zane added, "All we need now is the go-ahead to get Mark Black."

"Stay here. I'll be back," Dominic ordered.

Piper looked over at Zane. "Where'd he run off to?"

"Hopefully, he's getting us approval to roll."

The team opened the printed dossiers on Mark Black and went through them in detail, studying every picture of his face, memorizing each angle and look carefully. Zane hoped the knowledge would be put to use identifying the guy and not having to shoot him to keep him out of Iranian clutches. Persephone Black seemed like a nice lady who would appreciate getting her husband back in one piece.

Dominic was back within about ten minutes to announce that they had, indeed, been green-lighted to proceed with the rescue mission. He nodded at Zane. "You'll be the CIA liaison officer for this joint operation. Use your usual contacts."

Dominic passed him a Tyvek envelope taped shut, and Zane signed for it. He recognized a legend package when he saw one. Inside would be fake IDs, a passport, perhaps some jewelry or a distinctive possession, emergency phone numbers and email addresses to memorize, along with challenge-and-response codes to use with those emergency contacts. And most important, there would be a printed packet of information on his new identity. An entire team of cyberspecialists sat around day in and day out building identities just like this one and maintaining them for when operatives needed a quick cover story.

He would memorize everything inside the envelope over the next few days and accustom himself to answering to the new name inside. Goodbye, Zane. Goodbye, Amir, the wannabe terrorist. Hello, Rashid Farouk.

"The folks down in the photography shop would like to see you before you leave the building so they can get to work creating identification documents for all of you," Dominic commented.

Zane would undoubtedly get his hair dyed, wear colored contact lenses, maybe start growing a beard, and then he would be photographed for his—Rashid's—new passport, driver's license, library card and whatever other IDs were in the package.

Piper and her teammates were taken away to be fitted for their uniforms for the mission—costumes, actually. They would also be photographed for their fake IDs.

The hair dying, fittings and interminable photographs, fingerprints and even dental X-rays took the rest of the night. They reconvened back at the hotel in Torsten's room for breakfast and to quiz each other on their legends. Zane stared when Piper walked in. He'd assumed she would also go dark haired, but in fact, just the opposite had happened. Her hair, already antique gold in color, was now platinum blond.

"Well, hello, Barbie," he drawled.

She stuck her tongue out at him, while Rebel and Tessa laughed. Tessa, naturally olive complexioned and dark haired, had not had her appearance appreciably altered. Rebel, naturally a fair-skinned brunette, had been taken red haired. It was actually a good look on her.

He understood the thinking of the beauticians in the basement at Langley. Blondes and redheads were exotic creatures in a country like Iran, where most of the population was Persian in descent. Piper and Rebel would be treated like celebrities anywhere they went, but all that anyone would remember after seeing them would be their hair colors and not their faces.

The women all carried zippered vinyl clothing bags, which they hung in Torsten's closet. Their uniforms were already tailored and ready to go? That was fast. This mission must have a higher priority at Langley than Dominic had let on to them.

Now, why wouldn't Dominic be honest about something like that? Zane hated it when the higher-ups withheld information from field schmucks like him. The more he knew, the safer he was and the better he could do his job. But without fail, the brass kept secrets and played coy with the truth.

He sat beside Torsten, who was digging into his pancakes with gusto. Zane waited until the guy had slowed down to murmur, "Have folks in your intel channels given you any additional information about this op?"

Torsten looked up at him sharply. "Most of what the military has comes from your people. Why would we have more?"

Zane shrugged. "I know Dominic. He wasn't telling us everything. I got the distinct feeling that folks up the chain of command from us are holding back something important."

"Like what?"

"Maybe something about Black, or maybe about the facility he's supposed to inspect."

Torsten nodded. "I noticed how coy Dominic was about guessing what the Iranians don't want Black to see." He paused and then added quietly, "Only bit of hot intel I've seen recently on Iran has a major arms dealer coming back from the dead and supposedly doing a deal with the Iranian government."

"What dealer?" Zane asked quickly.

"Abu Haddad."

"Haddad? Well, hell. I was hoping that bastard was well and truly six feet under."

Torsten lifted his chin in Tessa's direction. "Tessa and Beau are the ones who took him out. We all thought for sure we got him, but apparently, he managed to slip away. Either that or one of his flunkies has resurrected his business and is invoking his name to get clients."

Zane picked up his cell phone, put it on secure mode and placed a quick phone call. "Hi, Antonia. It's Zane." He chatted with the Turkey-Cyprus-Greece specialist for a few minutes and then casually shifted topics. "Hey, Toni. I heard a rumor that Haddad may be back in business. Has anything crossed your desk about him recently?"

The analyst expressed surprise that Haddad was alive but had nothing else.

"Do me a favor," Zane added. "Don't mention his name in connection with mine. No need to go out of your way poking around to find out more."

"You don't want me to raise any red flags?" the woman asked shrewdly.

"You know me too well," he replied ruefully.

"If I happen to run across any information, I'll pass it your way."

"Thanks, love."

Piper's eyebrows raised fractionally across the room.

Zane disconnected the call and said to the group at large, "Antonia has been around practically since the CIA was founded. I'm convinced she personally knows every single person living in Greece today. And she is related to at least half of them by blood. Last time I heard, she has about thirty grandchildren."

Piper's expression abruptly shifted to one of total disinterest, and Zane glanced over at Torsten, who was, indeed, looking back and forth between him and Piper.

"Did she have anything to say?" the major asked.

"No. Which is telling. She knows *everything* about Turkey. Whatever's being withheld from us is happening at a very high level."

Torsten swore quietly. "There's possibly nothing on earth I hate worse than going into a mission half-blind."

Zane laughed without humor. "I dunno. Direct congressional oversight on a mission sucks pretty hard."

Torsten groaned. "God save us all from meddling politicians."

Around midmorning, a call came in to Zane that the airplane and two pilots requisitioned by the agency would arrive at Dulles International Airport in a few hours. They would cross the Atlantic and stop in Europe for twelve hours of crew rest for the pilots and then continue on to Tehran.

Zane asked the group, "Any preference as to where we stop over in Europe?"

Torsten pulled up a map on his laptop, and a good-natured argument ensued. It was eventually settled that they would stop over at a US Naval facility in Sicily. It was far enough off the beaten path that casual informants shouldn't spot them, and the food was apparently first-class. Mount Etna, the volcano that rose up to tower over Sicily, had been quiet recently, as well.

The entire group went to the Pentagon to work out in its gym before their ride arrived, and Zane took pleasure in being less shocked than the other gym rats as Piper, Tessa and Rebel commenced tossing around weights like candy and generally embarrassing the men in the big facility.

A group of silent men working out together in one corner recognized Torsten and invited him and the women to come over and play with the big boys. Zane was just as happy to stay on his treadmill, stretching out his legs for a quick hard run today.

As they rode in the van back to the hotel, the women talked excitedly about getting to work out with and measure themselves against a SEAL team. He was gratified when Piper slid her hand surreptitiously between them to squeeze his in reassurance.

No need for her to worry. He was confident in his own masculinity.

They each went their own way for supper, which meant he was able to collect Piper and take her to that jazz club downtown. They sat on the same side of a banquette table, and he lounged back, listening to an improv band while she half lay on his chest, relaxing.

He couldn't remember ever being this at peace in his own skin.

He couldn't ever remember being this scared.

Which was exceedingly strange to him. He didn't do scared. He'd stared down fanatics and terrorists; he'd been chased by spies and run for his life without ever feeling half this terrified.

But then, he also didn't spend much time living in his own skin, either. He'd spent a good chunk of his adult life pretending to be someone else.

"You're messing with my head, Piper," he murmured as the level in the bottle of wine in front of them dropped.

"You're messing with mine, too," she replied.

"How?" they both asked simultaneously.

"You first." He beat her to saying it.

"I wasn't looking for a relationship," she confessed. "I'm still not looking for one. But here you are, and I have no idea what to do about you."

He set down his wineglass and twined their fingers together. "I would never come between you and your work. I have a decent idea of how hard it was for you to land an assignment with the Medusas. It's a once-in-a-lifetime opportunity."

"You're not wrong. I've devoted my entire adult life to this goal," she replied. "But then, I imagine you had to do the same to become what you are, too."

He shrugged. "It's possible that it was easier for me to hide behind all those other personas rather than face my own life and deal with it."

"Is there some trauma in your past? Something that made you want or need to run away from it rather than face it?"

He replied quickly, "Nothing like that. My family is affluent. Successful. Relatively normal if you accept the premise that no family is actually 'normal' and that all families have their problems."

"What problems does your family have?"

He shrugged again. "Nothing radical. My father is a control freak and ordered around my mom, my brother and me. My older brother went along with the program and did what he was told. I…didn't."

She nodded. "Rebelled as a kid. Check." A pause. "Did you get in trouble with the law?"

"No. My old man was the district attorney and was always able to have a word with the police chief and get any charges dropped."

"What kind of stuff did you do?"

"I drove too fast and drank too much. Partied too hard and made too much noise mostly."

"Why the choice of your current employer?" she asked curiously.

"They were looking for risk takers. People who could function in danger and were willing to put their necks on the line. It seemed like a good fit at the time."

"And now?"

He looked up, making eye contact with her. "For the first time, I'm questioning my life choices."

She jolted. "Why? Because I'm a bad choice?"

"Not at all. Because I may actually have found something—someone—worth living for. Someone more important to me than my job."

"Oh." Her gaze slid away from his, and in the dim lighting he wasn't sure she blushed. But he thought she did.

After a long pause, she looked back at him. "You said before that I'm messing with your head. Is that what you meant?"

"Partially."

When he didn't explain, she asked hesitantly, "What's the rest of it?"

He sighed, "This is going to sound stupid, but I have no idea who I am."

She frowned. "How's that?"

"I went straight from college to the agency. All that

growing up and self-discovery you're supposed to do in your twenties didn't happen for me. The next thing I knew, I was pretending to be all these other people."

He tossed back the rest of his wine and refilled their glasses.

"The thing with deep cover is you have to become your legend. You don't get a break to go home and put your feet up on a coffee table, read your mail and catch up on your life. You don't report in to your boss or touch base with your colleagues. Anything that might link you to your real life is strictly off-limits. You're cast adrift without any anchor whatsoever to your reality."

"That sounds scary," she murmured.

"After a while, it becomes normal. You stop thinking about your real life, your real family and friends, your real identity. You become the cover story."

"Would you say you actually became a white supremacist or a religious fanatic?"

He took another slug of the excellent wine, swirling it around in his mouth and savoring its dry bite.

"While I was that other person, I was both of those things. I had to be. There's no room in an undercover operation for hesitation or equivocation. You have to commit to the role, both in action and in thought. You have to believe you're that other persona."

"I don't think I could do that," she replied.

"It's like being a method actor and completely immersing yourself in the role."

She smiled sadly. "I still couldn't do it."

"I'm starting to wish I hadn't done it," he replied in a low voice.

"Why not? You've done your country a great service. You should be proud of your work."

"But at what cost? I don't even remember who I am

anymore. I don't know what I think, what I like or dislike, what I believe in. I'm…empty."

"How do you feel right this minute?" she asked urgently.

He considered for a moment. "Relaxed. Happy. Relieved that I get to spend more time with you before our careers rip us apart. Worried about the mission."

"Why are you worried?" she asked quickly.

"I'm a known Iran expert. I have to assume that Mahmoud sent photos of me back to his superiors. After I escaped with you, he also surely told them I was at best a traitor to their cause and at worst a plant of some kind. The odds of me being recognized when I enter Iran are fairly high. And the consequences of that…" He shrugged.

"You'd be lucky if they only killed you," she finished for him.

"Exactly."

"How good is the disguise the agency worked up for you?"

"It'll have to be good enough, won't it?"

"Can I help you be less recognizable?" she asked.

"I don't know."

"What if we pose as a married couple? That would throw them off, wouldn't it?"

"Our IDs would have to be redone—"

"Not necessarily," she interrupted. "You know us aggressive, out-of-control American women. We don't take our husbands' names anymore. It's scandalous. All that would have to happen is one of the cyberidentity folks would have to enter a marriage license for us in some database." Warming to her topic, she added, "We could have eloped to Las Vegas recently."

"It might help. And it would have the added benefit of forcing you to stay near me during the mission."

She reached in her purse for her cell phone and placed a call. "Beau, it's Piper. I need you to marry me."

Even Zane heard the squawk at the other end of the phone.

"Not like that," she laughed. "I need you to plant a marriage for me in whatever system it needs to be planted in. Yes. Part of a cover legend. Zane. His name will be Rashid Farouk."

She glanced up at him. "How's that spelled?"

He relayed what was on his new passport, and she relayed it to Beau.

She put her phone away and picked up her wineglass. "A toast. To our long and happy fake marriage, Mr. Farouk."

"To us, Mrs. Farouk."

Except it didn't feel the least bit fake as they clinked glasses and drank, smiling deeply into each other's eyes.

Chapter Seventeen

Piper tugged at the annoyingly tight red suit the CIA had seen fit to provide for her. "When I signed up to be a Medusa, I didn't think I would end up saving the world in pantyhose and high heels."

Zane and Torsten laughed, and she threw them a dirty look. "Next mission, you two get to wear the pencil skirts and stilettos."

Zane threw up his hands. "No, thank you. I don't know how women stand upright in those monstrosities, let alone walk in them."

She glared at him. "Clearly, it's because we are the superior gender and have exceptional balance."

He grinned. "You'll get no argument out of me."

Tessa rolled her eyes. "It's this stupid hat that's going to be the death of me."

All three women had been given dopey little red pillbox hats that had to be pinned to their hair to even stay perched on their heads.

Torsten grinned. "Think of them as your big red buttons. Someone hits one of those, I give you full permission to take out the transgressor."

"Done," Piper muttered.

"You may regret telling them that," Zane commented. The two men traded wry smiles.

"How much longer till we land?" Piper asked no one in particular.

Torsten got up and walked forward past a half-dozen plush armchair-style seats to ask the pilots. He wore an identical uniform to those of the two men in the cockpit, and his hair was cut to match theirs. She had to admit he wore a suit well. But then, all military men tended to. They had the right physiques for it.

"About an hour left," Torsten announced, returning through the snazzy, tricked-out passenger space. "Any last-minute questions before we land?"

Piper shook her head. They'd been over the mission parameters so many times she could probably recite them in her sleep. Zane sat across from her, wearing an exceptionally well-cut suit. He was posing as a sales representative of the TrevAir Jet Manufacturing Company. Poor guy had had to memorize more information about airplanes in the past two days than she could even begin to imagine.

Luckily, her job was to act like a bubblehead and flirt with the Iranian officials. The challenge would be to flirt enough to disarm them without flirting so much as to offend them. Zane had spoken with all three women at length about it, explaining that, as infidels, they would not be perceived as fully human. They were something…less. Particularly with the ultraconservatives who tended to populate the government.

He avoided using words like *whores* or *sluts*, but Piper got the idea. And it left a sour taste in her mouth.

The descent and landing at Mehrabad, in downtown Tehran, went uneventfully. Out her window, Piper spotted a row of tan C-130s, American military cargo planes sold to Iran in another age, when the shah was still in power and a friend to the United States. On the other side of the runway from the military ramp was a blocky, ugly 1970s-style terminal. And in the distance, dry, dark mountains rose above the skyline of Tehran. High-rise apartments and offices rose in clusters growing out of the lower, older sprawl of the ancient city. The contrast was stark.

The airport's tarmac was crowded with business jets from all over the world, every major aircraft manufacturer angling for this lucrative contract with the Iranian government. The Medusas had timed their arrival for after most of the other airplanes arrived, giving them a big, chaotic crowd of jets and crew members to blend into.

The air tasted like bitter dust and thick diesel exhaust. A wall of city noise struck Piper as she paused on the top of the steps to the jet—vehicles and people living in overcrowded proximity. Over eight million of Iran's not quite seventy-five million citizens lived in Tehran.

They passed through customs control without issue. The immigration officers had spent the past two days checking in crews for the air show and were overworked and sloppy.

Thank God. Piper noted that the customs agent didn't look twice at Zane with his black hair, dark beard stubble and thick, horn-rimmed glasses, nor at his papers declaring him to be the crew's translator.

The first hurdle was crossed. She and Zane had made it into Iran without incident. Now to make it out the same way.

Piper rolled around the unfamiliar gold wedding band on her left ring finger and glanced sidelong at him. She murmured, "Should I drop back three steps behind you as befits a proper wife?"

"Don't you dare."

He had a quick conversation in Farsi with two cab drivers at the front of the taxi queue outside the main terminal, and then he loaded Torsten, Tessa, Rebel and one of the pilots in one cab, and Piper, the second pilot and himself in the second. She was careful not to touch him because he'd stressed that public displays of affection between men and women were deeply frowned upon.

The taxis delivered them to a nearby hotel, and Zane efficiently checked them in and passed out room keys. Piper followed him to their shared room.

The decor was hopelessly outdated, but the unit was clean. She commented, "Well, it's better than that last place we stayed in."

He shot her a rueful smile. He'd also told everyone to expect their hotel rooms to be bugged and to guard their speech accordingly. "Are you tired, darling, or would you like to go out and see a bit of the city?"

They had a short window of three days to find Mark Black and arrange to sneak him out of the country. Which was to say they didn't have a minute to spare. "Ooh, I'd love to go sightseeing," she gushed. "Just let me get out of this uniform and into something a little more appropriate."

Appropriate being loose long pants, a high-collared blouse, a loose long sweater and a scarf tied around her head. Thankfully, it was a cool day in the city and she wasn't going to swelter under all the clothing.

Zane gave her a quick once-over and nodded in approval at the modest attire. He drew her into his arms for a quick kiss that ended up being a long, slow affair that left her rethinking having turned down a nap with him. She was pleased to see him breathing a little hard when he finally broke it off.

"I can't ever get enough of you," he whispered against her temple before he stepped back from her and opened the door.

"Ditto," she murmured as she moved past him into the hall.

Tehran was crowded and dusty, but the streets were bustling and energetic.

"I've never seen traffic this bad," she commented as she watched a group of pedestrians nearly be run down by several motorcycles diving between gridlocked lines of cars.

"The city was designed for about three hundred thousand cars but has more than five million vehicles on the road. You do the math."

"Aren't you just a font of information?" she teased.

"We'll have to take traffic into account when we…need to get anywhere."

He was referring to their plan to kidnap Mark Black back from the Iranians. Torsten had wanted to rent a large, covered truck to move the whole team covertly, but now Piper understood why Zane had insisted that motorcycles would be more practical.

They walked to the bazaar, an old but charming covered market in the old city. A huge white dome decorated with blue and gold mosaic tiles rose over the ancient wooden structure, shading the heart of the open-air marketplace.

"You look like you need a cup of coffee," Zane announced as they wandered through the shops, full of textiles, brass and cheap electronics, while the scents of cinnamon, saffron and sewage swirled around them.

"Um, sure," she replied.

He steered her into a grimy little coffee shop with plaster walls painted peach, faded turquoise ceilings and cobalt blue tables. This country was a full-on assault to her senses, noisy, brightly colored and smelly. Zane tucked her at a table in a dark corner and then went to fetch tiny cups of what turned out to be tactical nuclear espresso.

Thick and strong and bitter, it nonetheless left a pleasant aftertaste, and she definitely felt the zing of its caffeine punch within a few minutes.

Zane lingered over his cup of coffee and then wandered

away again, bringing back sweet pastries this time, and warning her to take her time eating hers.

"What's up?" she muttered from behind unmoving lips.

"Contact's late."

Whoa. This was a meeting, then? She smiled and nodded, leaning back in her chair and feigning exhaustion and relief to be seated and resting. Zane picked up a newspaper abandoned on the table beside them and began browsing through it.

"Can you read that?" she asked, eyeing the Arabic script.

"Of course I can. Just because my family lived in the United States for a while doesn't mean I didn't learn my family's native tongue."

"I'm sorry. That was stupid of me. Of course you would have learned your family's language and culture."

He shrugged. "It came in handy in college in my Middle Eastern studies."

He said that like she was supposed to know what he'd majored in at university. Oh, right. They were married. Did he think they were being eavesdropped on, even here? She had to give him credit; he was flawless at maintaining a cover.

"And here I thought I knew everything about you," she replied.

Approval shone in his eyes, but he said smoothly, "I have to keep a few secrets from you, darling. How else will I keep you on your toes?"

They traded affectionate smiles that felt entirely genuine, and he went back to reading his newspaper.

Thankfully, she still had a few bites of the dry, stale cinnamon bun left on her plate when a young man approached their table. Zane stood up, exclaiming in pleasure, and hugged the man, warmly inviting him to share a cup of coffee with them.

She'd already noted that the locals generally seemed animated and demonstrative. They tended to talk loudly, laugh a lot and argue good-naturedly. Although the greeting was wildly out of character for reserved Zane, it was wholly in keeping with how everyone else was behaving. Yet again, she was impressed to death by how well he blended into his surroundings. The man was *really* good at his job.

Zane bought a round of espresso for all three of them, and Piper braced herself to have the jitters for hours to come.

The new man was introduced as Samir—an old friend of the family—although what family was never specified. And she didn't ask.

Samir and Zane chatted in casual, quick Farsi for perhaps ten minutes. Just long enough to finish their coffees and trade pleasantries. Then Samir excused himself, citing not wanting to be late for a class, and rushed off. As far as she could tell, not one bit of useful information had been exchanged. There had been no message passed, no dead drop, nothing that would help them find Mark Black.

Zane was in no hurry to leave, but when they finished their drinks, he led her outside once more. "Wanna see something amusing?" he asked her.

"Sure."

They walked a few blocks until they came to a blocky office building made of pink brick with iron bars on the windows. "What is it?" she asked.

"It's called the US Den of Espionage Museum."

Her gaze snapped back to the facade. "Is this the old US Embassy? Where the hostages were taken?"

"The very same."

"Well, that's…gruesome."

"You should see the inside. There's a huge painting covering a wall, of the Statue of Liberty with a skull face." He muttered under his breath, "It's creepy as hell."

"No, thanks."

"That's okay. I want to show you the Negarestan Garden, anyway. It's only a few blocks from here."

The garden turned out to be more of a park, but it was green and shady, with fountains sending the sound of tinkling water into the air. It was a pleasant break from the cars, jostling crowds and thick traffic fumes.

"What are we doing here?" she asked from behind unmoving lips.

"Dead drop to fetch," Zane answered in the same fashion.

The CIA must have arranged this before they left Washington. Efficient bunch, those spooks.

They stopped in front of a turquoise blue pool of water shaped roughly like an embellished square, with elaborately swirled and curved edges in the ancient Persian style. "Let me take your picture in front of the fountain," Zane announced.

"Uh, sure." She took her place, obediently smiling. She suspected he had spotted someone following them and was snapping a picture of the unlucky tail.

They strolled a bit more, and then he suggested they take a rest on a bench under a row of young trees beside a long, narrow lawn. "I gather grass is a bit of a luxury in this part of the world?" she commented.

"Water's in terribly short supply. Hence grass is, too."

Zane leaned back, stretching his arm across the back of the bench behind her but not touching her shoulders. Still, the move was possessive, and sent warm fuzzies through her tummy. "It's good to be home," he sighed.

"Do you miss it?" she asked, playing along. Rashid

Farouk had been born here, according to his legend, which she, as his "wife," had memorized along with her own.

"I miss the big family gatherings. And the food. There were always cousins around to play with. Although there were also always aunts and grannies around to grab your ear and tell you to behave, too."

She smiled wistfully. "That sounds nice."

"It was a good way to grow up." He paused, then added, "You'll see for yourself in a few days, when you meet my family."

They'd agreed that it would look strange for a native Iranian not to visit his family if he was in the country. The CIA had undoubtedly arranged for some family in the suburbs of Tehran to pose as his relatives and go through the motions of preparing for a big family get-together. She'd already figured out the agency was nothing if not thorough in building cover legends.

"Would you ever consider moving us back here?" she asked Zane speculatively.

"Would you come with me if I wanted to live here?"

"Of course. You're my husband. I'll follow you to the end of the world and back."

His gaze snapped to hers, and the look they traded was loaded with intensity. And questions. Did she mean that for real? What would their life together be like if they were really married?

A slow smile unfolded across his face, growing to encompass all his features. "I think it's time for us to go back to the hotel, Mrs. Farouk."

"Indeed, Mr. Farouk."

They left the gardens, and he surprised her by hailing a cab. In a hurry to get her into bed, was he? More warm fuzzies coursed through her. Good. She was in a hurry to get naked with him, too.

Not that a cab ended up being much faster than walking. The traffic really was incredible. Their driver yelled out his window and honked, and she was pretty sure he went the wrong way on a one-way street before they finally made it back to the hotel.

When they got back to the room, Zane announced that he wanted a shower and disappeared into the bathroom. After a few minutes, he called, "Can you come scrub my back, wife?"

That was a strange request. Nonetheless, she played along and slipped into the fog-filled bathroom. The shower ran loudly, but he sat on the toilet, fully clothed and holding a wrinkled strip of paper. He passed it to her, and she realized it was thin onionskin that could fold into a tiny space.

Holding it open, she read aloud. "'MB, guest of honor. Appears at Club Musika Retro tomorrow. Don't miss it— one-time show!'"

She looked up at Zane, frowning. He stood, took her in his arms and whispered in her ear, "MB is Mark Black. *Guest of honor* means he's under arrest, as in he's a guest of state security. Club Musika Retro—CMR—Center for Materials Research. Tomorrow is when he's due to inspect that facility. And the one-time show comment undoubtedly means that he's expected to see the facility only once and then disappear after his report on the CMR is delivered to the Iranian government."

"How did you know to pick this up?"

"Samir showing up at the café meant the message had been successfully dropped. All we had to do was go collect it."

"Was the pickup point prearranged?"

"No. Samir and I talked about playing as children in the park and he remembered that fountain and liking to sit and listen to the sound of water."

She smiled at Zane. "Well, aren't you clever."

He smiled back at her, and then he stood up, drawing her into his arms. Their smiles mingled, turning into a kiss fully as steamy as the shower.

Breathless and distracted, she pulled her mind back to business with great reluctance. "What time will Black be at the lab tomorrow? How much security will be around him?"

"No idea. If the CIA's informants knew it, that information would also have been in the note. This is the part where we get to improvise."

"Weapons?" she asked in a low voice.

"Gunnar's going over to the airport later today to get the equipment out of the plane."

That had been the hardest part of getting ready for this trip—asking the manufacturer of the airplane to quickly build in a hidden compartment large enough to carry all the operational gear for an entire special operations team. Apparently, a team of cabinetmakers had worked around the clock to finish the construction and installation.

She asked, "Do we have wheels yet?"

"No. We have to go take care of that tonight. We have supper with the Iranian contract officials this evening, and after that, we'll need to go over to Club Musika Retro in case the message was discovered. We'll sneak out of there, get transportation and then meet up with the others."

She nodded in understanding.

He said gently, "Time for you to leave the bathroom if we don't want to arouse suspicion. If you want to take a nap, I'll join you when I'm done in here." His hands fell away from her and he stepped back, but reluctantly. Her heart warmed. She knew the feeling.

When she glanced back over her shoulder at him as she slipped out of the bathroom, though, his eyes were alight with the promise of delights to come.

Yes.

She stripped out of her tourist clothes and washed off with a damp cloth. Refreshed, she lay down on a mattress only marginally softer than concrete. But having slept on concrete recently, she was able to perceive and appreciate the slight difference.

She was half-asleep when Zane slipped under the sheet beside her, gathering her into his warm, slightly damp embrace and murmuring, "I never get tired of how you feel in my arms."

She noticed he made no effort to keep his voice down. *Right. Act married for the people on the other end of the bugs in the walls.*

"I never get tired of being in your arms, my love."

His gaze snapped to hers, and a slow, possessive smile took over his features. He liked the *L*-word, did he? She'd never been in love, but she was starting to wonder if it didn't feel pretty close to how she was feeling now.

"You're so good for me. You ground me in the present," he said, staring at her significantly. Clearly, he meant more than that. But, leery of any bugs, he wasn't going to say anything more aloud. She got the message, though. In the midst of running from cover story to cover story, she reminded him of who he really was. She grounded him in his real identity.

"I hope you'll always do the same for me," she replied carefully. She wasn't likely to spend the majority of her career in undercover roles, but she was likely to spend a lot of time away from home in dangerous places doing dangerous missions. She, too, could use the reminder that moments like this were real and waiting for her when she got home.

"Always," he agreed solemnly.

Had they just agreed to try a long-term relationship with each other? If only she could ask him outright!

Instead, she kissed him passionately, pouring all the feelings she dared not speak aloud into their kiss. She desperately hoped he felt her genuine desire for him, her wish to be with him, her willingness to commit to a full-blown relationship.

She traced her hands across his muscular shoulders and relished the smoothness of his skin sliding under her palms. He was so warm and vital, and he made her feel vibrantly alive.

He smiled at her, a whole host of emotions flitting through his expressive eyes, and she smiled back.

"Don't let me lose myself," he breathed.

"Never. I'll be your anchor as long as you need me to be."

They made love slowly, tenderly even. When it had shifted from great sex to deeply emotional lovemaking, she wasn't sure. But this was entirely different than what they'd shared the other times they'd been together—and it had been pretty special then, too.

In the midst of a dangerous foreign land, they created between them an island of safety and belonging. If only she could tell if it was a real promise. Had some sort of deal been sealed between them or not?

Or was she interpreting great sex by a considerate lover to mean more than it really did? Assailed by doubts and bedeviled by her silent hopes and dreams, she made love to him with all the intensity of feeling that she could express. No surprise, she felt tears on her cheeks when they finally fell back on the mattress, side by side, to catch their breaths.

Regardless of what it meant for the long term, it surely had satisfied the curiosity of whoever was listening on the other end of the bugs. If that didn't sound like a married couple genuinely enjoying each other's company, she gave up.

They had time for a short nap together before Zane's alarm clock blared, announcing it was time to dress for dinner.

The supper meeting with government officials responsible for choosing which airplanes to buy was a complete bore to Piper. She was expected to smile politely, look nice and say nothing. At least she got to dust off her rusty Farsi as she listened to the conversation flowing around her. Zane was kept busy through the meal discussing airplane performance parameters and dancing around possible discounts that the aircraft company—ostensibly a Swiss firm and politically neutral—might be willing to slip to the Iranians on the down low.

After the interminable meal with course after course of heavy sauce-laden fare, each spicier than the last, Zane finally escorted her out of the restaurant to the hotel lobby, where Tessa and Rebel were waiting.

"Shall we go, ladies?" Zane asked.

He led them outside, hailed a cab and gave the name of the nightclub, Club Musika Retro. The odds of the dead-dropped message being intercepted were low, but just in case, they needed to follow through with visiting what turned out to be a discotheque, complete with mirror balls, flashing lights and dreadful Persian remakes of Western music from thirty years ago. Piper was totally going to have a headache before they got out of here.

Under the cover of the pounding noise, she leaned over to ask Tessa, "Did Gunnar get the toys okay?"

"No problem. Did you get a nap this afternoon?"

Piper felt her cheeks heating up and hoped her teammate would put her flush down to the mass of hot bodies around them. "Um, yes. A nap. Uh-huh."

Tessa grinned knowingly. "Makes life easier when you finally work out all that romantic confusion, doesn't it?"

"I'm not sure it's all worked out. And it's not as if we can have heart-to-hearts about it here and now."

"He's crazy about you. Never takes his eyes off you. Always looks half enthralled and half ready to leap to your defense at the slightest provocation."

Piper stared at her teammate. "Really?"

Rebel jumped into the conversation, rolling her eyes. "The poor guy's completely head over heels for you."

Piper knew the feeling.

Zane came back from the bar to their booth, juggling four sodas without ice. "We're in luck," he announced. "There's a men-only hookah lounge in the back. I'll slip through there and head out to pick up the keys to our motorcycles. You three party hard while I'm gone, and don't forget to flirt with our tails."

"We were followed?" Piper exclaimed.

"They picked us up leaving the hotel," Zane retorted.

"You'll have to teach us how to spot them better," Tessa interjected. "I didn't see anyone, and I was looking."

"Me, neither," Rebel admitted glumly.

Zane murmured, "Once we get home, it would be my pleasure to up your field ops games. In the meantime, it's the two guys on the bar stools right where the bar turns toward that wall."

"One guy has his back to us and the other is facing us?" Piper responded. "Big, beefy dudes in suits, with the funny bulges under their left arms?"

"Those are the ones," Zane laughed over his tepid drink.

Piper sipped without relish at the flat, oversweet soda. Zane stood up and dropped a chaste kiss on her forehead. "Don't have too much fun without me."

"Ha!" she replied in fake indignation. "Do you know who you're talking to?"

He looked around at all three women. "Yes. I do. Hence the caution."

Piper rolled her eyes at him and grabbed Tessa's and Rebel's hands. "C'mon, girls. I feel some *Saturday Night Fever* moves coming on."

All three women actually danced carefully, not wanting to draw too much attention to themselves. They followed the lead of the local women in how to dance. It wasn't just that Iranian women moved only a tiny bit. They also looked strange doing it in clothes that would not have been out of place at a Catholic school dance presided over by nuns. Piper and her teammates wore thick leggings underneath calf-length skirts, long-sleeved turtlenecks and sweaters over those.

When traditional, Iranian-flavored music came on, everyone on the dance floor, male and female, shifted to more traditional Middle Eastern dances. The young men twirled cloth handkerchiefs over their heads, while the women mostly clapped and laughed.

Piper and the other Medusas joined in for close to a half hour with no sign of Zane. Then Rebel leaned close to Piper to shout in her ear, "Problem—our tails are looking at their watches and at the entrance to the hookah lounge."

Crud. A distraction was called for.

"C'mon!" she shouted at her teammates. They made their way across the floor until they were directly in front of the tails. And this time, when an American dance tune blared, they broke into American-style dance moves, still being careful not to do anything that might be perceived as overly provocative. Zane had warned them that nightclubs were a recent experiment by the government and tightly monitored for obscenity.

Piper hoped that, by ignoring their tails and dancing in a tight triangle facing one another, they wouldn't get arrested by whatever religious police might be lurking in the corners.

"There's Rashid," Rebel called to Piper, just as the song ended.

Thank God. Piper was nearly out of dance moves that wouldn't get her arrested. The women strolled back to the booth to rejoin Zane, who brought them another round of drinks. This time he set down bottles of water. They all sipped, using the bottles to shield their mouths from any lip readers or cameras.

"Success?" Piper asked him.

"Indeed. Having fun?"

"I'm ready to get out of here. Our tails are enjoying watching our, um, tails, a little too much."

Tessa added, "We're supposed to meet the boss in an hour. We'll need that time to make sure we're not followed."

"We'll split up to leave," Zane commented lightly from behind his water bottle. "Our minders will be forced to split up, too, and it's a lot easier to lose a solo tail than a team who can pass you off from one person to the next."

Piper asked her friends, "Do you girls know how to get to the rendezvous point?"

Rebel grinned. "I speak Arabic. Even if we get lost, I'll be able to make myself understood enough to get directions. That, and I memorized a map of the city. We'll be fine."

Piper lifted her bottle one last time. "All right, then. We'll see you in an hour or so." She drained her water and nodded at Zane. Time for the new Medusas to go into action for the first time as a real team on a real mission.

Chapter Eighteen

Zane watched Tessa and Rebel slip out behind a couple that actually looked quite a bit like himself and Piper. He was impressed at how quickly the two women managed to exit the bar without looking like they were in the slightest hurry. It was a departure worthy of an experienced CIA operative.

Even better, one of the two men seated at the bar left moments after they did. The lone tail left behind in the club looked disconcerted. Excellent.

"Time to go," Zane muttered to Piper. "Before our friend has time to call in reinforcements."

She gathered her sweater and he ushered her outside, making no secret that they were leaving the club. The moment they stepped out into the cool evening, he and Piper turned left, hurrying away from the noisy disco.

He lengthened his stride to a near run, relieved that Piper could keep up with him. They swerved into the first alley they came to and took off running. She ran lightly on the balls of her feet, making very little noise. Thank God for her excellent training. Or more accurately, thank Torsten.

However, when they dodged out of the far end of the alley, she tugged his sleeve for him to stop. He glanced at her and was shocked to see a pair of black, rubber-soled loafers emerge from somewhere under her coat. She changed shoes quickly, threw a dark scarf over her blond hair and nodded her readiness to proceed.

If he'd thought she was quiet and fast before, she was twice as silent and quick wearing flats instead of high heels. Which was fortunate, because he ran her all over the old city, winding through warrens of narrow streets, narrower alleys and connected courtyards.

He defied anyone to successfully follow the two of them without revealing himself or herself as they darted across the city on foot. The tricky bit was actually going to be circling back to where their motorcycles were waiting for them.

He and Piper slowed down, moving stealthily as they backtracked into the old city. At this time of night the walls and tall iron gates, so abundant in Tehran, were mostly closed. It turned the streets into long tunnels with a single entrance and one exit. Their only option was to sprint down each street, slowing only to slip around corners into a new tunnel and then sprinting down it.

Eventually, he found what he was looking for. A gate stood open into a courtyard bordered by several old apartment buildings only four or five stories high. Tehran sat on two major fault lines, and these old buildings were squat and built of heavy stone to survive earthquakes.

As they darted across the deserted courtyard, Piper snatched a woman's chador off a clothesline. The traditional garment was made of a large semicircle of black cloth. Piper wrapped it loosely about her head and upper body, letting it fall nearly to her knees.

Following her lead, Zane stripped off his blazer and exchanged it for a sweater drying on the same line. It was still damp and smelled like lye, but it changed his physical appearance and made him look even closer to native.

They darted to a gate on the opposite side of the courtyard, at the end of a dark tunnel through one of the buildings. He paused to peer out before stepping into the street with Piper.

They continued to peer around corners and randomly pause in dark doorways to check behind them for the next several minutes. Even he didn't spot anyone following them. They were in the clear.

He approached a row of motorcycles, chained together and parked in front of a small storefront with its metal grate pulled down and locked. Using the key he'd collected earlier, he unlocked the motorcycle on the end and relocked the chain looped through rest of them.

He threw his leg across the seat, and Piper climbed on behind him, clasping her arms around his waist. He picked up the ratty baseball cap hanging from the handlebar and tugged it down low on his head. The street was rather quieter than he would like, but there was no help for it. He started the engine, and it roared to life, sounding shockingly loud in his ears.

He pulled away from the curb and turned the corner.

"Hide your face," he ordered Piper tersely.

She instantly buried her nose against his back, letting the flapping chador do the rest. Her entire torso pressed against his back, and she felt warm and feminine and sexy. Memories of their afternoon in bed flooded through his mind's eye, and he nearly drove over the curb in his distraction.

Dammit. Focus on driving.

"Good thing you're my wife," he muttered as he drove past a man in a dark suit standing on a street corner and looking around suspiciously. Maybe the guy was a state security agent, maybe not. But either way, Zane wasn't taking any chances with Piper's safety. "Otherwise you'd go to jail for holding me like this."

"I'd happily go to jail to keep holding you like this," she

muttered back. He wasn't sure if she'd meant for him to hear her or not, but her comment caused a burst of warmth in his gut nonetheless.

The strangeness of having a partner, and of worrying about that person's safety more than his own, struck him. It wasn't that he minded working with her; it was just weird not being a lone wolf.

Truth be told, he could get used to this business of working in a pack of wolves.

"Okay. You can sit up," he announced, when the guy on the corner disappeared from view behind them.

"I don't know," she murmured. "I kinda like it right here."

"Don't distract me," he half laughed.

She lifted her face, but her hands slipped lower, sliding below his belt buckle and coming perilously close to parts of him that were all too ready to perk up with interest.

Thankfully, they came into a more lit area soon, and she moved her hands back up to a more decorous position. He turned onto the Besat Expressway, then headed southeast out of Tehran on Highway 44. The idea was for the other team members to meet up and make their way out of the city center, where police and security forces would be thickest. The rendezvous point was in a small city called Mamazand, about forty-five minutes outside Tehran.

The Center for Materials Research, where Mark Black should be making an appearance in the morning, was just beyond Mamazand.

The trip out of Tehran and into the barren desert was uneventful. He guided the motorcycle to the house where their rendezvous had been arranged, and the tall iron-paneled gate, painted light blue, opened for him as he approached it. He drove into the courtyard and cut the engine.

Torsten locked the gate behind them as Piper climbed off the motorcycle, and Zane followed suit.

"Everyone's here now," the major said quietly. "We'll head out as soon as you gear up."

Piper had already moved over to the weapons and body armor laid out on the ground, stripped off her chador and was arming herself efficiently, stowing flashbang grenades, spare ammo magazines, det cord and other gadgets and tidbits in the utility belt she'd strapped to her waist.

Zane joined her, familiarizing himself with the equipment before stowing it on his person. "You look pretty comfortable with all this stuff."

"Tools of the trade," she commented with a shrug.

"This is the first time I've seen you in full commando mode," he commented back.

"Welcome to the Medusas in combat mode."

"You ladies really are full-blown warriors, aren't you?"

Piper stopped what she was doing to stare at him. "After everything you've seen me do, it's just now dawning on you that I'm a real soldier?"

He frowned. "It's one thing to know you can do all this stuff. It's another thing to actually see you do it."

"You saw me engage in a firefight with Mahmoud's guys. I killed Hassan, for crying out loud."

"I know. I know. But this…" He spread his hand over the tarp filled with weapons. "This is an imposing array of killing power."

"And that's why the Medusas are successful in general. People, particularly in places like this, can't compute that women can use all this gear effectively. Heck, you're American and have seen me in action, and you're still having trouble buying it. Imagine some Iranian dude who's never seen a woman say boo to a mouse."

He nodded, impressed in spite of himself. Only now

was he fully grasping the scope of her training. No wonder she'd been such an emotionally strong and mentally disciplined prisoner.

"I'm just glad you women are on my side in this mission," he said fervently.

Piper smiled. "Let's go find ourselves an American engineer and bring him home."

"Amen," Zane said under his breath.

PIPER SHIFTED SLIGHTLY beside Zane. Their surveillance hide was low to the ground and dusty as they peered over a slight rise toward the research facility Black would be inspecting any minute now.

The lab was a freaking fortress. Shortly after they'd arrived here in the wee hours, the team had determined that no way could they infiltrate the facility, snatch Black from his captors and make it out alive. The place bristled with electronic signals, there were cameras everywhere and alert Iranian Special Forces types were crawling all over the place.

The revised plan was to spot Black from here and follow him to wherever his captors took him next. They would have to keep him alive long enough to film him or have him type out an email. It would be during that transfer when the rescue team nabbed Black.

Problem was, they had no idea where the Iranians planned to take him after this. Which meant they were going to have to improvise on the fly. It was nobody's idea of a good mission, but it was the only option they had to save the guy.

Tessa's muttered voice sounded in Piper's earbud. "I've got dust on the horizon. Caravan of three SUVs inbound at high speed."

Torsten whispered, "That's probably Black. Get me license plates and a head count of people inside the vehicles when able."

"Working on it," Rebel replied absently. She was flying the team's tiny overwatch drone, while Tessa watched the live feed from the drone's high-powered surveillance camera.

In a few minutes, Tessa called out license plate numbers and started counting heads inside the SUVs. Four men in the first one. Three in the second…and a possible facial ID on Mark Black in the back seat with one other man. Three men in the third vehicle.

Black plus nine hostiles. Not bad. They'd been expecting more like a dozen guards.

Tessa, Rebel, Torsten, Zane and herself made five. Five on nine with their training and their equipment was a piece of cake. Assuming they could isolate the group transporting Black. And assuming the Medusas could engage in a firefight without excessively endangering Black. It was entirely possible that his captors would try to hide behind him. It was what she would do.

"I can hear you thinking, you're doing it so loudly," Zane murmured.

"I was just thinking about how I'd use Black as a human shield if I were the tango."

"How much training do you ladies have in close-quarters marksmanship?"

"I'm good down to about a four-inch-wide target. Tessa can shoot consistently into one-inch windows." Meaning if Tessa had a one-inch-wide target behind a hostage, she could still hit the bad guy without nicking the hostage.

"Nice," Zane commented. "I'll leave that shot to you and Tessa, then."

"Let's hope it doesn't come to that," she replied.

Silence fell between them as, in the distance, a puff of

dust became visible. She gauged that it was still several minutes out.

"Tell me something," Zane said in a low voice. "Do you enjoy doing stuff like this?"

"Love it. You?"

"This is a lot easier than being undercover. It's straightforward. Kill or be killed."

She smiled briefly. "We like to think in terms of kill... or kill."

He grinned. "Fair enough." A pause. "I like being here with you like this. I'm enjoying being part of a team."

"It's nice...weird but nice...having you here." She focused on the length of his muscular body pressed against her side and took comfort in his steady breathing and contained power. It wasn't that she needed a big, strong man to protect her. Far from it. But it was nice having a big, strong man work with her as an equal, respecting her capabilities and ready to cover her back.

"Vehicles are slowing," Tessa reported, at the same time as at least a dozen guards swarmed out of the lab to await the arrival of the caravan.

Zane muttered, "Black's sure getting the VIP treatment."

"The prisoner VIP treatment," Piper corrected.

They watched through their field binoculars as the SUVs halted in front of the lab and a Caucasian man was ushered out of the middle vehicle. Black was escorted toward the building.

Torsten said tersely, "He's ambulatory. Appears healthy. Anticipate an able-bodied hostage."

That was good news. Having to carry out a badly injured hostage slowed a team down. A lot.

Black disappeared into the building and Torsten started a stopwatch. The longer Black was inside, the more the CIA hoped he would be able to see and report on.

When Torsten's stopwatch hit the thirty-minute mark, Zane let out a sigh of relief. "Black's getting the full tour of the place. Which means he knows what the Iranians are so hot and bothered to protect that they kidnapped his wife."

"Why wouldn't they not let him into the lab at all and just coerce him into writing up a fake report?" Piper asked Zane.

"The report has to pass for real. He has to include enough technical details that the Global Atomic Inspection Team bigwigs believe he actually did the inspection. And for all the Iranians know, the West is watching on satellite feeds as Black arrives and goes inside the facility."

"Or a surveillance drone," Piper remarked dryly.

"Exactly."

They traded warm smiles. Zane seemed as happy to be here with her as she was to have him here. Something had shifted between them since they arrived in Tehran. They'd both settled into the idea of being in a relationship with each other, and they both liked how it felt.

Who'd have guessed she would find a man of her own who was okay with what she did and who she was? She didn't know where this would go or what the future would hold, but for once, she was hopeful. Maybe her dreams of someday settling down with a man who could accept her life choices, dreams of maybe even having a family, might come true, after all.

"Here they come," Tessa announced.

The lab's front doors opened and a large group of guards streamed out with Black tucked in their midst. Piper saw several of the guards glance up at the sky, and she grinned. The overwatch drone was barely a foot long, its underside was painted pale blue and it was loitering several thousand feet up, completely invisible to the naked eye.

Tessa reported that Black had again been loaded into the

second SUV, this time with three escorts instead of two. Piper and Zane slid backward from their hide and raced down the sandy hill to their motorcycle. They jumped on and took off down the road.

Their job was to get in front of the convoy in case it headed back toward Tehran. If it went the other way, heading away from Tehran, they would turn around and ride in the trailing position. It was also their job to hunt for a good spot to ambush the SUVs and to call for the actual attack.

"We're away," Piper reported into her microphone.

"First SUVs pulling out now," Tessa stated.

"In position to fall in behind them," Torsten reported. He, Rebel and Tessa each had their own motorcycle. That way, they could all carry weapons, ammo and gear in bags behind them.

As it was, Piper felt like a porcupine underneath her billowing chador. This morning, she'd added a maqnaeh to her clothing. It was a hooded scarf that had a tiny protruding bill, like a baseball cap. It would keep the chador from sliding down over her eyes and obscuring her sight. She also wore loose black trousers, black socks and her black tennis shoes. There would be no bare flesh to draw the attention of the religious police, no, sir.

Even though it was only midmorning, the day promised to be a hot one, and the sun baked her beneath the layers of dark clothing. No help for it, though. She needed the chador to cover all her weapons. Tessa and Rebel were similarly dressed.

Torsten had laughingly declared them all BBMOs last night: Badass Black Moving Objects.

Zane sped up as Torsten reported that the SUVs were driving back toward Tehran at nearly a hundred miles per hour. The wind tore past Piper, cooling her a little, at least. No way could they ambush vehicles moving that fast.

Which was, of course, the point of driving that rapidly. They would have to wait until the convoy slowed to jump it. When that SUV caravan hit the horrendous city traffic, it was going to have to drop to a crawl. That would be the best time to rescue Black.

She leaned forward and yelled into Zane's ear, "Slow down when we approach Tehran and let them catch up with us."

"My thoughts exactly!" he shouted back, without taking his eyes off the road.

Into her microphone, she called, "Have we notified the pilots to crank up the jet and be ready to go?"

"Affirmative," Torsten replied.

The roar of the engine beneath her lessened as Zane throttled back, slowing the cycle to a more sedate speed as they hit the suburbs. She kept watch over her shoulder for the SUVs.

"Convoy in sight," she reported over her radio.

"Let's let them get as far into the city center as we can before they make a turn away from the vicinity of the airport," Torsten ordered.

"Contact on the traffic jam," Zane reported. All of a sudden, their motorcycle slowed to a few miles per hour as they hit the wall of cars, taxis, mopeds and people that clogged the Tehran streets.

Piper took one last glance over her shoulder and spied the three black SUVs a dozen cars back. She dared not look back again lest the front driver see her watching him and grow suspicious.

"We're weaving through traffic to close the gap," Tessa reported.

Piper and Zane inched forward through an intersection. The SUVs cleared the traffic light.

"Caught by the light," Torsten grumbled. "Don't move until we've caught up to you again."

Zane reported tightly, "First SUV turned behind us. I'm going to turn now to try to meet up with the convoy at the end of the next block."

"Convoy in sight. We're turning, as well," Torsten responded.

A cacophony of car horns erupted behind them, and Piper looked back as Zane cut across traffic to turn the corner. She saw three motorcycles running the red light and cutting in turn—not that they made the congestion any worse.

"They're through the light and in pursuit of the convoy," she reported.

"Targets acquired," Zane stated as they shot out into the next street in front of the SUVs, but perhaps only a hundred feet ahead of them now.

"We need to take them as soon as the others are in place behind the tangos," she called in his ear, off mike.

"Agreed," he called back.

She clutched her chador close so it wouldn't flap and reveal the rifle strapped across her back. Zane wove expertly between lanes of traffic, ignoring the occasional shouted epithet. She was glad he was doing the driving. Even she wouldn't have been as bold as him.

They passed the SUVs going the opposite direction, and Zane made a quick U-turn. "Don't look at them," he bit out over his shoulder.

He actually drove directly past the SUVs, close enough for her to reach out and touch them. She turned her face away and counted the seconds until Zane muttered, "We're clear."

Into her mike, she said, "Call when in position."

"We're there," Torsten replied. "Anytime now."

"Next intersection," Zane said. "Hang on tight, Piper. When I tell you to, jump off the bike and make your move for the tangos. I'll cause a distraction."

"Roger," she replied in a clipped voice. Here it went.

"Now!" Zane called out.

She slid off the back end of the motorcycle, jumping clear of the rear fender just as Zane punched the throttle and slammed into a produce truck in the middle of the intersection. Somehow, as the bike slid under the truck's wheels, Zane came off it, and one of the wooden slats of the truck bed miraculously gave way, spilling melons all over the intersection.

The chaos was instant and spectacular. People shouted. Horns honked. Drivers got out of their cars to shout some more and wave their arms. Where Zane was in that mess, she had no idea.

Piper turned, ducking low between cars, and ran back toward the SUVs. She approached the second one from the passenger's side and pounded on the front door. The window started to roll down.

"Help! Help!" she screamed in her best Farsi. "My husband is dying! He needs a hospital. You have to drive him!"

"Go away," the man inside shouted back at her.

Through the open window, she spied Tessa pounding on the driver's window, and Rebel doing the same on the left rear-passenger door.

The doors of the front SUV opened. Tessa, hardly looking to the left, paused her tirade for just a second. Piper was at exactly the right angle to see Tessa fire a silenced handgun under her left armpit at one of the security guards emerging from the front SUV, shooting a dart coated with a high-powered chemical that caused instant shock and paralysis. The other two front guards went down, as well. Torsten and Zane had hit their targets successfully, too.

Time to cause total chaos. Piper pulled out two flashbang grenades and threw them as hard as she could in opposite directions. Other Medusas did the same, and a half-dozen explosions rocked the entire intersection.

As smoke filled the air, people screamed, abandoning their cars and running for cover. Whipping out her sound-suppressed handgun, Piper shot the front passenger in the temple—with a bullet—while Tessa took out the driver.

Piper had to expose herself to lean in the front window, and the shot was at an awkward angle, but she targeted the third guard, in the rear. She hit him in the face, and blood and gore exploded everywhere. Mark Black shouted from the back seat.

"Open your door, Mr. Black!" Piper yelled over the din. "We're Americans here to rescue you!"

The rear door opened and she moved swiftly to intercept Black before he could emerge from the vehicle. The four security guards from the rear vehicle had yet to be neutralized, and he needed to keep off the street until Torsten reported that the other tangos were down.

"Stay inside," she snapped at Black, who'd already started to climb out.

"Who are you?" he demanded, sounding close to losing his cool.

"I told you. Americans. Put this on." She handed him a maqnaeh. He merely stared at it, and she took it from him and yanked it down over his head. Leaning into the SUV, she sloppily wrapped a chador around his torso.

"What are you doing?" he asked.

"Rescuing you. Do what I say and don't ask any questions until I tell you we're in the clear."

"Rear guards are down," Torsten reported.

She didn't know how he'd done it and didn't stop to ask. "Come with me," she ordered Black. "Quickly."

He stumbled out of the vehicle, getting twisted up in the chador. She yanked it free and pulled it down around his thighs, then grabbed his hand and took off running along with the other panicked civilians.

Torsten fell in on Black's other side, and a woman in a chador closed in directly behind them, keeping up with the killer sprint Piper was forcing Black into. One of the other Medusas.

They turned the corner into a smaller street filled with fleeing people and made their way to one side, letting the flow of civilians pass by.

"Any sign of Zane?" Piper panted into her microphone.

Rebel answered, "I'm about to…" a pause, then the sound of a pop came over her mike. "…take out the cop trying to detain him." Another pause. "Zane's running."

"Turn left, Zane," Rebel said tersely. "Then take your second right."

"Get out of there, Rebel," Torsten ordered.

"On my way."

"Strip down," Torsten ordered. Piper took off her chador and maqnaeh, switching them out for a bulky, knee-length coat. It was wool and hot as blazes, but it allowed her to wear her utility belt and hide a short-barreled urban assault weapon across her back. She probably looked deformed, but whatever. She wasn't giving up that weapon until Black was on the jet.

They waited for a long, tense minute until Piper spied Zane's familiar face coming around the corner. In a few seconds, Rebel came around the corner in turn, stripping off her chador to reveal a red coat and a colorful head scarf.

"Move out," Torsten ordered.

Together, they moved back into the street, turning away from the accident, the smoke and the renewed round of chaotic screaming as civilians began to realize a bunch of men lay in the street and in their vehicles.

Quickly, they fetched Torsten, Rebel and Tessa's motorcycles, and the six of them climbed onto the bikes and drove away from the scene.

They headed directly for the airport and didn't stop until the tall hurricane fencing surrounding it was in sight. They swerved into a small grocery shop and headed for the restrooms in the back, the women piling into one room and the men in the other. Quickly, all three women changed into their flight attendant uniforms. When they emerged, Zane wore the suit he'd arrived in, and Torsten and Black wore identical pilot's uniforms.

Quickly, the women dumped all their weapons into the canvas bags their uniforms had been stowed in and passed the bags to Torsten and Zane.

"I can't go with you," Black announced.

"Why not?" Torsten blurted. "You'll die if you stay here."

"The Iranians have kidnapped a woman. They thought she was my wife, and they're torturing her. I won't let that woman die."

Oh, for crying out loud. Piper stepped right up to Black. "That woman was me. Look at me carefully, Mr. Black. I escaped my captors, and now I'm here to rescue you."

Black stared hard at her. Recognition dawned in his eyes. "How did you escape…and get all the way over here… Who *are* you?"

"Later," she bit out. "Right now, we've got to get you out of Iran. Your wife is in a safe house with the FBI guarding her, and she'd very much like to see you."

"Right, then," Black mumbled. "What are we waiting for?"

Everybody laughed and turned for the exit.

The young man at the cash register stared at them suspiciously until Torsten tossed a fat wad of bills across the counter on the way past. Avidly, the young man turned his attention to counting it.

It was awkward as hell climbing onto a motorcycle in a tight pencil skirt, and Piper had to hitch the stupid thing practically up to her hips. They'd better get to the airport soon because someone was sure to arrest them *fast* for this lewd display of legs.

They raced up to the guard shack where crews for the air show could access the flight ramp directly, bypassing the terminal on the far side of the airfield. The three women leaped off the motorcycles and yanked their skirts down hastily. Then, as a group, they approached the guard shack on foot with their credentials in hand.

The guard checked them off on a clipboard. Black had been given Torsten's credentials and stepped through to the other side of the shack with Zane and Piper, while the guard hunted through the clipboard in search of Torsten's new fake name.

"I'm sorry. You're not on the list," the guard announced.

Torsten frowned. "I've been back and forth through this checkpoint a half-dozen times. Hell, son, I remember you. Don't you remember me? I'm the guy who brought in the coffee and box of pastries yesterday morning."

"Oh, yes! That was you!" the guard exclaimed.

"Just write my name down, and when the next list of air crew members is printed up, add me to it. It was obviously a clerical oversight."

Piper was impressed to death by how casual and calm Torsten was. Not even the slightest hint of tension was visible in his stance or demeanor.

The guard waved Torsten through, and Zane breathed beside her, "Damn, he's good."

The group started the long walk across the ramp toward their ride out of here.

Another plane was just pulling in and parking, and Piper idly watched it as the steps lowered and a pair of men, acting a lot like security guards, jogged out and took positions on either side of the steps. A third man stepped into the doorway, and Piper gasped. Her footsteps slowed, and the others pulled ahead of her.

Zane, who'd kept pace beside her, glanced at her quickly. "What's up?" he asked out of the side of his mouth.

"Is that Abu Haddad?" she muttered back without moving her lips.

Zane glanced toward the new arrival and swore under his breath. "The mission is to get Black out of here."

"The jets flown in for the air show were granted diplomatic status. As soon as Black's on our jet, he's in Swiss territory and can't be touched," she retorted. "We can't get this close to Haddad and let him get away."

"Torsten will kill you."

"He'll forgive me if I take out Abu Haddad. He seriously hates that guy."

Ahead of them, Black jogged up the steps of their Swiss jet and Torsten waved for them to catch up.

"Do you still have the bag of gear?" she asked quickly.

"Yes."

"Come with me," Piper muttered, making a rapid decision.

"This is crazy," Zane warned.

"*Crazy* is my middle name."

"So I heard."

"We'll never get another chance like this. And isn't this what we've both trained for? To capitalize on opportunities that come our way?"

"That interpretation of our missions is open to debate—"

"I went along with your kidnapping. You need to go along with this for me."

"That's a low blow," he muttered.

"I'm right and you know it."

Zane huffed and then nodded tersely. She veered to the left, with him on her heels. They paused to peer under the nose of a low-slung business jet.

Three pairs of male legs were striding away from them, heading in the general direction of a big white hangar at the edge of the tarmac.

"C'mon," she called over her shoulder to Zane, taking off running herself, swinging wide of Haddad and his men.

She spied a maintenance pickup truck parked beside another plane and headed for it. She ran up to the driver's window and looked in. *Yes.* The keys were in the ignition. She and Zane hopped in, and she drove as fast as she dared across the open space between the planes and the hangars. She veered between two hangars and raced around to the back of the one Haddad and his men were approaching.

While she drove, Zane emptied the bag, slamming magazines into both assault weapons and laying out Piper's utility belt. She stopped the truck, snatched the keys out of the ignition, grabbed the gun and belt, and took off running after Zane, who was already racing for the man-sized entrance door.

He eased the door open as she swung into position behind him. Moving low and fast, he spun right, leaving her to spin left. They were in an office with a big window looking out into the hangar.

Two limousines with dark windows were parked off to the left side, and a sleek jet took up the right side of the hangar. Along the left wall was a second-story metal loft housing shelves full of tools and aircraft parts.

As Haddad and his guards stepped into the cavernous

shadows, a half-dozen men emerged from the limos, and four more exited the jet.

Zane swore under his breath. He must recognize them. Piper didn't know any, but this had to be some insanely high-powered meeting.

Haddad walked up to the group of men, shaking hands with several. The others, obviously guards, fanned out around them in a loose circle.

Zane ducked down below the windowsill and Piper knelt beside him. "We're badly outgunned here," he muttered. "What's the plan?"

"Take out Haddad and run like hell?" she suggested.

"The other men he's meeting with are a who's who of terrorists, arms dealers and criminals. We need to take out the whole bunch or we won't have made any difference at all."

She thought fast. "We'll have to split up. You tell me which targets are mine and I'll make my way to that platform on the left. It looks like there's a staircase up to it from an office. You stay here. Take your shots and then head back to the truck and get out of here." She passed the keys to him.

"I can't leave you behind!" he exclaimed under his breath.

"Either I get off my kill shots and make it off that platform to join you, or I die," she said matter-of-factly. "I'll take the five men nearest the jet. You take the others."

"I don't like this. Let's just leave. We can have the agency's eyes in the sky track Haddad after he leaves this place."

"This is a once-in-a-lifetime opportunity, and you know it," she whispered back. "Would your bosses deem the loss of two American agents' lives worth the trade-off of killing all the men in there?" she challenged.

Zane huffed. "Yes." He paused and then said grimly,

"But I'm taking the platform. You stay here with the easy egress."

"But—"

"I'm not arguing with you. That's my final take-it-or-leave-it offer."

It was her turn to huff. "Fine. Go."

"Give me three minutes to get into position and then fire at will. And, Piper?"

"Yes?"

He kissed her hard and fast, and then raced over to the doorway, stopping only long enough to say, "Good hunting. I love you."

She stared at the door in shock as Zane left the office the way they'd come in.

He *loved* her? What in the hell? Why on earth would he drop that bomb on her here and now? The only possible explanation was that he expected to die in the next few minutes.

No way did he get to make a declaration like that and then *die*! The big jerk hadn't even given her a chance to tell him she loved him back! Irritation rushed through her, along with furious determination to see to it that both of them got out of this alive so she could return the favor.

Swearing in a continuous stream under her breath at Zane, she moved stealthily into position by the window. She would take two quick shots from this corner of the window, and then would move to the other side for the next shots. The window was a good eight feet across and she calculated distances and angles from both spots as she waited for Zane to get into position. Using a glass cutter, she carefully and quietly scribed two small circles in the glass. Her first shots at each position should blow out the pieces of cut glass without shattering the whole window. In theory.

Zane should be past the long hallway behind several

more offices and on his way upstairs soon. She watched the metal staircase like a hawk and caught the barest hint of movement at the top of the steps. Dang, he was smooth. She lost sight of Zane as he worked his way into the stacks of spare parts. Her watch said he had one more minute to get into position.

She checked over her weapon quickly and then settled into her first shooting position, emptying her mind of everything but her targets and her weapons.

He loved her?

Well, she loved him, too—

Stop. Focus.

And then she inhaled, counted to four and exhaled slowly.

Showtime.

Chapter Nineteen

Tessa jumped as Torsten barked without warning, practically in her ear, "Where in the hell are Zane and Piper running off to?"

Torsten leaned across her, staring out the windows of the jet, apparently trying to spot his operative and the CIA liaison, who'd just gone AWOL without warning.

"She must have seen something," Tessa answered.

"But what?" Torsten demanded. "We have to get Black out of here before the Iranians decide to cause an international incident and storm a Swiss-flagged aircraft."

"It must be important or she wouldn't have run off," Rebel offered. "And the Iranians have no idea where Black is right now. We made a clean getaway. It'll take them hours to sort out where we went, even assuming they do have full closed-circuit television coverage of downtown Tehran. Which I highly doubt."

Torsten straightened to his full height and glared at both women. "It is unacceptable to go off script in the middle of a freaking operation."

Tessa replied gently, "Which means it must be a matter of life and death, or she and Zane wouldn't have taken off like that."

Her boss moved over to another window to stare out,

grumbling, "You Medusas are going to be the death of me yet."

He sounded ticked off enough that Tessa refrained from a snappy comeback.

"Son of a bitch," Torsten grunted. "There they are. Driving across the damned ramp in a truck like bats out of hell." He whipped around and pointed a finger at Black. "You. Don't move a muscle. You're a dead man if you set foot off this jet. Understood?"

"Um, yes," the engineer said nervously.

Torsten snapped at Tessa and Rebel. "Gear up, you two." He strode forward and poked his head into the cockpit. "If you gentlemen see anyone except me and my teammates approaching this jet, taxi out and take off. Immediately."

"We can't just take off. We have to get clearance first—" the copilot started.

Torsten cut him off. "You'll die if you don't get the hell out of here. Use this jet like a weapon, get to the runway and get airborne at all costs. Do you understand?"

The captain replied crisply, "I'm ex-navy. I hear you loud and clear."

Torsten grabbed one of the canvas bags of weaponry and ran down the plane's steps. Tessa and Rebel were close on his heels with bags of their own. He said tersely, "Last I saw, Piper and Zane were driving toward that big white hangar."

Tessa peered where he pointed. "You mean the one with all the security guards coming out of it right now to surround it?"

Torsten swore again.

"The guards don't look alarmed, at any rate," she reported.

Rebel spoke up. "There's a luggage carrier off to our

right. What if you drive that, boss, while Tessa and I hide in the back behind the curtains?"

"Done," Torsten replied. Quickly, he stripped off his pilot's uniform coat, leaving him wearing a white shirt and black slacks.

While he hot-wired the tug vehicle, Tessa and Rebel hid themselves in the covered luggage cart, carefully pulling the curtains closed and then quickly unpacking guns and the last of their concussion grenades. The luggage carrier lurched into movement.

"Here we go," Tessa muttered. "Charging into battle at a solid five miles per hour, wearing skirts and heels."

"And sassy hats," Rebel added.

"Torsten did say we could kill anyone who messed with the hats," Tessa retorted.

"Game on."

They traded grins, and then they both picked up weapons and put on their game faces.

PIPER DIDN'T EVEN have to think about which target to choose first. Haddad. The bastard had slipped through the Medusas' grasp once. No way was he doing it again. She aimed at his head, going for the kill shot. All the weapons provided for the Medusas would have been precisely tuned to fire true, so she would aim right at the middle of Haddad's face.

Her watch said Zane had ten more seconds to get into position and commence firing. She placed her eye on the rubber cup of the sight, counted down the remaining time in her head and exhaled. Three. Two. One.

Bang-bang.

Her shot rang out at almost the exact same moment Zane's did. Haddad dropped to the ground, a fine red mist hanging in the air where his face had just been. She'd hit him. Whether he was dead or playing possum, though, she had no way of knowing.

Men jumped all over the place, shouting and diving for cover, which she'd expected and anticipated. One of her targets dived behind a limo, taking cover from Zane, but still a clear shot for her. She exhaled and fired again.

Two down.

But then the security guards started shooting back. The window in front of her shattered, and she spun away, taking cover behind an old-fashioned metal desk. Rounds pinged off of it.

She slipped around the end of the desk and moved to the other firing position. She spied a target clambering into the plane, and then going limp on the steps. Zane must've shot him. She took aim at the man trying to climb over the body and shot again.

A pair of security guards took off running toward her.

Well, damn.

She took aim at one and shot him. He doubled over like he'd taken a bullet but then continued running.

She shot twice at the second guard, who staggered but also kept coming. New plan. She had to retreat from the office.

Grabbing her spare magazines of ammo, she flung the bag over her shoulder and ran out of the office, closing the door behind her. Darting down the hall, she tried a door. Locked.

Sprinting on, she tried the next door. And the next. Finally, an unlocked door. She spun inside, caught her breath for a second and then cracked it open just far enough to point her muzzle down the hall and see to aim.

The guards burst out into the hallway. She fired quickly, sending nearly a dozen rounds at them in a burst.

One man slid down the wall to sit motionless on the

floor, while the other cried out and retreated into the office. But she'd seen enough blood from the second guy to know he wasn't going to be chasing after her anytime soon.

This office had no window into the hangar. Checking the hallway quickly, she darted out and continued running down it. From inside the hangar, she heard car engines starting.

Veering into the next unlocked office, she was relieved to spy a window, and rushed over to it. She was just in time to see a concussion grenade explode directly in front of the first limo. Zane must have thrown that.

She also spied guards shooting up at the second-floor platform where Zane was trapped.

Oh, no, you don't kill the man I love.

Using the butt of her weapon, she knocked out the window glass and dropped into a firing crouch, spraying the backs of the shooting guards with a burst of lead. She was going through ammo fast, but this would all be over in the next minute. There was no use conserving ammo.

A power unit of some kind started to make noise from the jet, and she took aim at the tires, shooting out both nose tires and one set of main tires before returning her aim to the men, most of whom who were running around the hangar like panicked chickens.

What they were trying to accomplish, she couldn't tell. They certainly didn't have the discipline of trained Special Forces types. She picked off three or four of them before someone got wise to her new position and rounds started coming her way.

The red pillbox hat flew off her head. Good riddance. But she was more careful about showing herself as she shot at the melee in the hangar.

The jet's engines screamed to life, and the steps lifted as the passenger door closed. The plane started to taxi, leaving behind strips of rubber that had once been tires. They had to stop that jet!

She fired at the one engine she could see, but to no apparent avail. The jet rolled forward and was almost clear of the hangar when, without warning, a vehicle pulling a big metal luggage cart rolled directly in front of the aircraft.

The luggage vehicle slammed into the nose gear of the business jet with a screech of metal on metal. It startled everyone inside the hangar into looking that way.

Piper took aim and dropped two more men before the firefight resumed. She slammed her last mag into place.

Three men had been organized by a fourth, and raced toward the metal steps leading up to Zane's position. They moved out of her line of fire and she swore. Leaping to her feet, she jumped over the windowsill and ran toward them, firing in bursts at the men, heedless of her safety.

Nobody was killing her man! Not on her watch!

The trigger clicked and nothing happened. Out of ammo.

She continued running forward, reaching into her belt for a concussion grenade. Designed mostly to create noise and smoke, it would nonetheless have enough punch to knock a grown man off his feet at close range.

Arm raised and screaming like a banshee, she charged toward the last cluster of resisting guards.

ZANE SWORE AS he saw Piper charge out of an office near the far end of the hangar. He saw the moment when muzzle flashes stopped spurting from her weapon and she tossed it aside.

"Turn around! Turn around!" he shouted at her. But she either didn't hear him or didn't listen, because she was running straight at Haddad's personal bodyguards. They were the best-trained of the security types now littering the hangar floor in pools of blood. They'd stayed together, crouched over Haddad's body, and had dragged Haddad over to the limo in between shooting at him and Piper. They almost had their boss stuffed into the last limo.

It happened in slow motion below him. One of the men saw or heard Piper coming and pulled a sidearm, turning around to shoot her. Zane aimed and fired all in one frantic, blindingly fast motion, and the guy pitched forward. But not before his weapon discharged.

Piper spun to the side, hit.

No-o-o!

Off to Zane's right, a tremendous explosion rocked the whole platform beneath him. Bastards must have found the trip wire he'd left at the base of the stairs.

He grimly regained visual on Piper, and saw her right herself and alter course to charge the limousine. Zane pointed his weapon at the cluster of men beside the limo and mashed the trigger, emptying every round he had left at the guards.

They had the good sense to duck, which removed them from his line of fire behind the limo. He swore and stood up, coming out of hiding and racing for the stairs, yanking out his own sidearm as he went. Fourteen rounds. That was all his pistol held. And they had better be enough to get him to Piper's side and save her life. He leaped over the gap and the dead bodies left over from his trip wire trap and sprinted toward the woman who was his whole reason for living.

PIPER FELT THE round hit the meaty part of her upper left arm, but didn't register pain. Only a vague burning sensation. A few more steps.

In range now.

She lobbed a grenade at a cluster of men, who were now

crouching beside the limousine, unsuccessfully trying to manhandle another man's limp body into the vehicle.

She had one more grenade. She threw it with all her strength, drawing on everything she'd ever learned in fast-pitch softball in high school, and flinging the grenade through the open door into the black cavern of the limousine's interior.

The vehicle's windows lit up as the grenade exploded. The doors opened and the men inside poured out, coughing and doubled over.

She heard the pops of a nearby pistol, but couldn't see where they were coming from in the thick smoke.

She stumbled over something big and soft. A body. She dropped to her knees and searched the corpse by feel. Bingo. She felt the cold, hard barrel of a weapon. Scooping it up, she spun away from the cloud of smoke now enveloping the hangar.

Out of the fog and shouting and gunfire, a familiar voice merged from the din. "Get out, Piper!"

"You get out, Zane!"

And then she ran, zigzagging back and forth as she headed for the open hangar doors. As she got close to the light outside, she realized that her zigzagging had turned into staggering, first to one side and then the other.

She made out red shapes spilling out of a luggage cart and squinted, confused, as they rushed toward her.

"Get down, Piper!" one of the shapes shouted.

She dropped to the ground, but whether it was voluntary or her legs just gave out from underneath her, she wasn't sure.

In front of her, the red shapes erupted into flashes of light. She identified it fuzzily. Muzzle fire.

And then everything happened very fast. Someone came up behind her and scooped her off the ground. She bounced like she was on a trampoline. There was a luggage cart for a minute or two, and then the back of a pickup truck. And then they were racing across the airfield toward… the runway?

She didn't understand.

A male voice nearby murmured a continuous stream of soothing words. Something about hanging on and staying with him.

"Zane?" she mumbled as her eyesight gave out and gray crept across her field of vision. "You'll never get rid of me. I love you, too…"